W9-CAS-303

PUEBLO
Mountain, Village, Dance

50

Also by VINCENT SCULLY

The Architectural Heritage of Newport, Rhode Island
(*with Antoinette Downing*)
The Shingle Style: Architectural Theory and Design
from Richardson to the Origins of Wright
Frank Lloyd Wright
Modern Architecture: The Architecture of Democracy
The Earth, the Temple, and the Gods: Greek Sacred
Architecture
Louis I. Kahn
Arquitectura Actual
American Architecture and Urbanism
The Shingle Style To-day, Or, The Historian's Revenge

PUEBLO/Mountain,

Village, Dance

VINCENT SCULLY

THE VIKING PRESS New York

Book Design and Layouts by Libra Graphics, Inc.

First published in 1975 by The Viking Press, Inc.
625 Madison Avenue, New York, N.Y. 10022

Published simultaneously in Canada by
The Macmillan Company of Canada Limited

SBN 670-58209-3

Library of Congress catalog card number: 73-16935

Printed in U.S.A.

Chapter VII originally appeared in *Art in America*

Acknowledgment is made to the following for permission to quote from the works indicated:

The University of Chicago Press: From "The Bacchae," translated by William Arrowsmith, from *Complete Greek Tragedies: Euripides*. © 1958 by The University of Chicago. All rights reserved. Reprinted by permission of The University of Chicago Press.

Walker Art Center: "Men and Nature in Pueblo Architecture" by Vincent Scully from the 1972 catalog *American Indian Art: Form and Tradition*.

Page 390 constitutes an extension of this copyright page.

FOR THE AMERICANS
OF THE FOURTH WORLD

"I am living in poverty, but in peace,"
replied Masau'u. "If they wish
to share such a life, they may."
—Simmons, *Sun Chief*

And when the weaving Fates fulfilled the time,
the bull-horned god was born of Zeus. In joy
he crowned his son, set serpents on his head—

—Euripides, *Bacchae*, 100–102
(William Arrowsmith)

PREFACE

This book is written in love and admiration for the American Southwest and its people. It is primarily about Pueblo architecture and dances but is intended neither as a complete history of Pueblo buildings nor as a proper anthropological exploration of the mythology and ceremonials, of which the dances are only a part. Much fine work has been done along both these lines, and the reader's attention is directed to it.[1] Here is proposed only a general analysis of the form of the existing pueblos (though only incidentally as they looked in 1972 rather than, say, in 1900 or to Stubbs in 1950),[2] and of some of their dances in themselves and as they are framed by the buildings and as both are related to landscape forms. I think that the contemporary pueblos can be best seen and valued in this way and can, in fact, hardly be understood or sympathetically appreciated otherwise. The dances themselves I believe to be the most profound works of art yet produced on the American continent. They call up a pity and terror which only Greek tragedy rivals, no less than a comic joy, at once animal and ironic, that suggests the precursors of Aristophanes. And to the beginnings of Greek drama they are, I believe, fundamentally allied in a comparative sense. For these reasons, only enough reference is made to the grand, enduring, and much admired architectural remains of Anasazi prehistory, primarily of the so-called Great or Classic Pueblo period of c. A.D. 1100–1300, as seems necessary to approach the existing pueblos in their historical context and to set their position in a general art-historical development.[3] I also have something to say about Christian churches and Navaho hogans and, by way of epilogue, about the sacred tepee of the Mescalero Apache.

So approached, I hope that this topic as a whole can open up several wider avenues of thought about architecture—about, that is, all our natural and man-made environments and the meaning of human action in them. As such, this book grew directly out of my previous work in Greece, whose landscape the American Southwest strongly recalls, not least in the forms of its sacred mountains and the reverence of its old inhabitants for them.[4] Only in the pueblos, in that sense, could my Greek studies be completed, because their ancient rituals are still performed in them. The chorus of Dionysos still dances there.

As an art historian I feel that I must apologize for any trespass upon ethnographic ground, which is as little as I could make it, and for the occasional intrusion of the first person, which I have hitherto managed to avoid in my writing. It was the dances that drove me in that direction; I came to feel somehow that it was the only proper way to describe them. We see everything from our own psychic stance (as Taylor pointed out some time ago),[5] and it is at once inhuman and unscientific to pretend otherwise. Every ceremony, every dance, for example, also changes in some way each time it is performed, so that abstract generalizations can be historically misleading, despite their "structuralist" popularity at the present time. The question of feeling also arises, since we are involved here with works of art, which always deal with feeling and which must therefore be described in terms of our experience of them—an experience which probes as rigorously as possible toward that of the culture which produced them but which remains our own nonetheless. For this reason I have tried to write only about things I have experienced at first hand and have relegated much other material to bibliographical references.

Yet as the drums recede, a question relative to consciousness and the work of art may well be raised. Can the ceremonies of what, for lack of a more accurate term, Western European anthropology describes as a primitive people be regarded as works of art and described as such? Surely they can and must be, and they are indeed almost the ultimate works, since they directly form human behavior and distill, in the architecture of their natural and man-made spaces, a sculptural and pictorial essence of human action and of the structure of human thought. They, like all works of art, always flesh out at least two realities and live in two kinds of time—first in that of their people, and secondly outside and beyond it, capable of any number of unexpected effects upon others, able to endow themselves with a thousand meanings, and inhabiting the time of the watcher, or perhaps eternity alone.

I feel that I must say a word in appreciation of Americanist archaeologists and anthropologists, from whom I have received unfailing help and courtesy and who are interested enough in their subject to be willing to assume that even synaesthetic approaches may help illuminate it, if only by a little. Behind them in the Southwest stand giants, men like Fewkes, Hewett, and Kidder, who are unrivaled for brilliance and intuition in any field; and beyond them looms that unsympathetic titan Adolph Bandelier. We are invariably following in the footsteps of one or all of these men every time we climb a mesa or attend a ceremony, where we are in all likelihood joined by Parsons and others as well. One does not dare to claim fellowship with them but feels doubly joyful in the subject, knowing that they are there. I think here especially of anthropologists who have helped me directly, such as Marjorie Lambert, George Ewing, and Stewart Peckham of the Anthropology Laboratory of the Museum of New Mexico, Bertha Dutton of the Navaho Museum of Ceremonial Art, Alfonso Ortiz of Princeton, and Michael Coe of Yale. I owe much to many people: a special debt for counsel and hospitality to John B. Jackson of Santa Fe and Harvard, and warm gratitude to Frank Waters of Taos, to Edward T. Hall of Santa Fe and Northwestern University, to Tom Cummings of Ramah, to Leslie Koyawena of Shipaulovi and Albert Peywa, Jr., of Zuni, to Charles Di Peso of the Amerind Foundation and Douglas Schwartz of the School of American Research, to Harold Bloom, Robert Thompson, and Thomas Gould of Yale, to Peter Smith of Columbia, to Frank E. Brown of the American Academy in Rome, and to Robert Boissière and his wife, Ruth, of Santa Fe, who introduced me into their own foster family on Second Mesa and walked with me to the shrine of the Lions of Cochití. Bernard Second and Donni Torres of Mescalero were also of help. I do not know the name of the gentle and fierce old man at

Taos who showed me how he used to hunt with the bow; Philip Garvin took some pictures and taught me to rope. Melanie Simo did some drawings and maps; John A. Ford of the Chrysler Corporation made it possible for me to get to the snake dance at Mishongnovi in 1969.

Those who have over the years administered the archives of the Museum of New Mexico have been of enormous help to me; I have special cause to thank Sallie Wagner, Lucille Stacey, and Arthur Olivas, Photographic Archivist. I am grateful to my editor, Barbara Burn of The Viking Press, for her painstaking help. Without Helen Chillman of Yale, in this as in all previous work, I could hardly have functioned.

A grant from the Concilium on International Studies, Faculty of Arts and Sciences, Yale University, made this work possible, and the Walter McClintock Fund of the Yale Collection of Western Americana, under its enormously obliging curator, Archibald Hanna, paid for some hundreds of old photographs, many of which are published here for the first time.

Many other persons and institutions have contributed to this study, and I am grateful to all of them—as to my sons, Daniel, Stephen, and John, who helped in their own (respectively) architectural, classical, and anthropological ways, and to my wife, Marian, my stepdaughters, Ann and Maika, and my daughter, Kate, who loved to watch the buffalo dancing.

About the Americans with whom this book is concerned I feel an enormous ambivalence and the usual guilt, boring to everyone as such sentiments always are. I have told none of their secrets, in part because I don't know any and don't like to ask questions. But I have intruded into their plazas during the long dance days and, not of their blood, have been one more voyeur upon their culture and have written about it and speculated about them. I can only say that I have meant no harm. In my European-American way I have been driven to know, because what they are and do seems to me full of meaning and importance. My respect for their mordant intelligence and wit is as great as my perhaps rather urbanized amazement at their knowledge of sun, moon, stars, plants, animals, and all natural and living things. I can only extend to them in return my gratitude and my hope that having resisted European imperialism so long they will not let it pull them down in its very death throes now. Easy, though full of terror, to stand off pikes and bayonets and ignorant or venal bureaucrats and intolerant missionaries; harder, perhaps, to discover that the *bahána*, the long-hoped-for white brother, was a monster after all; but hard, so hard, to keep the electricity out, the television, the big real-estate money for leases to the various Colonías de Santa Fe and the geriatric new towns with their green golf courses in the arid land. During the next decade mass industrial society will literally flood the Southwest with its own indulgences and diseases, and I think that it will carry the Pueblos and the others away with it unless they are braver, wiser, and more selfless than any human beings we have known before. Perhaps they will be exactly that; if so, they will serve the rest of us Americans no less than themselves. Taos kept electricity out with guns—not for antiquarian reasons but for its very life. Cochití is gone into Cochití Lake, though it may not yet realize that fact. But Santo Domingo will never yield. Domingo will be around when everything else on the continent has fallen to pieces. The Hopi towns will endure—unless, of course, the incredible strip mining now taking place to the north on Black Mesa should lower the water table just a little. It could well do so, since it employs some millions of gallons a day of subsurface fossil water simply to float its pulverized coal some 275 miles to the Mojave generating station: cheapest to move it that way.[6] If the water table should subside a foot or so, the deep-dug kernels of Hopi corn will not be moistened in their washes but will turn the color of death and wither in the bleaching sand. And the Hopi will be gone. So that Las Vegas can spin its (I think we really must say) rotten wheels.

So I cite, not in apology but with a kind of bitter

pride, the restrictions under which this book took form over many years. No photography of any kind is allowed in the Hopi or the Keres towns. None at all, except under the most unusual and irregular conditions, for several of which I have cause to be profoundly grateful, though not, I hasten to add, to anyone named in this book. Zuni permits photography in the town but never of the dances. Taos and Acoma the same. The Tewa pueblos permit photography of some dances under certain conditions. These restrictions make it very difficult to show the essential visual relationships with which this book tries to deal. But I hope that the problem has been overcome. Old photographs help and are heavily employed here. There is sometimes an imbalance, with many photographs of towns and ceremonies about which I say little and few of some of those where I write a good deal. One can trade off to help the other in such cases. This often made synchronization with the text difficult, but it has been worked out as closely as possible. I approve of the restrictions in any event. We can only be glad that the surviving Americans became so canny at last. Otherwise, one is soon doing it for the camera rather than for the god, and that is the end of it all.

VINCENT SCULLY

New Haven, 1974

CONTENTS

PUEBLO
Mountain, Village, Dance

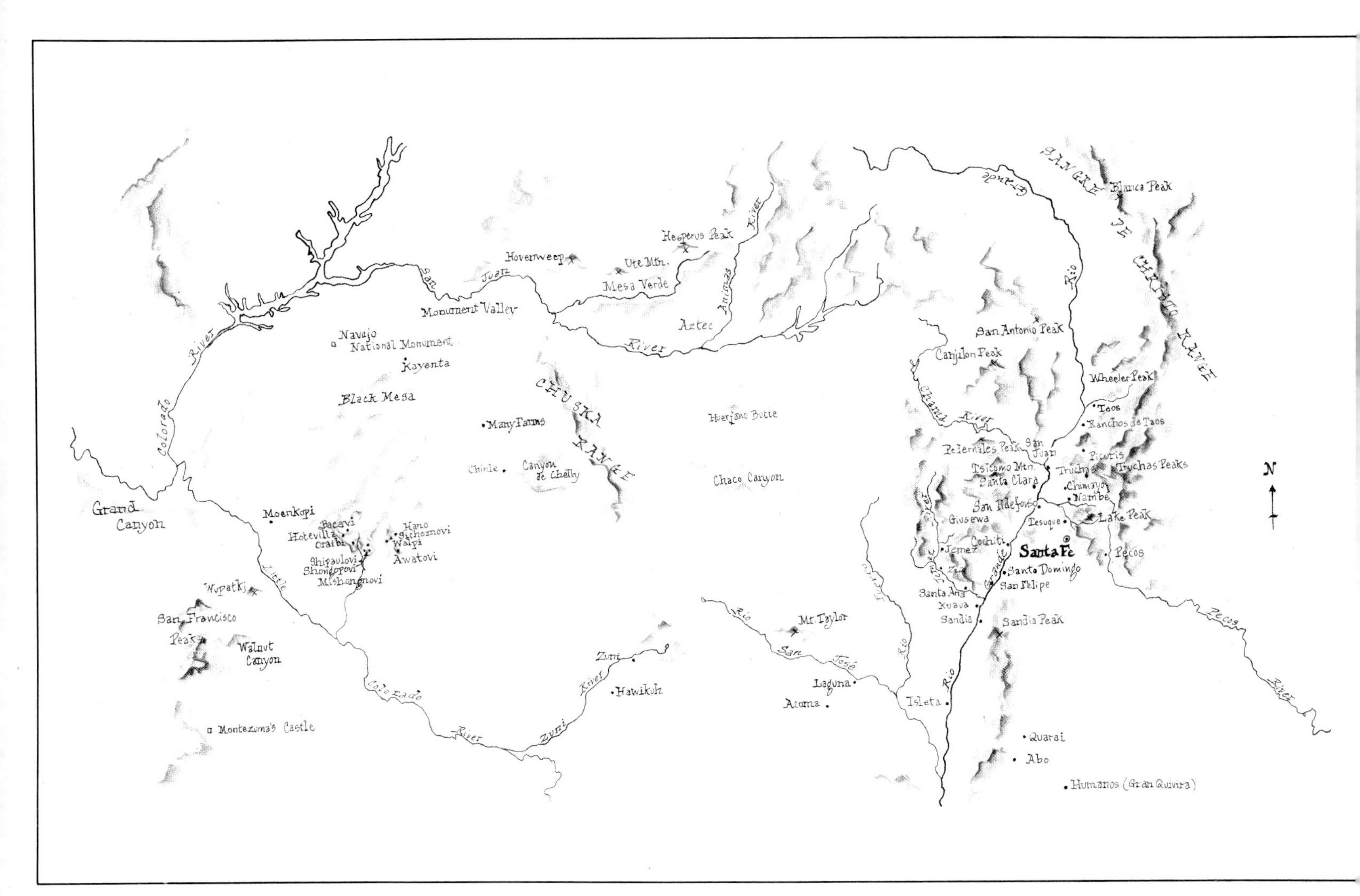

I:1 Sketch map showing most of the prehistoric and modern sites discussed. The topographical unity of this part of the Southwest and the beauty of its shape are immediately apparent in map form when the abstract grid of state boundaries is removed. (*Drawing by Melanie Simo*)

I

MEN AND NATURE—PREHISTORY AND THE PRESENT

The modern Pueblo Indians of New Mexico and Arizona are the direct heirs of a long tradition of human life on this continent (fig. I:1). There is no break between their prehistoric past and their present. They inhabit the same unit of time as their old ones, with the same view of life and the same laws as they. Only conquest divides their former and present ways, when a race of men descended upon them pale and glittering as from some polar star. Then all was changed—but for the Pueblos not destroyed. They mounted the first permanently successful American revolt on this continent, that of 1680, the only wholly efficacious Indian uprising. It is true that the booted men came back, but this time they came with considerable diplomacy, offering pardons, charters, and guarantees, most of which in this special instance have been more rather than less honored right up to now. So the Pueblos, of all the original North Americans, remain the most free. Their sovereignty, despite many pressures, is still fundamentally theirs. Their agricultural economy has protected them always and, though now dwindling somewhat, it still controls their most important possession: the incomparably rich and intricately constructed pattern of their ceremonial lives. The major reason for that obsessive ritual structure is the demanding presence of the Pueblos' other enemy, which is also their beloved mother and friend, the Southwestern land. Long ago it began to dry up, step by step, hardly perceptibly, with many shifts and starts. The Pueblos fought that process with every resource at their command, with terracing and canals, and with magic—with everything that could be reasoned out about the forces that shape reality as it could be known. So slow was the process of desiccation that the ceremonial pattern seemed always about to catch up with it if perhaps one more factor could be involved. Hence it grew elaborate, directing the actions of every critical day, perhaps of every moment in life, and erupting always in communal ceremonies of enormous power. So strong their shapes and songs, so reasoned into strength over the centuries, that they indeed seem always to be about to accomplish what their participants desire: nothing esoteric, only

I:2 The Grand Canyon from the North Rim at sunrise.

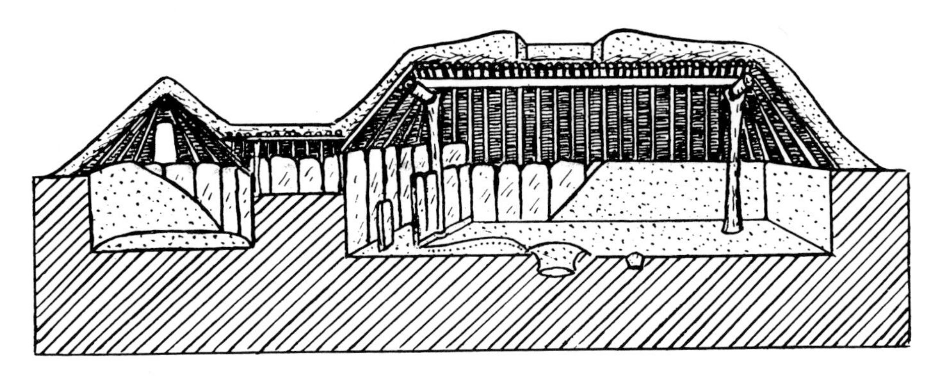

I:3 Mesa Verde, Colorado. Pit House, section. Modified Basketmaker. *(After Roberts, Courtesy Smithsonian Institution National Anthropological Archives)*

more life and growth for all living things. It is reality the Pueblos are after, so that they are in fact realistic, not idealistic. They are American empiricists, hopeful, reasonable, and hard. Something true and clear, massively unsentimental, runs through all their works, and this is, at bottom, the relationship between men and nature that they embody and reveal. In this they occupy a clear position in relation to the fundamental problem of human life: how to get along—which means in the end how to live and die—with the natural world and its laws.[1] It is the fundamental architectural question as well, because the environment inhabited by human beings is created partly by nature and partly by themselves. All human construction involves a relationship between the natural and the man-made. That relationship physically shapes the human cultural environment. In historical terms, the character of that relationship is a major indication of the character of a culture as a whole. It tells us how the human beings who made it thought of themselves in relation to the rest of creation. Are they, in their view, unique in the scheme of things, or have they no such conception? Do their buildings contrast with the forms of the earth or echo them? Primitive house types are normally too dominated by functional, structural, and internally symbolic preoccupations to be actively involved in evoking such relationships, though the actual congruence of shapes, deriving from purely practical considerations, may be startling. All this was generally true of the Modified Basketmaker villages of the Southwest (c. 450–750), one feels sure (figs. I:2, 3). Indeed, the profiles of their tiny pit houses were almost exactly those of the mighty mesas they rode and from the depths of whose canyons they had emerged, in their myths, to this upper world, this "fourth world" of earth, where they were greeted by the god Masau'u. But the vast majority of early civilizations—Mesopotamian, Egyptian, Meso-American (figs. I:4–7) and so on—fairly obviously set out to imitate natural forms in their monumental buildings and to geometricize them at landscape scale, so creating conscious images of mountain, sun's rays, river, swamp, and cloud. Other references are to the heavens; patterns are tied to the sun and the stars. Through all these links and images, human ritual borrows nature's forms and adjusts them magically to human measure and human ends.

The Greek revolts from this calculated symbiosis. Because the landscape is sacred it embodies its own divinity separate from man, who completes it—completes the structure of things as they are—by placing in it a house, a *naos*, as a shelter for his own image

I:4 Teotihuacán. Valley of Mexico. The Temple of Quetzalcoatl with the horned and feathered serpent, the Temple of the Sun, and the Temple of the Moon in the distance; the latter is placed directly on the axis of the ceremonial avenue and the cleft peak of the mountain, which is riddled with springs. (*Philip Teuscher*)

I:5 Monte Alban, Oaxaca. General view looking south. (*Photo courtesy Yale Slide Collection*)

I:6 Tikal. Petén, Guatemala. Mayan corbel-vaulted temples as mountain-cloud. (*Mary Elizabeth Smith*)

I:7 Tikal. Temple I (*Enrique Franco Torrijos. Copyright 1972 Editorial Herrero, S. A., Mexico 5, D. F.*)

of the god of that place. Then he surrounds it with columns, like images of standing men, and later in his history he describes them verbally in such terms (fig. I:8). But for the exterior body of the peripteral temple as a whole the Greek seems to have had only two special imagistic words: *aetos*, "eagle," for that broad triangle which the Romans were later to call the pediment; and *ptera*, "wings," for the peripteral colonnades. So, while the *aetos* may seem to echo mountain shapes a little, that is apparently not how the Greek primarily saw it. His temples embody not the natural, but the man-conceived divinity. They are heroic; they confront and balance the earth shapes but are not of them (fig. I:9). They are the eagles of Zeus, wingspreading, through whom mankind bursts free[2] (fig. II:15).

Western civilization has lived with that fundamental concept of freedom from nature ever since, despite recurrent appeals to "nature's god" and "natural law." Right now it is clearly abusing both according to a frame of reference which, whether Liberal or Marxist, has been largely shaped by nineteenth-century materialist thought. The industrial and scientific revolution was primarily directed against nature's boundaries, and it has pushed them back step by step. In the process it has tended to poison and ruin the natural world for the mass gratification of human desires. What nature's counterattack may eventually consist in is not our concern here.

Our problem is: How can we perceive the architecture of the American Indian, who has such an entirely different view of men and nature than the one we hold? We have even lost the Greek's constant awareness that nature indubitably exists. We ignore it; we confront it no longer. To the Greek the relationship was tragic; to us, trivial. Since this is so, how can we hope to penetrate even deeper to that landscape of the consciousness where we and the mountain are the same? Yet we must try to do so, because the American Indian world is a place where no conception whatever of any difference between men and nature can exist, since there is in fact no discrimination between nature and man as such, but only an

I:8 Paestum. Temple of Hera II with conical hill.

I:9 Paestum. Temple of Athena.

I:10 Hopi. Second Mesa. Mishongnovi in the foreground, Shipaulovi behind. (*Ben Wittick, Collections in the Museum of New Mexico*)

ineradicable instinct that all living things are one. And all *are* living: snake, mountain, cloud, eagles, and men.

Pueblo architecture itself can help us toward some understanding of this state of being. It is, first of all, much the most permanent of all North American Indian architectures, and is, therefore, always related to specific sites with their special sacred or, at least, religiously functioning landscape forms. Secondly, its ritual is still wholly alive and hence illustrative of how its architectural frame was originally conceived. That architecture is also described by a verbal language, whereby its visual language can be supplemented and clarified for our restless eyes: eyes not yet blind but much less connected in most instances with the intellectual centers of our being than those of the Indians still are.

Here even the apparent deficiencies of language serve our turn. Whorf tells us, for example, that the Hopi have no special names for special building types or building shapes or rooms except *yé·mòkvi*, meaning equally "inner room" and "cavern"; and *te'wi*, meaning both "setback," as in a building, and "ledge," as on a mountainside.[3] And in the latter meaning, so Mindeleff and Stephen told us long ago, *te'wi* is also used for the bench around the sides of a kiva's interior.[4] Even for that subterranean room, the center of religious life and ritual, there was no special term, and the word *kiva* is only a foreigner's corruption of *ki·he*, which means a building of any kind. From all this, no less than from the forms of Hopi architecture itself, it would seem apparent that buildings and mountains are all one for the Hopi (fig. I:10). Manmade structures are works of nature, too, no different in that from the homes of the bees. Looking like natural rock outcrops on the crowns of their mesas, Hopi towns are not exactly engaged in "fitting in" with nature, as so many Western romantic buildings have tried to do. They *are* nature, pure and simple, but their resemblance to the shapes of the earth is not

I:11 Hemis Kachina dance in a Hopi plaza. The photographs are combined to give a feeling of the plaza shape; hence the kachinas are doubled.

I:12 Pueblo Bonito. Keyhole doorway.

I:13 Pueblo Bonito. Rooms.

I:14 Pueblo Bonito. Doorways in upper floors.

accidental entirely either. It is to the Hopi, I think, at once an act of reverence and a natural congruence between two natural things.

But the matter does not stop there, because the Hopi know that, within nature, they as men are trying to do certain special things. They are hoping—as we have already noted, they are forced to hope—that they can affect the rest of the universe: can make it rain, for example. Out of conscious intentions of that kind, reinforced no doubt by complex human instincts toward formal symbolism and abstract elaboration, a peculiarly man-made construction is built up, in this case the great Pueblo ceremonial system, an order of thought and action which is magical and scientific all at once.[5] Pueblo architecture is that system's setting and its physical vehicle, and as such it is very clearly described by the special words relative to architecture that the Hopi do in fact possess. These are words which, in the case of buildings, directly denote physical elements such as doors and windows, and, in the case of the town as a whole, can name it and its major functional open area. Putting those words together can indeed do much to resolve the question that troubled Whorf concerning the Hopi's lack of space- and shape-descriptive terminology, because they unmistakably lay out for us the major environmental function of Hopi architecture, which is not to provide complex interior spaces or a

I:15 Pueblo Bonito. The wall. (*William R. Current*)

I:16 Pueblo Bonito. General view. Casa Rinconada across canyon.

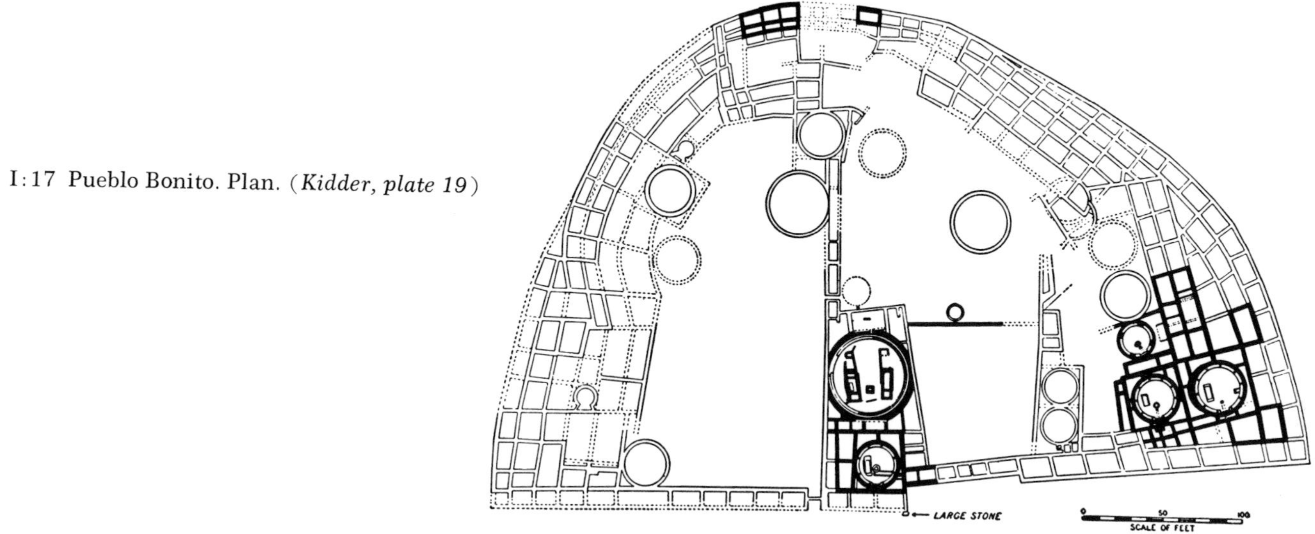

I:17 Pueblo Bonito. Plan. (*Kidder, plate 19*)

I:18 Pueblo Bonito. Reconstruction drawing after Jackson. (*Kidder, plate 19*)

variety of individually expressive buildings but instead to use buildings to frame a plaza in which ritual dances can be performed and from which they can be watched (fig. I:11). Using Whorf's list we find that all the words are there: *kí·coki,* "village"; *kí·sonvi, "plaza"*; and *te'wi* (again that "ledge" or "set back)," here placed along the house front, so that spectators can lean back against the *tek*^{w}*ni*, or "wall." This is capped, just about at the height of a file of high-masked dancers in the plaza, by the *kiqálmo*, the "eaves" or "cornice." Above it is the roof, *kí·àmi*, upon which more watchers stand, a frieze of men at the side of the dancers. And there is a word for "on the roof" to place them there, where they can see the sacred landscape as well. The human scale is precise, so that the buildings become an exact frame for ritual. The environment frames the act. Even a conscious sense of the plaza itself as a spatial volume may not be lacking, since the word *tek*^{w}*wánmène*, "encircling wall," exists to describe such a condition.

There is another important word, too, I think: *kiska*, a covered way between buildings leading into the plaza. Such passages can best be seen at Walpi and Shongopovi: at the former very deep, a good thirteen lintels long (fig. VI: 41); at the latter arranged in a splendid sequence of tunnels from plaza to plaza, with wooden boards spanning shallow trenches in the passages, which reverberate like thunder underfoot. In these passages is retained, I believe, a direct reference to the "Classic Pueblo" period of the "ancient ones," the Anasazi, when the village as a whole was all one house, the Great House, where the inhabitants went from room to room *en suite*, bending under the pine or cedar lintels that supported the many stories of wall above them (figs. I:12–15). Scores of prehistoric ruins show that

unified organization: many are in Chaco Canyon, for example, which the Hopi claim as one of their earlier homes.[6]

At Pueblo Bonito, as in the other vast structures of the eleventh to the thirteenth centuries there, the word *yé·mòkvi*, or some equivalent, must have functioned appropriately: almost all the rooms are deeply "inner" and "cavernous." *Te'wi* would have applied, too, as the rooms are set back in elevation to form sunny external ledges for outdoor living within the embracing D of the huge building's outer wall (figs. I:16–18). Across the canyon from Pueblo Bonito, the cliff opens in a cross canyon, and that cleft must have caught the eyes of the inhabitants on the terraces, but all the major relationships seem inward. The Great House does not appear to be turned outward to focus on any natural feature external to itself—except, of course, upon the regal sun. It is fundamentally symmetrical and complete. Unlike contemporary pueblos it cannot be added onto. It is a *Unité d'Habitation*, an internal world, a hive, a dizzying constellation of cellular units (fig. I:19). No throne rooms, or *megara*, as in the Bronze Age palaces of the Aegean, emerge among them; the principle is egalitarian.[7] Nor, unlike those palaces, does any special system of labyrinthine circulation other than that from room to room reveal itself in the depths of the ruins, though the dances of modern pueblos often show clear patterns of labyrinthine movement through the town.[8] Here such may indeed have taken place right through the deeply buried cells and along upper levels now lost. Ritual was surely focused on the cylindrical kivas which penetrate the body of the building and spatter its contained courtyard like enormous drops of rain. The kivas intensify the effect of an obsessive geometric order. When

I:19 Pueblo Bonito. From above. Note Great Kivas in plaza.

I:20 Chaco Canyon. Chetro Ketl. The string-coursed wall and the tall cylinders encased within the rectangular building may reflect Toltec influence. The Great Kiva is in the courtyard. (*Myrtle P. Vivian*)

I:21 Chetro Ketl. Cylinders inside cubes. Great Kiva beyond.

I:22 Chetro Ketl. The courtyard with colonnade, later walled up. Great Kiva on the right.

I:23 Aztec. Aerial view. A typically Chacoan symmetrical layout. Great Kiva reconstructed in courtyard. Three-walled sanctuary just out of the picture this side of ruin. (*Petley Studios*)

placed above ground among the dwelling and storage cubicles they are built upwards to whatever height is necessary to permit entrance and egress through their roofs, and they are packed round with earth to retain their original and, apparently, ritually necessary subterranean character. Stepped altars, mountain and cloud at once, would probably have been found in them, and the *te'wi* circled their walls, rock ledges deep in this ultimate cave. Yet in the floor the round, shallow, navel-like notch of the *sipapu*, symbolic of the place of human emergence from the earth, gave spiritual access to still another world deeper below. One descended into the kiva by ladder through the smokehole in the ceiling over the fire, which was shielded by a masonry deflector (which was also, perhaps primarily, part of the altar) from an air vent, called by the Indians a "spirit tunnel," in the wall behind it. In some areas that wall often flared out into a keyhole shape, perhaps to facilitate the spirits' passage (fig. I:31).

The largest kivas at Pueblo Bonito and elsewhere are of the so-called Great Kiva type, large and deep, with what may have been huge foot drums in the floor and with ceilings supported on four massive piers (figs. I:17–19). They were a traditional and well-established building type in Pueblo culture and were probably intended to serve a larger social unit, perhaps half the pueblo—a "moiety"—than the smaller ones, which were probably for the clans.[9] In their fully developed Classic Pueblo form, they could clearly have contained many people for many hours in elaborate ceremonies. Some of them, such as the central one at Pueblo Bonito (fig. I:19), the larger one at Chetro Ketl (figs. I:20–22), and the restored multileveled and antechambered cylinder at Aztec north of Chaco (figs. I:23–25), would appear to have been designed to serve the town as a whole, and to have been centrally placed so as to dominate the view from the living terraces.

The Great Kivas also seem to have eventually become the vehicle of two major developments in Pueblo architecture. These were: first, an opening out of ritual focus beyond the building to external

I:24 Aztec. Great Kiva. Interior reconstructed. (*Photo by Gene Aiken*)

I:25 Aztec. Great Kiva. Reconstructed interior looking toward upper sanctuary. (*Painting by Paul Coze*)

natural features (with, later, a concomitant loosening up of the massing of the Great House as a whole); and, second, the transformation of the Great Kiva itself into the plaza of the modern town. In my opinion it is likely that progressive desiccation, culminating in the decisive drought of the later thirteenth century, led to intensified attempts to draw yet more of the earth and the sky, as well as more of the larger human community, into the web of ritual. As Chaco's stream cut its arroyo and the water table fell, and as the scanty rain failed and the runoff from the side canyons was carefully husbanded, and as canals—if that is what some of those channels really are[10]—were built to bring water from considerable distances, so the Great Kivas began to be built out in space on their own. The ritual on their roofs thus began to call out to greater distances and to invoke striking natural features. Casa Rinconada, rising as a squat cylinder out of the earth, is placed on its own swell of ground across from Pueblo Bonito; it commands a sweeping view up and down the drying canyon and now draws Pueblo Bonito's own view with an almost axial directness across space (figs. I:19, 26). Kin Nahasbas, perhaps the first Great Kiva built to serve more than one pueblo, is set near the top of a distinctive natural cone, and it is inflected toward the startling Fajada Butte, which focuses the view eastward from it, while the drying stream runs snakelike far below (fig. I:27). There is also a kiva—though technically not a Great Kiva—topping a cone at the Mesa Verde (fig. I:28). Its excavator suggests that it may be using that natural feature like a Mexican temple base, and the same might be said of Kin Nahasbas.[11] Elsewhere, as below Shabik'eshchee at

I:26 Chaco Canyon. The Great Kiva called Casa Rinconada. Pueblo del Arroyo left distance; Pueblo Bonito center; Chetro Ketl right.

Chaco and at Nutria near Zuni, Great Kivas are built in clusters near the mouths of canyons as if to tap the water seeping through underneath.

Even more specialized structures, apparently of religious purpose, then began to be built during these climactic twelfth and thirteenth centuries: triple-walled towers for example; and they too were often sited to invoke a source of water (fig. I:29). One was touchingly placed right at the edge of the hopelessly deepening arroyo behind the Pueblo del Arroyo in Chaco;[12] another was raised behind the great house at Aztec, between it and the powerful irrigation canal which still brings some of the water of the Animas River down from Colorado high above the main channel so that green fields can be irrigated right up to the sand hills' edge.[13] North of Aztec, at the Mesa Verde, a special proliferation of ritual structures took place during the thirteenth century. It would appear that within not much more than a few generations all the new kinds of buildings were conceived and constructed and, together with the whole of the Mesa Verde area, abandoned. Some kiva-tower units were set forward on the tops of the mesas, as if to invoke earth and sky together in a kind of archaizing revival of the old unit-type dwelling (figs. I:30, 31). Towers echo them across space at Howenweep (figs. I:32, 33), sited as if to use the view toward the impressively shaped Ute Mountain near the Mesa Verde, as are several Great Kiva sites in the area. At the Mesa Verde itself, a spectacular bow-shaped labyrinth like a compacted abstraction of Pueblo Bonito was pushed far out on a prow of mesa where two canyons intersect deep in the earth below (figs. I:34, 35). It was called Sun Temple by its excavators,[14] and it was

I:27 Chaco Canyon. Great Kiva, Kin Nahasbas, with Fajada Butte. (*National Park Service*)

I:28 Mesa Verde site, 1086. An above-ground kiva tops the conical hill above this pass into the Mesa Verde. Its excavator suggests possible influence from Mexican temple bases.

I:29 Chaco Canyon. Pueblo del Arroyo. Three-walled structure.

clearly intended not only to enclose the worshiper but, from its roof, to carry his eye out above the earth; he was lifted to the clouds, the temple a platform to project him there and perhaps to draw them down. In all this, "Sun Temple," too, suggests Meso-America.

Another kind of specialization that took place at Mesa Verde in that cataclysmic century was the building of elaborate structures, with many kivas and towers, in the clefts of the mesa sides. It would be wrong, I think, to regard such complexes as Cliff Palace, Spruce Tree House, and so on, as simple cliff dwellings[15] (figs. I:36–39). The inhabitants of the Mesa Verde had lived in pueblos on the mesa tops for many centuries. Suddenly, very late in their history and just before total drought struck, some of them climbed back down the canyon walls to ancient clefts, of which a number had been used by their Early Basketmaker ancestors (c. A.D. 1–450) long before. Why did they do so? There is no hard evidence for the presence of wandering nomads in the area, certainly none for Navahos and Utes, who came much later. It is true that there is some evidence of violence, but it was probably inter-Pueblo in orgin. Competition for life must have become intense in those years, and the movement to the clefts may in part have had a defensive intention. Indeed, some tiny houses are stuck in dizzy cliffs far off by themselves. Yet many of the Great Houses do not seem especially defensible. Some of them could be traps; Spruce Tree House comes to mind as an example (fig. I:38). It may, however, be argued that at least one of the purposes of this kind of dwelling was ritualistic in character, and that it was connected with the rise of the specialized structures we have already discussed. Contact with the earth had to be renewed; it was perhaps mankind's first wholly conscious attempt to reach back out, or down, to mother earth in this area—his first major philosophical leap, or regression, not to

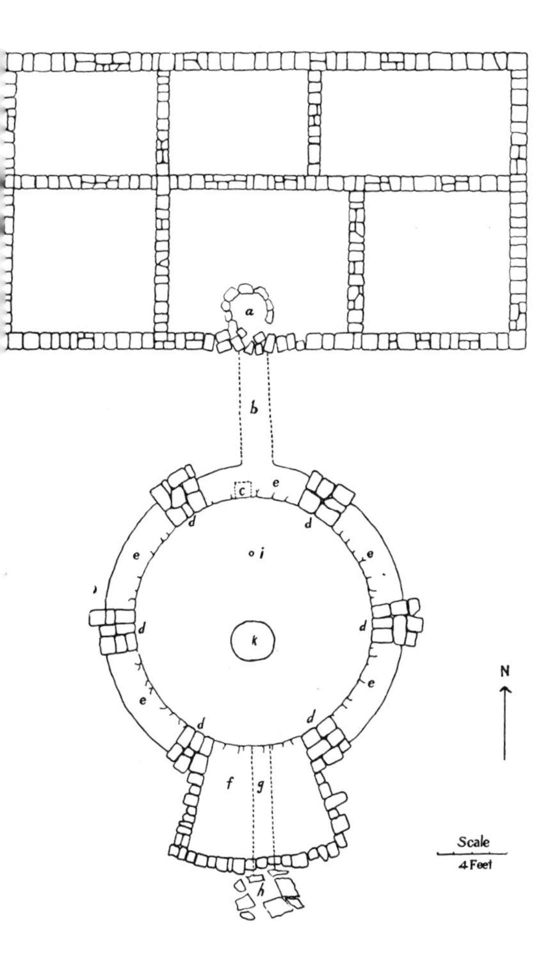

I:31 Ground plan of unit-type dwelling (after Prudden); note the keyhole-shaped kiva. (*Kidder, figure 11*)

I:30 Mesa Verde. Kiva and tower unit on mesa top.

separate himself from nature but to attempt a firmer grip on more of it. Nevertheless, he failed; both his egalitarian palaces at Chaco and his final kiva-tower palace-temples in the clefts went under, and he had to move on, bereft of his grandeur and his ritual setting and reduced to his sack of seed corn for planting. But those dry kernels were invincible in the end. He survived with them; and over the centuries his massed corn dances have celebrated their paramilitary power. So in Sophocles' *Oedipus at Colonus* (698 ff.) the citizens of Athens call out together to "the olive . . . terror of our enemies."

We should not underestimate the historical decisiveness of the drought and its implications. This reading of the Great Houses and of what happened to them suggests that the Pueblos had wrestled nature to the very edge of a humanistic consciousness—which is where some of their animal dances stand today—at which point the drought knocked their pretensions down. Men simply cannot stand up to the sky and the earth in the Southwest as they can in the Aegean[16]—not without a technology that tends to destroy nature, which did not become a problem in the area until modern times.

Nor can we look at Cliff Palace or Spruce Tree House at Mesa Verde without realizing their enormous and fundamental difference from the structures at Chaco (figs. I:14, 16, 18). There the house was enclosed in a constructed shell of wall, upstanding and abstract in form—thus very much a man-made shape

I:32 Howenweep, Utah. Square Tower canyon cluster, with Ute Mountain.

I:33 Howenweep. The Square Tower.

I:34 Mesa Verde. Sun Temple.

I:35 Mesa Verde. Sun Temple with canyon view.

and one that was compulsively elaborate, even precious, in its structure, with a thick, tapering mass and a fluid mosaic surface of small tabular stones (fig. I:14). In the clefts of the Mesa Verde that wall is entirely gone, and the Great House as a whole has no man-made shell whatever. The earth provides it now (figs. I:36–39). The towers of the house reach up to touch the earth, while their connected kivas probe similarly down below. What is up, what down? This is the true magic of the houses, a complex, highly evolved, and abstracted urbanism all slipped back into the earth as in some mad, modern science-fiction dream: lower Manhattan hidden in one titanic cleft to withstand—what? How the dances must have resounded on the kiva tops, drum and chant and foot-beat rolling back down from the cavern roof while the rest of the population packed the doorways around. The shapes and sounds of ritual had to have been profoundly intensified in this setting. There is surely a true delirium of man-made geometry in the cylinders, cubes, and towers, but the ultimate order is the cavern's, and to its preexisting shape the human geometry must eventually conform. That geometry was constructed with the honey-colored, hand-scaled blocks of masonry so characteristic of the Mesa Verde. The solidity, I think we should even say the dignity, of

I:36 Mesa Verde. Cliff Palace.

the material fabric of the building was still, as at Chaco Canyon, a matter of special significance to its builders. But in the cliff dwellings that other Anasazi —though some of them may have been fugitives from the Mesa Verde—built at the very end of the thirteenth century into the sides of mesas along the routes out of the area to the south, as in Betatakin and Keet Seel at Kayenta (figs. I:40–43), the masonry quickly became more casual in character: rough-cut and increasingly slapdash, developing rapidly toward rubble and mud.[17] There is a sense of haste, in which the fabric of the house was no longer of obsessive concern or ritual significance. The cavern, not the Great House, is now, or perhaps we should say once more, the primary physical and psychological protector of human beings. The majestic caves at Kayenta have special powers along those lines. They create enormously monumental volumes of space and suggest figural images at tremendous scale as well (fig. I:42). It would be hard to believe that they were not sought out largely for their ritual power. But like the clefts of the Mesa Verde they were not occupied for long. Down along this southwestward route into northern Arizona the kivas also soon lost their traditional circular shape and became rectangular like the living units. This had already begun at the Mesa

Verde in the rectangular Fire Temple and probably in other kivas in the narrower clefts. The cliff dwellings as a whole were also progressively loosened in massing. They relaxed and opened. With their rubble walls and corrals of jacal construction they began already to look much like contemporary Pueblo towns (fig. I:43). Moving in this southerly direction, the towns were in fact becoming Hopi, and there is no reason to doubt that the Hopi are the direct descendants of the Anasazi in this area. Some of them, it is true, may have come from the south and west, from Walnut Canyon or Wupatki under the San Francisco peaks, for example, from which the mesas of eventual refuge for those from north and south alike can indeed be seen not so far off across the Painted Desert (fig. I:1). In any event, the Great House in its old, abstractly shaped and heroic form, and the Great Kiva, too, had both disappeared long before the sixteenth century and the beginning of written history, and the Pueblo village had opened and stretched its body to create more communal plazas and for an easier adjustment to landscape forms.

The steps by which the prehistoric Great Kiva underwent its metamorphosis into the plaza of historic times are not all known. Kinishba, in the White Mountains of Arizona, a compact, single-building village with a tightly enclosed court (figs. V:64, 65), is often cited as a transitional example.[18] The tiny, deeply engulfed, but clearly main plaza at Zuni has always seemed to me another (fig. V:69). Finally we arrive at the fully organized *Ki'sonvi* of the Hopi villages, which we discussed before (fig. I:11). In them, too, is a board-covered *sipapu*, along with other relics of kiva furniture—including the *te'wi* as bench, now exterior. The pattern can probably be seen at its most fully evolved in the large plazas of the towns of the upper Rio Grande. Here again there is little reason to doubt the continuity with Anasazi prehistory, and

I:37 Mesa Verde. Cliff Palace and Canyon.

I:38 Mesa Verde. Spruce Tree House.

I:39 Mesa Verde. Spruce Tree House. Court with kiva.

I:40 Kayenta. Betatakin.
(*W. M. Cline Co.*)

I:41 Betatakin. Detail.
(*W. M. Cline Co.*)

I:42 Kayenta. Keet Seel. (*W. M. Cline Co.*)

contact with, perhaps some immigration from, Chaco Canyon and so on. Ortiz has shown how the plaza of Tewa San Juan makes use of all the major elements of the old Great Kiva, including as well the outward-reaching landscape focus of its developed phase. Now the plaza takes cognizance of four sacred mountains on the four directions, with four sacred hills standing before them along the same axes.[19] Conspicuous from San Juan are the horned Truchas Peaks, which the Tewa call Rock Horn Mountain,[20] and which

I:43 Keet Seel. Detail. (*William R. Current*)

Ortiz, who calls it Stone Man Mountain also, identifies as San Juan's sacred mountain of the east, upon which the long axis of its largest plaza is exactly oriented. When the long files of dancers fill that space, the architectural pattern is complete; the natural and the man-made together frame and encourage the human ritual act. All is one. The photograph from Tesuque, slightly to the south, shows those relationships well (fig. I:44). The ridge line of Lake Peak, Tesuque's sacred mountain of the east, is redrawn close at hand by the profile of the building, while the ranks of corn dancers complete the unison of natural,

I:44 Tesuque Pueblo. Corn dance with Lake Peak, sacred mountain of the east.

I:45 San Ildefonso Pueblo. Kiva with Pajarito Plateau and Jemez range with Tsi'como, sacred mountain of the west.

man-constructed, and human lines.[21] The same is true at San Ildefonso, another Tewa town, where the outlines and masses of the buildings trace those of the Jemez range, culminated in this view by Tsi'como, cloud gatherer, sacred mountain of the west (fig. I: 45). Here the kiva in the plaza lifts up like the old Casa Rinconada, but now with a stairway like a gentle memory of Mexico far off. It is framed in those stepped profiles which, like the altar within, are apparently intended to invoke mountain and sky together.

But Taos, as always, seems most dramatically to embody the ancient intentions, like a place of special power, a great Teotihuacán of the north. Its splendid, sweeping plaza is as imperial a container of pickups and trailers today as it was of horses and nomad booths in the past.[22] It grandly receives the full force of looming Taos Mountain, cleft, horned, and terraced, with its sacred Blue Lake cupped within its peaks (fig. I:46). The plaza taps the mountain's water, and the buildings to north and south open outward as if dancing to celebrate its flow, which rushes undying between them in a lively stream. The north building demonstrates what the "inner room" unit and its concomitant "setback" massing can do when they are freed from the old Chaco-like containment and when the sensitivities of a virtuoso community reign.[23] Together they organize an articulated mass which echoes the mountain and abstracts it to the measure of human units, picks up its beat in fact, exactly as the dancers do who move in file, stamping up and down before its face (fig. I:47). Between it and the mountain, the kivas, now also

I:46 Taos. Panorama with stream and Taos Mountain. (Note that this panorama crops North House and mountain.)

I:47 Taos. North House. *(Collections in the Museum of New Mexico)*

I:48 Casas Grandes, Chihuahua. Great House, left rear, ceremonial structures and mountains.

free of containment by the apartment block, are sunk deep into the earth. They are edged about with wooden palings like medieval palisades, and their ladder poles, heroic in scale, ride extravagantly high. Across the stream the southern building masses up into its own perfectly obvious pyramid, and it exactly mirrors and fits into the green or blood-red glowing foothills of the Sangre de Cristo beyond it to the east (fig. I:46). Southward, beyond a long, low range of buildings, the horns of the Truchas loom far off (figs. II:14–17), while westward behind the church all structures fall away to the high Rio Grande plain. Only the church, its form European in origin, stands up flat against the mountain (figs. II:18, 19), but here, as always, the Pueblos subdue and adjust its towered massing to the mountain's ridge line, just as, over the centuries, they have been able to gentle its imposed Christianity into their own pattern of belief.[24]

A comparison with Meso-America should be made here. We have already noted possible relationships with Mexican temples in the siting of ritual structures. It is also true that a certain knowledge of Toltec buildings such as those at Tula, Chalchihuites, and La Quemada may perhaps be suspected in some details of pier and massing at Chetro Ketl and elsewhere in Chaco Canyon, and perhaps in its mosaic wall facing generally.[25] And the Toltec period of the tenth through the twelfth centuries, exactly dated to influence the elaboration of Developmental Pueblo (750–1100) into Classic Pueblo architecture, would certainly seem to be that in which Meso-American culture reached out most effectively toward the north. But on the whole the Valley of Mexico—unless, as some have believed, it inspired the masked dances—seems to have affected Pueblo culture only slightly, providing sacred parrots perhaps, and copper bells.[26] In architecture, at least, the cultural impact was clearly much less than that which inspired the Mound

Builders of the Southeast to raise their Mexican-like temple bases to the skies. The deserts of Chihuahua were a formidable barrier, not a highway like the Gulf, and even when they were crossed by Mexican traders and settlers, the Pueblos seem to have retained their own special ways. At Casas Grandes, in Chihuahua, the two cultures can be seen juxtaposed, hardly overlapping but complementing each other, so that the Pueblo apartment house is placed to enjoy a view of the more-or-less Toltec-style temple platforms framed by the hills behind them (figs. I:48, 49).

Pre-Columbian Mexico monumentalizes, compacts, and abstracts. The setback organization of its temple bases tends toward the purely pyramidal. Its "inner room," where there is one, is only a tomb chamber far below, though its ancient hut type is lifted in masonry to the heavens. Religious specialization and hieratic political organization have otherwise gone far. Pre-Toltec Teotihuacán shows the archetype: compressed and compacted man-made mountains repeat and abstract the real mountains beyond them (fig. I:4). Together they describe the well-watered Valley of Mexico, as the mountain running with springs gives birth to a mass human population whose works can approach its own great scale, and whose horned and feathered serpent emerges hugely from the rock and pierces the sky. Much the same is true at Zapotec Monte Alban (fig. I:5), which rides its high ridge down between the two Sierras while its ranges of buildings echo

I:49 Casas Grandes. View from Pueblo Great House toward temples.

their coned and blocky masses and San Felipe del Agua looms northward over all. Where there are no mountains to shape the world, as in much of the Petén and in northern Yucatán, the Mayan temples ride above the trees like clouds and, indeed, breathe out a chill rain breath from their cool corbel-vaulted interiors. Their bases are springs to lift them there (figs. I:6, 7).

The Pueblo builder, after the hopes and experiments of his years of crisis, settled in the end for something less specialized, gentler, and more offhand. His largest building, that most at the scale of the mountains, remained his communal dwelling,[27] and his room units built to a looser massing than that of Mexico, no less pyramidal in fundamental intention, perhaps even more evocative of nature's shapes, but curiously reticent, deceptively casual in profile. His last Great Houses have thus been able to pass themselves off through all the centuries of bondage as simple accidents of conglomeration, not the passionate human contributions to natural divinity which they really are. When, today, the priests of Taos stand wrapped in their blanket-cloaks at the apex of their two buildings—and call to each other with strange, birdlike voices and observe the sun—they are surely carrying on a rite not unknown in ancient Mexico, and they are doing so from the same kind of place. Man-made, their platform is yet a cavernous mountain, so that the mountain, too, is theirs.

II:1 San Antonio Peak. Former sacred mountain of the north. View from the south.

II:2 San Antonio Peak.

II

THE RIO GRANDE—TAOS AND PICURIS

The Pueblo world of the upper Rio Grande has an especially clear and protective shape (fig. I:1). It is a long and comparatively narrow bowl defined by mountains in whose forms the Pueblos have chosen to read the lineaments of divinity. The two major ranges, which contain the sacred mountains of the east and the west for all the Pueblo towns in view of them, are the Sangre de Cristo on the east and the Jemez on the west. Southward, the valley falls away below Santa Fe to the vast buffalo plains that stretch toward Texas. There the protection of the hills is lost, and with the coming of the horse the nomads were eventually able to drive away the Pueblos who had settled there earlier. The plains became Apache, and, most of all, Comanche, land. Below the southeastward gap, however, one double-peaked mountain rises high, turtlelike as seen from the north, fanged in great Vs from the west (figs. IV:59; V, 20). It is Sandia, home of the twin war gods, sacred mountain of the south.[1] Far northward beyond the Jemez range and a little northwest of Taos, a perfect swelling mound of deceptively large scale rises out of the upward lifting plain (figs. II:1, 2). This is San Antonio Peak, or Bear Mountain, and, according to Harrington in 1916, the sacred mountain of the north.[2] By 1970, according to Ortiz, that function had been taken over, for San Juan at least, by Canjilon Peak (Hazy or Shimmering Mountain to the Tewa), which lifts somewhat southwest of Bear Mountain and culminates its own tangled and beautifully watered range[3] (fig. III:1). This tendency to drift southward had been characteristic of the Pueblos throughout their history. Indeed, one suspects that in this area the sacred mountain of the north may once have been the magnificent Sierra Madre, the Sierra Blanca (fig. II:3), in some ways the most spectacular presence in the whole Sangre de Cristo chain, and perhaps still the Navaho mountain of the east, which looms maternally about Fort Garland in Colorado.[4] At such a time, San Antonio would have defined that upper valley on its western side, while Mount Wheeler or one of the other peaks above Taos might have acted as its complementary guardian on the east.

Whatever the case, Taos (figs. I:46, 47; II:4–39)

is now the northernmost pueblo, sitting on what seems in wintertime to be the very roof of a Tibetan world. She holds her own sacred mountain with its sacred lake jealously to herself; her grip is firm (figs. II:4–10). Over the centuries the people of Taos built a series of villages directly in front of the mountain, each time moving a little farther down into the valley. Two general Pueblo characteristics are apparent in this. First is a compulsion to move the village periodically, if only by a little, and second is the special Rio Grande pattern that directs the village in a sequence of sites out of the foothills of the mountains toward the open plain. Among the other pueblos to the south that movement normally ended up right on the bank of the great river itself. But Taos—fortunately, because the Rio Grande runs deep in an awesome gorge through the Taos plain—never needed to move so far. She was doubly blessed in that her own stream from her own mountain always supplied more than enough water for her needs.[5] So she was able to shape her own integral balance between the natural and the man-made, the latter formed of the humblest material of all: mud, here liberally tempered with straw (figs. II:11–13). In a sense, the adobe of the northern Rio Grande represents the culmination of the prehistoric movement away from the fine masonry construction that we noted earlier. Now, instead of the tesserae of Chaco Canyon, or the mason's blocks of Mesa Verde, or even the rubble of Keet Seel, we have only wet clay, laid up in handfuls by the women and patted and smoothed as in the shaping of a pot. Adobe bricks were not introduced until Spanish times. The building's body remained fundamentally hand shaped, hand smoothed, a man-made earth form relating to the mountain. In this a comparison with Attica seems important (figs. II:14, 15). The horned and cleft

II:3 The Sierra Madre of the Sangre de Cristo from Fort Garland, Colorado. This is the Sierra Blanca, sometimes regarded as the sacred mountain of the east by the Navaho.

II:4 Taos. The North Building in the late nineteenth century. *(Ben Wittick, Collections in the Museum of New Mexico)*

II:5 Taos. Blue Lake in Taos mountain. *(Collections in the Museum of New Mexico)*

II:6 "Laos" at the San Diego Exposition of 1915. The point of the setbacks misunderstood; the other half of the architecture, the mountain, absent. (*Collections in the Museum of New Mexico*)

II:8 Taos in the snow.

II:7 Taos. Plan (1950). (*Stubbs, figure 4*)

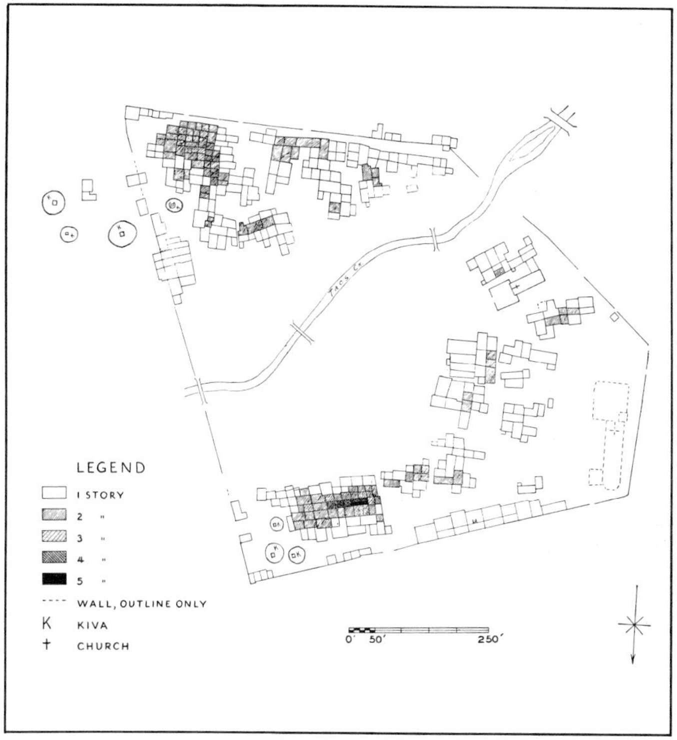

LEGEND
1 STORY
2 "
3 "
4 "
5 "
WALL, OUTLINE ONLY
K KIVA
+ CHURCH
0' 50' 250'

II:9 Taos. The South Building in winter from the west.

II:10 Taos. The South Building from the northwest on a summer afternoon.

II:11 Taos. Adobe wall, wood frame.

mountains rise much alike in both places, but the one at Taos is more dominant and the human works are part of it. They echo it in shape and color. Hymettos lies lower and the Parthenon rises free to the sky, self-contained as a ship, giving off the blazing light of sharply cut marble against the mountain's dark.

Yet the man-made part of Taos is rich in its own forms as well. Here the major contrast is between the prismatic setbacks of the adobe masses and the frame structures of the drying racks before them (figs. II:11–14, 16). This play of shapes was even more striking before doors were introduced into the adobe planes. Closed cubes are contrasted with open skeletons, the texture of strawed adobe with that of grainy cedar, the warm brown of mud with weathered silver. Now Spanish conical ovens play their part. The relationships are inexhaustible, and the modern tourist, his brain packed with Cubist images, runs amok with his camera, just as the first of the artists' colony at Taos ran wild with watercolor two generations ago. The forms are always changing as the light models them, shifting in tone, and they are eminently pictorial. But in the end they are stern and ritually fixed. One is led by the wooden frames into the canyonlike passageways trod by the dancers, below and through the house masses, which truly loom with

II:12 Taos. Adobe wall, wood frame.

II:13 Taos. Five views among the houses.

physical power, a little ominous and secret. A silent domical midden, forbidden to visitors, lies on the north. A view of the north house from the small plaza directly below it on the west shows its proud, flat-backed profile (fig. II:36). Here Chaco is at least remembered. The Great House now echoes the mountain in all its profiles but does not bend its back to do so, and the priest on its summit, as seen in this view, is standing on something much higher than one of the Howenweep's towers (figs. II:34, 35).

We have already seen how the buildings are related to the mountains to the east and south, as well as to each other and to the open western plain (figs. II:14–17). A tendency—which will be noted also in Hopi towns such as Walpi and Schongopovi—to mass up the most pyramidal of the buildings near the major kivas, is most fully developed at Taos. The north house, backing up its kivas as their ladder poles leap between it and the mountain (figs. II:37, 39), is matched on the south, where the climactic pyramid rises directly above other kivas similarly placed (figs. II:7, 17). Westward, as we saw, the church stands up facing the mountain and is splashed with Hellenic white; but here, as in all the pueblos, the old harmonic twin-towered façade of Western European church architecture is pulled into gentler undulations of outline to suggest rather than to oppose the mountain's form (figs. II:18, 19). It seems obvious too that the portico in front of the church is overtly intended to echo the mountain's profile. In this way, as in others, the intrusive European attitude, like the imperial European religion it housed, was deflated by Pueblo culture and drawn by it into a more naturally inclusive web of divinity. There is a clear contrast here with the church of San Francisco de Taos, which serves the Spanish community just down the valley (figs. II:20, 21). Its towers are aggressively European, however simplified and even gentle they may seem (like so much of New Mexican Spanish culture) when they are compared with those of the Cathedral of Mexico or Tlaxcala (fig. II:22), and they challenge the mountains with considerable machismo, but the

II:14 Taos. Panorama. (*Philip Garvin*)

II:15 The Parthenon on the Acropolis of Athens from the west, with the horns of Mount Hymettos and the conical hills of Aphrodite at Kaisariani. The Theater of Dionysos lies under the South Wall of the Acropolis.

II:16 Taos. Panorama from the northeast. Left to right: wall; South Building, Truchas Peaks beyond; church; corn-drying racks; North Building.

II:17 Taos. South Building from the northeast in winter light.

pueblo will not permit its church to do so.[6] It is not interested in heroic confrontation but in cooperative interplay. It wants to bring the force of the mountain to itself. Here again one recalls Teotihuacán (fig. I:4). Taos too has a great axis: its living stream (figs. II:7–19). Off that the buildings are deployed and, as at Teotihuacán, reciprocate with their own mountain masses. The enormous open plaza, which is one of the glories of Taos, is of course much less contained than Meso-American courtyards or even than most pueblo plazas, and one feels strongly that it is something special, unique in itself. It is hard to see a trace of the old Great Kiva in it. One senses that the two houses are sacred, and that they equally praise mountain and stream, but that between them is a strange, rather disquieting open space—like the empty plains which lie just beyond the mountain eastward. Strangers mill around and trade in it and sèt up shop, and the social dances are held there, the round dances and, today, the usual Plains "war dances" (figs. II:23, 24). The pole climb which is held in it is sacred (fig. II:25), but most of the dances of ritual and the sacred races are held, now as in the recorded past, tight up against the buildings, usually taking place entirely or at least culminating under the northern one (figs. II:26–32). And the beat of those dances is built into the architecture, which thus dances too. In Mexico, the fractured horizontal lines of the temple bases look as if their shapes had themselves been compacted by the pounding of massed feet upon them (fig. I: 4), but at Taos the looser, even lighter, step-back effect is more like a syncopated drumbeat embodied, hitting and lifting, striking, withdrawing. Again the contrast with eagle-winging Parthenon is strong; but there too a chorus of ancient lineage, the chorus of Dionysos, danced under the south flank of the Acropolis rock, like the dancers of Taos below their Great House. Beyond them both, their savage, sacred landscapes towered (figs. II:14, 15).

The hunting-dance days of winter are often of great cold, sometimes with enormous depths of snow. Even today Taos can be temporarily cut off by it, the mountain roads drifted over, the highway south through the narrow canyon of the Rio Grande packed

II:18 Taos. The church with the clouds.

II:19 Taos. The gate of the church's precinct with Taos mountain.

icy hard under a bitter Rocky Mountain wind. Temperatures may fall to thirty below. On such days a flat, white cloud often condenses on the summits of the sacred mountain and hangs like a gauzy rebozo over its face. All else is crystal clear, so that the deep, snowy canyons under the cloud can be seen from the pueblo, with the shadows cast by the cloud-cap riding across and into them, so emphasizing their depth, their remoteness, and their great scale. At such times the mountain possesses a double character, not only hunched over and brooding like a being which feels the power of the cold, but also opening up to show a wild environment high up near its summit, utterly different from, and perhaps even dangerous to, the human world of towns and cornfields down below. Now the mountain is animal land and animal mother, savoring the savage winter world of the wild. And when the hunted beasts and their Mistress in human form come down into the pueblo in the winter afternoon as if from that savage home, they pass the pitiful little wall of clay which is all that stands between the town and the mountain on that side (fig. II:37). It is only now that one feels a true purpose in that wall, drawing as it seems to do a fragile ritual line between the pueblo and the wild. Now the deer come down and dance in the plaza; they let you see them. Innocent, they bring their power openly down to you.

One guesses that all this may be among the reasons why the animal costumes of deer and buffalo alike have remained much more naturalistic at Taos than at any of the other pueblos farther away down the valley. The deer dancers of Taos dance in the full deer skin, the horned head held high, while the buffalo dancers wear the whole buffalo head, not merely a buffalo mane (figs. II:38a, 38c). The deer carry two fore-sticks but often walk with an upright gait like were-deer or like hunters masquerading in the bodies of their prey (figs. II:38a, 38b). And the deer are surely dead; the eyes are glassy, and from the open mouth a long red hanging tongue protrudes. Are they dead animals walking, or hunters entranced in the hide? Whatever they are, it is hunting magic pure, straight, and unsentimentalized. It is not

II:20 San Francisco de Ranchos de Taos.

II:21 San Francisco with the mountains (after stabilization in concrete).

II:22 Tlaxcala, Mexico. The cathedral.

II:23 Taos and nomads.

II:24 Taos. "Justice Day," 1968.

II:25 Taos. Pole climb on San Geronimo's Day, 1910. Note how the trees which have now grown up east of the pueblo emphasize the relationship between pueblo and mountain by masking the middleground. They are missed in this view. (*H. F. Robinson, Collections in the Museum of New Mexico*)

drama yet, I think, nor really ballet. Something has walked into the plaza. It is the deer, now dead, the ghost deer, whom you heard last night breaking the ice in the stream with his forefeet, driven down from the mountain by the cold. Or it is equally the *ur*-hunter himself, Bushman and Cro-Magnon, alive and mad in the skin of the dead animal he has come to know better than he knows himself (figs. II:38a, 38b) and thus is he. This is shamanism; it is all animal power in one way or another, man or deer the same. Under the hanging tongue of the dead beast the man's set face is seen.

The deer dancers of the Tewa pueblos, on the other hand, wear a costume wholly man-conceived as symbolizing not only deer but also, as at Santa Clara and Tesuque, for example, the green evergreen forest which is their ideal home. Those dancers, their ardent young faces painted black, deploy in brilliantly

II:26 Taos. On the day of a Comanche dance.

choreographed files to become not only the shy prey of the buffalo hunters but also the natural green environment in which those maned heroes and their accompanying Buffalo Maidens can act out their portentous, tragic rôles (fig. III:81). All this seems extremely sophisticated, citified, compared to Taos, which is by contrast primitive, or prehistoric, or perhaps only closer here to the wild nomad hunters of the Plains (fig. II:38c). But one wonders further if Taos is not also in part a cultural prisoner as well as a cultural beneficiary of its awesomely balanced setting, which is so much more dramatically focused, if no more ritually directed, than those of the other pueblos to the south. Is the mountain wholly master, or mother, to the town? Whatever the case, the Mother of the Beasts of Taos—two of whom come with the deer though none with the buffalo—is not a maiden, already an Artemis, as she is in the southern pueblos (fig. III:74), but an older, conical, massive woman, clothed in whitened buckskin and moving between the files of dancers seemingly without volition, remote as the snowy mountain behind her which she so closely resembles in her form. Up and down she passes between the poor dead shuffling deer or changeling hunters or whatever those horned, skinned creatures are. She is not virgin, emotional Artemis, however much Taos and Artemision are alike in dread at such times. She would not be moved like Artemis against Agamemnon to avenge the death of one of her young, however untimely. Old and young, she brings her animals in to men because all things die, young or old, in their season, each to some other, all in the end. She connects us, men, to the animal skin. She is Mother of all, of us and the animal. It is only hunting she knows, no ballet, no drama. Hence, if the Tewa animal dances are the creations of great

II:27 Taos. The dancing ground.

II:28 Taos. The dancing ground.

choreographers and costumers, of generations of Balanchines, say, and those of the Keres are dramas by Aeschylus after Aeschylus unnamed, so those of Taos are the blood dreams of shamans in the animal pelt, too deep down and unresponsive to civilized imagination to evoke anything other than—what? Awe and terror? Pity? Yes, for the lolling tongue and the glazing eyes, but no generous, self-indulgent tears like those the gorgeous Tewa masques can spring.

The buffalo bring the snow with their stamping. On January 6, 1974, Taos substituted a buffalo for a deer dance in a season of heavy snows; they danced along a broad avenue shoveled out for them between the drifts across the front of the north house to the church. Five deer walked with them, bemused between their files. It was a gray day. The mountain was monstrous, black and heavily charged with thick, dark clouds. Snow vapor poured eastward from across the plain, and when the priests began to call in the early afternoon from the summits of the houses under the stormy sky—voices heavier than in summer or only hoarse with cold—the first new snow began to spit like icy buckshot across the plaza. Soon the men, wrapped in their burnooses and carrying portentous-looking packages, began to file toward one of the kivas of the north house—toward a kiva of the south house too, but I, standing on the bridge over the stream by the wall and watching the north house, was unaware of this at the time. Unaware until I heard what was hardly more than a shuffling behind me, a drumbeat perhaps but as if far off, and turning saw—closer than the cattle which were at that moment drinking splay-footed at the holes in the ice of the stream—the whole buffalo heads, slanted up and questing in little steps, massed and coming up behind me (fig. II:38c). The empty eye sockets could not help but remind me all at once of Catlin's blinded buffalo at bay (fig. II:38d). It was the dancers of the south house, shepherded by their hunters in Plains-Indian braids and white buckskin, and with their engulfed deer—I saw the stag antlers rising above the muzzles, manes, and black buffalo horns—walking like fey captives among them. I fled. When they

II:29 Hidatsa dog dancer. (*Engraving after a painting by Carl Bodmer, Smithsonian Institution, National Anthropological Archives*)

II:30 "The Warrior of Capistrano." An Italic *devotus.* (*Museo di Villa Giulia*)

II:31 Taos. Dance under the North Building, date uncertain. (*Collections in the Museum of New Mexico*)

II:32 Taos. San Geronimo's Day races under the North Building, 1910. (*Collections in the Museum of New Mexico*)

II:33 Taos. Booths and priests.

II:34 Taos. Priests on the roof; the sun is declining.

reached the eastern corner of the north house, I against its wall by this time, the buffalo of the northern kiva joined them, passing close beside me, heads up and forward, some of them bigger than the red-ochred bodies which bore them. The two bands came together to form one herd—to be precise, one platoon, four across, ten deep—of dancers, filling the shoveled avenue. There were in all forty buffalo and five deer, four hunters driving them with wolfish cries and nine singer-drummers chanting out the old buffalo songs, each beating on a thin hunter's drum, a hand drum like those of the Plains, not the big booming parade drum of the other pueblos. Along the front of the north house toward the church the deer and the buffalo danced as a single broad body of brown and silver, a river of horns. Each buffalo carried one arrow—here seeming more a symbol of his fate than a weapon—the deer nothing but, as in a dream, their fore-sticks hanging, and the hunters each his hunting knife, bow, and buckskin quiver. Most of the buffalo were full-headed, a few only buffalo-capped and horned; a few others, especially among the tiny children at the end of the line, were merely hooded in brown buffalo mane, and some were single-horned: the Little Buffalo of legend. One grown man had only his long black hair streaming down. One wore, blindly, a fabricated hairy mask without eyes. Most had eagle feathers tied to their horns, and all wore white kilts, empty, unlike those of the other pueblos, of snake images upon them. The animals meandered a little in passing, but not much, and in front of the church they began their dance, partly bent over,

II:35 Taos. Sky altar.

II:36 Taos. Approach to west end of North Building.

always questing, stamping only with the right foot and that not raised very high. Indeed the step the little buffalo boys were doing at the end of the line looked much like a muted version of the generically "Plains Indian" war-dance step they all rather commercially know. Yet perhaps this too connects the dance with the curious buffalo-hunter orgy that Catlin recorded among the Mandans (fig. II:38c).

The Taos buffalo do not run in place, standing straight with knees lifted high like lords and hunters themselves, as the Tewa and Keres buffalo do, but, like the masked kachina dancers of the western pueblos, they simply pound their power into the dirt of the plaza, giving it to the pueblo, bringing the snow and spending themselves. Yet at that moment in 1974 the sun burst through, blasting under the dark clouds, lighting up the eagle feathers and the whole face of the pueblo as if by some cosmic electricity of animal power. And the power with which the animals of Taos endow the pueblo is surely that which comes from the warm life of prey. Whatever animal is, they bring: the flesh, the herd, the mass, the energy of all alike pounding the ground. They are in no sense individuals or heroes. They do not think or react, like the buffalo protagonists of the Keres towns. Nor do they mime out the godly splendor of hunting, as the Tewa Nijinskis do. They beat the earth to the drumbeat and hold their arrows and bob their great heads, and that is all.

On that day they danced one set in front of the church, and three times in sequence from west to east along the face of the north house, and then they split to dance each group one set at the very eastern end of its respective house. At last they stopped and

II:37 Taos. North House, stream, and mountain.

stamped in front of their kivas and were thereafter seen no more except, we are told, as they passed that night dancing from house to house, muzzles in the doorway, when Spanish and Anglo were far away.

It is clearly the animals that Taos loves, much more than she loves the corn.[7] She loves her buffalo herd and her horses, and she knew the horse nomads well. In February of 1968 I saw a Comanche dance there, with perhaps fifty dancers, mostly young, led by a boy in a fine Plains war bonnet. The Comanche dances that I have seen elsewhere, as in the Tewa pueblos, for example, seem a romantic evocation of Plains Indians heroics, where the village dwellers give over their town to a kind of symbolic rapine by themselves for a while. There may well be something else going on, perhaps the old scalp dance, but it is not strongly felt, at least not by me. But Taos is different, very close to the Plains indeed, with strong Kiowa and Apache connections. Its Comanche dance seems sterner and more businesslike, as drummers, dancers, north building, and mountain all throb together, and the long file of men and girls moves up and down the building's south flank, along an avenue leading, or at least aimed, toward the pass under the mountain which leads out to the Plains (figs. II:26–28). Out there Taos has its banner, the horned mountains above Blue Lake, standing out against the sky. It must have drawn the nomads in toward itself, their spotted ponies filing through the passes below the lake to issue forth at last into Taos's special, magically shaped, upland world. This is what towns do; they pull the nomad. So the Scythian king was fatally drawn to the rites of Dionysos at the Greek settlement of the Borysthenites, a colony of Miletus on the Black Sea.[8]

After three sets of dances in the morning and three in the afternoon on that particular day in February, everything suddenly changed. Beings of some sort appeared all at once, unexpectedly, out of a room in the west of the building, opposite to the way the dancers had come from the kivas on the east. They were two mature, strong men, richly feathered and painted parti-colored, with one side of the face mottled white to match the other side of the body. They were led on leashes by maidens, and they danced between the files of dancers back and forth before the chorus standing on the east. They danced crouched over, questing, holding long stiffened banners like veils before their faces. They danced sniffing, led by their maidens like hounds. Indeed, their costumes and stance were much like those recorded by Bodmer in his famous painting of the Hidatsa dog dance (fig. II:29). While this was going on, two dogs were temporarily trapped by the younger dancers at the opposite end of the double column, within which they corraled them for a few moments and poked them, not hard, with their sticks (figs. II:27, 28). It was then that one especially noticed that most of the sticks had mid-nineteenth-century bayonets fixed to them, with what might have been rabbit fur wrapped like scalps around the other

II:38a Michael Naranjo, Deer Spirit, bronze, 1971. (*Photo courtesy* Art in America)

II:38b Bushman cave painting. (*Willcox, plate 31*)

II:38c George Catlin, Mandan Buffalo Dance, lithograph, 1844. *(Yale University Art Gallery, The Mabel Brady Garvan Collection)*

II:38d George Catlin, Buffalo and Wolves, lithograph, 1844. *(Yale University Art Gallery, The Mabel Brady Garvan Collection)*

II:39 Taos. North House and kivas.

II:40 Taos. The western plain.
Taos has its own buffalo herd.

II:41 The Sangre de Cristo from the Arroyo Seco. The spring is under the rock mass to the left.

end. The young dancers made the dogs crouch and move, a little like the two "dog dancers" themselves; they yipped a bit, mostly in surprise, and then were let go. Like Bandelier shocked by the Pueblo clowns long ago, I was surprised into shock by this: cultural preconceptions are hard to set aside.

Yet the man-dogs somehow remain ambiguous and not entirely sympathetic figures. Stooping down between the rows of dancers, they were indeed most beautifully caparisoned—with flaring feathered headdresses and many bells—dressed gloriously but with some fundamental dehumanization, too, and held as it were tolerantly on their leashes by their bell-cheeked girls. Bent over they stamped, questing left and right on the ground. They were animals, obsessed on some errand pursued with the nose. Beyond them the old priests chanted, scattering their cornmeal, singing with what seemed like compassion, even sadness; again the note of tolerance was felt. Toward them the young men skirmished, demented in their olfactory trance, always restrained by the leashes. The girls seemed superior, even smug, though I do not think that we should surmise from that any reflection on the dancers except as they are being handled as rather abnormally dedicated beings: the very Dogs of War, the famous Dog-Soldiers who leashed themselves in place to die and whom these dancers represent on the Plains. Extravagantly feathered, they recall the Italic *devotus* with his enormous hat (fig. II:30), and like him they were intended to call attention to themselves and to unnerve the enemy with their fanatic devotion to death.[9] Taos may be more complex than the early Romans in her assessment of this state of mind, but she too seems to be turning these mad young men on her enemies through this ceremony. It is known that the bayonets used in the dance belonged to American troops of the period of 1847, when Charles Bent, the first Anglo governor of the territory, was killed and scalped along with some of his men in one of several revolts at Taos.[10] After him no governor until David F. Cargo would visit there; it was a kind of tradition. It has also been rumored that the scalps are still around somewhere, and that they too perform on their poles on some frozen night under the moonlit mountain's neutral eye. In rather different vein is the reminder that the Spaniards used dogs against the Indians in war. So one wonders why, with old American bayonets on the ends of sticks wrapped with rabbit fur, the dancers frighten the poor dogs of the plaza, whom normally they so utterly ignore. Perhaps only to awaken their dog spirits and to help them lend power to, or borrow it from, the dancers—who, at the conclusion of the ceremony, are led out in a fast-stamping circuit of the wintry plaza and finally back into the cold lairs of the north house once more.

Taos is always complicated and remote. On July 25, 1971, I saw a women's dance on the afternoon of the day of Santiago's fiesta. Down in Spanish Taos, La Raza was whooping it up for its warrior saint with booze, mariachis, and so on. And in the morning Taos put on its own big pan-Pueblo fair with commercialized though often very beautiful wares and not so beautiful dances. It was a typical Taos performance, brilliantly exemplifying the two sides of the pueblo's life, both of which are clearly embodied in its architectural form. First is Taos the sharp trader, Honest John, friend of all nations—the marketplace for Kiowas, Comanches, Apaches, Spaniards, and Anglos now. The space used for these activities is the huge, spreading plaza, which thus comes into its own. Full of automobiles and campers, booths and stalls, it looks better than at any other time—marvelously ample and properly filled (fig. II:23). So while the church raises its sky altars to the slowly gathering western clouds, this Taos offers expansive midday hospitality to everyone. It puts on Plains Indian war dances at eleven or so, photography permitted; a public-address system amplifies the whole business. Blue Lake comes in for its share of comment (fig. II:24). This is the open, rather specious Taos, kidding and exploiting us all. It may make us forget how sacred Blue Lake really is and that the critical ceremonies of summer take place up there[11] (fig. II:5).

But by four in the afternoon on that July day when

the dip of the sun into the far, empty west became just perceptible, Taos changed again, and its mysterious playacting men in their Arab-like burnooses (unique, I think, in North America) began to gather on the tops of the two great houses (figs. II:33–35). They seemed to be observing the sun, and they called out in rather hectoring voices into space, calling each other or the gods. The tone was like that the Hopi priests often use to the kachinas, embodiments of divinity; it was set on a rising note of rather exasperated exhortation. (The gods can be quite dense by contrast with mortal beings, so mindlessly powerful are they. Men and animals need brains to get along.) Vast space was felt in the priestly presences high up and in their distant voices. One was aware of the westering sun and the lengthening shadows. Just as they seemed to approach the horizontal, a bunch of men came out, wrapped in their burnooses and carrying one great drum and their stools. They took position by the church and began to chant, almost inaudibly and with a feeble drum beat. It was very different from the sonorous drum of the Keres pueblos and the dramatic, dancing chant of their entering choruses. This was shockingly casual by comparison. Disappointment is felt and is augmented when the dancers appear: in this dance they were all women, dressed in immense, high, white moccasins and flowered bright dresses, ribbons hanging down the back, no *tablitas*, or sky altars, on their heads, just hair rather commonly waved or, more rarely, long and straight. They danced minimally, milling about, looking embarrassed, exactly as Waters described them in the summer dances. They did a very muted but typical pair of corn-dance songs: one moving, one in place. The milling was apparently meant to represent the great marching prance into the plaza of the Keres corn dances. Then they did the same dance four times in the south building—in its interstices as it were. By the last set they were a little way out into the open plaza beyond a strongly projecting and, for Taos, unique kiva at which they had performed their third dance. Then they walked diagonally across the main plaza and danced four times in the interstices of the northwest group of buildings (figs. II:7, 36). They were tracing a labyrinth which wound through the whole body of the pueblo like the *Salii*, the Leapers, winding twice yearly through Ancient Rome and dancing the archaic *tripudium*, the triple stomp, before various traditionally sacred altars.[12] Before the third dance on the northwest, the women were joined by one typical male corn dancer. He was very cool, hardly moving at all, but his single movement up and down, vertical and bouncy (like that of a Leaper perhaps?), wholly set off the women's big-blossomed roll from side to side. It focused the whole thing and impregnated the body of the dance with new life, much as Balanchine often uses one male lead to do.

At last the dance moved out toward the main plaza again. As it went on, the chants became stronger, especially the great approach song. The women, their dresses now shining incandescent in the declining sun, were moving to their task, faces set. Finally they crowded right up against the great north building and danced three sets down the avenue in front of it, exactly as in the Comanche dance of 1968 (figs. II:26, 27, 28). By the last set, best seen from the low wall that bounds the pueblo on the east, they were a rich line of color in shadow under the darkening mass of the building with the sun sliding down westward behind it (figs. II:37, 39). The labyrinth had now found its object in the ultimate building-mountain mass, and the dance was holding on in that place toward the climax of the day.

At supper time the dancers went into one of the northeast kivas for a short while and ate there. Then they came out and danced the sun down with three more sets along the building's flank. As the last set ended, the sun had just sunk on that bearing behind the peak of the building; the shape had become cosmic. Taos Mountain was now balanced off the apex of Taos by the declining sun, and it was the dance that fixed its moment there.

Soon the far-off splendid sun would slide back down the westward-tilting plain to shoot its last rays straight back up along it, so flooding the mountain from below and bathing it red in the blood of Christ with the last light of evening (figs. II: 10, 40). It is no wonder that so many sensitive and religiously minded people have fallen under Taos's spell. She gives the impression of being able to sustain a dialogue between earth and heaven that can make the sacraments real to men. At another level her secrecy, her disguises, and, especially, her indefatigable trickery intrigue our imagination as they suggest shamanistic styles of religious practice now normally unconscious or long gone.[13] Taos attracts Jungians, especially, like flies to compost, and indeed everyone who is attracted to the mystery of humanity's buried thoughts. It therefore seems wrong to leave her without referring to D. H. Lawrence, whose spirit haunts the place and who created its contemporary literary aura. It is curious that Lawrence should have written his great book about American culture in England in 1917–1918, before he came to America, but he then rewrote it at his ranch in the Sangre de Cristo in 1922–1923.

In that monument to the human intuition, *Studies in Classic American Literature*, upon which all sober American studies programs were later to be based, Lawrence invoked what he called the *daimon* of the American continent as the ultimate source of power for its people. That *daimon* he surely came to know in New Mexico, about which he wrote in his article, "New Mexico," of 1928–1931, "I think that New Mexico was the greatest experience from the outside world that I have ever had. It certainly changed me forever . . . the moment I saw the brilliant, proud morning shine high up over the deserts of Santa Fe, something stood still in my soul, and I started to attend." And in the same article, after writing brilliantly of the dances "with the timeless down-tread, always to the earth's center," he says ". . . and I had no permanent feeling of religion till I came to New Mexico."[14] Yet it was hard for Lawrence to sustain that mood, and sometimes, especially in his fiction, it was a more narrowly demonic *genius loci* that he perceived. There he tended both to romanticize and to fear the Indian. There is, for example, a cavern above the Arroyo Seco on the west flank of the Sangre de Cristo which he transported to Chihuahua as the setting for the human sacrifice of the heroine in his story "The Woman Who Rode Away."[15] The Taos Indians have legends of that kind about the cavern, and its aspect amply suggests them. It lies under a savage boss of somber rock, like a stone axhead sunk into the earth. Southward from the rugged mass a gentler ridge slopes up, the two between them swinging from westward into a wide set of horns (fig. II: 41). Clouds normally gather over the savage one while the other is clear. The cavern lies behind a waterfall, rich in minerals, which in the full fall of winter flashes like a mirror across the plain.[16] A gigantic boulder lies behind the shining curtain just in the cavern's mouth. It was across this crude monolith that Lawrence, with his sometimes distressing imagination, had four, almost naked Indians hold the naked lady down.

Lawrence's shrine near his ranch farther northward along the mountainside is beautifully sited, though perhaps equally uncomfortable in the end (figs. II: 42, 43). It is a little rustic temple, apsidal: just one small room with some awful paintings and a sort of monstrance purporting to contain the appropriate ashes. It faces out through a gap in the pine forest toward what Lawrence called, in "New Mexico," the "lofty, indomitable desert," the upward-swelling ocean of the Rio Grande plain. Frieda Lawrence's aggressively framed gravestone lies before it, appreciatively signed by Angie, her third husband, and severely compromising the view, while on the gable of the shrine an ambiguously busted, epicene eagle reigns: Lawrence as Phoenix rising from the fire.[17] It is a queer place, and profoundly un-Indian. But it is intelligently expressive of Lawrence with his heroic cum antiheroic postures, his magnificent grasp of landscape's religious power, and his terror of what he called "merging" with it. Hence once again the eagle, Melville's "sky hawk" which, to Lawrence's joy and horror, the hammer of the Indian, Tashtego, had

II:42 D. H. Lawrence's shrine on the Sangre de Cristo with Frieda's grave.

pinned with the American colors to the foundering *Pequod*'s mast. "What splendour!" Lawrence had written of his desert. "Only the tawny eagle could really sail out into the splendour of it all."

The tiny pueblo of Picuris, of the same language group as Taos, lies embedded in the Sangre de Cristo to the south (figs. II:44–58). It is built on a swell of earth on the slopes of a beautifully shaped mountain. A cylindrical kiva culminates the town; it rises directly above the older, now largely archaeological, quarter and rests exactly in the mountain's heart.[18] From it the eye is led across space to Jicarita Peak, lifting in that view as a pyramid just left of the Truchas Peaks on the Sangre de Cristo summit. The mountain shrine of Picuris is up there on the Jicarita, and the young men run races to it on their feast days. Races also take place beside the stream below the town, and after them a chorus approaches the village singing and waving, in their season, the appropriate boughs of autumn and spring. The church, as they approach it, offers an excellent example of the transformation of a towered Spanish-baroque façade composition into a pueblo sky altar which at the same time reflects the profiles of the ridge line with which it is seen[19] (figs. II:46, 56). Later the dancers descend into the kiva in the vague little plaza. It is entirely below ground and engulfs the dancers with nothing at all to show thereafter—only the empty surface of the earth, life, as once in Pueblo myth, all deep below (figs. II:57, 58).

Picuris, tiny, poor, almost extinct—and now seeking to revive itself a little with handicrafts, fishing permits, hokey-hey postcards (fig. II:53), and movie making—is still perfectly set, locked until death in its landscape's arms.

II:43 Lawrence's shrine from the rear.

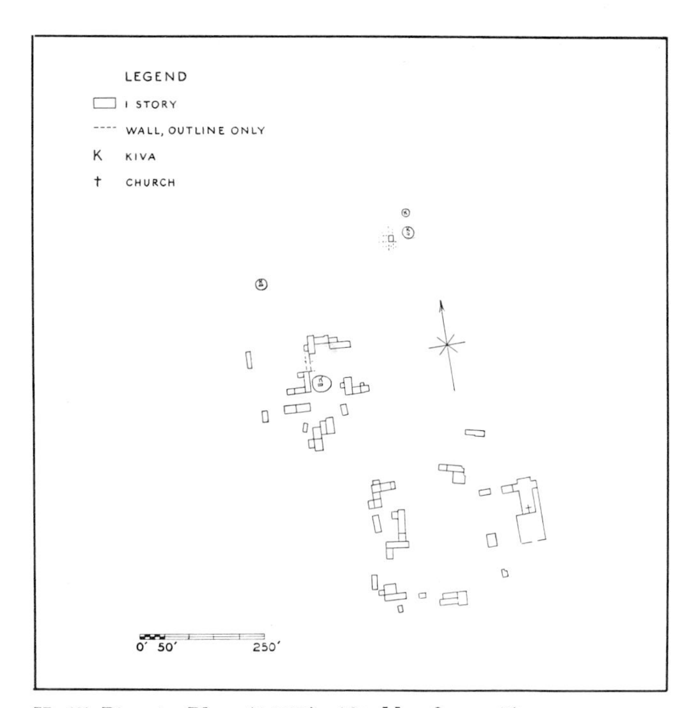

II:44 Picuris. The site from the south.

II:45 Picuris. Plan (1950). (*Stubbs, figure 5*)

II:46 Picuris. The church and the mountain.

II:47 Picuris. The cylindrical kiva with corral and mountain. Ruins of old pueblo to left of kiva and below it.

II:48 Picuris. The graveyard beyond the kiva, under the mountain.

II:49 Picuris. Cylindrical kiva with mesa to the south. Jicarita and Truchas peaks to the left.

II:50 Picuris. The cylindrical kiva with Jicarita and Truchas peaks.

II:51 Picuris. Old house with the Jicarita.

II:52 Picuris. Old town. Underground kiva with ladde
poles reconstructed. Not sacred.

II:53 Picuris. Inside the reconstructed underground kiva.
Not sacred.
(*Bob Petley*)

II:54 Picuris. Races on saint's day.

II:55 Picuris. Bringing in the boughs on saint's day.

II:56 Picuris. Entering the church with boughs.

II:57 Picuris. Descending into the kiva in the plaza on saint's day.

II:58 Picuris. The kiva in the plaza. Everyone below ground.

III

THE RIO GRANDE–THE TEWA TOWNS

The Tewa towns are at present San Juan, Santa Clara, San Ildefonso, Tesuque, and, barely, Nambé and Pojoaque. The latter was in fact "revived" in 1973 and performed a Comanche dance that winter, its first public ceremony in a hundred years. The Tewa occupy the perfectly defined bowl of high valley between the Sangre de Cristo and Jemez ranges above modern Santa Fe. It is the most purely circular landscape space in the Pueblo area. The first three towns are set closer to the Jemez along the Rio Grande, the others nearer the Sangre de Cristo on the Tesuque and Nambé creeks (fig. I:1). San Juan is the northernmost and the best documented, through the recent work of Ortiz, in terms of the ritual meaning of its topographical setting. Its four sacred mountains have already been mentioned, as have the four sacred hills that lie before them. To trace those relationships down to modern San Juan is to follow the Tewa out of the hills and down through the valley of the Chama southeastward to the banks of the Rio Grande.[1] Again, the sequence is from the mountains to the plain. One could start where Canjilon, now the mountain of the north, rises cool and gentle above the high green meadows of its lovely range (fig. III:1). Sliding down toward the Rio Grande from it we come to La Madera, above which one of the sacred hills almost closes the pass. Ortiz is careful not to describe those hills too closely, but it is not hard to find them. The shape is typical: the Tsin, the sacred hill, is essentially flat topped, like an altar or a pueblo itself (fig. III:2). Behind it the higher serrations of the mountains emphasize its flat-topped form. Directly below it an awesomely twisted gray gorge tears the earth. It is the point of egress from the underworld of the Keres people, the Tewa dryly say. From the altar hill of La Madera we see down into the valley almost to San Juan; it is the perfect waystation of a cultural migration. But there are other ways down from Canjilon too. Straight southward down the Chama, on the axis of its pass, the magnificent Pedernales Peak stands alone before the mass of the Jemez like a gigantic Mexican temple

III:1 Canjilon Peak.

III:2 La Madera. San Juan's sacred hill of the north.

base (figs. III:3, 4). It is not now named as a Tsin by the Tewa, but there are proto-Tewa remains all around its area, and one can hardly help surmising that it may well have been an altar hill itself at some earlier time. The second hill, that of the west as La Madera is of the north, is the great butte which sails down toward the Chama near Abiquiu, flat topped too, caverned and cleft with burgeoning *potreros* on its seamed flanks, opening amply and looking both to the Jemez and down the cleft of the Chama toward San Juan on the Rio Grande (figs. III:5, 6). It will be noted that no flat-topped altar hill lies directly between San Juan and Tsi'como, the sacred mountain of the west, which rises conspicuously above it (fig. III:7). Some pull from the two old shrines still holding the northern passes and almost redundant in placement must still be functioning here. To the south, the altar hill is Tuñjopiñ, Black Mesa, with several shrines on its summit, and around whose massive hub all the Tewa world spins like a wheel. Black Mesa is indeed the central monument of the Tewa landscape. It most eminently has the compacted, horizontally fractured, and compressed character that the Mexicans built into the bases of their temples (fig. III:62). The cornice is heavy; it weighs down, crushes the main mass. Only one route, that on the south, leads like a

III:3 Pedernales Peak from Canjilon Mountain. Valley of the Rio Grande far left.

III:4 Pedernales Peak from the north.

III:5 El Rito. San Juan's sacred hill of the west from the northeast; Jemez range beyond, Pedernales Peak far right.

III:6 Abiquiu. Sacred hill of the west from the southeast.

stair to the summit. There were, we are told, several shrines in the long, lion-colored grass up there.[2] Only one is clear today, a boulder partly worn, partly carved, in circular indentations to suggest a staring facelike mask. It is surrounded by a rough ellipse of black stones like pieces fallen from a star (figs. III:63–65). It lies in the high grass, its gaze fixed upward. If there has been rain the eye sockets are full of water and move with the clouds. All of the upper valley is visible from here, but the Pajarito Plateau is especially close, with Tsi'como riding above it.

In my opinion, though, San Juan's own most significant relationship does not really seem to lie with the Jemez right on top of it, but with the Sangre de Cristo eastward across the valley (figs. III:8, 9), upon whose crest the splendid rock horns of the Truchas open directly on the axis of San Juan's plaza. They are savage horns of power. The modern Spanish town, tough Penitente Truchas, lies just under them on the heights and is stunned, barbarized by them (fig. III:10). And far below them, standing visibly before them very roughly on the axis from San Juan, rises the sacred hill of that direction (figs. III:11, 12). It is the perfect truncated pyramid which rises above the Christian Santuario at Chimayo, which is now, as it was then, a place of medicinal earth and healing. When the horns of the sacred mountain rise, as they do here, above the sacred cone, we are at Knossos, Phaistos, Mycenae, Eleusis, and Athens—to name only a few of the Aegean sites so favored.[3] The towers of the Spanish church at Tsi'mayo may perhaps in this case even be regarded as adjusted to the sacred phenomenon; they lock the building into the V cleft between the Tsin and its adjacent mesa[4] (fig. III:13).

Ortiz tells us that there is an earth navel, a *sipapu*, in the plaza behind the church at San Juan, and he points out that the corners of the plaza are open,

III:7 Looking west toward San Juan and the Jemez range along the axis of the plazas. Church tower of Chamita center under Tsi'como.

much as pueblo masonry walls are not bonded at the corners[5] (fig. III:14). In this way one supposes that, despite the major organization of the town into parallel rectangular plazas running east and west, other lines of force can be received from the four directions upon which the sacred mountains and their temple-hills all rise.[6] So San Juan does not gather up into clear masses like Taos. Only in its best days did a multistory unit of houses rise on the side under Tsi′como to praise it, backed by a high, mesa-like old church, now gone (fig. III:15). Even then the houses were mostly of two stories with one deep setback and a clear cornice line (fig. III:16).

As the Rio Grande pueblos so open themselves they also allow their own fabric to become progressively less massive, more offhand, even sloppy in detail (fig. III:17). Their adobe is supplemented with cinder block and stucco and with various kinds of porches, windows, and metal frames. At the present time, the pressure of the modern technological world and its junk culture plays a certain part in this development. But historically it had, as we have already noted, a deeply ritualistic point. It is as if the buildings of the pueblo had finally come to have meaning only as they functioned as space definers for ritual action and collaborated with the sacred landscape to

III:8 San Juan. The Rio Grande (from the site of Onate's capital at San Juan de los Caballeros) with the Sangre de Cristo range. Truchas left, Gap of the Sun right center; Flower Mountain (Baldy) and Lake Peak form the V shape to the right.

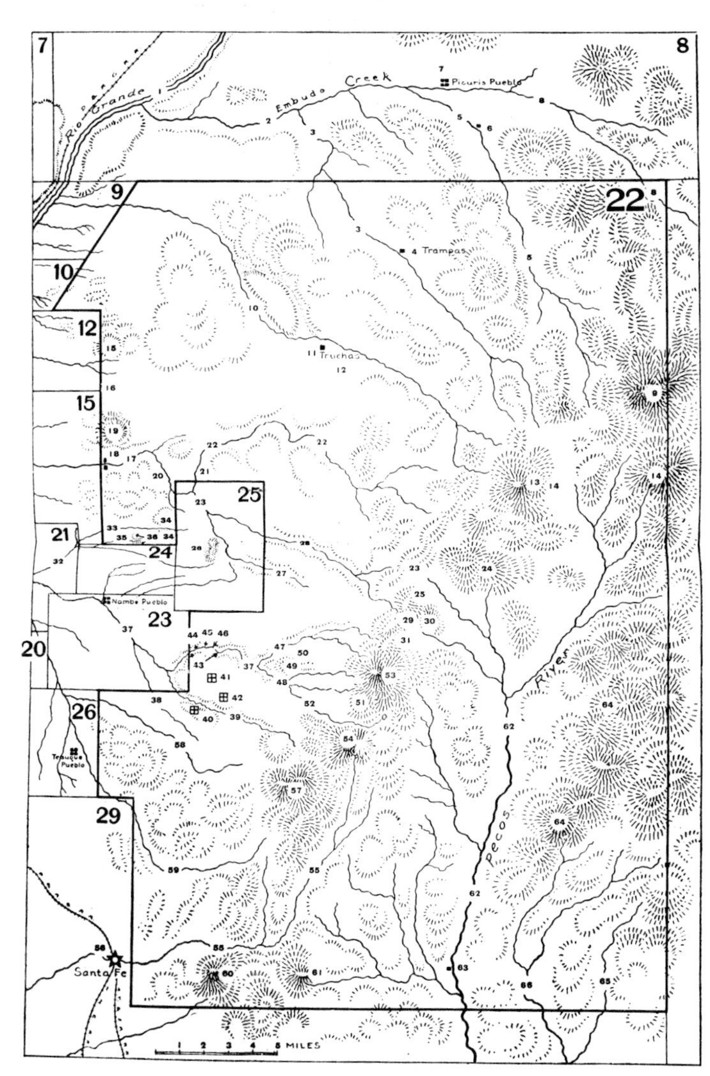

III:9 The Sangre de Cristo south from the Jicarita (9) to the Truchas (13), to the Gap of the Sun (29), to Baldy (53) and Lake Peak (59), and to Santa Fe's range (57–60). Note the Pecos drainage. *(Harrington, map 22)*

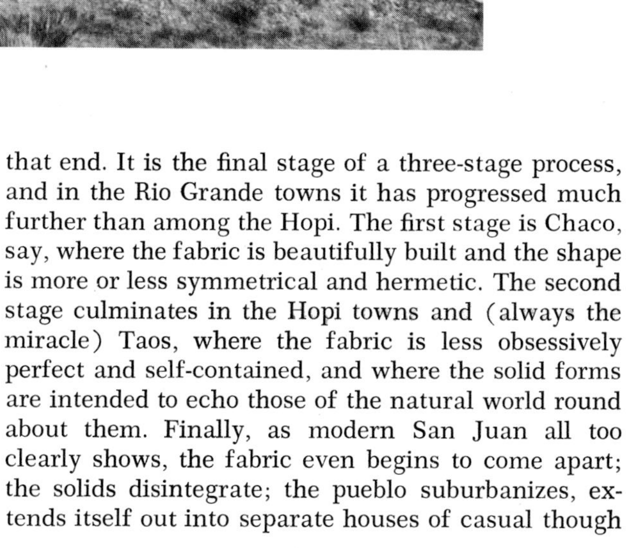

that end. It is the final stage of a three-stage process, and in the Rio Grande towns it has progressed much further than among the Hopi. The first stage is Chaco, say, where the fabric is beautifully built and the shape is more or less symmetrical and hermetic. The second stage culminates in the Hopi towns and (always the miracle) Taos, where the fabric is less obsessively perfect and self-contained, and where the solid forms are intended to echo those of the natural world round about them. Finally, as modern San Juan all too clearly shows, the fabric even begins to come apart; the solids disintegrate; the pueblo suburbanizes, extends itself out into separate houses of casual though

III:10 Truchas under the horns.

III:11 Tsi'mayo. The sacred hill of the east and the horns of the Truchas on the axis from San Juan.

III:12 Tsi'mayo. The sacred hill of the east in shadow; Truchas Peaks left; Flower Mountain (Baldy) and Lake Peak far right distance.

III:13 Tsi'mayo. El Santuario under the sacred hill.

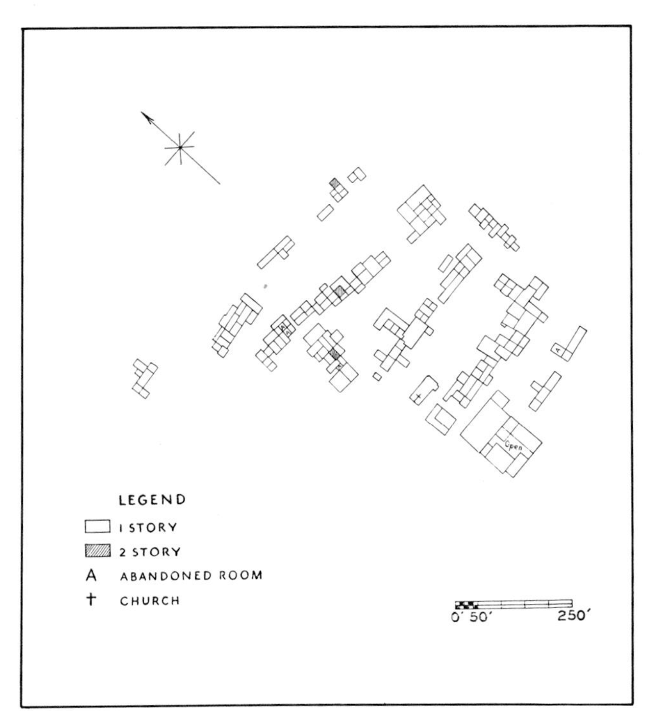

rarely aggressive form, and may seem to become even a tragic rural slum—but in fact does not do so, because however much has been lost, its fundamental reason for being is still built into it. The ritual framework and the connections with the sacred earth are as alive and functioning as ever, and it is in this way that modern pueblos such as San Juan must be experienced and valued.

For this, no time is better than the saint's feast day, which falls on June 24 at San Juan. Sometimes there will be days of dancing, a buffalo dance on the twenty-third perhaps, a Comanche dance the next day (fig. III:18). In the morning the saint's image is escorted from the church of the Spanish-American community of Chamita, which lies on two sides of San Juan. It is carried with European snare drumming to its leafy

III:14 San Juan. Plan (1950). (*Stubbs, figure 8*)

III:15 San Juan, c. 1920, showing multistory house on the west. (*H. F. Robinson, Collections in the Museum of New Mexico*)

bower, the *kisi*, on the south side of the northern plaza. Then, later, from the kiva built into the house blocks beyond that plaza on the west, toward the Truchas, the Comanche will sally forth, skirmishing down between the houses: wild, intrusive, disquieting. The nomad raiders are in the town. They are not, I think, as quietly sinister as those of Taos or as grandly expressive as those of San Ildefonso; they employ fewer banner bearers and less complex cavalry wheels. But they complete the pueblo's relationship to the landscape as they wind their labyrinthine pattern through it (armed *Salii* in blood-bright tunics) and move down the axis of the plaza toward the horns of the Truchas and dance before the *kisi* with the dome of Tsi'como rising behind them.[7] Their dance is especially packed and rich in the southern plaza with

III:16 San Juan. The second plaza, c. 1920, looking northeast. Truchas Peaks just out of picture to the right. (Charles F. Lummis, *Collections in the Museum of New Mexico*)

III:17 San Juan. Second plaza looking east in 1971. Note direct axis to Truchas Peaks and loosening of village fabric since 1920.

(a)

(b)

III:18 San Juan. Saint's Day, June 24, 1968. Comanche dance. a) Second plaza, saint's bower, *kisi*, right; b) from the east, churches and Tsi'como to the left, Spanish-American church (Chamita) with tower; c) the dance; d, e) detail; f) Comanche entering second plaza from the west; g) standard bearer; h) in church plaza, the women; i) in church plaza, the men.

(e)

(f)

(c)

(d)

(g)

(h)

(i)

(j)

(k)

(n)

III:18 *continued.* j) The children; k) standard-bearer chorus; l) standard bearers advancing; m) standard bearer and churches; n) dance approaching churches; *sipapu* near tree left; o) the Pueblo church; p) returning to kiva on east side of pueblo; q) dancing in front of the kiva.

(p)

(o)

(l)

(m)

(q)

III:19 San Juan. The general store. (*T. D. Anderson*)

III:20 Santa Clara. The axis down the plaza east to the Sangre de Cristo range. Kiva right.

the *sipapu* behind the pueblo's church, while Chamita's tower looms brittle beyond them. It is a tall, stiff Gothic creature like one of Archbishop Lamy's French priests.[8] Its prickly presence is much less generous than the round-arched façade of golden stone which gives some noble breadth to Lamy's cathedral in Santa Fe, and it cows the pinched, tight-gabled Gothic chapel which serves the Indian community across the road. No gestures to the landscape here, no ridge lines brought gently into the town. No machismo either. They are high collars and tight shoes, both these Jansenistical buildings, and they appear at their most inappropriate when the dances are taking place. On the other hand, the general store (boots, slickers, and sides of bacon) is one of the strongest and most delightful survivors of a now almost vanished Southwest (fig. III:19)—or was, until it was destroyed by fire in 1973, after the above lines were written.

A little way south on a rise above the river the pueblo of Santa Clara invokes the horns of the Truchas much more dramatically than does San Juan. Santa Clara is higher, so that more of the mass of the Sangre de Cristo is visible from it and therefore seems closer at hand and more looming (fig. III:20).

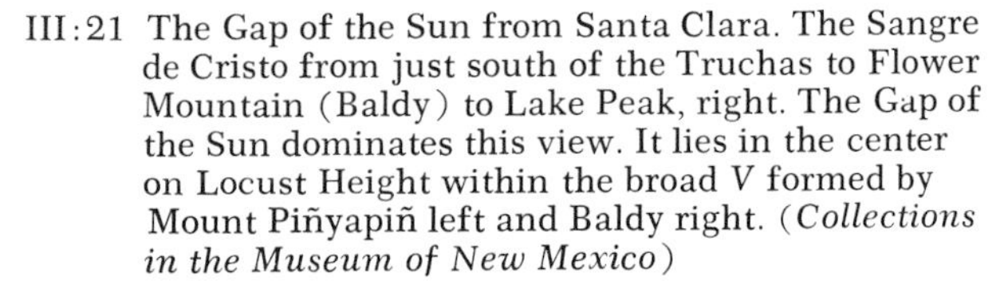

III:21 The Gap of the Sun from Santa Clara. The Sangre de Cristo from just south of the Truchas to Flower Mountain (Baldy) to Lake Peak, right. The Gap of the Sun dominates this view. It lies in the center on Locust Height within the broad V formed by Mount Piñyapiñ left and Baldy right. (*Collections in the Museum of New Mexico*)

III:22 Santa Clara. (*Collections in the Museum of New Mexico*)

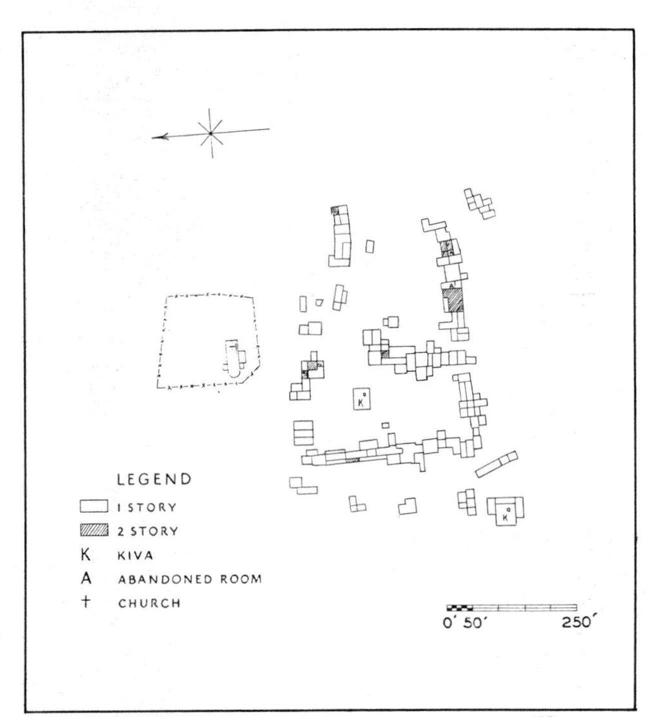

III:23 Santa Clara. Plan (1950). (*Stubbs, figure 9*)

The view generally swings from the Truchas south across lifting and subsiding summits to Lake Peak. It focuses especially on the wide cleft south of the Truchas, which Santa Clara's people call the Gap of the Sun and within whose broad and gentle horns their most significant sunrises take place[9] (fig. III:21). At the same time, the church at Santa Clara is still blessedly Spanish-Indian, and it flings up the corners of its façade as if it were echoing that gap, and the Truchas, and indeed the whole challenging range across the valley (fig. III:22). Not to carry a metaphor too far, it lifts its arms to the summits. In that gesture most open and splendid, it receives the rising sun. The deep double lift of its profile, so appropriate in this relationship, should be contrasted with the lower, wider, stepped affair at Picuris, where it is the rather

III:24 Santa Clara. The north kiva from the south.

III:25 Santa Clara. The kiva from the northeast with the saint's *kisi*.

III:26 Santa Clara. Buildings on north side of plaza across from the kiva, c. 1920. Now partly ruined. Photos of harvest dance taken through drying racks center. (*Collections in the Museum of New Mexico*)

III:27 Santa Clara. Corn dance, 1969. a) In the plaza with *kisi* and kiva; b) revering the saint; c) out and away; d) toward the kiva.

(a)

(b)

flatter ridge line behind it that is being invoked (fig. II:46). Santa Clara also has a splendid, centrally located, rectangular kiva with round buttressed corners at ground level and strongly defined horns up above (figs. III:23–26). It articulates two of the main plaza spaces.[10] That to the north contains the *kisi*, the saint's leafy shrine at her festival dances (fig. III:27), but almost all the dances flow in and out of at least four plazas. On feast days four kinds of dances may succeed each other. They may coil out from the tiny first plaza to the broad one on the east, then up to the saint's *kisi*, then on to the south side of the central kiva. Other sequences have also been observed.[11] The principle of the labyrinth, at any rate, is strongly suggested (fig. III:23). A fine head-shaking buffalo dance is splendidly climaxed outside the robing room south of the kiva, from which, down the sloping plaza to the east, the summits of the Sangre de Cristo stand out very plain (fig. III:28). When the people of this kiva conclude their dance they may take station for a while on its roof and so stand out against the sky above its clear-cut profile (fig. III:29). The other kiva is embedded in the houses on the southwestern side of the town and is seen with the first sandy foothills of the Jemez behind it (figs. III:30, 31). Southward, beautifully made corrals once more point up the importance of the wood frame in contrast to the adobe cube, and they lead the eye across the green, watered fields of the river valley to the squat mass of Black Mesa, apparently as sacred to Santa Clara as to San Juan (fig. III:32).

But it is with the Jemez range that Santa Clara has its closest traditional, if not visual, connections. In one sense Santa Clara is more locked into the western mountain than San Juan, which is still pulled in ritual and memory toward the old route down the Chama from the north. Above Santa Clara the first steps of the Jemez, the Pajarito Plateau, are cut into great mesa-potreros, like aircraft carriers, sailing out below the higher peaks, riddled with prehistoric cave

(c)

(d)

dwellings on their southern flanks and, in many cases, with fine prehistoric pueblos on their tops. Directly above Santa Clara and included in its reservation lies Puye, the most complete and expressive of all the ruins in that area[12] (figs. III:33, 34). This time the relationship to Knossos is exact (figs. III:35, 41, 42). Each has a long rectangular courtyard with an entrance at one corner; from here the axis of view runs diagonally down the length of the court toward a stairway that opens the building mass at the other end: for Knossos on the south, for Puye on the west. Beyond on that axis rises for Knossos cleft and conical Mount Jouctas, where Zeus was buried, and for Puye the dome of Tsi-como, sacred mountain of the west, above whose summit the great rain clouds of summer gather almost every day (figs. III:37, 38). Upon its smooth, heart-lifting peak there is a shrine, where even Taos Indians can still be seen going with their sanctifying cornmeal. (Picking flowers, they gratuitously insist they are doing, if they cannot avoid meeting other climbers on the way.) Douglass called the sanctuary a "world quarter shrine" and believed that it was intended to invoke rain; Ortiz regards it as an earth navel, open toward the Tewa villages.[13] It is, in fact, a small hollow from which what seem to be two or at most three shallow and rather indistinct short trenches have been dug out on the bearing of several pueblos: certainly Santa Clara, San

(a)

(b)

(h)

(i)

(j)

(d)

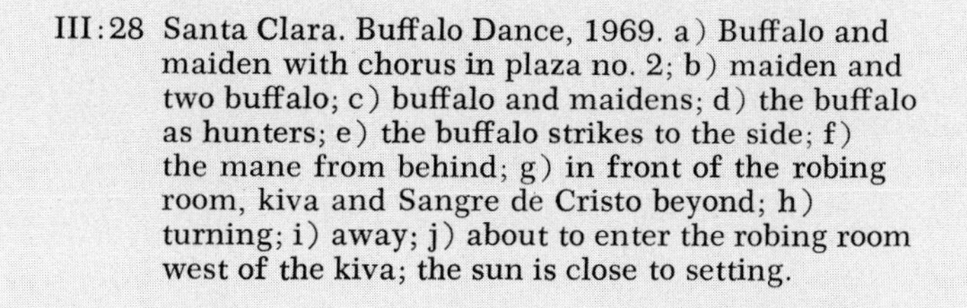

III:28 Santa Clara. Buffalo Dance, 1969. a) Buffalo and maiden with chorus in plaza no. 2; b) maiden and two buffalo; c) buffalo and maidens; d) the buffalo as hunters; e) the buffalo strikes to the side; f) the mane from behind; g) in front of the robing room, kiva and Sangre de Cristo beyond; h) turning; i) away; j) about to enter the robing room west of the kiva; the sun is close to setting.

(e)

(g)

(f)

(a)

(b)

III:29 Santa Clara. Harvest Dance, 1969. a) In the small plaza; b) in the small plaza, beginning to coil; c) out to the large plaza; d) in the plaza with the *kisi*; e) the same (detail); f) in front of the kiva; g) on the roof.

(g)

(c)

(d)

(f)

(e)

(a)

(b)

(e)

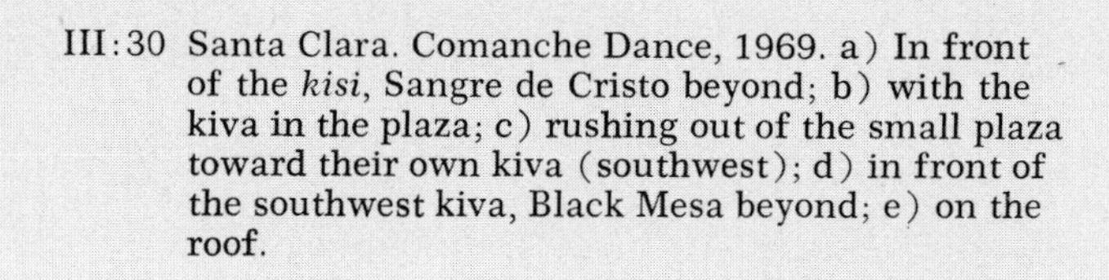

III:30 Santa Clara. Comanche Dance, 1969. a) In front of the *kisi*, Sangre de Cristo beyond; b) with the kiva in the plaza; c) rushing out of the small plaza toward their own kiva (southwest); d) in front of the southwest kiva, Black Mesa beyond; e) on the roof.

(c)

(d)

Juan, and San Ildefonso (figs. III:39, 40). It was once believed that Taos to the north, the Keres towns well to the south, and perhaps even the Navaho to the west, were involved here, and all of them may indeed make offerings, but in 1968 at any rate there were apparently no trenches leading toward them. An eyed boulder like that on Tuñjopiñ lies staring upward not far from the hollow. Now, from the summit one can see the rape of the Jemez forests, which the Department of the Interior has allowed. Hidden from the main roads below, the devastation lies under the eyes of whatever gods inhabit Tsi′como, and awaits their judgment in time.

Puye receives Tsi′como's full force in its courtyard, exactly as the courtyard at Knossos receives that of shrined Mount Jouctas beyond it (figs. III:41, 42). Unlike Greek temples, which came to balance the sacred mountain mass with a man-made one (fig. II:15), Puye and pre-Greek Knossos alike simply focus on the natural form by directing their hollow courtyards toward it, so that it is the force of nature that dominates all. So it does in the dances that are held at Puye every July.[14] They have been commercialized to a certain extent and their sets are very short, not repeated all day long as in ritual they normally have to be. But when the horned buffalo of Santa Clara dance directly before the mountain's face, their eagle feathers flying under the dark clouds, the hairs can indeed rise along our napes, in memory of the bull-masked king and his Bronze Age Cretan dancers with the horns (figs. III:43–48). We are most obviously forced here to that fundamental question of history: whether it is a matter of multiple human invention that similar images arise far apart in space and time according to common types of human need, reverence, and desire, or whether there was some vast Stone Age diffusion long ago, so that the bulls of Altamira and Lascaux are the sires of them all.

As the eagle dancers crouch and rise, wings lifting for their great dance in which, to the tapping, lonely drums, they wheel all silent through immensity (fig. III:49), we realize how high we too are on Puye's

III:31 Santa Clara. The southwestern kiva, c. 1920, with sand hills below the Jemez. Corn dancers. (*Collections in the Museum of New Mexico*)

III:32 Santa Clara. Black Mesa (Tuñjopiñ) from Santa Clara. Fields and Rio Grande between.

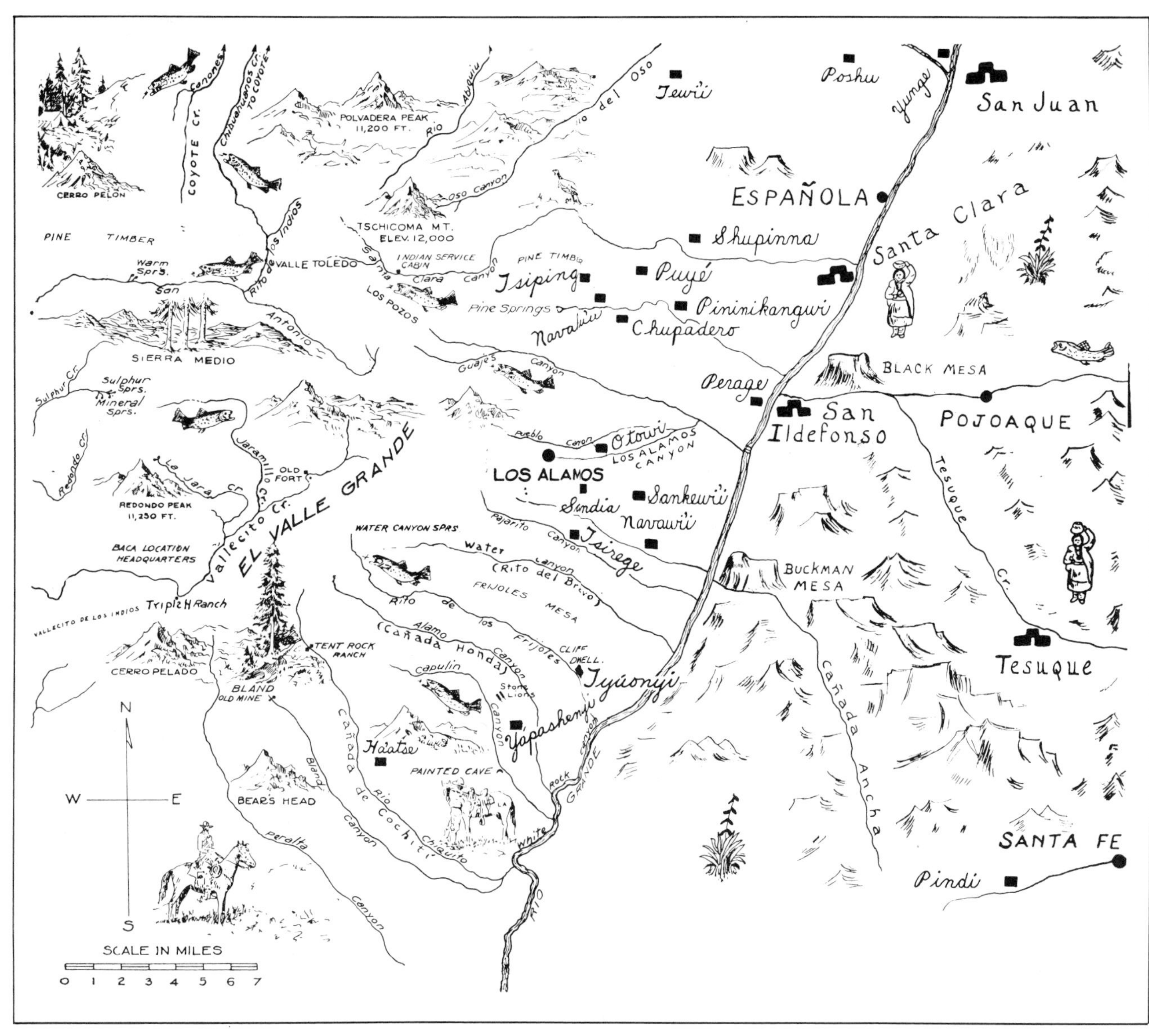

III:33 Pajarito Plateau, the Jemez range, and the Valley of the Rio Grande. (*Hewett, endpaper*)

III:34 Puye and Tsi'como.

III:35 Puye. View west down plaza toward Tsi'como.

III:36 Puye. Kiva, Great House, and Tsi'como.

III:37a Tsi'como. The summit, July 1968.

III:38 Tsi'como. The summit with cairn, looking west.

III:37b Tsi'como. The summit, two minutes later.

III:39 Tsi'como. Eyed Boulder near shrine.

III:40 Tsi'como. Earth Navel shrine: hollow with new prayer sticks and cornmeal forward, trenches running out on both sides of tree.

plaza and how lifted by it to the sky (fig. III:50). As it anchors itself to Tsi'como it also sails eastward out and away from it, directing our eyes toward the Sangre de Cristo, whose whole range south of Taos seems displayed before us: the Jicarita, the Truchas (their cleft directly on axis from here), Santa Clara's own great Gap of the Sun, Baldy, Lake Peak, on down toward Santa Fe (fig. III:51). We are nobly placed; this must once have been the finest site of the Tewa world: an ample town of golden rubble masonry, with good caverns and houses along the warm southern face of the mesa to supplement the plaza grouping on the top (fig. III:52). Now Puye plays a strange intermediate role, no longer inhabited but still at least partly sacred, still a great platform better related to the wholeness of divinity than is the modern town of Santa Clara on the river below it.

The pueblo of San Ildefonso across the river also had its prehistoric ancestors on the Pajarito Plateau:

III:41 Puye. The plaza, July 1968.

III:42 Knossos. The Palace. View south down the court toward Mount Jouctas.

Tsankawi is one; probably Otowi as well, the latter with some colossal carved heads on its mesa sides but somehow hard to find since the massive intrusion of Los Alamos into the area.[15] At Tsankawi, as at Puye, there was a town on the potrero top; it too invoked Tsi'como, here somewhat to the north (fig. III:53). A lovely little humpbacked flute player, beloved by the Anasazi, was carved into the tight natural gate that led up the mesa to the town (figs. III:54, 55). A serene arc of cave dwellings, supplemented by masonry construction, curved along the southern façade of the mesa at Tsankawi, too, and called Black Mesa into view in the plain (fig. III:56). One tends to wonder at all these places why human beings ever left caves like these: perfectly scaled dwellings, dry, snug, sunny, and naturally terraced. They usually look out across the old stream beds where the patches of corn once grew in the sun, and the northern face of another potrero often shaped and maternalized the

III:43 Puye. Buffalo dance I.

III:44 Puye. Buffalo dance II.

III:45 Puye. Buffalo dance III.

III:46 Puye. Buffalo dance IV.

III:47 Knossos. Relief of charging bull in North Portico. (*Hoegler, page 60*)

III:48 Puye. Buffalo dance V.

III:49 Santa Clara. Eagle dance. (*Collections in the Museum of New Mexico*)

view. Certainly there is no sequential development of departure from the caves; they were not abandoned for the mesa tops. At Puye and Tsankawi the two were occupied together. At the Mesa Verde, as we have seen, many of the inhabitants left the towns on top and returned to the clefts in full urban splendor when renewed contact with the earth apparently seemed mandatory to them. But the pull of the river in the drying land was too much for anyone to resist in any locality. So from Otowi and Tsankawi the inhabitants moved down to San Ildefonso, where what seem to me to be the finest of all the Tewa dances take place. I am surely influenced in that opinion by the fact that San Ildefonso is somewhat more eloquently placed than Santa Clara or San Juan; its relationship to the landscape is more wholly visible from the town and clearly echoed in the plaza (fig. I:45). It is a great, dusty plaza, hot and yellow in

III:50 Puye with the horns of the Truchas.

the sun. One splendid cottonwood remains to it. It was once divided in half in a moiety dispute, and when the transverse range of houses was torn down it took on its present expansive scale[16] (figs. III:57, 58). Most moving is the cylindrical kiva which strongly echoes the Pajarito Plateau and Tsi'como above it (figs. I:45; III:59, 60), not to mention the tiers of clouds that billow above the sky-terraced parapets of its stair. The church is so placed beyond the pueblo as to contain that view with its façade (fig. III:61). It has been rebuilt many times; in its present, recent form the lift of its rounded center piece is emphasized rather than, as at Santa Clara, the gesture of its horns[17] (fig. III:22). In this way it echoes Tsi'como's dome as Santa Clara echoes the Truchas Peaks and the

III:51 Puye. View east toward Sangre de Cristo. Notch of Truchas Peaks on center axis. Gap of the Sun to the right.

III:52 Puye. Kiva and houses on the mesa's side. Sangre de Cristo beyond.

III:53 Tsankawi. View northwest toward Otowi and Tsi'como.

III:54 Tsankawi. Humpbacked flute player.

III:55 Tsankawi. Humpbacked flute player on left in pass to mesa top.

sun's gap. We note how European architectural terms no longer apply to these façades. We cannot speak of pediments, cornices, volutes, or akroteria. Kubler employs the term *parapet*, which is neutral enough; but again, exactly as with Hopi architecture, the nomenclature, even for the Spanish churches in the pueblos, most properly becomes what we might call American Natural rather than European Academic.

Black Mesa lies exactly on axis to the north of the plaza (figs. III: 62–65), thereby creating a clear cross-axis of two landscape directions now that the central range of buildings is gone: northward to the Mesa, westward to Tsi'como (fig. III: 58). Here, as always, the plazas of the pueblos seem willing to adjust their main axes of orientation a good deal in order to fit in with the landscape and to invoke its forms. Yet they also seem to be squared with the points of the compass whenever possible and to be inflected more strongly north-south if possible, like the Minoan palaces before them. San Ildefonso as it now stands is a perfect union of celestial and terrestrial focus.

III: 56 Tsankawi. Cliff dwellings on the south face, Black Mesa and the Sangre de Cristo beyond.

III:57 San Ildefonso with the Rio Grande and the Jemez, c. 1920. Note anglicized church and central range of houses. (*Collections in the Museum of New Mexico*)

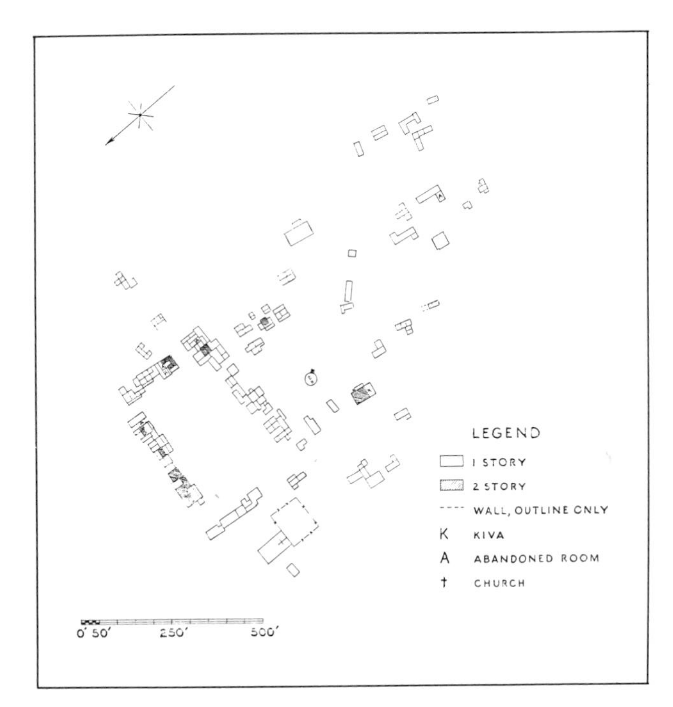

III:58 San Ildefonso. Plan (1950). (*Stubbs, figure 10*)

III:59 San Ildefonso. Kiva (more or less unused now: a monument) and robing room with Jemez and clouds. (The cubical, the cylindrical, and the diagonal with related natural forms.) Old photograph. (*Collections in the Museum of New Mexico*)

III:60 San Ildefonso. Butterfly dance. Old photograph. (*Collections in the Museum of New Mexico*)

On January 24, its feast day, San Ildefonso performs two great dances that explore the dual nature of man: a Comanche dance, where he is a crazy hero, an Achilles, and an animal dance, where he calls the animal families back to himself once more. The latter is a hunting dance, but it is one which seems much more complex and less basic than that which is so eerily embodied in the animal personifications of Taos. It has few elements of dramatic conflict in it, either, so that its mood also seems less that of a stern mystery play, like those at Keresan Santo Domingo, than of a lyric, suggesting an ode on the immortality of the herds and an elegy that laments their passing. Indeed, the mood of the public dances at San Ildefonso, which is the home of artists, anthropologists, and nuclear workmen, is somehow always Theocritean—knowing, a little nostalgic, almost romantic.[18] So the Comanche dance is at once the most splendid and the most psychologically penetrating of that type to be found among the pueblos. It takes shape in long lines directly across the face of the northern buildings, among which the governor's office is placed (figs. III:66, 67). Black Mesa, heavy browed, looms behind the buildings, which are designed to emphasize a lateral stretching as if to provide a complementary base for its bulk.

III:61 San Ildefonso. Church as reconstructed by 1970.

III:62 San Ildefonso. View north toward Black Mesa. Note intermediate range of houses now gone. Old photograph. (*Collections in the Museum of New Mexico*)

III:63 Black Mesa (Tuñjopiñ), the Eyed Boulder, and rock circle.

The dancers descend to the plaza from the rectangular kiva built into that range. They sweep out with their fine slender American pole banners held out like lances before them (figs. III:68, 69). These can remind us of the long lances carried by the *Salii*, but they are used like guidons to point a direction, to change front with a flourish, and to dramatize that wheel from line into fours which is as characteristic of this dance as it was of the drill of old cavalry units.[19] It must always have been one of the most efficient ways for advancing cavalry to change direction fast and to get the hell out of there in a manageable column. So the dance, though on foot, is charged with a horseman's swagger—with his menaces, retreats, and bridlings.

The Pueblos were clearly taken with Comanche horse culture, exactly as the Anglos after them were to be, and they understood what it could mean in terms of pure fun to be free from tilling the soil and to ride around and behave like madmen and invade

III:64 Tuñjopiñ, the Eyed Boulder, and the Rio Grande.

towns and yell in triumph at their taking and drag the women away. They dance out these feelings in the Comanche dance. But they are Pueblos and therefore eminently sane despite everything. So in the last set, when they crown the kiva top and scream and wave their banners over the plaza (fig. III:70), in that moment of exquisite male triumph the leader takes the woman's headdress off his female partner's head

III:65 Tuñjopiñ, the Eyed Boulder (detail).

III:66 San Ildefonso. Comanche dance, January 1968, with Black Mesa.

III:67 San Ildefonso. Comanche dance. Entering the north kiva.

III:68 San Ildefonso. Comanche dance. Old photographs. (*T. Harmon Parkhurst, Collections in the Museum of New Mexico*)

III:69 San Ildefonso. Comanche! Old photograph. (*T. Harmon Parkhurst, Collections in the Museum of New Mexico*)

III:70 San Ildefonso. Victory. Old photograph.
(*Collections in the Museum of New Mexico*)

(a)

(b)

III:71 San Ildefonso. Animal dance, January, 1968. a) Leaving the robing room; b) entering the plaza.

(c)

(d)

(e)

(f)

(g)

(h)

III:71 *continued.* c) With the Pajarito Plateau; d) the buffalo advances; e) changing front, "meandering"; f) the other animals are running bent over on their fore-sticks, here a splendid elk; the buffalo dancer stands tall; g) the buffalo turns; h) the principals come forward; great elk left.

(i)

III: 71 *continued.* i) Leaving the plaza; j) returning to the robing room.

(j)

(or at least did so in 1968) and puts it on his own and dances in it.

What is he saying? That girl-men once ran the Tewa scalp dance, as they did those of the Cheyenne?[20] That the killing of other men is a homosexual act—as Shakespeare interpreted the motives of Achilles? Or only that war and rapine are silly after all? Whatever it is, it seems right at the time, intelligent and cleansing after the aggressive postures of the dance.

Each set of Comanche dance is matched on San Ildefonso's feast day by a set of animal dance, which moves in an arc around the cylindrical kiva and so calls to the Jemez with its own voluminous, rather than simply linear, form (figs. I:45; III:71). The crowd of dancers, first seen, is breathtaking. They are painted black, and are feathered and horned. Their eyes look wild under the paint; they are not masked—no kachinas visible east of Zuni—but changed, barbaric, just enough possessed by their animal embodiments to bring some old terror with them into

III:72 San Ildefonso. Buffalo, maidens, and chorus. *(T. Harmon Parkhurst, Collections in the Museum of New Mexico)*

III:73 San Ildefonso. Buffalo, maidens, and the hunter. *(T. Harmon Parkhurst, Collections in the Museum of New Mexico)*

III:74 The buffalo and the maidens. (*Collections in the Museum of New Mexico*)

(a)

(b)

(c)

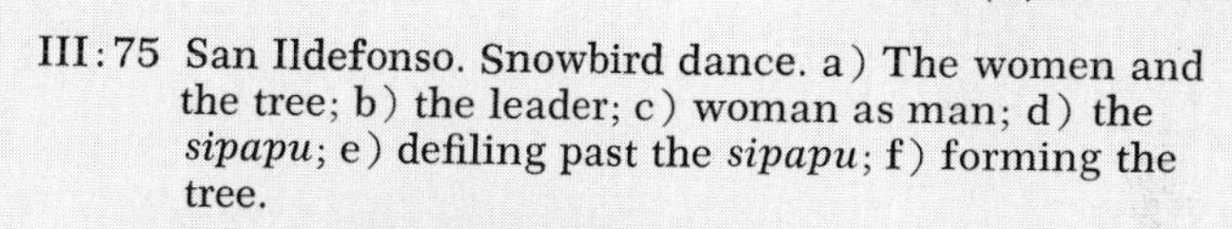

III:75 San Ildefonso. Snowbird dance. a) The women and the tree; b) the leader; c) woman as man; d) the *sipapu*; e) defiling past the *sipapu*; f) forming the tree.

(f)

(e)

(d)

III:76 San Ildefonso. View east toward the Sangre de Cristo from rooftops east of plaza. Baldy and Lake Peak (and Tesuque) behind sand hills straight ahead. Santa Clara's Gap of the Sun to the left. (*Collections in the Museum of New Mexico*)

III:77 Lake Peak looking from the south to the north horn and northward along the Sangre de Cristo range.

III:78 Lake Peak. The lake below the twin peaks.

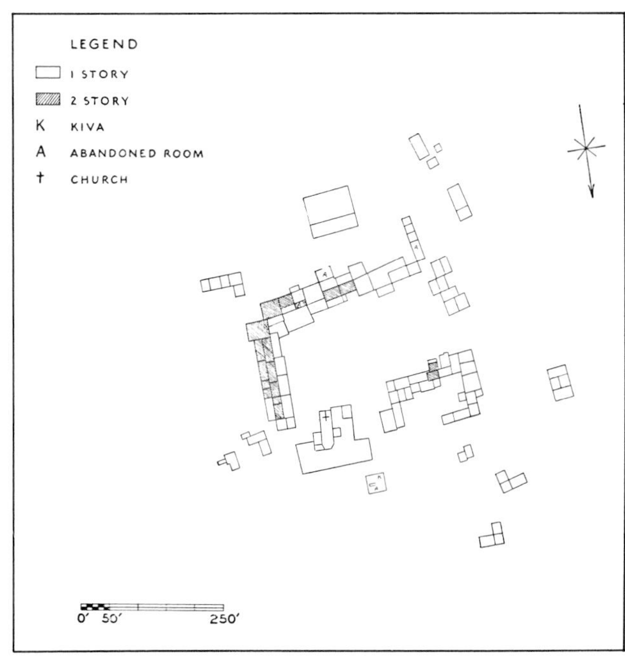

III:79 Tesuque. Plan (1950). (*Stubbs, figure 12*)

the plaza. But again, the final mood is idyllic and nostalgic. All dance together—buffalo and elk, buffalo maidens and hunters—side by side in files.[21] The chorus sings the great buffalo songs much like those of the Keres, with their long sad notes and distant haunting calls. But dramatic conflict, as I have mentioned earlier, is not very developed. Several other kinds of animals do appear, as in the Keres dances, but while there is some interaction, perhaps even some passages of competition between buffalo and elk, there is no clearly developed struggle between them and the chorus, which dances with them too. It is a golden memory of animals and men with the blood between them removed.

Two major things, it seems to me, must strike the contemporary observer. First is the revelation of how herd beasts may have come to be regarded as gods by so many ancient peoples: not merely through shamanistic identification, but because, as the animal dancers lean forward on their two sticks, rumps in the air, and dance en masse with the bells on their hocks all jingling, one feels what it must have been like when the herds ran in their thousands unceasing,

each one like all others, a hundred leaping up when one went down (fig. III:71f). They are not like us, men must have thought at some point; our food, yes, our brothers, too, but unchanging, untouchable, immortal. The dance embodies this.

Second is the end of the dance, when the song is overtly sad, reflecting, one feels sure, both modern nostalgia and some dark, ancient lament. Now it is clear that the animals have gone away, can never be called back. The gods have left us. The gods are dead. We have killed them now, and they will never return. There are no animals in this last set. It is danced close to the robing-room door beside the cylindrical kiva; this time they wait and sing a long while, repeating the sad calling song many times before they pass within at dusk, not mounting to the upper room as before but disappearing into the black shadow of a cavernous chamber.

They also dance more purely buffalo dances at San Ildefonso, in which two buffalo are the center of attention in every set. In these they employ two buffalo maidens, like all the other Tewa and unlike the Keres, who normally, though not invariably, use only a single girl (figs. III:72–74). The maiden's power as Nature is so total that she is more to the point danced singly, I think.[22] And the buffalo dance as a whole can be best seen and described in the Keres towns. But the maidens and the buffalo of San Ildefonso, the man-beasts wearing eagle feathers on their horns and the horned and feathered water serpent, Avanyu, on their kilts, are as touching here as anywhere, embodying as they do the grandeur of the animal and the innocent beauty of the maiden who holds his death in her hand (fig. III:74).

One winter I saw the women of San Ildefonso dance a snowbird dance in honor of a child (fig. III:75). The great potter, Maria, danced with them, at least in the chorus, in her old age. This time it was the cottonwood that served as the natural focus for the form: a file of women dancing in their soft steps out into the plaza to coil below the tree's spreading crown, the navel of the earth under their feet, and Black Mesa out beyond them to the north (fig. III:62), its eyed boulder in San Ildefonso's keeping. That noblest of sacred hills is being invoked, too, as the child is presented to all hills, grasses, birds, and beasts for their consent to its being, its life introduced to the cosmos and all living things.[23] So the dance gently unfolds and opens, circling under the great tree, filing quietly across the plaza. It is a dance of birth, giving, and confidence in life. The leader is young, straight-shouldered, and vigorous (fig. III:75b), but it is the old women dancing in it who bring tears to the eyes.

At Tesuque, the Jemez and Black Mesa have both dropped out of sight, and all visible links are to the Sangre de Cristo range (fig. III:76). The main gap in the plaza, to the northeast (fig. III:79), leads the eye directly to Lake Peak, which is Tesuque's sacred mountain of the east rather than the Truchas Peaks, which here lie farther off to the north. From Tesuque, Lake Peak seems a tight, slightly cleft cone (fig. I:44). Climbed, it shows two immense and wild horns of

III:80 Tesuque. The church and range of buildings with the house of the governor.

(b)

(a)

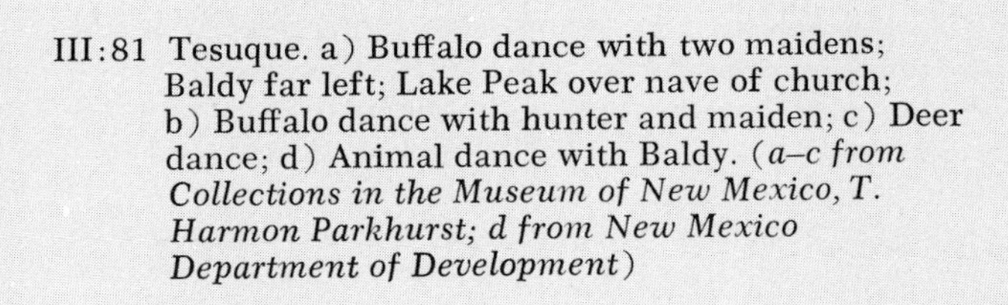

III:81 Tesuque. a) Buffalo dance with two maidens; Baldy far left; Lake Peak over nave of church; b) Buffalo dance with hunter and maiden; c) Deer dance; d) Animal dance with Baldy. (*a–c from Collections in the Museum of New Mexico, T. Harmon Parkhurst; d from New Mexico Department of Development*)

(c)

(d)

rock, below which a perfect lake is cupped almost at the summit (figs. III:77, 78). On the other side the eye goes out across a wilderness of dark forest land in which the Pecos River rises. But on the side toward the Rio Grande the mountain is a chalice, lifted to hold the sacred lake just below the sanctifying peaks. The whole is a shrine. Westward, Tsi'como gathers its cloud cover; lightning flashes far across the valley. Tesuque lies closer in the plain below.[24] Its church is so placed as to dominate the gap to the mountain, or at least to participate in it, and the flat, stretched plane of its façade is emphasized by the only white paint in the village. Its profile seems to me exactly that of Mount Baldy, which it thus assists in complementing Lake Peak to the right. Tesuque had an earlier church with a balcony and two short, horned corner towers[25]; the present example has been simplified to the point where it can exercise its functions of framing and echoing with maximum directness and subtlety.

The whole plaza at Tesuque is a subtle affair of delicately scaled buildings with light wooden porticoes set off by the plane of the church, whose own massing with its dependencies is especially lucid, delicate, and crisp (fig. III:80). Many splendid dances are performed in the plaza, and the relationship between natural and man-made in their setting is especially generous, sweeping, and serene (figs. III:81, 82). Here the buffalo beat the ground in the presence of church and mountain; the deer run in their files with the Bighorn sheep before the white façade, and the eagles lift to the wide sky.[26] The lines of corn dancers pick up the long low profiles of most of the buildings that define the space[27] (fig. III:83). Their *kisi* with its embowered saint is set up on the south side of the plaza, with only sand hills (and the insane government-issue metal water tower, instantly struck by lightning upon completion) visible behind it. The lines of dancers make a clear rectangle with the hills when they face each other before the shrine. When

III:82. Tesuque. Eagle dance I and II. (*Collections in the Museum of New Mexico*)

(a)

(b)

III:83 Tesuque. Corn dance, June 1968. a) The plaza looking east; b) the plaza looking west, the approach march; c) the drummer; d) the chorus; e) lines dancing through each other in front of the *kisi* on the south side of the plaza.

(d)

(c)

(e)

III:83 *continued.* f) lines dancing through each other front of the *kisi* on the south side of the plaza; g) men and women dancers; h) the church an Lake Peak; i) with Baldy and Lake Peak still i snow; j) the saint returning to the church.

(f)

(g)

(h)

(i)

(j)

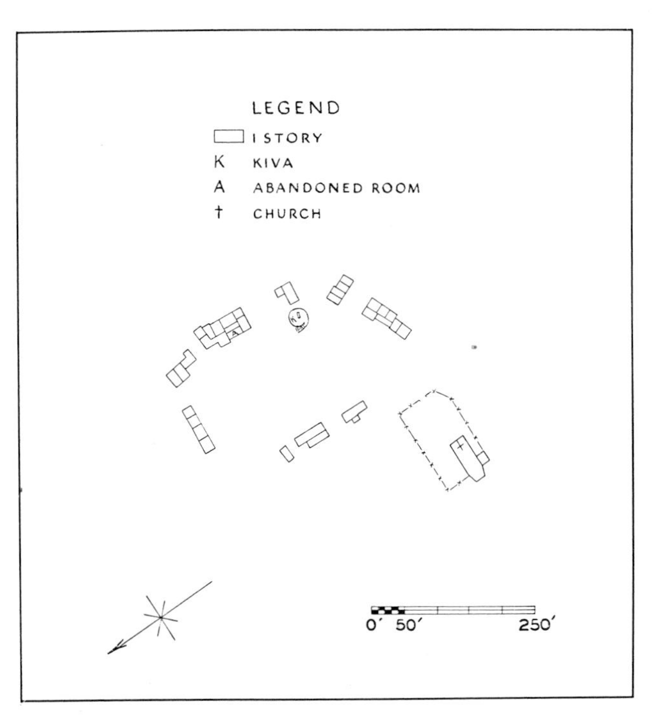

III:84 Nambé. Plan (1950). The pueblo has since deteriorated markedly. (*Stubbs, figure 11*)

they turn and dance out eastward, their movement reverberates in houses and church alike, and in the looming ridge lines of the sacred range. They start in the morning with some of the urban air of Santa Fe still holding them apart from each other and from the place. Most of them work in the city, more or less proletarianized. So they tend to smirk and twitch a little, especially some of the young ones, embarrassed and awkward as the dance begins. As the day goes on they pick up the beat together. Their faces change; they become part of their bodies, like the faces of archaic Greek *kouroi* (fig. III:83g). They reflect the mind's nervous life and the glances of others no

III:85 Nambé. The kiva.

longer. The communal action of the tribe, the rhythm of the planting and the growth of the corn are, after all, what the corn dance is about. At Tesuque the alchemy of the dance makes that come alive again for individuals who are for the most part farmers no longer. It makes them into a Pueblo people once again.

So Tesuque, though small, is still a place, and I do not believe that the rather suburban arc of concrete-block houses which has been laid out behind the sand hills hurts it at all. True enough, the pueblo has leased away hundreds of acres of its birthright out of sight among the sand hills and across the highway upstream for a housing scheme called the Colonías de Santa Fe; but this act of doubtful wisdom does not affect the physical character of the pueblo at the present time. The same cannot be said for Nambé, which has been utterly destroyed by government housing. The design of the individual units is degrading, and their scattered placement suburbanizes the village entirely. The old town had largely disintegrated in any event (fig. III:84), and was well on that road to oblivion so recently traveled by Pojoaque and other Tewa pueblos—but from which Pojoaque, as mentioned earlier, has so miraculously returned.[28] All that is really left to Nambé is a noble kiva, with a contained curving stair which stretches the mass into one of the most sculpturally plastic in the Southwest (figs. III:85, 86). It stands out grandly before

(a)

(b)

(c)

III:86. Nambé. Hunting Dance before kiva. Baldy and Lake Peak beyond. a, b) The animals, in this case deer, "meander"; c) running in place. (*T. Harmon Parkhurst, Collections in the Museum of New Mexico*)

III:87 Nambé Falls. Fourth of July under the two hills.

III:89 Nambé. The old church, which collapsed in 1909. (*Kubler, figure 198*)

III:88 Nambé Falls. Buffalo.

III:90 Spanish Nambé. The church.

III:91 Santa Fe. The Sangre de Cristo with its Sierra Madre above Santa Fe. From the southwest. Arroyo Hondo among foothills far right.

III:92 Santa Fe with its Sierra Madre. There were pueblos in this area. Arroyo Hondo among the foothills right. Plains open beyond. Urbanization should go no further in this area, but the plain will soon be filled with new developments.

III:93 Arroyo Hondo near Santa Fe. View across site toward Sangre de Cristo. Conical hill with shrine right.

III:94 Arroyo Hondo. Some excavated rooms with the conical hill.

the twin mountains of Baldy and Lake Peak, between whom a deep cleft, marking the headwaters of Nambé Creek and called "Puerto Nambé," forms a strong V. That same effect is repeated at the very foot of the mountains in the gorge at Nambé Falls. There the pueblo puts on a Fourth of July festival under two mounded hills which are as looming and shaggy as the buffalo headdresses which toss in the dance before them (figs. III:87, 88).

The old church at Nambé faces the mountains across the plaza with the kiva between them.[29] The strong central triangle of its bell tower and the angle of its flanking horns once suggested a reflection of Baldy and its flanking peaks (Lake Peak cleft to the right) as they rise up behind the kiva on that bearing (figs. III:86, 89). The roof collapsed in 1909, after which the church was given the disastrous tight-gabled, tin-roofed treatment and is now virtually dead. The other church near Nambé is Spanish-American; it stands up on a considerable rise and confronts the mountains (fig. III:90). Like San Francisco at Ranchos de Taos, it has two strongly articulated towers, in this case with the deep void of a porch between them to dramatize their heavy mass. There is little modulation or inflection of any kind here; the proportions are gross and rather brutal.

III:95 Arroyo Hondo. Sweep across the site from the conical hill. Cerrillos (Turquoise) Mountains to the left with Sandia beyond them. Jemez center. Foothills of the Sangre de Cristo far right. (*Philip Garvin*)

Southern Tewa once lived in the area of Santa Fe and out toward the open plains below it, but they are all gone now (figs. III:91, 92). One of the finest sites in that area is now being excavated above the Arroyo Hondo, just forward of the red hills south of Santa Fe[30] (figs. III:93, 94). An enormous sweep of landscape is visible from it, with the Jemez range seen now in an angle toward its more southern aspect (fig. III:95). A conical hill rises directly south of the town, and a small rock shrine lies just below its summit, inflected toward the conical Turquoise Mountains above Cerrillos and toward Sandia, sacred mountain of the south (figs. III:93, 94, 96). The sweep of the Rio Grande valley below La Bajada between Sandia and the Jemez is perceived far off in this view (fig. III:95), and down there, marked and glorified by Sandia but dominated in fact by the southern bastions of the Jemez, lie the great Keres towns.

III:96 Arroyo Hondo. The shrine looking south toward Turquoise and Sandia mountains and, left, the open plains.

IV: 1 Cochití and the Jemez from across the Rio Grande. The pueblo lies under water tower far left. Sacred formations of the Jemez far right. Most of the foothills from center to far right are to be covered with a suburb-like town (Cochití Lake) for 52,000 people.

IV: 2. Cochití Lake. Three views in 1971.

IV

THE RIO GRANDE—THE KERES TOWNS

The towns of the Keresan people deserve to be called great—especially the largest of them, Santo Domingo, which is an implacable bastion of Indian life and ways. Cochití, it is true, egged on by the Bureau of Indian Affairs, recently committed an act of suicide when it deeded off most of its land, including a couple of critical shrines, as the site for a new town of some fifty-two thousand people (fig. IV:1). That thing, called Cochití Lake, is now taking shape, damming the Rio Grande and looking a lot like Southern California (fig. IV:2). A slogan, "New Mexico, Land of the Seven-Day Weekend," is emblazoned with similar legends on its adman's billboards. The thought seems inadequate to the place, somehow, and to the unrelenting labor through which human beings have lived with dignity in it for so many centuries before our own. Above the billboards the mountain shapes which gave focus to the Keres world still stand out against the sky—a great cone to the left, a cleft pyramid rising in the center, a long stretched slope to the right, where the shape has often been described as that of a crouching rabbit[1] (figs. IV:1, 23, 29). In and under that general formation all the topographical features that are sacred to the Keres and remind them of their history are clearly in view. The Keres, like the Tewa, descended step by step from those mountains, and when they raise their eyes to them today the old beloved places have their placards in the precipices and the peaks. High up somewhat to the north rises an isolated cleft peak, the very heart, the Sierra Medio, of the Jemez range, which lies on the long axis of Frijoles Canyon, the site of one of the earliest of the proto-Keres settlements and now a national monument named for Adolph Bandelier[2] (figs. III:33; IV:3, 4). Indeed, if one looks closely from somewhere near Cochití, the rocky debouchement of Frijoles Canyon into the snake-haunted White River Canyon of the Rio Grande can also be seen. Up that canyon under the horns, the space opens to a grassy meadow once planted with corn and beans (fig. IV:5). There the major settlement, Tyuonyi, lay directly under a mighty prow of rock which plunges like the bow of a ship into the canyon.[3] The kivas in the enclosed plaza of the Great

House were supplemented by another out in the meadow where there was also a curious paved circle like a threshing floor (figs. IV:6, 7). All of these man-made forms are dominated and sanctified by the rock prow, and by the weirdly eroded spires of stone that stand below it (figs. IV:8, 9). Around them and it fine cave dwellings of all kinds pock the mesa's sides at several levels (fig. IV:10). One was partly built

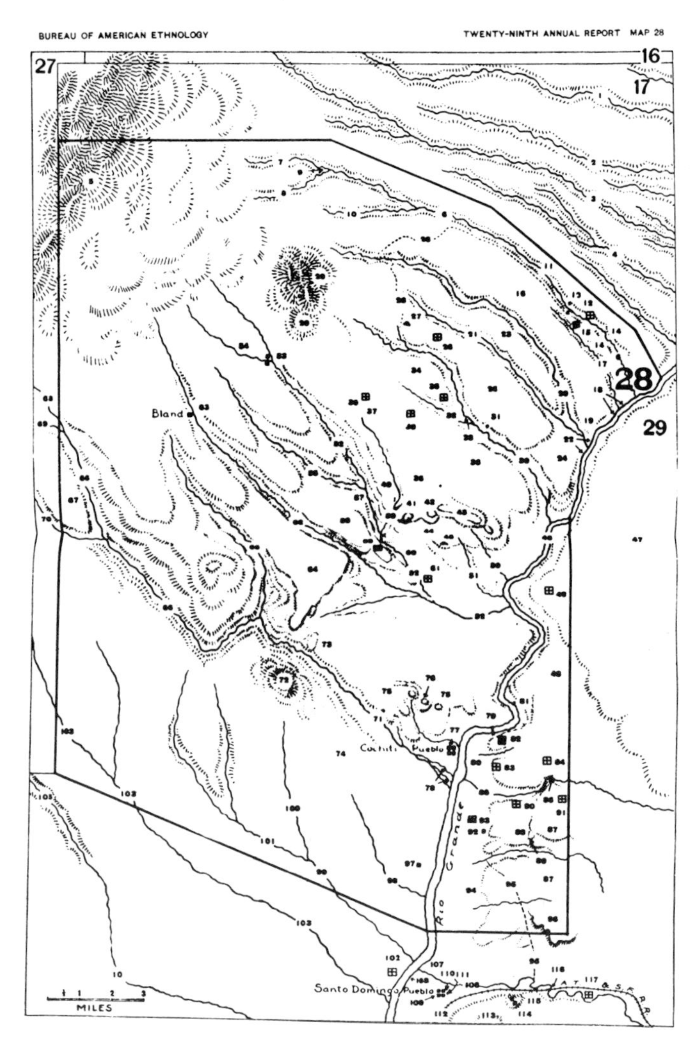

IV:3 Map of the Jemez range and the Pajarito Plateau on the side toward Cochití. Theresan mountains (5), Rabbit mountain (29), Rito de los Frijoles (6), The Lions of Cochití (27), Stone Lions of the Potrero de los Idolos (45), Painted Cave (31). (*Harrington, map* 28)

IV:4 Rito de los Frijoles. (Bandelier National Monument) The axis of the canyon with the twin-peaked mountain dead ahead.

out in a long house along the prow's southern flank (fig. IV:11). Farther up the canyon a kiva was dug and built into the floor of a cavern high up toward the mesa rim. Here we feel ourselves in the heart of the mountain, lulled and cooled by trees and water but very high (figs. IV:12, 13). Other sanctuaries, like those at the Mesa Verde, but here simple rings of stones, were sited on the mesa tops in view of the great canyons and the cleft peaks alike. But of this whole sacred area Frijoles Canyon is the literal paradise, a true *paradeisos*, a walled garden—the Garden of Eden for the Keres in sober fact. It is not easy to understand why they left it. The stream does not dry up at any time; the winter weather, though it brings plenty of snow with it, is bracing rather than otherwise. The growing season, however, cannot be long.

IV:5 Rito de los Frijoles.

IV:6 Rito de los Frijoles. Kiva in the valley. Shrines on mesa above. Tyuonyi directly ahead under rock prongs. Cave dwellings to the right and along face of prow.

This may be why the Keres moved away at last. It looks now as if they did so long before the Navaho began to raid in this area, so that nomad pressure probably cannot be blamed. The Cochiteños told Lummis that they had moved eight times and that Tyuonyi, their second town, had been destroyed by their "brethren,"[4] which could mean Tewa, as Bandelier more or less indicated in his sensational novel *The Delight Makers*.[5] For whatever reason, the Keres traveled across the potrero tops, down into the awesome Alamo Canyon (fig. IV:14) and up to the Potrero de las Vacas, where they built another town, whose unexcavated ruins are visible today and whose name, Yapashi, derives from the shrine of mountain lions couchants which are carved in the living rock slightly above it (figs. IV:15–19). They are often called "The Lions of Cochití," but it is an all-Pueblo shrine and is probably venerated by Navaho as well.[6] It is for all hunters; the lions lie in the stretched-out crouch of cats before they spring. A circle of rock slabs protects their sanctuary, and a tree grows beside them, camouflaging their bodies with its dappled shade. One cannot help but recall the combination of twin lions and column which meant the mountain goddess and the Mistress of the Beasts at Knossos as at Mycenae (fig. IV:18), and of the tree where Apollo was born, saluted by the lions of the goddess on Delos.[7]

One is stirred again by the recurrence of heraldic themes in human art. Here the seat of the lions is high, and the breeze must crackle with many scents of deer as it ripples down across their backs from the pine forests of the heights, and slides, heavy with cattle smells, up to their muzzles from the plain. The horns of deer lie as offerings beside them. Feathers have been offered there as well, one from an eagle

IV:7 Rito de los Frijoles. The kiva and the prow.

IV:8 Rito de los Frijoles. Tyuonyi under the prongs.

who sailed high overhead in the current above Alamo Canyon and wheeled and dropped it at a Hopi call.

There is another pair of mountain lions carved in rock and surrounded by slabs on the Potrero de los Idolos farther down toward Cochití (fig. IV:20). In some ways these forms, though cruder, have more sphinxlike power in them than those of Yapashi.[8] But their shrine has been disturbed and one of them was almost entirely destroyed, blown and levered out of the living rock by some fortune hunter long ago. A painted cave is not far away; conspicuous among its images is a long, feathered serpent of the kind that is found several times among the petroglyphs of the Pajarito Plateau (figs. IV:21, 22) and is ubiquitous elsewhere in the imagery of the prehistoric Southwest.[9]

Down below lies modern Cochití (fig. IV:23). The

IV:9 Rito de los Frijoles. Tyuonyi and the south wall c the canyon.

IV:10 Rito de los Frijoles. Cliff dwelling above Tyuonyi; entrance to caves, sockets for beams.

two cylindrical kivas of its moieties stand on the side toward the mountains[10] (figs. IV:24–26). As always, their ladder poles rise high into the air; they are the only forms in an Indian pueblo which, except for the corn dance standard, shoot up to pierce the heavens. Southward, the main plaza is gently sunken. It is almost square but is subtly relieved and opened at all the corners. The shapes of the Jemez can be seen over its northern houses, and once again they are generally echoed in the architectural forms (figs. IV:27, 28). In winter the animal dancers emerge from a rectangular kiva or robing room which is adjacent to the cacique's special shrine or headquarters to the southeast of the plaza, and they walk into it on the northern bearing toward the mountains. Indeed, all dancers seem to enter the plaza in that way. In the animal dance the chorus takes station on the east side. On February 18, 1968, it was made up of perhaps thirty men who seemed to be hunters with guns and bows; and it was led by a man in blackface, wearing a derby hat and carrying a guitar. Who was he? "He thinks he's Amos and Andy," one of the members of the chorus gratuitously, and without doubt mendaciously, suggested to me. The black slave Estevan always comes to mind, perhaps irrelevantly, at such times, but 1968 was also the Black Power year, and the teen-agers in Cochití were going around done up like Rap Brown.[11] Was there any connection? The Pueblos were at least considering possible alliances with black activists at that time. Later they seem to have backed off from them.

There were also two buffalo maidens, as among the Tewa, but such is unusual in Keres practice.[12] In any event, whether with two maidens or one, the principals, who also include the two buffalo and a hunter in buckskin like a Plains Indian, act out as always their special Keres tragedy of nature and death together, while the pairs of other animals, deer, elk, mountain sheep, and so on, frisk and flee in a circular pattern around them (figs. III:71f, 71g, 71j, 72–74). Never touching each other, except when the buffalo maiden reaches out with her stiff bouquet of evergreens and eagle feathers to lead him back to his fate,

IV:11 Rito de los Frijoles. Looking east back down the canyon. Long House along face of prow on left.

buffalo and maiden dance reciprocally in advance and retreat, while the hunter more or less follows their motions as a kind of separate, slightly foreign, rather entranced, background figure. It is clear that the buffalo regard themselves as lords and hunters; they dance upright like men and carry bows and rattles. Here at Cochití the theme of their death is not overly developed. They count coup on the other animals and, it would seem, bring them to life again. This happens most tremendously after the eighth dance. By this time it is lateish winter afternoon. The animals are all massed outside the robing room. They dance bent forward over their fore-sticks, balancing on them while their hind legs run with all their ankle bells jingling in unison (figs. III:71f, 81, 86). Then the buffalo dance with their strong, stamping, shoulder-lurching step—knees high, deep drums pounding as their feet pound the earth—up and down the line of animals, touching them with the bow. Then they dance back up again, all the animals dancing faster and faster now, running with their galloping beat in place, the bells sounding like thousands of animals running far off. And the buffalo touch them with their black rattles from which long black hairs trail—and gesture with shoulder, arm, and bow: Come on, come on. Run. Run. And all run faster to-

IV:12 Rito de los Frijoles. The Ceremonial Cave.

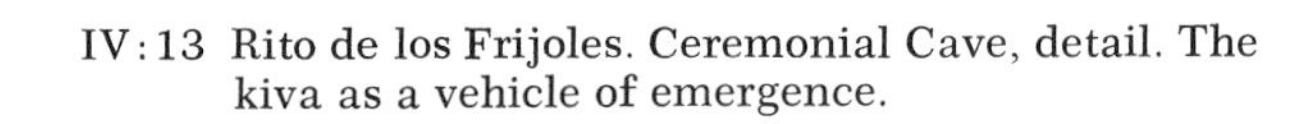

IV:13 Rito de los Frijoles. Ceremonial Cave, detail. The kiva as a vehicle of emergence.

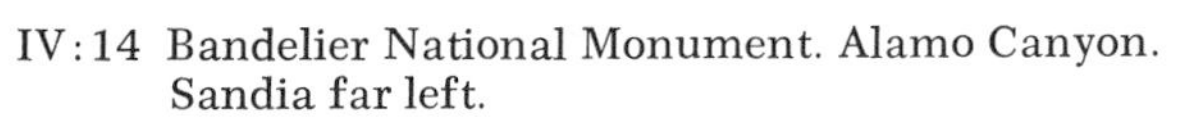

IV:14 Bandelier National Monument. Alamo Canyon. Sandia far left.

gether, all the antlers tossing and the backs moving in unison, the buffalo beside them running in place, enormous black shaggy headdresses, godlike, knees high. And the drum stops. Silence. And they go into the room.

On February 25, 1968, they danced the buffalo dance again and this time with only one girl dancer; she was magnificent, a buffalo maiden wise, compassionate, beautiful, and exact. Because of her the last act was more moving than ever; her gesture of blessing (and condemning) the buffalo on the forehead with her sacred bouquet was exquisitely gentle and kind. She encompassed the death and resurrection of the animals and then death again with that gesture, bringing the herds along to their fate, great buffalo too, up and over the hurdle of death, firmly and kindly with her bundle of feathers and evergreen. She was as fine a dancer as I have ever seen anywhere, but an actress most of all, playing a lovely and terrible role: Artemis and Athena, Mistress of the Beasts and palladium of heroes, loving and treacherous, serving only the law of things as they are (fig. III:74).

The chorus was huge that day; one man was dressed as a woman, with sunglasses and pocketbook. Otherwise it was made up of every conceivable kind of Indian, with one Spanish-American but no Anglos that I could see. The sense was of the purity of the animals and of the dedicated dancing hunters set off by the confusion, perhaps even the evil, of mankind. Surely the animals seemed lucid and natural and the chorus wild, aggressive, crazy with passion sometimes, and very complicated. But only the dark races were represented (though no black man today); the white man was clearly excluded from the communion and, however it was couched, the prayer.

In the summer festivals at Cochití the corn dancers emerge toward noontime from one of the round kivas, women and men together. The men are stripped to the waist wearing only a white Hopi kilt and with lots of evergreen tied to their arms. They wear parrot feathers in their hair and skunk fur around their moccasin heels, and hold a rattle in one hand and evergreen in the other, with a turtleshell rattle gurgling away behind one knee (figs. IV:32–34). The women are in the traditional black dress, leaving one shoulder bare, hair generally long, feet bare, ever-

IV:15 Bandelier National Monument. Yapashi. The Lions of Cochití in their enclosure.

IV:16 Yapashi. The Lions.

green in each hand, the *tablita*, itself a stepped sky altar, on the head. They walk down from the kiva in two files—two men side by side, two women behind them—down from the mountains toward the plaza in front of the church, where the first dance will take place. Here the relationship of the church profile to the shapes of the Jemez is most obvious (fig. IV:29). The gate into the sacred precinct echoes them too. Lummis saw this and drew and photographed it. On his drawing with the gate he altered the Jemez just a trifle to make everything utterly identical (fig. IV:30), and he wrote, "On the west the broken masses of the noble Jemez Range pierces [*sic*] the clouds . . ."[13] So much the more grotesque it was when the old adobe church was remodeled later, its horns ripped off, a tin roof with a tall belfry stuck on it (fig. IV:31). When the belfry began to shake the church apart in the wind, it was replaced by a stubby one. The adobe wall around the cemetery was replaced by a wire fence.[14] Better counsel finally pre-

IV:18 Mycenae. The Lion Gate, detail. (*Gordon Sweet*)

IV:17 Yapashi. The Lions camouflaged.

vailed and the church was restored pretty much as it was originally meant to be. So today, as in Lummis's time, when the great banner of the corn dance is lifted before it, it can play the part in relation to the sacred landscape that it was so long ago adapted to fulfill. They are in unison, like most of the dance.

The corn is the life and the glory of the pueblo. Every corn dance has always seemed to me as much in praise of the power of the polis, almost as much military, as agricultural in character. Almost everybody seems to dance in it who can lift a foot. The plaza is never still. First one kiva dances, then the other, coiling around through it in a labyrinthine pattern, their banners passing each other as one group enters and one goes out. Sometimes they overlap. Sometimes, in the last set, they dance together, so that the whole plaza is one sea of evergreen and cloud altars, with drum beat and singing, like an imperial cornfield growing in sun and wind between the houses. But the first dance, here and in all the Keres

IV:19 Yapashi. Lion.

corn dances, is in front of the church. The first movement is the entrance in column of twos, in a kind of almost-in-place double-time march for the men and a shuffle (their feet must never really leave the earth) for the women (fig. IV:32). It is an army advancing behind its banner. Then it halts. The lines face each other and two other dances take place, one more or less slow, the other one fast (figs. IV:33, 34). That is the climax, and it comes on in that beat which al-

IV:20 Potrero de los Idolos. One of the Stone Lions, c. 1890. (*Charles F. Lummis, Collections in the Museum of New Mexico*)

IV:21 Bandelier National Monument. The painted cave, with horned and plumed serpent. (*Harrington, plate 18*)

IV:22 Petroglyph of Avanyu, the plumed water serpent, at Tsirege, also on the Pajarito Plateau. (*Hewett, figure 18*)

ways says *Indian* to those who know no more about them than whatever the popular European culture may provide. It pounds the earth, as the lines wheel through each other, the banner sweeping low across them, the men's arms bent at the elbow and pumped straight up and down, the rattles like rain splashing downward, the drum thundering and calling to life, exaltation, victory, growth most of all, being. The beat of the corn dance is life, repetitive as the heart-beat, interminably insistent as the pulse of the sun in the corn. And when that beat hesitates, as the drummers make it do at intervals, the heart skips, misses. Will it pick up? Then those great drummers, architects of life, reverse the drum in that splendid split second and hit the other side on a shriller note with a faster beat and all comes up again: the corn starts up its cosmic clock, the human heart swells on again in glory.

IV:23 Cochití. The pueblo in middle distance, the formations of the Jemez beyond.

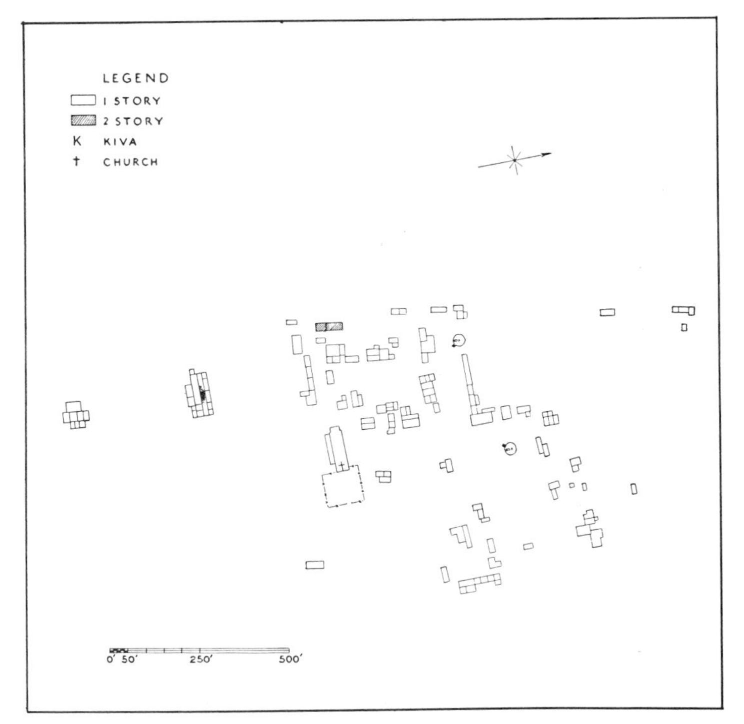

IV:24 Cochití. Plan (1950). (*Stubbs, figure 14*)

IV:25 Cochití. Aerial view in 1947. (*Collections in the Museum of New Mexico*)

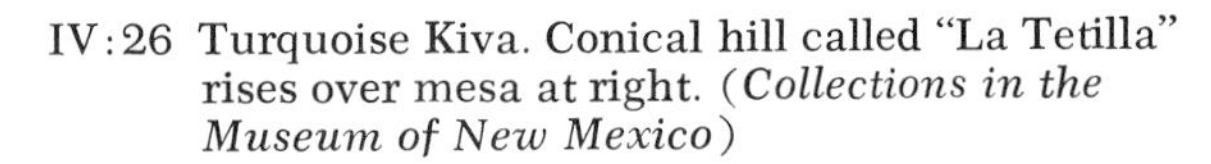

IV:26 Turquoise Kiva. Conical hill called "La Tetilla" rises over mesa at right. (*Collections in the Museum of New Mexico*)

So it continues all day in the blazing sun by church and mountain and most of all in the plaza of the town. Other ceremonies may be connected with it on feast days. The Spanish horsemen who guard the saint may come out near midday with their Spanish snare drummer to be driven around the plaza, stalked by the governor carrying his two silver-headed canes of office, one from Abraham Lincoln, the other from the emperor of Spain. It is a long day; dancers and spectators alike change during it. It has all the boredom of life in it, all the heat and difficulty of its middle parts, and then, as promised, fulfillment toward evening. Perhaps even rain, coming down like smoke upon the dancers while they cry out in triumph and joy. Finished, there has been a shape made, a day carved by men who salute with their banners the sun at its zenith and dance it to its declining and, rain or no, to the first puffs of coolness in the later afternoon.

But Santo Domingo is greater: larger for one thing, but harder, too, and, unlike poor Cochití, never trusting the white man in anything, under any circumstances anywhere. Its layout is stern, strict, and grand.[15] Long lines of houses, some still set back in two stories, stretch out with long streets between them (fig. IV:35). They are, of course, only intervals between the house masses, not designed streets in the European sense. All is laid out close under low hills to the east and extends from them toward the Rio Grande and the wide fields, beyond which the sacred formations of the Jemez are still well in view (figs. IV:36, 37). The corrals along the western side of the town have developed considerably since the old photographs were taken and are now a splendid maze. Those on the east under the hills are as elaborate as ever. The central interval of the pueblo is somewhat wider than the others and slightly sunken, concave like a very long canoe (fig. IV:38). It is the dance plaza. One kiva stands at the end under the sand hills, whose forms it echoes, and the slant of whose sides is picked up by the ladder poles (figs. IV:39, 40). Another kiva just barely intrudes the monumental scale of its cylinder into the space of the

IV:27 Cochití. The plaza in 1908. Women's dance. *(H. F. Robinson, Collections in the Museum of New Mexico)*

IV:28 Cochití. The sacred formations are just coming into view on the right. (*Collections in the Museum of New Mexico*)

IV:29 Cochití. Mission of San Buenaventura about 1890, with the formations of the Jemez. (*Collections in the Museum of New Mexico*)

IV:30 Cochití. The Campo Santo and the Jemez range. (*Charles F. Lummis, 1888, Collections in the Museum of New Mexico*)

IV:31 Cochití. The church as remodeled in 1912; it has now been restored to earlier state as in figs. 29–30. (*Collections in the Museum of New Mexico*)

plaza on the south side halfway down; it is a marvelously disquieting geometric apparition (fig. IV:41a). The west end of the plaza is terminated by a flat building which is repeated by two flat planes of far hill slope across the Rio Grande (figs. IV:38, 41a). From the rooftops farther mountains are seen, especially the great turtle of Sandia off to the southeast, and all together Sandia and the Jemez and the nearer hills work plastically with the advanced and recessed building masses.

At Santo Domingo the corn dance fills the plaza with hundreds of dancers of all ages, from ancient grayheads with vast potbellies to children a few years old[16] (figs. IV:41a–h). But its strength is deep in middle-aged men and women and in teen-age dancers, boys and girls. The whole population seems solidly one, dancing with set faces through the blinding dust storms of spring afternoons and in the furnace heat of summer and then, perhaps, with raindrops exploding around them late in the August day. Far off the lightning may be seen flashing around the shrines on the Jemez, and the fire watchers start up and shield their eyes to see if the last strike left fire behind it.

Santo Domingo's corn dance is the greatest of all,

IV:32 Corn dancers in approach dance to front of church in 1888. Note Kusha'li (koshare) side dance. *(Charles F. Lummis, Collections in the Museum of New Mexico)*

IV:33 The corn dancers, 1888, now in second dance with the gate to the Campo Santo and the Jemez range. *(Charles F. Lummis, Collections in the Museum of New Mexico)*

but the type has already been described. A further word should be said about the chorus. It is made up of men in bright shirts and Spanish trousers, often white and incandescent in the summer light, singing and dancing behind the drummer in a bent-kneed step and lifting and lowering their hands with evergreen in them as if describing and praising the life and growth of the corn (figs. IV:41a; III:83d). There are also many koshare, members of a special priestly society, Bandelier's "delight makers." They are painted white with stripes of black with corn shocks (the universal Pueblo symbol of the clown) sticking straight up from their stocking-capped heads (figs. IV:41c, 41g). They dance their own way through the great ranks, directing events, aiding dancers with equipment, fooling about a bit like the Zuni mudheads and the Hopi clowns in the rare intervals between sets, and swaggering rather ominously about, always hurrying as if on some errand, running here and there with a bugle and a drum, popping in and out of the kivas, running down the stairs—but mostly freer than others and dancing with their space-devouring stride past the more rooted dancers.

Santo Domingo's hunting dance of late February is this continent's most searching mystery play.[17] As Greek drama grew out of the animal chorus of Dionysos, so here Thespis, in the person of the buffalo, is just on the brink of stepping forward as a tragic hero who will say no to fate and nature's law. Under the horns of Mycenae was nurtured, in the Greek imagination, a race, the Atreids, who were fated to smash every old way and all of nature's balances in their will to break free. Here it is not a man but the dark animal, hunter and hunted, who steps forth

IV:34 Corn dance, 1888. The standard is swept lower over the dancers, their lines pass through each other in the deeply inflected climactic song. (*Charles F. Lummis, Collections in the Museum of New Mexico*)

IV:35 Santo Domingo. Aerial view (1950). (*Stubbs, plate 13*)

from Dionysos' train: son of Zeus, snake-blessed, and horned[18] (fig. III:74). It is he who bears the burden of awakening and seeks to exercise choice and to cheat the common death that awaits us all. Why is it he? Perhaps originally because of all great living things on this continent he was the greatest, greater than man, whom he nourished. His shape is archaic, or rather, prehistoric: a mountain at the shoulder sloping down to tapering haunches beneath which the small hooves are gathered closely together. He bunches, exactly as the artists of Altamira pictured

IV:36 Santo Domingo, c. 1920. Corrals and horse parade in foreground. Church to right. Irrigation ditch divides this area from the town, the Rio Grande and southernmost foothills of the Jemez beyond. A swing to the left would bring Sandia into view. (*Collections in the Museum of New Mexico*)

him on the bosses of their cavern's roof so many thousands of years ago. The enormous head hangs low, and below the sharp, strong horns the face is masked in thick, curled wool with circular cutouts for the round brown eyes. In his thousands his gallop shook the earth, his multitudes pouring over the land like a river or an avalanche. But the individual presence is arrestingly melancholy; one can somehow believe in a tragic awareness imprisoned within it—especially if, in the course of business, one has come upon the wholly terrible Oedipus image that Catlin saw[19] (fig. II:38d). Now it may go further, because it was also he, at once the most numerous, the most essential, and the most kingly of us all, who also most conspicuously had his Fall and his Dorian invasion, so that upon his glory and his fate, as upon that of the Achaean lords, the deepening tragic consciousness of a later age was founded.

The dance is tremendous in power (figs. III:71a–j). Like Domingo itself it is big; its chorus is several hundred strong, with lots of guns and plenty of blanks shot off. Again, its members are made up to resemble all kinds of Indians from Apache to Eastern Woodlands, I think; and no Anglos. The two buffalo are heavy, black, and splendid, and the buffalo maiden is impressive too, but, as one might have predicted, not tender like the girl at Cochití but unreachable, implacable like her town. The other animals play their rôles with enormous theater: brave, noble elk; quick, nervous deer; twitchy goats; all acting and reacting like old troopers to the myth. In February 1968, they did the killing and resurrection ritual described at Cochití in the second and third sets in the morning. Then they danced outside the kiva and quit for lunch. In the afternoon they danced six times. The first was a line dance, the second a tug of war. By the second

IV:37 Santo Domingo in the nineteenth century. (*Ben Wittick, Collections in the Museum of New Mexico*)

IV:38 Santo Domingo. The main plaza looking west more or less as at present, though a gap has since opened in the center of the far side. (*Collections in the Museum of New Mexico*)

IV:39 The main plaza looking east in the early twentieth century. (*Collections in the Museum of New Mexico*)

IV:40 The kiva at the east end of the main plaza under the sand hills. (*Collections in the Museum of New Mexico*)

dance another actor had stepped forward to join the buffalo, the maiden, and the buckskin hunter. He was a spearman stripped for war, painted black with white stripes and carrying a spear and shield. He looked like death, the pure killing fever boiling out of the chorus when the blood is up, the real doom thing, the death. The third set was in fact an orgy of killing, and he danced wildly through it all. The blanks were shot off in fusillades, the antelope reeling, the buffalo frantic, because it was in this dance that the chorus began to shoot at them, the buffalo, and they raged back at it, their headdresses tossing in what seemed a sea of horns. When that occurred, the black spearman took their part and struck at the chorus with his spear. In the fourth set there was a jousting between buffalo and elk, and a great song for it like an account of combat between heroes, much more European in character, more literary and imagistic than most of the music. The great bull elk has his manhood, too, it seemed to say, and in that beat (figs. III: 71d, f). During the dance two antelope panicked and tried to escape and ran out of the plaza, to be harried back shortly. Late in that set, the black dancer did a curious thing. He stuck his spear point into the chorus and somebody tied what appeared to be a can of sardines on it, and he ran over and threw it in what looked like a gesture of contempt at some elders of the tribe who had seats in the plaza and who fell all over themselves to pick it up. (Herds wiped out? White man's lousy rations?)

(a)

IV:41 Santo Domingo. Corn dance, early twentieth century. a) Chorus to the left, standard in front, with koshare; it is the approach march into the plaza, perhaps from the cylindrical kiva that can just be seen at left; b) still the advance behind the banner; c) still the advance; note the fast-moving koshare; d) now the dance is in place, the men pounding the earth, the women caressing it.

(b)

(c)

(d)

(e)

(f)

(g)

IV:41 *continued.* e) Corn dance with eastern kiva; note scale of watchers on roofs; the *kisi* is in the middle of north side; at present it is normally placed farther east toward the kiva; f) the dancers rest on the kiva while the other half dances; g) koshare on an errand; h) dancing in front of the church in the first set; here perhaps most of all the army of Domingo is felt. (*b–d, f photos by Nathan Kendall, Collections in the Museum of New Mexico*)

(h)

IV:42 The church as it was. Note sky altar. (*Kenneth Chapman Coll., Collections in the Museum of New Mexico*)

In the fifth set so great is their fear that the buffalo turn on each other; they jostle and thrust. Each then tries to get away—away from the other and out of the plaza—but the maiden leads them firmly back to their destiny and they take up their dance in the rhythm of their natural running once more. This is where it is most moving, as all living things take up their fate together. The sixth and last set was more conventional and had the longest and loveliest dancing of the herds in their immortal companies—bells jingling, great drum booming, earth shaking, all the great plains thundering with life (fig. III:81c). The buffalo danced again like lords and comrades down their two lines, the maiden in front, the buckskin hunter, always inconspicuous, following her (fig. III:73). In the final set at the kiva, all the animals were shot and carried into the chamber.

It was the grandest and most complete of all the animal dances, austere and terrible, passionate and frightening in this deeply serious pueblo. The long plaza was crowned with its long cornices of watchers on the roofs in rich mulberry reds, purples, blues, and greens. The earth color of the adobe is thus set off and the architectural frame is finally completed as it is meant to be. Below, in the dance, the mood is Aeschylean. What occurs is truly awful. The proud kings are brought low, but worse than this, they betray each other and try to flee like the poor antelope, and in the end, weapons and all, are butchered like the others and carried as meat away.

So it is the maiden who conquers. She remains queen despite the heroes' challenge, and she is always untouched, gentle, and impassive. Nature personified, tyrant mistress of all, the true, ancient *pótnia therón*,[20] she gives her orders to her horned consorts with the touch of her feathered evergreen bough, waits for one instant to see that they are carried out, and then goes her way: ordering all, demanding all, reconciling all, healing, commanding, and leading each animal and hunter to his fated rendezvous and to his ending.

East of the irrigation ditch behind Domingo, the church is laid out facing west, with a broad horse plaza beside its long southern flank (figs. IV:35, 36). It once had a very expressive façade, climaxed by what can in this case only be called a cloud altar lifted above the sand hills[21] (figs. IV:42, 43). It has now been somewhat remodeled but is still painted with horses (fig. IV:43). That is appropriate enough, because it is the horse which dominates the games and rituals that take place in the open field beside it (fig. IV:44). On the afternoon of July 25, 1968, I saw footraces between men, boys, and girls run there, the track lying diagonally across the field. But then at least one hundred horsemen took it over. They massed near the church and started a mounted game involving a cloth roll or doll. An enormous horseman

IV:43 Santo Domingo. Façade of the church in 1915, showing horses.

IV:44 The site of the races and chicken pulls south of the church.

received it, I think from an old priest (a war chief perhaps), and then rode up to another rider and beat him brutally with it. The victim, seizing the roll, is supposed to make off with it if he can, but the others are on him. They pull and tear at it in a great scrum. If he or another breaks loose with it he rides off across the field like the wind. Or if he cannot get loose, the whole packed mob may push close up toward the irrigation ditch and, seeking to avoid it, turn to the side in six or seven close-sliding horse-planes like those of the Parthenon frieze (figs. IV:45, 46). Then it breaks up and somebody is loose and his horse runs. The rider sits well back, legs long, slashing at pursuers. Pueblo? Comanche? Athenian?

Then they do it all over again, this time with a chicken. The riders sit in a semicircle facing the south flank of the church; they talk quietly and smile. The old one gives the brutish one a live chicken, and he rides along the line with it and calls somebody out and hits him with it quite gently and he takes it—still very much alive and in good shape—and goes up to still another man and smashes him with it, it squawking, blood on the shirt now. The assailed man tries to grab it and after a couple of blows normally does so, and they try to tear it apart between them, standing in place.[22] If successful, they ride with their piece hanging up to the ditch and hand it across the water to a female relation or throw it to somebody. The church bell may be ringing continuously during the pulling or a drum beating steadily all the while.

Then some men hoist up two poles out near the center of the course where the footraces were run. A rope is tied between them and a chicken slung by the feet head down to that. All the horsemen ride around it in a tight catenary curve, with a few ki-yis in good old attack-on-the-wagon-train style. Then they fall into file (Indian file) galloping and ki-yiing and the drum beating—beating a cavalry beat, a fast, insistent rhythm that gets you excited and keeps it up like a charge (doom, doom) but not deep (more like a rub-a-dub-dub, dub, dub, dub) and they ride hard, one after the other and around again, under the rope, trying to grab the chicken, which the men at the vertical poles twitch up out of the way if they can. But they get him eventually, in terrible pulls, riding like hell, one hand stretched high. It is death—an execution. The chicken dies in what must be excruciating torment. By this time they are all excited and may pursue the man who gets it or a piece of it well out of the plaza—even through the ditch between them and the spectators, scattering them like quail and fighting down in among the shiny parked cars (not many) and running, slipping (by now, raining), splattering the mud. What abandon they have, tearing at each other; they don't seem the same people. Other heroes arise among them—one slender young man with wild eyes, long hair, and a headband, gets at least four cloth dolls and chickens, his horse thundering across the wooden bridge, he grinning like a movie star. When they hit that bridge en masse, it's cavalry.

The wildest variation of the game involves a live chicken given to a rider who must take off with it instantly, as with the cloth roll. Then there is the strung-out gallop of scores of ponies chasing him, rushing all out—around the whole plaza, around the church—he leading long enough, if he can, to throw it into his own corral. Otherwise—scrimmage.

When I left, toward 6:30 p.m., they were solemnly—no sound being made, the other horses standing still—solemnly tearing chickens apart again. There was a dark grand sober view of it from the east, looking back into town. But in general the spectators have their backs to the town during this ceremony and look out toward the backdrop of low hills with the major architecture and indeed the savage game itself being Spanish derived: the church painted with horses, the jacal horse corrals, the broad cavalry exercise plaza, even the chickens who moisten the earth with their bleeding.

It may indeed be a fertility sacrifice, but much more than that is released in it; the sober, calculating Pueblo man becomes a centaur for a while. It is breathtaking when they circle the corrals and swing down into the great space. It is what we have always regarded as Plains Indian to the life—and the terror of cavalry, more properly of wild horse nomads, in

IV:45 The Parthenon. North Frieze. Multiple planes of horsemen. (*Hirmer Fotoarchiv*)

IV:46 The Parthenon. West Frieze. Horseman striking back at other riders. (*Hirmer Fotoarchiv*)

IV:47 San Felipe and Black Mesa from across the Rio Grande.

IV:48 San Felipe. The town and the church.

IV:49 San Felipe. Northern kiva with hills across the Rio Grande. Old photograph. (*Collections in the Museum of New Mexico*)

IV:50 San Felipe. Houses and fences.

IV:51 San Felipe. Festivities on the day of a chicken pull.

IV:52 San Felipe. Aerial photograph (1950). (*Stubbs, plate 14*)

IV:53 San Felipe. The town from the south, looking over the range of houses across the plaza to north range; Black Mesa left. (*Ben Wittick, Collections in the Museum of New Mexico*)

the massed skirmishes, pursuits, and sudden charges. What we forget in our automobile world is that horses are *fast*, faster than cars in their proper scale of space. There is a terrible deathly grandeur in the circle of horsemen in the ride under the hung chicken, but always as they group and crush at the ditch and the first rank turns to keep the ponies out of the water and away from the people and the others turn after in flat multiple planes, then the Parthenon frieze is not only recalled but brought to life, explained. It is, like this, an order of form not rigid but taking shape from its own inner dynamics, and therefore full of accident and variety within the ritual frame that calls it forth. Infinitely particular it can be, and even casual, but it is inexhaustibly fertile, both in disciplined force and resourceful device, because it is passion that moves it and the cooperative rhythm of a whole people that gives it form.

If Santo Domingo is Classic (generally Severe Style, perhaps), San Felipe has always seemed neoclassic to me. Everything is perfect there, done just right, crisply formed, the site especially so. It is dominated by another Black Mesa, a big low one now that runs out from the southeastern flank of the Jemez range (figs. IV:47–51). The pueblo was located on its summit until about 1700. Now its plaza lies under the mesa's bulk and is marvelously shaped by it (figs. IV:52–54). Its plan is almost square with a very regular definition by houses.[23] Reflection shows that what appears to be the casual painting of some of the house façades seems in general to correspond more or less to the Keresan colors of the four horizontal directions: north yellow; west blue; south red; east white.[24] The four corners of the plaza are the actual directions for the Keres—again the open corners—with the middle of each façade the middle of that direction. The

IV:54 San Felipe. The plaza with Black Mesa.

orientation here is almost exactly squared with true north, with Black Mesa lying to the west. It completes the whole form, and the houses under it respond to its mass. It falls away on a strong diagonal toward the south, and medium-sized dances seem to take place more to the north of the plaza as if to participate in the mesa's superior formal definition of it at that point (fig. IV:54). The lines of dancers going down toward it act to supplement the house fronts in shaping the spaces. A number of small winter dances are staged in this way.

The church at San Felipe is especially dramatic. It is placed facing east toward the Rio Grande exactly at the point south of the plaza where Black Mesa splits into a deep gorge (figs. IV:55, 56). The façade of the church is stretched laterally as if to complement that void, and its two bell towers, especially before they were somewhat stiffened in a recent renovation, are tautly stretched and pulled as if under tension themselves.[25] Here the long body of the church seems to rush out of the gorge to the kachina mask of its façade. On San Felipe's feast day, May 1, its saint is ushered out of this church to his shrine in the plaza by the black Spanish horsemen and snare drummer mentioned at Cochití. Then the first of the moieties comes on in its approach march toward the church façade, before whose voids and twisted towers under the mesa the corn-dance banner seems as effective as it did before the church and mountains at the other town (figs. IV:32–34). The manner of its bearing is of planting and lifting, as in growth or advance (fig. IV:41a–c). It is exhausting to handle; its bearers are normally changed each time. It never touches the ground but is used to bless the dancers and is swung very low over them and the singers. Its parrot- and hummingbird-feathered top flutters like water drops from an aspergillum, as its bending, pliant pole is sometimes swept almost horizontal. It has been called a war standard,[26] (fig. IV:41h) but it does not billow like European battle flags, like smoke or cloud, but bends and dips like a plant or a man. It claims no dominion over the earth, as do their spreading folds, but claims to quicken it and is vibrant with vertical energies, like a phallus or a corn stalk. It is not baroque like our flags, full and open in space, but contained within itself and piercing. This is seen even better when it is carried by its bearer dancing into the plaza under Black Mesa as a great wheel of dancers turns before it, spreading out as they dance and the mesa flooding down (fig. IV:54), while, palpitating with the drum beat, the red or yellow feathered head of the banner pierces, pierces, rising up through the dark body of the mesa like the life force growing, always in victory. Beyond, it tackles the clouds, and swept down low again it rises once more, its Dorian headdress waving (fig. IV:34).

Always, on the rooftops and under the cornices, the spectators complete the architectural frame. However impure, in the old pueblo sense, the individual buildings may be, does not matter too much (fig. IV:54). The whole is functioning still as it was meant to do.

IV:55 San Felipe. The church with its plaza and Black Mesa.

In that plaza, on February 25, 1968 (I was running madly back and forth that day between here and Cochití, the back wheels of the old Chevy taking off sideways in the gravel with an admirable Larry McMurtry–type grasp of the mythic ironies involved), I was privileged to see what I thought must have been a special San Felipe variant of the Jemez bull dance.[27] When I arrived, two impressive rows of elders wrapped in blankets were sitting near the south side of the plaza. Out in the middle in front of them a round dance of Mexicans in big sombreros seemed to be going on. A couple of pseudo-black men in bib overalls were dancing too. The drummer was a short man in shirtsleeves with a black spade beard and a Lincolnesque top hat. They all danced around with a tight one-knee-straightening step, turtle clackers clacking. In the next round they brought out a bull, a man in bull costume, that is, black with white spots, like the Jemez bull. He chased everybody around for a while and then knelt and was harangued by the appropriate priest. Then he got up and chased everybody again, back and forth, especially the elders. This was the best part. They scattered before him, these heads of state, falling all over each other while the spectators roared with laughter. One decrepit old man tripped in his blanket and people came near to falling off the roofs laughing. (A good cure for Executive paranoia, I should think, this common submission to reality and derision. We could stand more of it.) Kids fled delightedly in splendid terror. Dignified men, guests, everybody ran in delicious panic. Run for your life, one entirely respectable old gentleman said to me, the bull is loose. Finally they chivied the bull back into the kiva and took a lunch break. Then there were two dances of those Mexicans, one round, the second linear, with a scraping instrument rasping a notched stick to supplement the turtleshell clackers on the right leg. No drum. Very impressive, ironic even, rather cold and dry. Then the bull again. They blessed him with cornmeal at the kiva and tied things on his head and off he went, lurching up ominously and

IV:56 San Felipe. Church and mesa before recent repairs. (*Collections in the Museum of New Mexico*)

IV:57 Sandia and the Rio Grande from Kuaua, the Coronado National Monument.

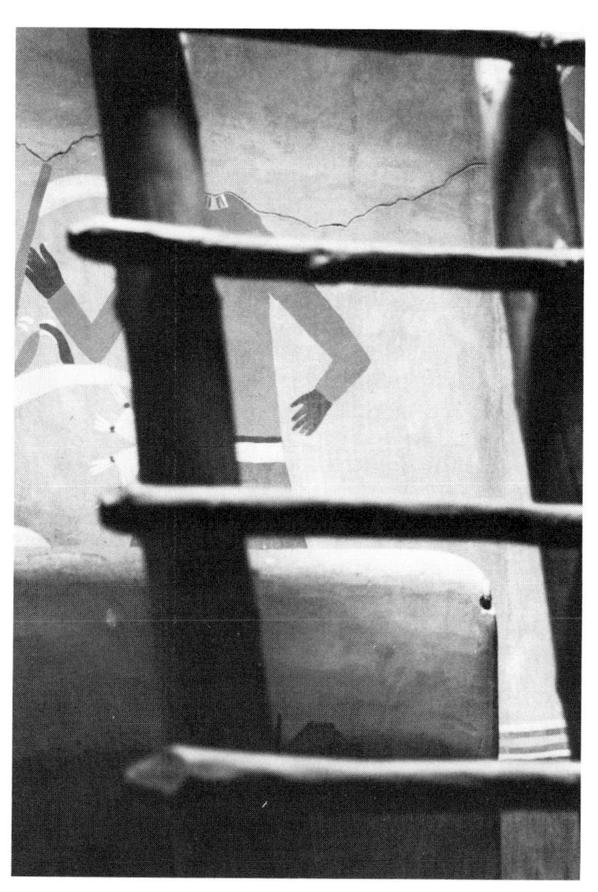
IV:58 Kuaua. Kiva with paintings.

IV:59 Kuaua. Sandia.

starting to zero in on somebody and everybody yelling, Oh, oh, and running. Soon, however, he was quelled by the priest. He was gentled and knelt, and everyone went in and touched him and sprinkled cornmeal and prayed over, for, or to him in a crowd around his recumbent body with its awful spots. Then he was gently led—he following with little steps, head bobbing peaceably up and down—into a house under Black Mesa while the chorus sang (in English), "Away, away, we're going back to Mexico." Then "Adios" they cried, and waved. The elders replied in Keres (I presume) and off the travelers went. While they were out a man sitting on the bench next to me, a Pueblo, asked me if I could change a dollar because they would be back with "all kinds of things to sell. They are from old Mexico." He wasn't trying to kid me, but did he really believe it? I don't know. I changed it for him, and indeed they did come back with suitcases full of stuff which had been given to them during the day (I believe). They laid out their wares in the plaza; junk mostly for kids: crackerjacks, rubber balls, plastic combs, and oranges. But one cannot help thinking of Casas Grandes, and the mummified macaws and the lovely little copper bells hawked up out of Toltec Mexico for Pueblo buyers. What memory of enormously ancient routes of trade across what deserts may not be present here? And with this Spanish bull. Whatever the case, I, the only Anglo, looking over the shoulders of people into the suitcases, was soon kicked out of the plaza. "Out, buddy," a fellow, no more offensive than all cops are to the poor and to strangers, said to me and tapped me on the shoulder. So it is a rite, a sacrament, that is taking place, not just a rummage sale. There is some element of belief that ties it all together in relation to Mexico: costumes, bulls, and trading wares.

IV:60 Sandia, as seen from Santa Ana.

From the roofs of San Felipe, another smaller Black Mesa stands up to the north (fig. IV:53), while Sandia looms to the southeast. It is the great mountain all along this more southerly part of the valley. The ancient pueblo of Kuaua with the historically important kachina paintings in its kiva, lay entranced above the shining river under its enormous spell[28] (figs. IV:57–59). It is also an important presence in the view from Santa Ana (fig. IV:60), which lies along the Jemez River hard under the southern flank of Black Mesa, almost directly opposite San Felipe, the body of the mesa lying between them (fig. IV:61). Santa Ana had been abandoned for some years, its people working their farms down on the Rio Grande and returning to the pueblo only on main feast days. It was always kept in good repair, and one has the feeling that, in this day of the pickup truck and excellent roads, many of its inhabitants have moved back to the pueblo and commute to their farms down below. Still, the town has a museum air, clean and shiny. Of its two round kivas, one is embedded in the town, the other set out on the edge of the river toward Sandia[29] (fig. IV:62). Their placement is a mirror image of those at San Felipe. But Santa Ana's

IV:61 Santa Ana under Black Mesa.

most notable feature is its church, which here, in contrast to the one at San Felipe, lies parallel to the mesa behind it and almost exactly copies its form[30] (figs. IV:63, 64). I use such an uncompromising word because the church is not only long and flat-topped like the mesa but is also chopped at the choir in exactly the same planes as those in which a section of the mesa terminates above it (fig. IV:63). At any rate, it strongly stretches out before the mountain and under the clouds, and its façade is kept flat in elevation and so is subordinate to that wonderful stretch, as of some fine animal or simply the special force of nature that it is (fig. IV:64).

The major event at Santa Ana is the corn dance of July 26, which is much like San Felipe's in neoclassic exactitude. Here in the first set the standard is carried magnificently up the hill toward the mesa with the

LEGEND
I STORY
2 STORY
K KIVA
A ABANDONED ROOM
† CHURCH
0′ 50′ 250′

IV:62 Santa Ana. Plan (1950). (*Stubbs, figure 17*)

white clouds boiling up over the fresh white walls of the campo santo and the church. After the last dance of the morning the two Spanish horsemen, masked like highwaymen, may come out as they do at Cochití and San Felipe. Here, though, they seem dark with evil—not delightful Santiagos like those described by Lange[31]—and they are whipped around the plaza by a sinister white-coal-scuttle-masked clown got up otherwise very dingily like Cochití's gray, awful Rivermen, who make naughty children scream. The snare-drum tattoo snarls incessantly as the horsemen are harried, and the governor with his canes follows tensely, watching them all the while. The crowd is silent. It seems to sense that alien forces are being released for a calculated period, brief but dangerous. One needs no knowledge of history to feel menaced; the costume of Spanish Mannerist black is a lump of sick darkness in the pueblo's luminous dust, and horse and rider is a scampering hybrid outside natural law.

Farther up the Jemez River poor Zía crowns a bluff (fig. IV:65). Again there are two plastically cylindrical kivas (fig. IV:66), both on the side toward Sandia, now quite far away, and a church prone on the other end as if lying through and into the mesa.[32] Its façade, facing toward the high peaks of the Jemez, now also distant, and seen against the open sky, recalls that of Santo Domingo as it was and is crowned with much the same kind of cloud altar. The winds of winter sweep across it from the Jemez as across the backs of the stone lions up above; the church, too, crouches, and its very low, drawn-out profile just calls to the long low mesas to the north[33] (fig. IV:67). The plaza is delicately formed, its axis north-south between the straitly massed houses along the ridge; the house

IV:63 Santa Ana. The church with Black Mesa.
(*Collections in the Museum of New Mexico*)

IV:64 Santa Ana. The church with foothills of the Jemez in the distance. (*Collections in the Museum of New Mexico*)

IV:65 Zía. General view from the west.

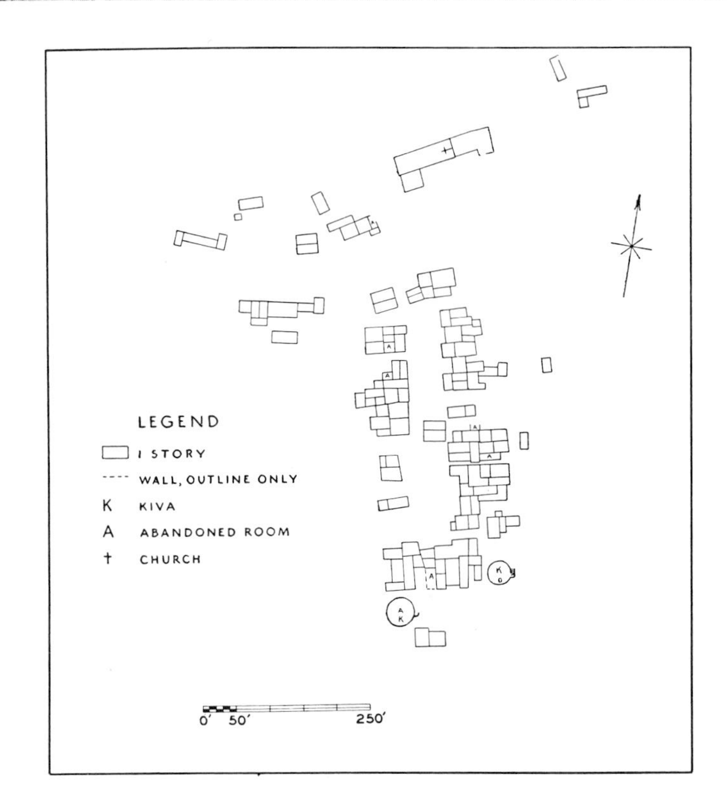

IV:66 Zía. Plan (1950). (*Stubbs, figure 18*)

IV:67 Zía. The church. (*Collections in the Museum of New Mexico*)

which divided it in Stubbs's time (fig. IV:68) was gone in 1968, and, to the south, the kiva which was in ruin then had been rebuilt (fig. IV:69). But Zía is poverty-stricken. I saw a sad dance there at Easter time, when about seventy men and women were called out by a priest from the southeast kiva and filed up from the lower southern half of the plaza to coil into a circle on its higher northern section, near a circular pile of stones like a little hearth. Perhaps it was an earth navel like those in the Tewa towns. Most of the women were in the usual black dress but without *tablitas* or evergreen; some had shawls flung over their shoulders. The men wore suits or sweaters, but all had beautiful high white moccasins with black soles. They held hands and moved very slowly counterclockwise, singing a rather lugubrious song. The slowly wheeling circle was beautiful in the high plaza under the sailing clouds and against the hills far away, and it recalled Zía's long-standing reputation for eloquent dances. After the second song the older men around the drum came forward, and all together said a long, very low-voiced prayer with their heads bowed. It was depressing. All at once they looked like poor farmers rather than ceremonially rich Pueblos like the San Domingueños. Instead of making it happen, as they were doing on that day and indeed always do at Domingo, the impression, perhaps a mistaken one, was that they were begging for it to happen: a thing hard to bear after witnessing the other. Once again I was struck by the decency of magic, the

IV:68 Zía. The plaza, looking north toward the church. The house in the center is now gone. (*Collections in the Museum of New Mexico*)

IV:69 Zía. Kiva above the river. (*Collections in the Museum of New Mexico*)

self-reliance involved in it. One takes the responsibility on oneself to perform the ceremonies correctly so that they must have the proper effect. The corn is danced up in the plaza, and if it is danced exactly right it cannot help but grow. One dances it up the whole day through and never flags or tires. It rather puts one off the Christian way of praying for things; there is a reasonable quid pro quo in this way. Better, as Lévi-Strauss so fundamentally pointed out, it shows us that magic is much the same kind of detailed, rationalized structure that science is, and so illuminates for us the human reasonableness of what we call the primitive mind.[34] Of course, neither magic nor science can make the corn grow if you have no cornfields, and this is Zía's problem. Like Santa Ana, she does not possess adequate farmlands nearby, but in her case she is too far from the Rio Grande to own them there, so that in a sense, despite her other dances, the very essence of what is left to her culturally is her slow wheel under the open sky.

In a larger sense, it is possible that it was difficult for Pueblo civilization as a whole to sustain itself in the Rio Grande area outside the great hollow formed by the Jemez and the Sangre de Cristo ranges. Some pueblos did so, of course, but with a very few exceptions they are all gone. It is hotter and drier down there, and eventually the Spaniards and then the horse nomads came, but perhaps it had simply spun too far out of paradise and was too irremediably far away on the periphery of the shaped world.

V:1 Jemez. (*Lithograph by R. H. Kern, 1847*)

V

JEMEZ, PECOS, SANDIA, ISLETA, LAGUNA, ACOMA, ZUNI

T Jemez is the language affiliate of another pueblo, Pecos, now extinct, whose survivors it received and which, on the other side of the Keres and Tewa worlds, occupied what might be described as much the same kind of topographical position as Jemez: just on the wrong side of a sacred mountain range (fig. I:1). It was wrong only as things turned out historically, there being nothing ecologically faulty with the sites themselves. Jemez, indeed, is still there, pushed deep up the gorge of the Jemez river on the west side of the range. It stretches out westward below the mountains' slopes into its own rather enchanted valley, its long, straight plaza aiming out toward fantastic mesas across the way[1] (figs. V:1–6). Kern's lithograph of 1847, though much exaggerated, catches the effect (fig. V:1). There is a strong rectangular kiva on the main street (fig. V:4) and still some setback second floors to the houses, though nothing like the beautifully terraced structures which formed the terraces as we see them in old photographs (fig. V:5). The flat façade of the present church, a successor to several older ones which are now problems in archaeology, is shaped up into a pointed arc which reiterates the profiles of some of the larger conical hills across the way[2] (fig. V:2). Here the bull dance begins as the congregation leaves the church on the feast-day morning of August 2. The father blesses him, poor beast all leprous and spotted, and he takes off after the children while the priest follows the saint over to his kisi at the low, western end of the plaza and then, his white ankles vulnerable below his rough brown robe, departs. Come back, poor Irish priest, one's instincts say. But tradition is stronger and probably more tactful. The conquerors finally decided that they did not wish to know what happens now. The elders are singing through the village and the world is turning back to the way it used to be—no, only to its other side, which among the pueblos has never died. The children flee before the bull in shoals and shriek and fall in ecstatic piles. At last the bull is tired out and blessed and led away and the corn dance begins, the standard dancing tremendously down the long plaza on the wrong side of the world (fig. V:6).

Jemez, like the Keres towns on the other side, had its predecessors up in the Jemez range. Giusewa, the site of a very early Spanish mission church, is one of them.[3] There is also a sacred cave up there, where important Basketmaker remains, including a mummified maker of baskets, were found.[4] A young fellow and his girl were camping out in it when I visited there in 1971. It is cut into a steep slope above a saltpan dam in the Jemez River, and it looks up toward the heights to the double-peaked mountain which culminates the view (fig. V:7, 8). The flat-topped shoulder across the canyon from it has to me a very Tsin-like air.

It we continue up the mountain, we come at last to the great open meadow-crater of the blown-off peak, the famous "Valle Grande" (fig. V:9). What a pure, empty space it is, this widow's walk above the rooftree of the world. Soon, sloping downward, we come back to Bandelier, where it all began for the Keres on the other side. If we look up from that eastern slope we can see Lake Peak again across the way, and if we can be transported somehow to the other side of it, to the valley of the Pecos River on the east, we can look back up at the Sangre de Cristo from Lake Peak to the Truchas along the axis of the courtyard at Pecos, great pueblo, fighter of Comanches, and now gone[5] (figs. V:10–13). To me, Pecos recalls Puye in the clarity of its courtyard, once beautifully colonnaded, and in its exact focus on the sacred mountain form. Pecos, though, does not direct itself toward a solid mountain dome close at hand but aims instead straight up the gorge of its own river valley, looking up toward what the Tewa call the "dark" side of the Truchas Peaks where the river is born.[6] The great Gap of the Sun, whence Santa Clara's sun will rise, is also identifiable in the view, but no sun can rise due north for Pecos there. It is outside the sacred precinct of the Rio Grande, and though it does its best to hold on to that power it accepts its destiny, too, and its courtyards flood out

V:2 Jemez. The church, about 1910. (*Kubler, figure 173*)

V:3 Jemez. Plan (1950). (*Stubbs, figure 13*)

LEGEND
1 STORY
2 STORY
K KIVA
A ABANDONED ROOM
† CHURCH
0' 50' 250'

V:4 Jemez. Main plaza, looking west. Kiva right, c. 1925. (*T. Harmon Parkhurst, Collections in the Museum of New Mexico*)

V:5 Jemez in winter, c. 1920. (*T. Harmon Parkhurst, Collections in the Museum of New Mexico*)

V:6 Jemez. Corn dance, c. 1925. (*Kenneth Chapman Coll., Collections in the Museum of New Mexico*)

V:7 The Jemez range from the sacred cave above the salt dam. The horned summit.

V:8 The Tsin-like hill.

V:9 The Valle Grande of the Jemez summit.

southward to look down the river valley toward the buffalo plains[7] (figs. V:14, 15). To them it opened too soon for the pueblo's security. Out there the horse eventually gave mobility and confidence (they could, after all, flee if things went wrong) to the various tribes of nomad raiders. Pecos was tough, though; she harassed some of the other pueblos herself and was often in league with the Apache against the Spaniards. She felt strong in her sacred snake and her especially potent bull and buffalo dances. So she fought them all out at the plain's edge and almost won but, carried away by a fatal mixture of exasperation and success, most of her men finally followed the Comanche far out onto the plains and never returned. At last, in 1838, her handful of survivors joined their relations at Jemez, bringing the bull mask and the bull dance with them.

Out there off that southeastern slope of the Sangre de Cristo the pueblos could not long survive. Abó, Quaraí, even fabled Gran Quivira, are all good ruins now (figs. V:16–19), with the monumental carcasses of their churches, looking like recent Frank Lloyd Wright ruins, standing watch over them. More to the point, of course, those high, straight masonry walls

V:10 The Pecos Valley, looking north toward the pueblo and the Sangre de Cristo, from Lake Peak left beyond the Truchas, right. Gap of the Sun center.

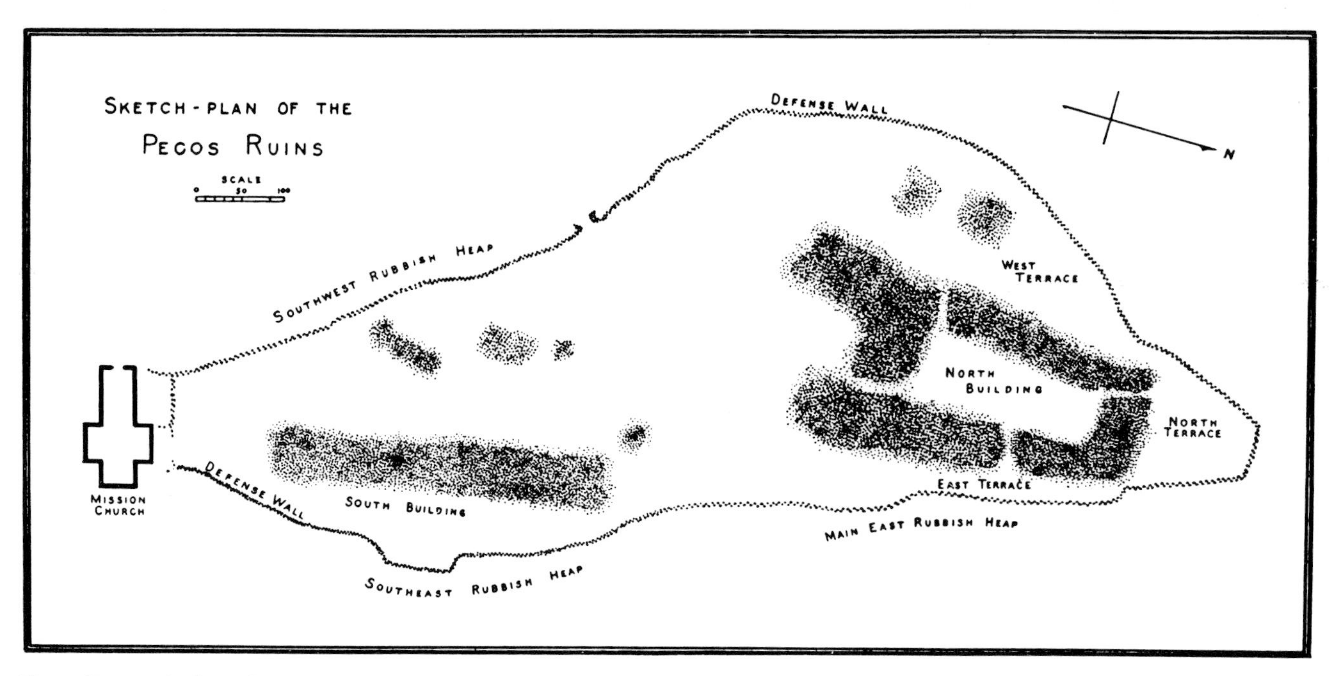

V:11 Pecos. A plan of the Pueblo with the mission church. (*Kidder, plate 7*)

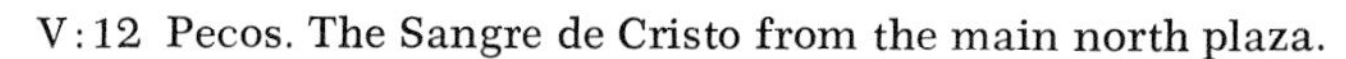

V:12 Pecos. The Sangre de Cristo from the main north plaza.

V:13 Pecos. The axis of the north plaza.

recall those of Chaco Canyon: nothing similar in the southwest in the intervening centuries and nothing quite so monumental since that time.[8] These are the lost and fabulous cities, sad ghosts at the edge of the plains. Beyond them far southward looms the Sierra Blanca of the Mescalero Apache, their executioners, but so far as pueblos are concerned, none at all. It is fundamentally empty still. One feels it on the plains; it is not Pueblo land even though in their great days they dared it. These high plains do not welcome roots, except those of the buffalo grass; they have always called their creatures to movement, first in the sweep of the herds and then in the horse and the automobile. They belong to the nomad.

It is as if Sandia were the last anchor to the closed and favored place. It is a mountain that radiates power. If we look at it from Kuaua, for example, it can be seen to be made up of at least two great masses, the larger one behind rising to the summit, the other a sharp ridge of rock sliding before the main mass (figs. IV:57–59). Precisely where those two fall into axis symmetrically with each other to form an enormous cleft and horns, there exactly the pueblo of Sandia lies[9] (fig. V:20). Tiny, it puts on splendid buffalo dances, as well it might under those dark twin peaks. Its church, again, as at San Ildefonso, standing to the side, does its best to echo the looming profile that fills the east with grandeur[10] (fig. V:21). The plaza shifts off an exact axis in order to direct itself toward the mountain, with a strong rectangular kiva placed between them, its ladder poles aiming up at the angle of the horns (figs. V:22, 23). There can never have been much question at Sandia where to go or what to do. Its place is cut out for it, and small as it is, it sustains itself wholly today.

The southernmost pueblo to keep going in its tradi-

V:14 Pecos. View back down the north plaza south along the river valley opening southeastward to the buffalo plains. Mission church oriented athwart that axis.

V:15 Pecos. Reconstructed kiva (not sacred) on east side of village just inside boundary wall. Interior and view south.

tional site along the river is Isleta, an enormous village as pueblos go.[11] It is Tiwa, too, like Taos, Picuris, and Sandia. The river is close and the fields are rich but the mountain is far away (fig. V:24). The town is already like something in Chihuahua: an enormous plaza surrounded by clear, separate, one-story, color-washed cubes of houses (figs. V:25–27). And a church which, having no mountain to refer to except at a considerable distance, widens out uniquely as a mountain mass itself and serves as a natural anchor and a ridgeline for the empty plain of the square (figs. V:28, 29). In its colonial form Isleta's profile was indeed like a whole man-made range of mountains rising and falling on the square's horizon as if reenacting

V:16 Abó. Mission and pueblo.

V:17 Quaraí. The mission and the plains.

V:18 Quaraí. The mission. Nave.

V:19 Gran Quivira (Humanas). Pueblo and Mission.

V:20 Sandia. The pueblo under the mountain. Church left. Note axis of road to central horns. That is the major axis of the pueblo as a whole.

V:21 Sandia Pueblo. The church from the Pueblo.

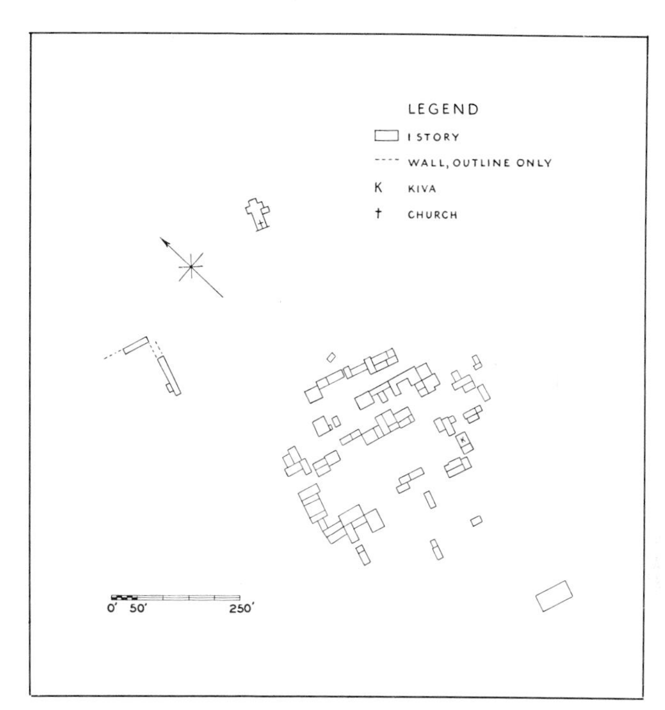

V:22 Sandia Pueblo. Plan (1950). Note that the plan is inflected off the east-west axis in order to aim the plaza at the mountain. (*Stubbs, figure 6*)

V:23 Sandia Pueblo. The plaza with kiva and mountain. (*Drawing by Melanie Simo*)

V:24 Isleta. View across the pueblo from the southwest.

V:25 Isleta. Plan (1950). (*Stubbs, figure* 7)

V:26 Isleta. The plaza in 1929. (*Collections in the Museum of New Mexico*)

V:27 Isleta. The plaza in 1968.

V:28 Isleta. San Antonio de Padua. a) Colonial form; b) in 1922; c) in 1930. (*Collections in the Museum of New Mexico*)

(a)

(b)

(c)

V:29 Isleta. San Antonio de Padua in 1971. View north across the plaza.

the entire length of the Sangre de Cristo far in the Tewa north. Later remodelings have progressively lost that marvelously serrated quality, but they have all aimed at building up the church's massive façade laterally, like a plastic surrogate, near at hand and at more immediately graspable scale, for Sandia and its fellows too far away.[12]

The pueblos south and east of Isleta are all gone. Westward we leave the Rio Grande, to find pueblos only where they possess very specially favored situations of their own. Laguna, first, is really a Spanish town, founded by them in 1699 to effect a synoecism of pueblo settlements.[13] It stands in the heart of a pass to the west surrounded by broken mesas. Its aspect is strongly Mediterranean; it crowns its hilltop in a European way (fig. V:30). The cubes of its buildings march up to the church, which dominates the massing of the whole (figs. V:31–33). Its belled sky altar façade rings changes on the profile of the peak of Mount Taylor as it can be seen above the nearer mesa tops to the northwest.[14] Mount Taylor is the sacred mountain of the south for the Navaho, into whose domain we are moving now, and it seems consciously evoked here at Laguna as well. Inside the church much the same shapes are painted around the nave walls (fig. V:32c). The plaza is strictly laid out at a slightly lower elevation.[15] It is defined in part by a kind of low free-standing wall with its own *te'wi* (if we may be allowed that Hopi word here), which shapes the space into a quite regular rectangle (figs. V:34–36). Moreover, unlike the Rio Grande pueblos, Laguna leaves the plaza open at only two of its corners. It seems likely that by its bench and enclosure alike it is linked more closely to the old Great Kiva than are the larger, looser plazas of the Rio Grande. It seems to represent older traditions than they. Yet there is a kind of Spanish feeling in its enclosure and regularity as well, just as the high frontispiece of its church is especially sensitive in a way both Indian and European, mounting up tremulously so that not only the sacred mountain but also the shifting clouds are physically embodied in it with an eloquence far beyond that of the simple step convention more normally found (fig. V:33). It becomes a person, peering out over its precinct wall like a kind of creature, with a biological quality rare but already noted in some of the liveliest and most intensely sited of the churches: Santa Clara, San Felipe, Santa Ana among them (figs. III:22; IV:57, 63, 64).

Beyond Laguna, and southward in its own great valley, cloud-scraping Acoma rises on the back of its enormous boulder to stare spellbound at the hypnotic Mesa Encantada across the way[16] (figs. V:37–51). Mount Taylor, too, is much in view from Acoma, its peaks standing very clear right above the middle of the long flat-topped mesa lines that define the northern horizon (fig. V:43). Acoma echoes those ridges in long ranges of houses, once with beautiful three-storied setbacks, which are now seen only in old photographs[17] (figs. V:37–41). Those east-west ranges are cut in the center by a wider, shorter cross axis of space which is the main plaza (figs. V:38, 43, 44). It has a short, free-standing *te'wi* in it. Still, a really quite Mediterranean type of square develops at that point, with some two-story buildings (one just remodeled to become so again) still remaining to de-

V:30 Laguna. Mount Taylor in the distance.

fine it and a general sense of closed, Spanish-Italian rather than open, plaza-like urbanism. But since a similar kind of enclosure was noted at Laguna as well (figs. V:34–36), we must ask ourselves if the Mediterranean reference is not less than half correct and if it is not primarily a closer connection with the old Great Kiva than that of the Rio Grande towns which is operating here. Kinishba, not so far away, down in the White Mountains, again comes to mind; the square is tightly enclosed there also (figs. V:64, 65). We will find the same thing in the main plaza at Zuni (fig. V:63)—again, as at Laguna, with only two open corners. So from Laguna westward we move somehow closer to the old Anasazi world in its later prehistoric phases. At Acoma we have also passed out of the Rio Grande area with its round kivas and are coming into the orbit of the square kiva as found in the Hopi towns and, as at Zuni, here built right into the house blocks (fig. V:40). Laguna, apparently

(a)

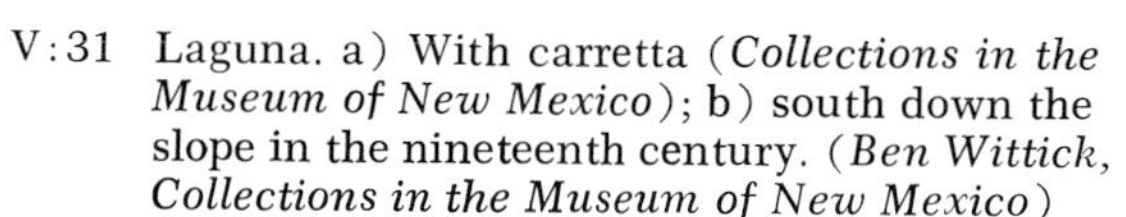

V:31 Laguna. a) With carretta (*Collections in the Museum of New Mexico*); b) south down the slope in the nineteenth century. (*Ben Wittick, Collections in the Museum of New Mexico*)

(b)

(a)

V:32 Laguna. San José and Mount Taylor. Sky altar in several modifications. a) Early view; b) another modulation; c) interior murals with related shapes. (*Photo of early view by Ben Wittick, c by T. Harmon Parkhurst, all are from Collections in the Museum of New Mexico*)

(b)

(c)

because of a religious schism, seems to have no kivas at all.

The effect of the plaza at Acoma is urbane if now slightly museum-like. It is being cleaned up for tourists, while its people live most of the time at Acomita, McCarty's, and other settlements near their fields along the San José River. In a sense, the cross axis at Acoma is ultimately defined by the broad façade of its church, San Estevan, the noblest in the Southwest, which faces out toward the Mesa Encantada across its own campo santo south of the house rows[18] (figs. V:45–49). The tragic rigor of the relationship between Spaniards and Pueblos seems built into this mission. It is a grim fortress whose long nave parallels and clarifies the profiles of mesas and houses, but whose flat, wide-towered façade cuts right across that communal axis to show one monumental face in opposition to all. No sky altars, no modulations, no creature qualities except some deep, stern sorrow. Most of all, there is what comes to be the archetypally American abstraction of form, as clear, for example, in the Lee Mansion of Stratford, in Virginia, as here. In this characteristic development European forms are simplified, clarified, and primitivized, partly because of frontier conditions, partly on purpose. Instead of opening, as it might have been, to the new continent, these buildings deny it, tight and pure. The result is abstract order, simple geometry, and a closing of the form.[19] These qualities were to be of considerable importance in American architecture later, and they characterize Acoma, and—except that the simplification of European-Mexican precedent is naturally common to all—they seem in direct contrast to the pueblo modulation

V:33 San José in 1971. With clouds.

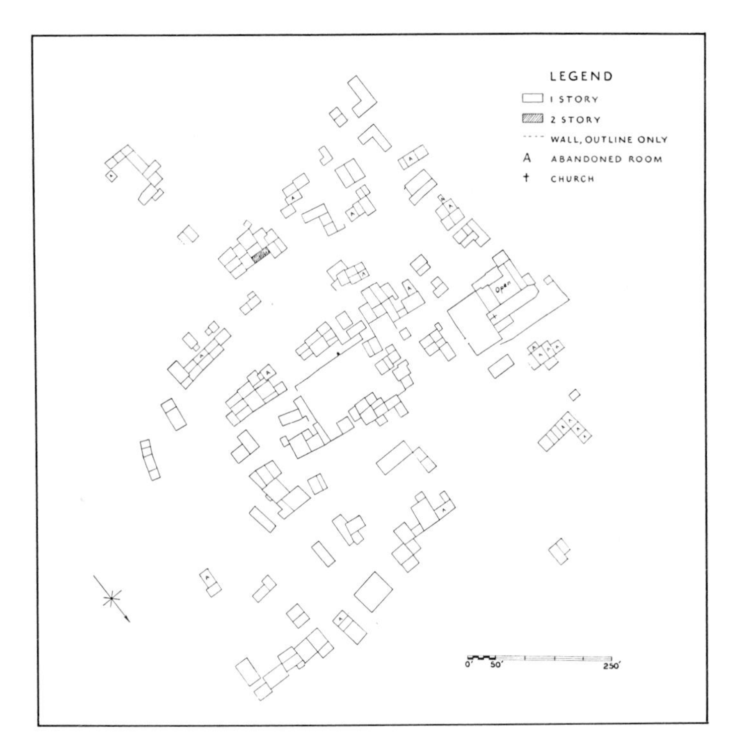

V:34 Laguna. Plan (1950). (*Stubbs, figure 19*)

V:35 Laguna. The plaza from the northwest.

V:36 Laguna. The plaza from the west.

of church façade to cloud and landscape which is so obvious at Laguna no less than along the Rio Grande. Yet are they so? What else could San Estevan be in this landscape but broad and flat profiled; a sky altar might have seemed feeble in relation to all the blocky mesas and the wide-spreading horizontals. But San Estevan is also a monument to the terrible series of confrontations between Spaniard and Indian that took place at Acoma. Its size alone is an indication of what agony its building must have caused the Indians as they dragged dirt, stone, and long beams up from the valley floor. Now they possess one of the essential American monuments, with a high, shadowed space inside (fig. V:48) and a sad brown face turned on the Enchanted Mesa, blindly, as if confronting the ultimate in Tsin-like hills (figs. V:47–49).

But all of Acoma is grand, perhaps its vast natural cistern most of all, a lake of pure water lying deep in the open rock face below the summit, where it slopes vertiginously off northward, with a view toward the Mesa Encantada and Mount Taylor above the horizon (fig. V:50). Acoma, seen from the pass off to

V:37 Acoma. From the west. (*Ben Wittick, Collections in the Museum of New Mexico*)

V:38 Acoma. Plan (1950). (*Stubbs, figure 20*)

V:39 Acoma. House ranges looking east. (*Ben Wittick, Collections in the Museum of New Mexico*)

V:40 Acoma. Kiva. (*Collections in the Museum of New Mexico*)

(a)

V:41 Acoma. Two ceremonies. a) Corn dance; b) St. John's Day in the nineteenth century. Mr. Bibo, only Anglo governor of the pueblo, waving left. (*Photo of corn dance by Ben Wittick, both photos from Collections in the Museum of New Mexico*)

(b)

V:42 Acoma. Sheepfold.

V:43 Acoma with Mount Taylor. The cross-axial plaza left. (*Ben Wittick, Collections in the Museum of New Mexico*)

V:44 Acoma. Bench and new two-storied house on the plaza. Mount Taylor behind.

V:45 Acoma. San Estevan. With convent. (*Ben Wittick, Collections in the Museum of New Mexico*)

V:46 San Estevan. Façade with Campo Santo.

the northwest, stretches the vision no less than the imagination (fig. V:51). The east-west spread of the valley is so ample, with the boulder carrying the town and the Enchanted Mesa lying so far apart, that it is difficult to keep the two forms in focus in one perspective all the time. It is hard to take them in at once, so broad and fair their golden shape.

Zuni is even more. It stands farther west on the banks of its own river, which is, alas, on a natural route down toward the southwest, toward western Apache country, San Xavier del Bac, and Sonora (fig. I:1). It was Coronado's route to the north, and Estevan's before him, so that the first white man whom the Zunis saw was a black man whom they treated as an intruder and killed. (That the Franciscans gave his name to the church at Acoma is a curious coincidence only.) What Estevan's timorous companions said they saw, "cities of gold," is understandable in that landscape. The Zuni land is a fleet of mesas, riding in widespread formation over the landscape like huge ships in a tremendous sea (figs. V:52, 53). This is Cibola, a golden armada in the declining sun, gathering from far off as if upon some signal pitched beyond our ear, and crowned with cities splendid in lighted air:

> ὦ ταὶ λιπαραὶ καὶ ἰοστέφανοι καὶ ἀοίδιμοι
> Ἑλλάδος ἔρεισμα, κλειναὶ Ἀθᾶναι,
> δαιμόνιον πτολίεθρον [20]

God-filled, renowned, violet-crowned, and shield: Zuni is all these, too, though in the last not as effective as Athens. Still, she bore the first brunt of the Spanish onset, her men held down with pikes in the burning houses of Hawikuh.[21] Now she theoretically allows no Spanish-Americans to witness her ceremonies, and she has killed plenty in her day. She has only one major town, Halona, which is modern Zuni, and some suburbs, but is in control of her squadron of mesas still. Most striking is the sacred mountain (so noted on a signpost by the main road: Sacred Mountain, it says, and points), Towayalane, Corn Mountain, which rises to the east and opens toward Zuni as a kind of am-

V:47 San Estevan, Façade, detail.

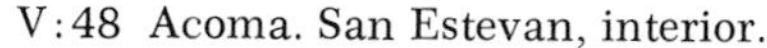

V:48 Acoma. San Estevan, interior.

V:49 Acoma. Campo Santo, pueblo, and the Mesa Encantada.

phitheatrical mesa with two horn- or feather-like piers of rock (figs. V:53, 54) rising out of its heart.[22] In line between them on the axis from Zuni the center of the world is a sharp cleft in the mesa's cornice; below it the "mother" rock folds under, and there the ithyophallic fetishes are offered, while down below, right in the center of the town, the twin-horned towers of the church have always done their best to imitate the natural sacred forms[23] (figs. V:55, 56). All of Zuni rose, and today, despite the loss of upper stories, still does rise, in terraces sloping up to westward and keeping the sacred mountain in view[24] (figs. V:57–61). The fabric of the town has been cut down, opened up, and suburbanized, but its rather purple-colored stone masonry is of good blocks, and the larger urban structure is still there as well. It is a great midden. We cannot help but wonder what sequence of Troys awaits exploration down below. Zuni (Halona = Anthill) has an ant shrine and, watching files of ants disappear underground there, one wonders what ancient ollas, rooms, and eye sockets they explore. Yet the town should never be excavated, because it still functions exactly as it was intended to do. If the beautiful setbacks and many of the sky-hung terraces are gone, there is still easy access to the roofs, from which the whole ceremonial structure of town and mountain is perfectly clear to see.

It takes a stranger a while to discover those relationships. The urbanism has to unfold at a footpace and in relation to the ceremonies which direct its form. For example, on July 11, 1970, I wandered by chance into the tiny but clearly main ceremonial plaza at the lower level (figs. V:62, 63) and sat down in there with the women and children and watched the last set of a kachina dance of twenty-two kachinas, with two mudhead women, stocking-headed and fish-eyed, and ten mudhead clowns (*koyemshi*) of pure

red-brown earth color with flat black kilts and under-masks: the gods and the first men and women erratically formed and unfinished, together.[25] The dance stopped exactly at the moment when the sun sank below the horizon (behind one of the western mesas, in fact). One could tell that from below as the light flicked off the spectators standing on the roofs above. The next day I found my way to that level. From the present ground level on the north side of the village an alley led in toward a broad flight of four stairs which mounted to the kiva top (figs. V:66, 67). From there the whole splendid panorama of town, church, and sacred mountain swung into place (fig. V:68). Instantly I thought of Knossos and Phaistos (fig. III:42), and of the watchers on the roofs seeing the horned bulls below and the horned mountains together.[26] The plaza lay below, already beginning to shadow, while the majestic landscape, dominated by the mountain, was in full late-afternoon glow. It was just the time when the sinking of the sun, the beginning of its slide out of its full tyranny, began to be felt.

The kachinas could be heard chanting in the kiva directly underfoot. Then they emerged, led by the war priest, a trim, clean-cut man with a sky-altared bowl of cornmeal in his hand. The kachinas were twenty-two again, rising as if out of the earth in front of the mountain and then descending by ladder to the plaza-court (figs. V:69, 70) where they were joined by the two mudhead women. Then they began to dance—the usual kachina dance, packed in a solid file, close front to back, leaning flat-backed slightly forward from the waist and dancing the knee-straightening step that makes the turtle rattles clack and the masks dip up and forward, and all of them turning always close back to front in definite communal beats (figs. I:11; V.73; VI:53, 54). The whole is one organism, like a single feathered serpent, as all

V:50 Acoma. Natural cistern, Mount Taylor, and the Mesa Encantada.

forces of movement ripple as one through its long body, and the feathers crown its single back. There is one mudhead drummer with a loose huge drum, and all the dancers sing deeply behind their masks, a resonant thunder unearthly and grand. These are not like the unmasked dancers which are the only kind we outsiders can see along the Rio Grande. The kachinas are not actors or participants; they are the gods, or their stand-ins, or something so close as to be indistinguishable from them. At Zuni, some of them may be ancestors too. Theirs is not normally a mystery play, like the Keres animal dances, or a great act of creativity and power, like the corn dance. It is simply the gods being present, expending their energy in the plaza, driving it, like the beasts of Taos, into the town. They are in that sense a machine, a dynamo: the gods with the first misshapen men, the mudheads, abetting them.

As the dance went on, the sun could be felt slipping down and the shadows slowly rising. On the third set the ten mudheads joined them. After each set the kachinas left by the south passage, rested for a time along a street to the east and then coiled around to reenter the plaza from the west. In the intervals the mudheads put on their own kind of satyr play and developed a beanbag game wherein they hit each other with a small pillow (fig. V:71). Later they did a burlesque kachina dance and satirized a Rio Grande corn dance and a Christian prayer.

At the beginning of the second dance, about six o'clock, the church bells struck the hour (about twenty-four times or so it seemed) and then began a Muzak-type concert with "Come to Jesus" and another rather saccharine hymn. One sensed, perhaps wrongly, a certain rivalry with the dance. But the deep chant coming up out of the depths of the village made the carillon seem unreal, weak, as if untrue. One had the feeling that Christianity as interpreted here, whether by Catholics or Protestants, is simply not real in this landscape and under these circumstances. Compared to the depth of the dance, it seemed at the moment superficial, even laughable, but it helps us, I think, to understand the Pueblos even better. This is the dry southwest, where men must dance the rain out of the sky, or pass away. No amount of prayer will do so, or will satisfy their human longing to be a functioning part of things.

Now as the dance went on one could feel the sun deeply sinking and the shadows creeping forward, finally toward the slopes of Corn Mountain itself (fig. V:68), while the kachinas danced in the darkening court below, seeing neither sun nor mountain but as it were keyed into (one almost said, controlling) their relationship. We are reminded of the summer dance at Taos, but this one is more intense. Its force constantly rose until the sixth and last set, when there were many birdcalls and animal noises, and, just as the sun slipped and the light left us completely except on the very tip of the mountain, the dance stopped. But then, the shadows thick below, they broke yesterday's pattern and the priest led them around and they danced again, masks gleaming like the snouts of predators up out of the darkness. It seemed a marvelously right thing to do: having set the sun, now braving the dark. And in that last dance there below, as in an open kiva, they, the gods or their simulacra, embodiments of human imagination and desire, seemed especially to embody all the riches their scarred and tragic landscape had to offer: the eagle, the snake, and the fox, the colors of sand and sky, feathers and foxtails, the big staring scale of the masks, and evergreen above all—all set off against the pure mud and black of the mudheads and their shapeless, unfinished, first-monster-man forms.

At last they stopped and climbed back up the ladder to the kiva top, all waning light now, and climbed

V:51 Acoma. Right far distance, with Mesa Encantada left. Panorama from the northwest.

V:52 Zuni. The buttes.

V:53 Zuni and Towayalane. Corn Mountain, on the day of Shalako, 1971.

V:54 Zuni. Towayalane, Corn Mountain. Ben Wittick called it Thunder Mountain. Zuni in the distance. (*Ben Wittick, Collections in the Museum of New Mexico*)

V:55 Zuni. The church in the late nineteenth century. *(Ben Wittick, Collections in the Museum of New Mexico)*

V:56 Zuni. The church with Corn Mountain.

V:57 Zuni. The view of Corn Mountain from the roofs. (*Ben Wittick, Collections in the Museum of New Mexico*)

V:58 "Across the roofs of Zuni." (*Ben Wittick, Collections in the Museum of New Mexico*)

V:59 Zuni from across the river. (*Ben Wittick, Collections in the Museum of New Mexico*)

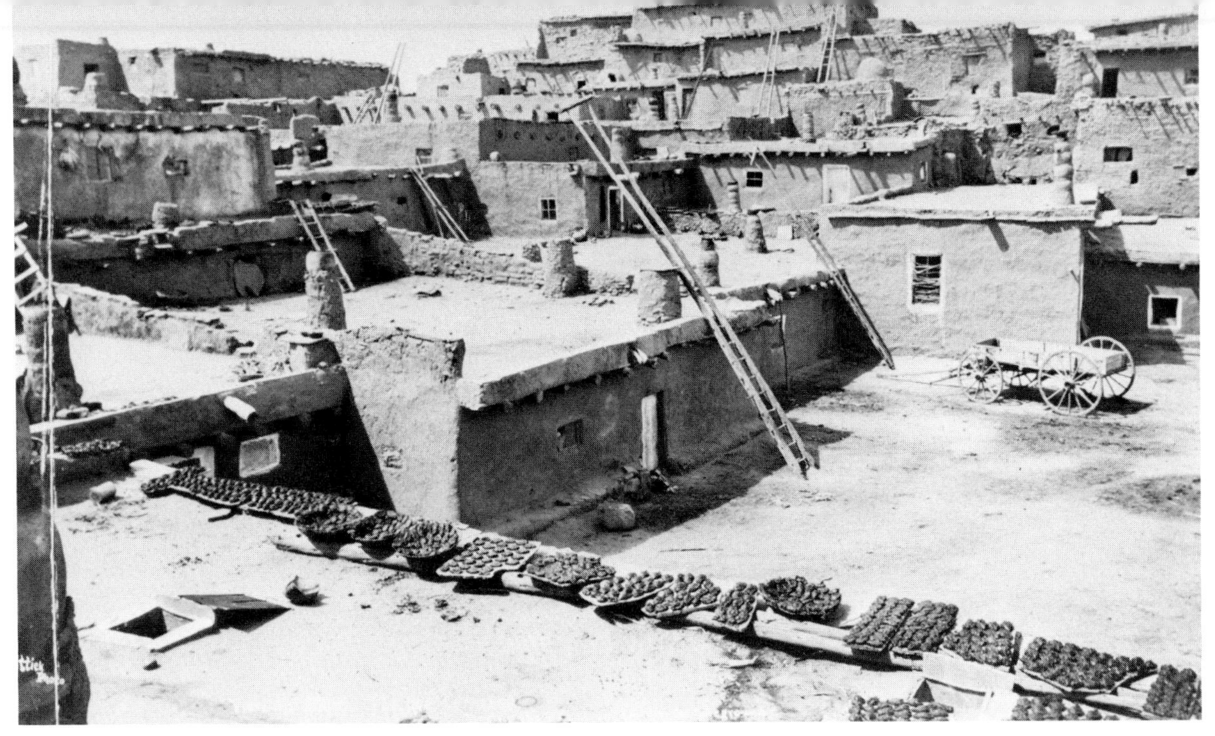

V:60 Zuni. The five-level terraces of nineteenth-century Zuni. (*Ben Wittick, Collections in the Museum of New Mexico*)

V:61 Zuni. Room. (*Ben Wittick, Collections in the Museum of New Mexico*)

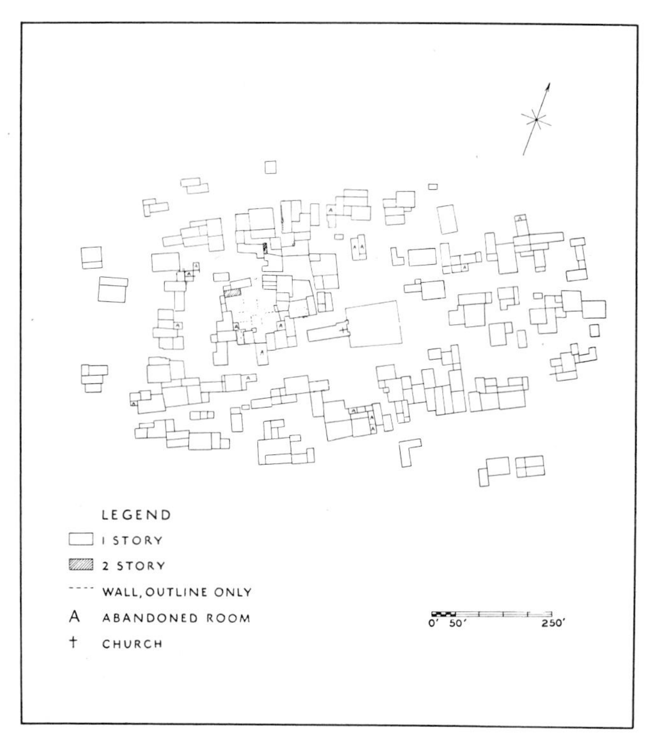

V:62 Zuni. Plan, 1950. There are, I think, five kivas besides the main one in this central part of the town as of 1971, though Stubbs shows none in this plan. (*Stubbs, figure 21*)

back down into the kiva as if descending into the darkening mountain itself, while the mudheads went trailing off in the gloaming across the main road, just tapping their beautiful long drum once in a while, and in that dying light looking terrific in their bloomless black and deep earth brown.

In summer the Zuni dances almost constantly for rain[27] (figs. V:71–73). Clown kachinas with twists of corn shock in their hair are ordered around by mudheads and dance with reeds and run little burlesque-shalako races. As one watches them over the days the subtle beauty of the little plaza impresses itself on the mind. The proportion of the windows is important; during the dances the frames are removed, and a whole filling of plum-colored dresses can be seen inside (figs. V:68–70). Alongside the raspberry-colored masonry the dun or rose-tinted stucco of the kiva is stretched laterally, with horizontal windows set off by the ladder. The whole space of the plaza, perhaps forty by fifty feet in dimension and delicately varied in definition, can indeed be felt as a close descendant of the Great Kiva, with the top taken off and opened (though perhaps those were too) to everyone. Here the court of Kinishba is very close indeed in scale and detail (figs. V:64, 65).

In Zuni's plaza one soon comes to love, fear, and value the mudhead clowns (fig. V:71). They eat junk off the ground, play awful games with Coke bottles, sing "Jesus Loves Me" and Gregorian chants, teach young koshare-costumed boys how to do things, communicate in nonsense language, and make fun of everybody around—of you if you are not careful. They are the teachers, like the Hopi clowns. We should not romanticize them. They enforce communal discipline —which is even more formidable in Pueblo society than it is in the United States—through ridicule (as we do: kidding, we call it), and they make fun of those who are different from us and make us feel good and special thereby.[28] But they do more than that: they really make us laugh. They reconcile us to life and nature through laughter, and they kid the messengers of the gods as well. They loosen everything up, all of creation, of which we are a part, so that it (we) can lose its inhibitions and *rain*.

One of the most important pilgrimages made by the Zuni is that to their sacred salt lake some forty-five miles far down across the hot desert to the south —far below the sad Texan homesteaders at Fence Lake, far down in elevation below Zuni's height so that it blazes in the sun down there. To arrive in summer is to have accomplished a journey, and as one tops the rise above the lake the perfect culmination comes into view: backed by a cleft mountain, two black cones of volcanic ash rise above the mirror of the white salt water (fig. V:74). The sharp black and white which appears in so much Pueblo symbol-

V:63 Zuni. The main plaza. Two views of the kiva from the entrances.

ism is archetypally created. One of the cones is exact and closed. The other has blown its top and now contains an almost circular pool in its depths, like a water kiva with bench-like ledges under water around the sides. It is the home of the gods of war, so Stevenson tells us.[29] But the lake and the cones as a whole are sacred to Ma'me, the salt-mother, and this is in line with the fairly universal human identification of earth cones with female symbols and with the tumuli of heroes.[30] It is Ma'me, according to Stevenson, who leads the war gods to the place in Hopi myth. There, in her body, she contains them.

From somewhere in this sacred southerly direction, though not from here, the ultimate messengers of divinity, the Shalako, come to Zuni in the depths of wintertime.

O Shalako

About four o'clock on the cold and windy afternoon of December 11, 1971, the Shalako first appeared on Greasy Hill, moving south in a long file in the saddle behind the water tanks. Around them clustered their attendants, about half their size, so that the fundamental character of the Shalako apparition was already set: tall beings, like wingless birds, leaning slightly forward, moving with small prancing steps, high above everyone, eagle-ruffed, horned, and with two high feathers calling to the twin feathers of stone which project up out of the heart of the Sacred Mountain itself (figs. V:54, 75). Their eyes are eager and their long beaks project forward, sometimes clacking with a pronounced snap. They are beings

which at very first glance tell us their character: well intentioned, too simple-minded to know their own strength, eager to do the right thing, interested in everything, liking each other, infinitely trustful of man. Messengers of the rain gods, Stevenson tells us they are.[31] But they seem also a more general embodiment of nature as these fundamentally sane and kindly (though warlike and formidable) Zuni people believe her to be: noble, dumb, and beautiful, amenable to proper attention, capable of blind benevolence —all embodied in these giant flightless birds.

The procession moved down the south slope of Greasy Hill, the men chanting and swinging their bull-roarers, the beaks snapping, and the people at the southernmost Shalako house (it turned out to be the *koyemshi* house in fact, with five other Shalako houses only, and one Council of the Gods house) lining up to bless it with cornmeal.

As the procession passed on southward toward the village the Council of the Gods came marching in at a diagonal well in front of the Shalakos and headed on a vector leading toward the traditional footbridge into the pueblo. Soon they came to the bridge, just as snow began to spit frigidly out of the northwest. (It had been hanging around the San Francisco Peaks all day.) Then the gods crossed, great Sayatasha first with his deer-bone clackers and his single horn (fig. V:76). Then Hututu and so on, the young fire god Shulaawi'si conspicuous among them, spotted red, white, and yellow over purple, lean and adolescent, moving straight shouldered and fast, like a cadet[32] (fig. V:77).

The group wound through the pueblo in a labyrinthine course, planting whatever they plant at the five excavations before the five kivas, with what seemed to me a special and unusually short stop at the

V:64 Kinishba. The transitional Great House pueblo in the White Mountains near Fort Apache, Arizona.

central plaza and the sixth, main kiva. By this time a few of the Navahos were beginning to act up a little. Their disrespectful behavior at Shalako is apparently traditional with them.

Finally the gods reached the house prepared for them near the northern edge of the village. They entered through the roof and after some backing and filling were installed in the long central room along the wall near the altar, sitting in a row bundled up in rugs (fig. V:78a). They pushed back their masks so that they looked startlingly like high-coiffed Mayan nobles and then, with a row of men on chairs facing them, they chanted for hours. Later they were to dance till dawn with a final beautiful ceremony on the roof at sun-up—much like the kiva-top ceremony at Hopi after the Niman dance. In the meanwhile, though, just as dusk was coming down, the Shalako began to cross the footbridge, one after another in file. They were crossing in the face of the watching village multitude at exactly the right time, at dusk, so that they were only barely visible: tall, haloed, not

V:65 Kinishba. Two views in the court. Note similarities to Zuni's main plaza.

V:66 Zuni. The passage to the roofs above the main plaza from the northwest.

V:67 Zuni. The stairs to the roofs above the main plaza.

V:68 Entrance to roofs above the main plaza from the northwest with the church and Towayalane Corn Mountain Kiva below.

V:69 Zuni. The dance plaza from the west.

V:70 Zuni. The plaza from the south.

wholly seen but looming and emitting, at intervals, their resounding snap.

Then, under cover of their attendants and the gathering night, the Shalako bearers squatted down and slipped out of the effigies, leaving them sitting, now at about man-height, in a row of six facing the village on this side of the footbridge. As each bearer disengaged, he (now anonymous) and the attendants, of whom Stevenson said that one was an alternate bearer, came bustling across the bridge, attired like Renaissance bravi, some swathed in black cloaks like banditti, others broad in belted velvet shirts, rosettes on the wide shoulders.[33] With no trousers, only G-strings, the effect is of tights: very Spanish-derived. They wore white caps like abstracted Renaissance helmets, and with a spike, more elaborate than the deerskin snoods Stevenson showed.[34] They swaggered past into the village and disappeared, leaving the Shalako effigies glowing white and silent in the darkness. Then the police drove the people away.

Later one finds a Shalako house, in this case Serafino Eriacho's, the paramount in the village, apparently. A deep, high central room was flanked by two side rooms which looked into it through wide interior glassless windows (fig. V: 78b). An altar stood at the end of the large room on the long axis from the entrance. Guests, uninvited and invited, were eating in the side room on the right from darkness on. At last, about 8:00 p.m. or so, a great wild singing approached from the south, and there appeared a crowd of people with two Shalakos and their attendants. The south doors of the house were removed and the Shalakos took position before them, leaning forward eagerly, protruding eyes staring into the house. Some singing, with strong choruses, took place, and finally first one Shalako and then the other leaned in under the doorway and, filling the long room, trotted majestically forward to take position by the altar. Then the attendants stretched out their black blankets and the Shalakos sank down behind them, and their bearers unobtrusively slid out from underneath and mingled with the attendants. The two effigies, now man-size again, sat there impassively until about 12:30, when the blankets were raised and the bearers entered the effigies once more. Then nothing happened until about 1:30, when a drumbeat started and a song rose and, finally, finally, a blanket was raised and a Shalako rose behind it, towering now to the ceiling, head turning, eyes staring with their characteristically searching, innocent, slightly retarded light.

Soon the great bird leaned forward and danced out with little steps, a kind of very restrained prancing up and down the open center of the room. Soon it was joined by one of the bravi, holding a yucca wand (or club) and dancing with a sideways step musingly up and down the room, passing and repassing the Shalako and ignoring it. He was the other bearer.

V:71 Mudheads (*koyemshi*) in the plaza with clown kachina. Note the changes today. (*Ben Wittick, Collections in the Museum of New Mexico*)

V:72 Zuni. Dance in the plaza behind the church, c. 1910. (*Collections in the Museum of New Mexico*)

V:73 Zuni. Long-haired kachina dance. (*Ben Wittick, Collections in the Museum of New Mexico*)

Eventually the Shalako stopped and faced back toward the altar and stuck its head forward and dipped and clacked its beak as if (the music rising) saying, I'll try, I'll surely try, and then it ran forward, teetering with fast little steps, swooping, as if practicing for what was to take place the next day, when it was to essay its final enormous act of demented dexterity, accuracy, flight, and faith in mankind.

On this night four other houses had one Shalako apiece (one Shalako house not having been completed in time that year), of which one Shalako dipped and swooped and snapped in a much more bravura style than Serafino's did. The Council of the Gods went on to its noble greeting of the sun at dawn, and the *koyemshi* in their house danced and kidded around and made fun of Hututu, who caught a cramp. Meanwhile the women fed their crowd of self-inflicted guests stewed mutton and good bread and strong coffee, and the girls were beautiful leaning in the interior windows like Rembrandts, and the Navaho behaved pretty well because the police were terrifyingly in evidence, moving around in threes—Zuni police, Gallup police, and sometimes MPs or something similar—pushing through the crowd and sniffing, probably more for pot than for Jim Beam. The guests need something, surely, trailing exhausted as they do from house to house in the blinding cold. This year the snow had blown away at nightfall, and after an hour or two of softer overcast weather the north wind blew the stars all clear, frosty and biting as diamonds, twinkling and freezing, while Orion leaned like a long Shalako over the southeastern quarter of the sky. It was all much as Stevenson had described it—though she is weak on the actual physical events. It was a debauch with the Zuni under pressure from their ritual to be kind all night long to Navaho and whites, the former characteristically "mean," the latter tending toward unlovely collapse.[35]

At noontime of the following day the spectators, many of them tired out and perhaps slightly disaffected by now,[36] gather on the south bank of the river near the footbridge to witness the final act: the so-called races and the departure of the Shalako to the south. Magnificent early photographs by Ben Wittick show long ranks of spectators on horseback waiting for the Shalako to cross (fig. V:79). The watchers are not so beautiful now, and where they once stood has been partly built up with suburbanized houses, but the bank is still open and broad with a large open plaza or field, beyond which the great Sacred Mountain with its twin plumes stands high. By midday this year one Shalako (the one perhaps from the single constructed Shalako house on the south bank), was crouched without its bearer facing eagerly as always toward the bridge and flanked by its attendants. Long after one o'clock another Shalako was seen high above the crowd moving east along the north bank toward the bridge. Some feeling of awe reawoke in the spectators; it was a special presence coming, one outside normal judgment, perhaps a god (fig. V:80). Arriving at the bridge, the Shalako was harangued for a long time by the priests and finally came across to join its fellow, preceded and surrounded by its own kiva attendants (fig. V:81). After an hour or so, the Shalako had all crossed over, the last one eagerly clacking and the others responding, all standing by this time, there having been considerable rising and falling behind the black cloaks. The Shalako greeted their last comrade with pleasure and excitement; it is one of their many disarming characteristics that they love each other and are happy and relaxed to see each other. This seemed especially true after the twenty-odd hours of earnest effort they had just put in trying to keep abreast of what men wanted them to do. Now they had had a hard day and were ready to depart. Soon the gods came across the bridge, moving fast as always. Sayatasha was in the lead, almost running with that implacable bent-kneed stride of his, clacking his bone clappers. He was followed by the others and, last of all, moving very smartly at a quick walk, came the sun priest followed by the fire god, Shulaawi'si, with his whole deerskin (full of seeds, says Stevenson) hanging head down off his left shoulder. Everything about him was still young, ardent, devoted.

By this time, as I had forgotten to note, the backers

of each Shalako had dug two holes out in the field in front of the Shalako line, six on one side, six on the other. The gods then came and blessed each hole in some complex pattern, all still moving very fast. Then, everything still moving with dispatch, the climax came. The Shalako ran. And they were no longer diffident or practicing. They were running as fast as they could, abandoning themselves to their task, all their total disequilibrium balanced by forward movement (figs. V:82–84). They ran in crossing patterns, leaning well forward, legs taking small steps but very rapid ones. The effigies teetered; they seemed now especially armless, wingless, and top-heavy, and they were really trying very hard. So running, they planed in on their two holes (two to each kiva, clan, or whatever) and were eagerly, even rather hysterically, received in the arms of the attendant at each one. He steadied them over it, and into it they shat, or laid an egg, or simply dropped down between their legs—something (prayer sticks, it is said) which the attendant then quickly covered up and buried. It all happened quickly and surely at just two holes apiece, and it was thus totally different from the interminable waits and repetitions of the earlier ceremonies.

As the teetering towers ran past each other, little legs twinkling underneath, there was always the possibility that they might fall. Apparently it is bad luck if they do so, but none did this time. So the singing and drumming were surging and happy, and there was a kind of mad joy felt in everything, in the

V:74 Zuni. Salt Lake. Natural "water-kiva" is in the hollow cone of ash to the right.

Shalakos weirdly interlocking, victorious races most of all, balancing simplemindedly and in goodness of heart very close to chaos. In this way the whole day-long ceremony climaxed, economical and clean, in one swiftly formed labyrinthine jewel of movement under the mountain's eye. It was the happiest ending I ever saw. Then the Shalako, clacking, delighted with themselves, bent-kneed, dipping a little, began to file off toward the south, back toward Greasy Hill, and the people grouped in two lines to bless them with cornmeal. The lowering sun was shining through their radiant diadems as they drifted toward it, and their two top diagonal feathers stood out for the last time against the mountain's two-feathered heart. For the Zuni there were days of festival and mudheads still to come,[37] but one could not help but be sorry to see the Shalako going: few beings so loving, few one has liked so well.

V:75 Shalako preceded by his alternate. (*Stevenson, plate 61*)

V:76 Sayatasha and Hututu, followed by two warriors (*Stevenson, plate* 63)

V:77 Shulaawi'si (*Stevenson, plate* 62)

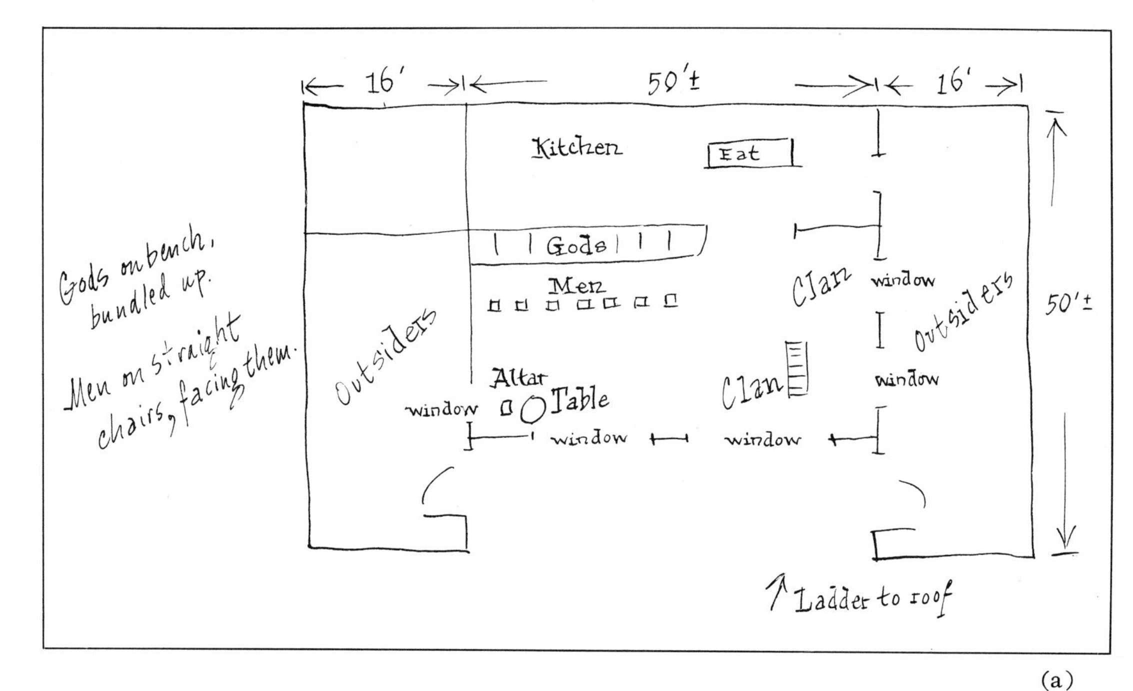

(a)

V:78 Zuni. a) The Council of the God's house. Sketch plan; b) Serafino Eriacho's Shalako house. Sketch plan. (*Drawings by Melanie Simo*)

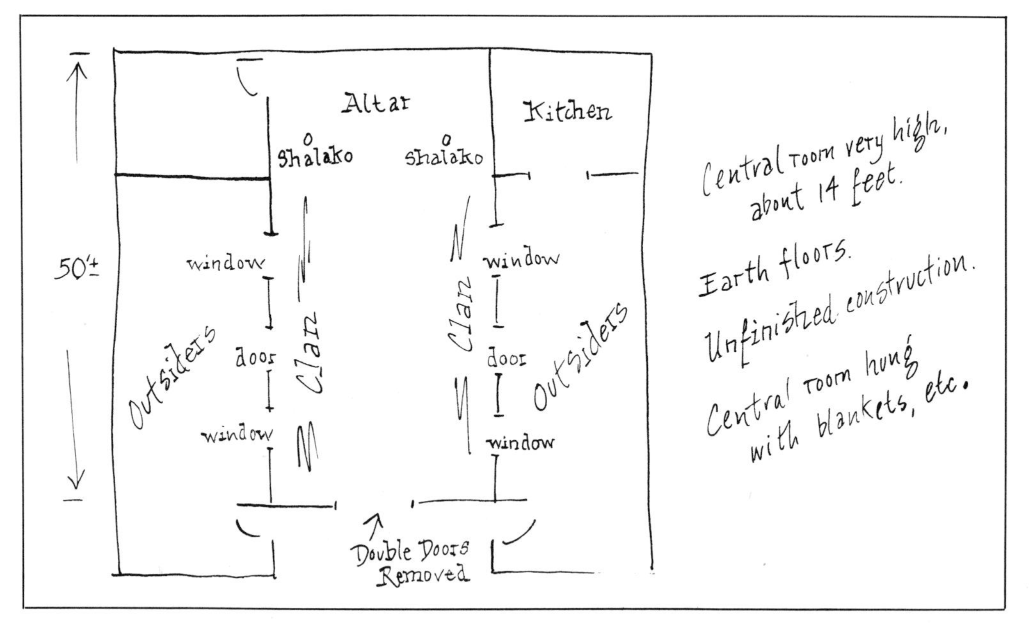

(b)

V:79 Zuni. Waiting for the Shalako to recross the river for the final race, 1896. (*Ben Wittick, Collections in the Museum of New Mexico*)

V:80 Zuni. The Shalako crossing, 1896. (*Ben Wittick, Collections in the Museum of New Mexico*)

V:81 Zuni. The Shalako and their attendants, 1896. *(Ben Wittick, Collections in the Museum of New Mexico)*

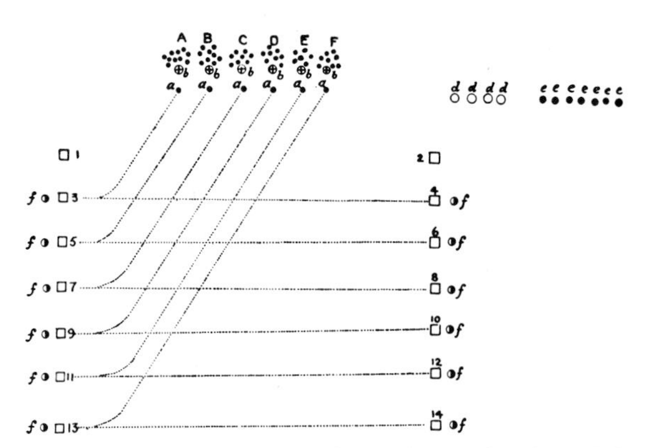

FIG. 8—*a*, personators of Sha'läko with effigies; *b*, alternates of the Sha'läko; *A, B, C, D, E, F*, groups from the ki'wi'siwe; *d*, Ko'mosona, Ko'pekwin, and two Ko'pi'läshiwanni; *e*, first body of A'shiwanni; *f*, Sha'läko managers; 1, 2, square excavations in which the Council of the Gods deposit te'likinawe; 3, 4, 5, 6, 7, 8, 9, 10, 11, 12, 13, 14, square excavations in which the Sha'läko deposit te'likinawe. The ki'wi'siwe*a* are paired as elder and younger brother, and the excavations are visited in the following order: A, People of the He'iwa ki'wi'sinĕ; B, people of the Mu'he'wa ki'wi'sinĕ; C, people of the Chu'pawa ki'wi'sinĕ; D, people of the O'he'wa ki'wi'sinĕ; E, people of the Up'tsannawa ki'wi'sinĕ; F, people of the He'kiapawa ki'wi'sinĕ; 3, 4, excavation for the Sha'läko of He'iwa ki'wi'sinĕ (elder); 9, 10, excavation for the Sha'läko of O'he'wa ki'wi'sinĕ (younger); 5, 6, excavation for the Sha'läko of Mu'he'wa ki'wi'sinĕ (elder); 13, 14, excavation for the Sha'läko of He'kiapawa ki'wi'sinĕ (younger); 7, 8, excavation for the Sha'läko of Chu'pawa ki'wi'sinĕ (elder); 11, 12, excavation for the Sha'läko of Up'tsannawa ki'wi'sinĕ (younger).

V:82 Shalako race. The Shalako then race back to their starting point so that the pattern interweaves. *(Stevenson, plate 257)*

V:83 Zuni. The final race. One Shalako is just approaching his attendant; another has just dropped his offering and his attendant is covering it up; another is down staring his attendant in the face. (*Ben Wittick, Collections in the Museum of New Mexico*)

V:84 The Shalako are running. (*Stevenson, plate 64*)

VI

THE NAVAHO HOGAN AND THE HOPI TOWNS

The trip south from the Mesa Verde and Kayenta toward the Hopi mesas is across one of the most beautiful landscapes on the continent (fig. I:1). Below Mexican Water the afternoon sunlight is reflected from the mesas and the wind-rounded rocks in a soft red glow (fig. VI:1). It is an indescribable color, not blinding but effulgent and warm. There is in all likelihood a lavender sky. The hogans of the Navaho who moved into this area, probably early in the eighteenth century, look exactly right under the glowing mesas and bluffs. North of the Canyon de Chelly the red mesas fall away, and the desert becomes vaster, duller in tone. Here the Canyon de Chelly pushes deep into the tough, brush-covered Chuska range. It glows with its own benign, rosy light, a watered sanctuary (fig. VI:2).

The cliff dwellings there can only be described as country houses[1] (figs. VI:3–6). Though representing habitation as old and constant as that of the Mesa Verde, they quickly elicit a projection of modern or at least romantic consciousness from the contemporary observer. This may be in part because they seem so much like rural hideaways, modest in scale, climbing the talus slopes and boosting themselves up into the clefts. The sweep of the sides of the canyon is enormous around them, a great swirl of red sandstone, water- and wind-gouged and smoothed. One also has the feeling that the ruins *use* the canyon—especially, like the lovely White House (figs. VI:3–5), choosing sites in bends for views down the shining stream. Perhaps it was mainly in such places that the forces of erosion worked most deeply, so that the appropriate clefts may have tended to be gathered there. But the canyon as a whole is uniquely blessed by the earth's beauty and protection. One would guess that the two qualities were equally valued by the people, Pueblo or Navaho, who lived in it (fig. VI:7).

The Anasazi used it hard and, as Hopi, returned to plant there after they had generally left for the south. Probably the Navaho drove them out at the very last. Indeed, this whole sweep of desert is the Navaho's best area. It is surely his most beautiful one with the

VI:1 The Navaho desert north of Chinle. Hogans.

VI:2 Canyon de Chelly. View from the mesa rim.

exception of the spectacular Monument Valley to the northwest; and there the farming is not much good. Here the town named Many Farms speaks for itself, and the red earth off the eroded bluffs is being tractored into new rich fields in several places. Sheep can be run almost anywhere, and just to the eastward the heights of the Chuska range offer water and grazing for cattle (fig. VI:8). But it is the gaudy quality, the insolent insouciance of this stretch of desert, which is most wholly Navaho (figs. VI:9, 10). It has somehow entered into him, and is indeed like one of his costumes, colorful and high crowned, this high-spirited, violent, and clean-aired place. Here he feels himself in the center of the world and spreads out his own sacred mountains around him; perhaps the Sierra Blanca (way over above Fort Garland) for the east, Mount Hesperus (La Plata Mountain) northeast of the Mesa Verde for the north, Mount Taylor for the south, and the San Francisco Peaks for the west,[2] with Huerfano Butte above Chaco Canyon (and just visible from Pueblo Alto on the rim) set in what any map can show us is the hub of the universe (fig. I:1). All this topographic orientation is quite Hopi, one feels, just as the sand paintings which are one of the major works of Navaho art are in the end Hopi inspired. On those paintings the earth is depicted by the Navahos, too, as a mother, with all the sacred mountains in place as her internal organs, all the colors of sky sliding across her, the ocean around her, and the corn stalk growing up through her body, its silky tassels her lungs (fig. VI:11). The sun rises eastward between the horns of her head, while the moon is born with the first sons and daughters out of her body below.[3] At the same time, the Navaho can

show this identical world on an illustrated tourist map, jazzy, but very informative, with the profiles of the four sacred mountains carefully depicted in the margins—but which the Tribal Council will not permit us to reproduce.

Yet if the light goes, the Navaho becomes uneasy. The night holds many terrors for him, haunted by spirits and worse, by beast men perhaps and unfriendly souls and unmentionable dangers.[4] The Navaho make all the noises of darkness in their night dances, especially in the *yeibichai*.[5] These are for the healing of individuals: the sickness of one may pull all down. There is good reason for the Navaho to feel some uneasiness, in view of the fact that he is almost the only one of the Indians of North America to live alone. He does not gather willingly in villages like the Hopi and almost everybody else, including all those swaggerers on the plains. Instead, he occupies his own tiny hogan alone in the vast expanse with his nearest neighbor set at what one might call a family's grazing distance away from him (fig. VI: 12). Only in this way could his dry rose-and-amethyst desert be occupied—by this willingness of men to spread out across it in order to make do with the scanty water. Each hogan is thus a little haven of warmth and coolness, a cavern whose domical exterior, somewhat like the old Basketmaker pit houses (figs. I: 2, 3), respects the shapes of the bluffs on the horizon.[6] But it is much more than this, being nothing less than a universe within itself, an interior space perfectly shaped to glorify the individual man (figs. VI: 13–16). Sitting, he has a whole horizon's circle around him at the reach of his arm. Standing, his head almost touches the apex of the wood-framed

VI:3 Canyon de Chelly. The White House from the rim.

VI:4 The White House with the stream.

dome—the archetypal dome of heaven which is filled by his vertical stance. Dead, it ends with him; its north side is broken out to release his soul. Proud the hogan, nurturer of heroes within, and recalling their Bronze Age tumuli,[7] but almighty small in the unrelieved dark of the desert night around it (fig. VI:17).

The Hopi and their Anasazi ancestors before them loped across this desert to find good growing spaces in protected spots, from Mesa Verde to Kayenta and the Canyon de Chelly, from Wupatki, perhaps, and so on. Finally they found their mesas and took root there till the ending of their world. The Navaho, coming later but clearly driven by desire no less than by necessity, spread out across the open expanse, and when he was forced to give up his raiding life he made his pattern of farming and grazing fit the desiccated landscape he was allowed to own. He seeded the desert lightly with himself and now covers almost all of it with a pattern so gentle that it can hardly be seen as we go hurtling by (fig. VI:18). No wonder the Navaho is fearful sometimes in the darkness, and dances at night in far-gathered groups for the health of the lonely soul.

Even the "squaw dance" is a curing ceremony, and a war dance too; it is sometimes held for persons who have been in contact with whites.[8] I attended one on the high ground south of Gallup (north of Zuni), which is apparently famous for violence. As usual, I saw none but was kidded a lot by the men and, as is the custom, had to pay not to dance. This seemed the wiser course, since an undercurrent of sexual rivalry, as of tomcats in the moonlight, was to be felt

VI:5 Canyon de Chelly. The White House, two views.

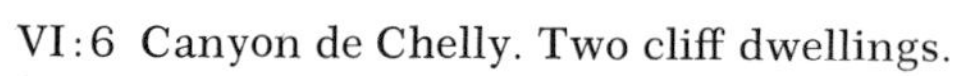
VI:6 Canyon de Chelly. Two cliff dwellings.

VI:7 Canyon de Chelly, Navaho hogan.

VI:8. The Navaho reservation. A branding in the Chuskas. Two views.

VI:9 The Navaho desert on the road to Rough Rock.

VI:10 Navaho at Chinle Trading Post in 1902. (*Ben Wittick, Collections in the Museum of New Mexico*)

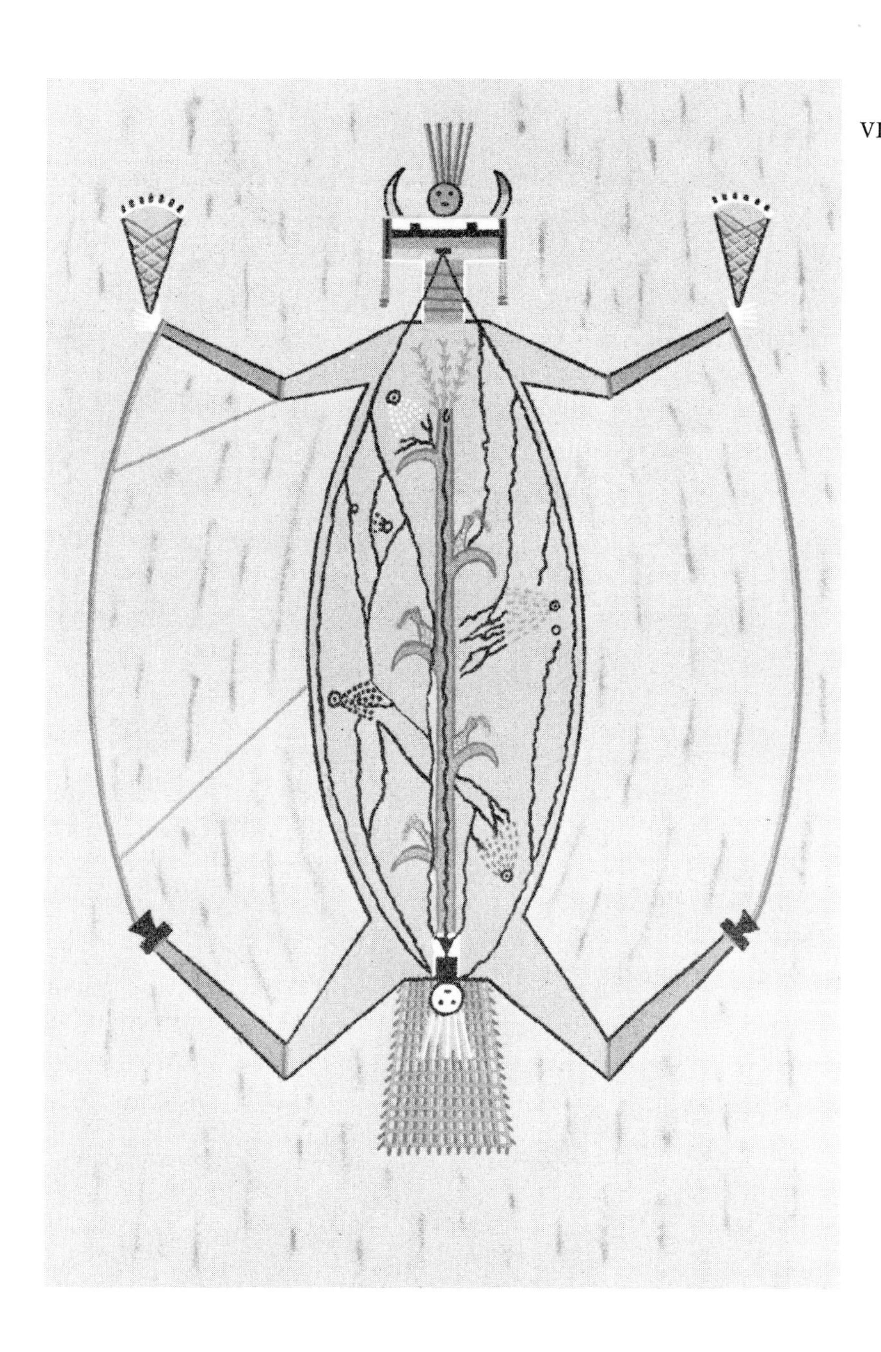

VI:11 *The Earth Mother.* Sand painting by Fred Stevens (Gray Squirrel). Mr. Stevens' description follows: "This is a Navajo Indian sand painting of the Earth Mother. Blue tips on the horns represent turquoise, or worldly wealth. Yellow part of the horns represents pollen, or everlasting life. The Figure (blue disk) between the horns represents the sun, with its rays radiating from it. The bars across the face of mother earth are white dawn, black darkness, blue haze, and yellow twilight. Bars on each side of face are red afterglow and black darkness. Red bars on throat are wind clouds, with blue sky. The yellow parts of the arms and legs are the yellow patterns of all vegetables. Blue part represents vegetation. Blue and red lines on elbows are plant blossoms. She carries vessels, one in each hand, of seeds of all food and medicines. Stripes on sides represent corn. White and black on top represent blossoms of all plants. Corn stalk represents spinal column of the earth and food. The mountain alongside the corn tassel is the Sierra Blanca Mountain. The heart of the earth. Yellow circle on mountain top represents medicine plant. Gray mountain on right top side of corn is Mount Taylor, and represents one side of the liver. The small circle alongside is the gall bladder. Mountain on left lower side is the La Plata mountain, and is the other side of the liver. Small peaks near La Plata Mountain are Huerfano peak, representing a kidney. Mountain at lower right foot of the corn is San Francisco peak, representing the bladder. Black lines on earth are water and veins. Water is the blood. Silk of corn is the lungs. Black circle at base of corn tassel is the breath of the earth, and the little winds. Black square at base of corn is the house of the wife of the sun. Triangle above the black house is the cloud. The white face at base is the moon. Yellow and white stripes coming out of moon are the first sons and daughters. The gray and red checked tail of the earth are rainbows, clouds, and fogs. The feet are clouds, stripes at knees are rainbows. All gray strips around earth is the ocean water. This painting is all hand done out of pulverized natural colored sand stones and silicon." (*Joseph Szaszfai*)

VI:12 Navajo Winter Hogan. (*David Muench*)

(a)

VI:13 Navaho Reservation. Frame of an old conical, forked-stick hogan in Monument Valley. All hogans face east. a) Sunrise b) the sun penetrates the hogan and models the interior.

(b)

round about. There was a great conical bonfire; above it one lone star wheeled through the darkening sky. Soon the moon rose. The circular linked-armed shuffle of the dance I thought very sad, a joyless round. The songs of the men before and after were, to me, unutterably lonely, crying as they did with coyote voices under the vast sky. Though sung by groups, they were not the deep communal Pueblo chants but true cries of individual isolation, beyond which, however, an animal brotherhood screamed.

The Hopi are entirely different.[9] Their villages stand in the last farthest place where men could get away from other men but still live in villages and grow corn[10] (fig. I:1). It is the southern edge of Black Mesa, from which three long fingers of flat-topped ridge push farther southward above the desert[11] (fig. VI:18a). Far to the southwest the San Francisco Peaks can be clearly seen (though not so easily photographed) from the mesas looming above the horizon, and they became the Hopi's ultimate Sacred Mountain, where men were born and whence their gods or ancestral spirits (or messengers of the gods, or representations of the gods), the kachinas, come and still have their home (fig. VI:60). Southeastward from the mesas another long finger of ridge pushes out across the empty plain. It is in fact made up of many separate

VI:14 Hogan. Interior.

VI:15 Hogan. Detail.

buttes and cones (isolated White Cone is one), but from the villages it looks like a notched calendar stick, and the sunrises, some of them critical, move down across it in wintertime[12] (fig. VI: 19). Farther out before this ridge a formation like a great pair of horns or wings flares in the immensity. It is in fact two curving buttes, now called "The Giant's Chair" and "Montezuma's Chair," but from the mesas they appear as one. The horns of the Navaho earth mother framing the sunrise are recalled (fig. VI: 11), as well as Santa Clara's Gap of the Sun far away (fig. III:21). All the old Hopi villages have the horns firmly in view. "There we catch eagles," a Hopi on Second Mesa told me when I asked. Eagles are messengers to the gods of the sky, and they are usually though not invariably sent reverently smothered back to them after the Niman (home) dance in July.[13] Consequently, the butte shape might perhaps be described with equal relevancy as wings. Such identifications of landscape shapes by a people are usually multiple in any event. However, the first great Hopi ceremony of the winter solstice, called Wuwuchim, is dominated by the Two Horn Spirits (fig. VI: 20), who are beings of special sanctity and power and in whose company great Masau'u, god of the earth and of death, and protector of towns, kindles the sacred fire.[14] Again, as in the Aegean, the horn seems to be the basic transmitter of creative power from the earth to man.

VI: 16 Navaho Reservation. Forked-stick hogan and Sweat Lodge at the Navaho National Monument.

If some of the Hopi migrated to their new homes from the prehistoric settlements to the south, they would have crossed the delicately colored desert under the great buttes and seen the mesas themselves opening out before them like some enormous animal body on the northern horizon, tawny as a lion. Some immigrants may have approached the mesas from the southwest, from old Wupatki and Walnut Canyon, and some, as their migration myths claim, from as far away as the lovely cliff dwelling in the Verde Valley called Montezuma's Castle, with the smoky mirror (Tezcatlipoca—the mists of winter mornings slipping across its face) of the cenote called Montezuma's Spring not far away (fig. I:1). The whole feel of the mesas, supplemented by the Hopi's own mythology, confusing though that can be, is of a modest flood of clans down from the north, the last of the Anasazi, moving out in the teeth of the big drought, occupying Kayenta for a while, and always the Canyon de Chelly in one way or another.[15] Finally, perhaps in competition with other clans for a watered place—since this was all surely long before the time when the Navaho came—they found their way to the ultimate outpost, right here. This is where everything stops. Just enough water seeps out of Black Mesa in the sand washes, and wells up in tiny springs, to grow deep-planted corn and water a field or two of squash or beans, and even a few melon patches and peach trees (fig. VI:21). A farmer coming out upon these mesas and looking out across the empty desert before him must have known that he had to take his stand at this place or die. And the heraldry of the horizon must have encouraged him to suspect that if he stood fast the gods might help him here: their home the San Francisco peaks, their sign the eagle-haunted horns of power (fig. VI:19).

The pattern of the Hopi settlement of the mesas tends to confirm these views. First (before 1150) was Shongopovi (some call it Schomopovi now), or rather the earlier Maseeba below it, now destroyed.[16] Here the mesa, Second Mesa in this case, floods farthest out above the desert (fig. IV:18a). All the water that there is in the mesa above should be expected to seep out here, and southward the horns are close and the San Francisco Peaks ride high (fig. VI:23). It is strategically the right place to seize, to hold the whole area. Next it was Oraibi's turn (c. 1150); it was settled after Maseeba but is still partially inhabited and is therefore the oldest continuously lived-in place within the confines of the present United States. Did the Hopi go there from Shongopovi or come in as new clans from the southwest? We do not know. But some men at least coming along the southwestern side of big Third Mesa and getting out as far as they could toward the desert wings to the east and stopping there, with the San Francisco Peaks, a link perhaps with old memories, still strong on the right hand (figs. VI:24–30). At any rate, Mishongnovi was soon settled (c. 1200) on the other finger of Second Mesa, beautifully sited for everything (figs. VI:31–33). It is interesting that it was doomed Awatovi which was settled next (c. 1332).[17] Why? Perhaps because this seemed to the Hopi a necessary if risky leap to a good broad mesa

VI:17 Navaho Reservation. Hogan and horses near Lukachukai.

(a)

VI:18 a) Hopi Reservation. Navaho Monument. b) Sketch plan of Hopi towns. (*Drawing by Melanie Simo*)

VI:19 Buttes in the desert.

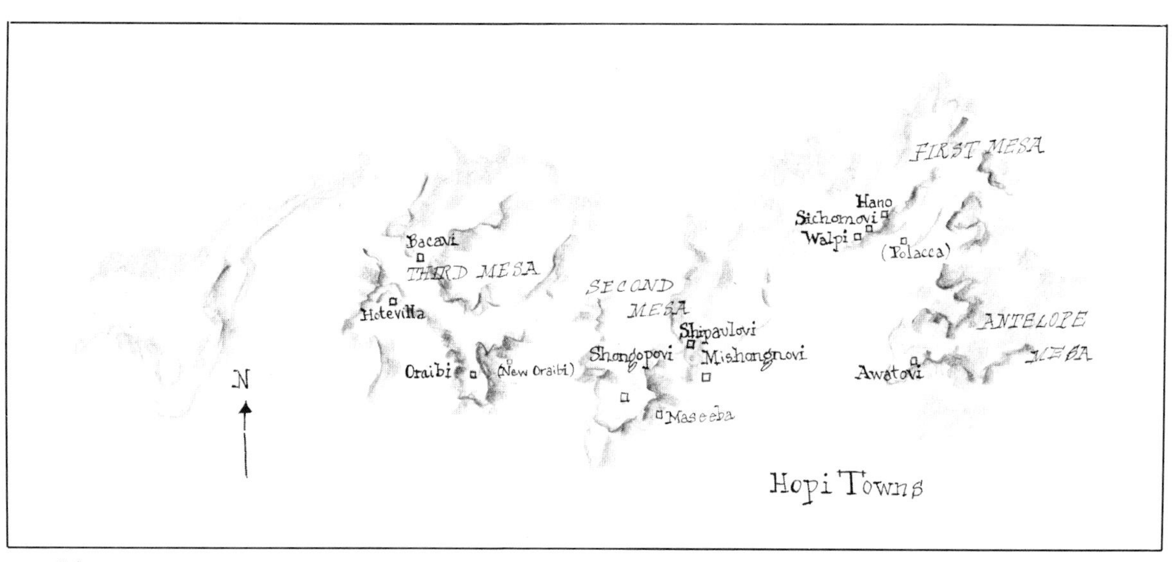

(b)

very close to the calendar ridge and the symbols of power (fig. VI:34). Awatovi was built well over on the southeastern edge of Antelope Mesa and so on the side away from the other towns. Alas, it was apparently too far away, because it alone of all the Hopi villages received back Spanish priests after the revolt of 1680 (in which all the churches were destroyed), so that the other towns came upon it by surprise and leveled it and killed most of its people and, it would appear, ate some of them.[18]

Next Walpi took position, in 1417, back on First Mesa (figs. VI:35–41). It was the first of the existing settlements there (Sikyatki, farther north, was abandoned), and like Shongopovi and Mishongnovi it moved to the very peak of the mesa in fear of Spanish reprisal after the Revolt, but it eventually came under increasing Navaho pressure too. Shipaulovi, perched on the tiny tip cone of Mishongnovi's branch of Second Mesa, was also founded after the Revolt, as was Hano on First Mesa, settled by Tewa fugitives from the Spaniards who, it is said, were permitted to fix themselves there to guard the trail[19] (figs. VI:42–45). Then, later, Hopi Sichomovi filled up the space between Hano and Walpi and, much later, in the late nineteenth century when fortification was no longer useful, Moenkopi, which, according to Hopi legend had been occupied during the original migrations "for a while" (Simmons, *Sun Chief*, p. 420), was replanted way back down out of the sacred area in the richly watered wash below Tuba City (fig. VI:22). Then Oraibi began to fall apart, and New Oraibi, suburbanized, grew up below it, and Hotevilla, founded by "hostile" antiwhite exiles from Oraibi, backed off northwestward from the view of the wings, though not of the peaks, toward more copious seepage, and Bacavi gave up the whole orientation and tucked itself

VI:20 Two horn Priests of the Wuwuchim Ceremony. Oraibi, c. 1900. (*Courtesy of the Mennonite Library and Archives, North Newton, Kansas*)

back into the body of Third Mesa with a restricted view. But the fields of Bacavi, and especially Hotevilla, are so well watered that one wonders why the settlers of Oraibi did not fix there in the first place (fig. VI:21). I think the answer must in part be that these places are not sanctified like the others. They are not locked into the promising landscape shapes. In the first instance they must have been deemed less trustworthy, so that it seemed better—even if the local water was somewhat less—to found the village in a place of power and to trudge daily the four or five miles to the watered fields. I do not mean to give the impression by this that Hotevilla and Bacavi are not good towns. They are, and not only prosperous but ritually and architecturally impressive as well. Hotevilla has a subtly defined plaza near its highest point, while the rest of the village progressively opens out down the gentle slope into single-family houses of good masonry. Below it are terraces almost Japanese in elegance, giving away to westward, where there are more fields of corn growing, even out on the plain. There are kivas, too, very sculptural ones on the edge of the mesa, looking toward the kachina peaks. I once saw a fine Niman dance in the plaza there. And Bacavi, I think, has the best dancers of all the villages in a purely choreographic sense. I saw a hair-raising Long-Haired Kachina dance there in 1968—the deep chorus, brave in the morning, brooding toward evening, telling more about prehistory throughout the long day than can normally be learned elsewhere. In the end it rained in long wild dark sheets like the curtains of the Long-Haired Kachinas' hair (fig. V:73). All this took place in a rectangular plaza which subtly slid open toward the new northeasterly view back through the canyons in the body of the mesa. Out there the kivas boldly took their new stand.

But the traditionally placed villages, always with the exception of Awatovi, are different. They all have a marvelously intricate relationship with each other and with the sacred forms to the southwest and southeast. There are interlocking lines of sight from village to village and to the peaks. Intersecting fields of fire as of a Main Line of Resistance cannot help, un-

VI:21 Fields under third mesa.

VI:22 Moenkopi.

VI:23 Second mesa. The side of Maseeba, with the horned buttes.

fortunately, but come to the modern mind, and one guesses that perhaps these lines of sight are exactly that in a magical sense, a system of defense and a way of connection, denying the approach ground to every kind of physical and metaphysical foe. Perhaps something like that had functioned between the Great Houses in Chaco Canyon, especially after such Great Kivas as Casa Rinconada were built (figs. I:16, 26).

Of all the villages, Oraibi, now approaching ruin, is the oldest, and the insistent urbanism of the Hopi intention is still clearest of all there. It is placed on a very spearpoint of mesa thrusting out at the great horn-wings which lift before the rising sun in that direction (figs. VI:24, 25). And by this act here and at Maseeba, sanctioned by Masau'u, the Hopi began "in poverty but in peace," to make the "fourth world" their own. Now Maseeba has been moved and Oraibi is dying. But its dilapidated kivas still project their ladder poles to the sky, and the ruined streets retain an urban scale, which most of the living pueblos have lost by now[20] (figs. VI:28–30). Oraibi's upper stories are still there in many cases, though in ruin. They have not been so generally removed as in the other more viable towns. Hence, after the desert, Oraibi feels like Manhattan, its man-made canyons engulfed below the high houses. Not so long ago Oraibi looked from a distance a little like an Arab town (fig. VI:26), with high urban cubes recalling those of the Hadramawt, in every way a compact massing of urban forms.[21] One suspects that the memory of the prehistoric Great Houses was still alive in the Hopi when they first built on the mesas. The development we traced earlier from the Mesa Verde to Kayenta and so on has now gone further. The House has opened up into lanes of houses, and the Great Kiva has become the plaza, and the whole has been penetrated by space and is opened to space, as to the great shapes on the horizon. It makes wider contact with the earth, and its own fabric loosens and begins to dissolve in a pattern we have already noticed along the Rio Grande. The tension between the older closed and the newer opening way is beautiful to see. That is to say, Oraibi is like one mass chopped through laterally three or four times (fig. VI:27). Whatever

VI:24 Oraibi with the buttes.

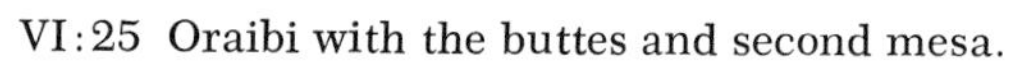

VI:25 Oraibi with the buttes and second mesa.

VI:26 Oraibi from the south in the nineteenth century. (Old photograph.) (*Collections in the Museum of New Mexico*)

VI:27 Oraibi. Aerial photograph, 1950. (*Stubbs, plate* 25)

VI:28 Oraibi. A street in 1919. (*Collections in the Museum of New Mexico*)

VI:29 Oraibi. Kivas, c. 1900. (*Ben Wittick, Collections in the Museum of New Mexico*)

VI:30 Oraibi. Kiva, 1911. (*Collections in the Museum of New Mexico*)

intervals result are used as the plazas. There is no sense of actively shaping a volume of space as there is in some of the later towns like, for example, the latest of all, Hano, Sichomovi, and Shipaulovi. And in them one wonders whether a century of Spanish contact may not have played some part, since they were all founded after the Revolt. Again, though, the old Great Kiva issue is raised, especially for Shipaulovi, so neatly enclosed and *kiska*ed it is. Mishongnovi's plazas, too, are more enclosed than those of Oraibi. Whatever the reason, there was a definite movement toward defined volume rather than mere street interval in the later towns.

Great Shongopovi is still fundamentally like Oraibi, but it is stiffened up, another neoclassical town.[22] It is in fact the conservative bastion of the Hopi: the Vatican, some of the most sophisticated among them call it. In this it recalls Santo Domingo, though it has little of Domingo's dourness. Its form is strict, like Domingo's, with three clean rows of houses and a pyramidally massed central house rising beside a kiva in the wider interval like one of Camillo Sitte's churches picturesquely placed to define and divide a square[23] (figs. VI:32, 33). But here the masses are awesome in character if not in size. The masonry goes from fine pebble work and lots of stucco to rubble and big blocks. The first court at Shongopovi looms around the observer; the kiva under the pyramid is complex with several levels, stairs, and so on. Right alongside the pyramid a covered passageway, the *kiska*, leads on into the next court (where once I saw four enormous eagles tied, leaping terribly against their leg tethers together), across which in turn another covered passageway is to be found, here spanned by the volume of a room. Underfoot the passageways are paved with boards over a channel in the earth. They reverberate to footsteps like a drum and recall, as mentioned earlier, what may have been monumental foot drums in the Great Kivas, while the *kiska* reminds us of the subterranean spaces and the labyrinths of the Great Houses themselves. Can the pyramidal mass in the first court represent influence from Mexico, or the

VI:31 Second mesa. Shongopovi right, Mishongovi and Shipaulovi left, with corn twins. Site of Maseeba just under Shongopovi's ridge.

Hopi's memory of such influence in halcyon days passed by? Again, if so, the shape has become casual; the pyramid is there, though unlike those of Mexico it is asymmetrical and a dwelling. But it is the monumental heart of the village: a firm combination of pyramid and kiva at the center. All the other kivas at Shongopovi are out where they can pick up the view to the peaks, the wings, and the calendar ridge.

The same combination occurs at Walpi, which should therefore be considered out of strict chronological sequence now. Walpi is almost one solid mass on its narrow mesa[24] (figs. VI:37, 38). There is more or less of a roadway on the west, but the plaza, if it should be called that, is along the open east, where all the kivas are placed. The major dance plaza there is defined by a natural rock of mad device, called Snake Rock, and in its presence Walpi's especially famous snake dance, so well photographed at the turn of the century, took place (figs. VI:39, 40). It is clearly strong medicine, and quiet, wrapped fetish bundles can be seen lying in its hollows. Again the eastern

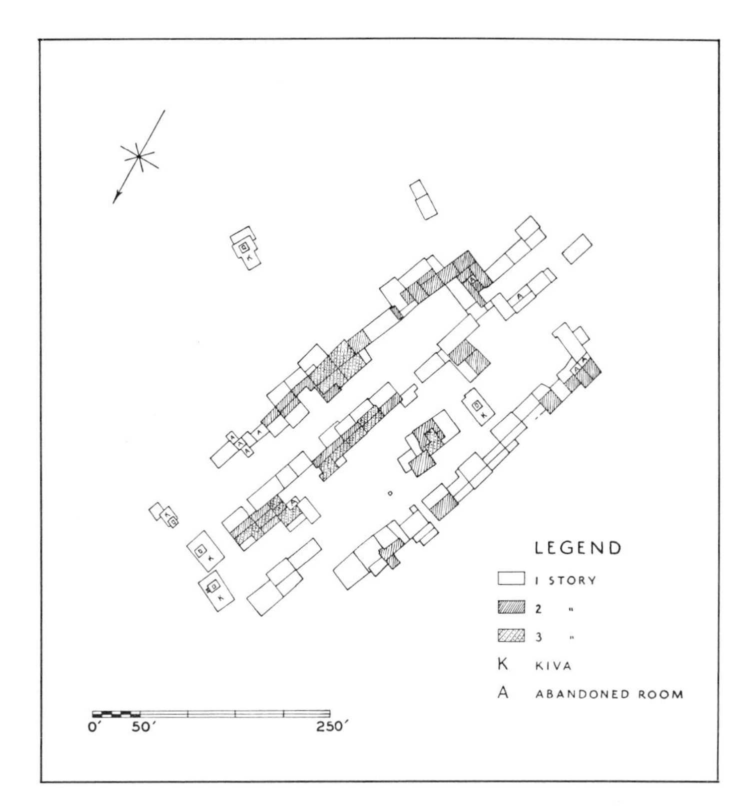

VI:32 Shongopovi. Plan, 1950. (*Stubbs, figure 26*)

VI:33 Shongopovi. Pyramidal building with kiva beyond.
San Francisco Peaks in distance. (*Paul Coze*)

ridgeline and the great horns define the view from here and from the kivas, and directly behind the Snake Rock plaza the town masses up to its highest, three- or four-storied elevation. Once again that massing is a stepped-back, more or less pyramidal affair (fig. VI:41). This time the *kiska* is directly under the pyramid, and it is the most monumental passageway in all modern pueblo architecture. Supported on thirteen pine lintels, it thrusts a dramatic hollow under the town's climactic mass. Once again, kiva, dance plaza, pyramid, and passageway are grouped together.

But there is more than this to the architecture of First Mesa. Walpi is poised on its southwestern tip, held out before the desert and the San Francisco Peaks. Behind Walpi are the other two towns, and they are its exact opposite and complement. Where it is mostly solid, they are both surprisingly spatial affairs of long shifting plaza-hollows, defined by separated sliding blocks of houses[25] (figs. VI:42–45). The pattern looks like that of an early De Stijl painting by Theo van Doesburg. It is indeed a rhythm as of a dance, but the Hopi (and Tewa) intention is not abstract. The relationships are to the landscape and so ultimately to the gods; they are also to each other, a communal relationship. Hano and Sichomovi, unlike Walpi, are both low one-storied towns and, so far as we can tell from old photographs, they always were—except at the very northern tip of the mesa where Hano started off with a strong three-storied mass, an anchor for the long leap southward down the mesa top (fig. VI:44). From it the long low buildings,

VI:34 Awatovi with the "Calendar Ridge."

(a)

VI:35. First Mesa. a) From the east at Rodeo; b) from the desert.

(b)

VI:36 First Mesa and windmill.

shaping the longitudinal hollows of the plazas—moderately extended in Hano, marvelously stretched at Sichomovi by a long continuous house façade on the southwest side (fig. VI:43)—lead out along the ridge through what is in fact a long, rather narrow slot of landscape space, defined by Second Mesa to the right and Antelope Mesa to the left (fig. VI:42). So all is being directed high in space as in an arrow flight toward Walpi (fig. VI:45), which is thus doubly made to stand out as a solid pyramidal object before the sacred landscape forms far off on the horizon (fig. VI:46). It is a construction that is somehow worked out between three villages to allow them to interact with each other in order to act out, focus, and control the sacred drama of the landscape in which they are set. The talus slopes are skirted in shiny tin cans, with the sad suburb of Polacca spilling down messily below them.

It is on Second Mesa, at Mishongnovi and Shipaulovi, that one feels the far-off quality of the Hopi towns most fully. There the villages seem most like the rock itself, building up to natural pyramids, and the stone is most golden or, as Lawrence put it, most like dry bread crusts[26] (figs. VI:31, 47, 48). The fine twin shafts of Sacred Corn Rock, recalling the rock twins in Towayalane's heart (fig. V:54), stand over the

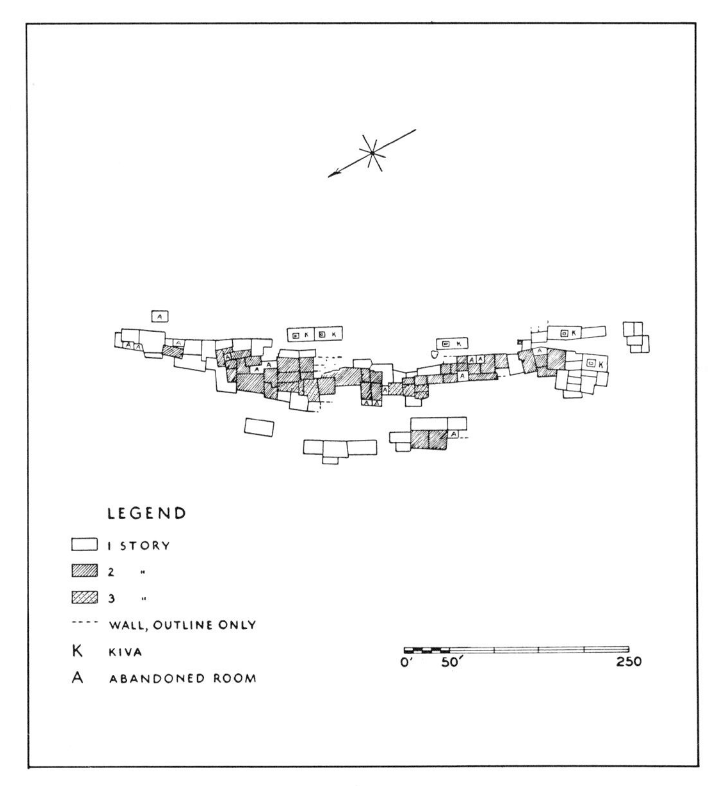

VI:37 Walpi. Plan (1950). (*Stubbs, figure* 22)

burial ground just below Mishongnovi, and they give a special scale to the view southward toward the desert horns (figs. VI:49, 50). On Second Mesa, too, the villages on their high and narrow cones seem to be sailing over the desert (fig. VI: 51). This is especially true as the clouds gather on summer afternoons and sail across the sky so that their shadows chase each other across the desert floor. From the villages one has the illusion that it is the mesa which is moving, as if it were sailing above the earth. It is indeed the ultimate Hopi position: far away, poised in space and waiting out what they believe may be the last age of earthly man. It is severe, this place of waiting above that desert which all the earth may one day be. The technicolor splendors of the northern Navaho landscape are gone. These are the monotone colors of dry tan stone and heat, and the only drama is that of the sailing clouds.

When the kachinas dance in the tiny, clearly shaped plaza at Shipaulovi,[27] highest of all, their file must be seen not only as it echoes the buildings' cornice lines but also as it packs the space ship of the village with all the riches of earth and of earthly divinity as if to transport them in it to eternity[28] (figs. I:11; VI:52–54). They fill up the monotone plaza with evergreen and white kilts and great masks and feathers and colors, and with their deep voices as well. There never were so rich a people as the penniless Hopi when the vessel of their village is so packed with the planet's life.

It can be packed with laughter too. One Sunday in June 1968, I was privileged to see the Hopi clowns perform during the intervals of a kachina dance at Shipaulovi[29] (fig. VI:55). They were from First Mesa, I was told. Today they were satirizing social workers and the agents of the Bureau of Indian Affairs. At other times they have taken off hippies and missionaries, tourists, and especially all Indian lovers, always. This time they produced white men and women in dead-white crazy supercilious masks who went hustling about the plaza making the Indians clean it up. Fix this, fix that. They brought out trowels and tried to cement over irregularities in the *te'wi*, of which there are plenty. Soon they started looking the Indians themselves over for structural defects and discovered that they had navels and tried to cement those over too. Then they insisted on bathing the Indians. "I'm no Navaho," screamed one as they dragged him to the tin washtub. Then the social workers began to get interested in the Indians' private parts and started fooling around trying to get their pants off. Come on. (Lots of projection—no pun—here, which always gives me a pain, in Indians as in anyone, but as a ballet it was funny.) They de-bagged them finally and the spectators—the Hopi that is, it was old stuff to the white kids—started to shriek with

VI:38 Walpi with the buttes; (*2nd photo Ben Wittick, Collections in the Museum of New Mexico*)

VI:39 Walpi. Snake Rock in 1917. (*H. F. Robinson, Collections in the Museum of New Mexico*)

VI:40 Walpi. Snake Rock in the nineteenth century. (*Ben Wittick, Collections in the Museum of New Mexico*)

VI:41 Walpi. The pyramid and the *kiska*. (*Ben Wittick, Collections in the Museum of New Mexico*)

VI:42 First Mesa. In order from near to far: Hano, Sichomovi, Walpi, in landscape (© *By Bob Bradshaw—Photo By Kinnear*)

VI:43 First Mesa. Hano left, Sichomovi right. Aerial photo, 1950. (*Stubbs, plate 21*) (*Collection, The Museum of Modern Art, New York, Lillie P. Bliss Bequest*)

VI:44 First Mesa. Hano looking north. Note kiva poles right distance. (*Ben Wittick, Collections in the Museum of New Mexico*)

VI:45 Sichomovi, looking south toward Walpi. (*Ben Wittick, Collections in the Museum of New Mexico*)

VI:46 Walpi. San Francisco Peaks right, horned buttes left. (*Bradshaw Distributing Co.*)

VI:47 Second Mesa with the Corn Twins.

VI:48 Second Mesa from the south, Mishongnovi above.

VI:49 Second Mesa. Calendar Ridge, two views. Corn Rock.

VI:50 Corn Rock. Detail with buttes.

VI:51 Shipaulovi center and Mishongnovi left with the "Calendar Ridge" and the buttes.

delight. The women covered their faces and peeked, but it was all so artfully done that there was nothing to see. Bandelier records the antics of Keres clowns with Victorian horror: copulating, masturbating, sodomizing, or pretending to do so—all probably for pedagogical or apotropaic purposes.[30] But there is in fact no real grossness in the Hopi clowns, at least there was not on that day. True, it all ended Aristophanically with a great orgy of screwing. The Indians humped the social workers up off their feet, shouting "Homemakers—homemakers," which is apparently what the poor things were supposed to be. The wives finally rushed out to rescue their men and dragged the white hussies out of the plaza while the kachinas came filing back in through the opening in the plaza's northern corner. They were led by their withered priest, ancient and bent way over, totally ignoring the clowns, scattering his pinches of cornmeal before him. I am told that the following year they made fun of the priest. (He was enormously old. When a man's time comes do the clowns somehow tell him to go?)

I also spent a night in one of Mishongnovi's kivas, but I tend to count it a Shipaulovi experience, since it was a joint dance and I was invited to it by Shipaulovi people. There through the late night and early morning the two priests sat and smoked ritualistically and spat ceremonially on the stove, and the women who had arranged this series of dances sat massed along the rear, with other guests on benches along the sides (fig. VI:56). The benches (the *te'wi* again) along the far side were reserved for the dancers but were taken by mistake by what the Hopi at any rate call hippies, wrapped Indian-like but unfortunately not Hopi-like

in blankets. The priests said nothing at first, but the women carried on until they stirred themselves to make the hippies move. A number of them passed out (zonk) later. After a long time steps were heard on the roof and unearthly voices called and were answered by the priests, and down the ladder they came, one after the other, a mixed bag of kachinas, with every kind, it seemed, of animal mask and feathered splendor. It was pure force filling the kiva, embodied in beings unknown, impossible to describe but larger than human life, animally and spiritually vibrant, vivid, and enormous. And then the great, booming, brain-drowning Hopi drum began to blow the roof off in overlapping puffs of power, and the

VI:52 Shipaulovi. Aerial view, 1950. (*Stubbs, plate 23*)

VI:53 Kachina Dance, 1911. Not Shipaulovi; probably Oraibi. (*Collections in the Museum of New Mexico*)

VI:54 Kachina Dance. Probably Oraibi. Note single drummer, priest, women with gourds. (*Collections in the Museum of New Mexico*)

VI:55 A Hopi clown. (*Kenneth Chapman Coll., Collections in the Museum of New Mexico*)

VI:56 Interior view of a Hopi kiva, c. 1890. (*Photo courtesy Smithsonian Institution National Anthropological Archives*)

kachinas lifted their right feet and their rattles and then both came down together and they began to chant and to dance in their close-packed, knee-straightening file around the far side of the room, jumping foxtails pressed up against the noses of the watchers on the side benches. The whole volume of space was packed with kachina sound and bodies alike, group after group of them all night long, their presence choking, stupefying. The kiva was like a pressure cooker in which the ingredients of reality were being boiled to a magic heat, charged not only with mankind but with every imaginable living thing and all hopes, ideas, memories, and desires.

Below Shipaulovi, but farthest out along the ridge on its own peak, Mishongnovi rides (figs. I:10; VI:31, 47, 48). Its organization seems a synthesis between the more or less open parallel ranges of Oraibi and Shongopovi and the more shaped courtyards of Shipaulovi and the two later First Mesa towns[31] (fig. VI:57). Here, too, there is as always the feeling that the Hopi would, like all the Pueblos, prefer to lock the court exactly into the major points of the compass, though whether the axis runs east-west or north-south does not seem to matter too much, and any variation that the terrain requires will be made.[32] Mishongnovi's exactly east-west plaza is magnificently

VI:57 Mishongnovi. Aerial view, 1950. (*Stubbs, plate* 22)

VI:58 Mishongnovi. The plaza looking north with Snake Dance *kisi* on left. (*Ben Wittick, Collections in the Museum of New Mexico*)

framed by what were once quite high and strict building masses (fig. VI:58). In it, and as most obviously in all the Hopi plazas, is a small rude altar and the boarded-over hole of a *sipapu* that booms when stamped on. A smaller plaza is almost filled by a major kiva, recalling the single kiva inside the town at Shongopovi, while the other kivas are set out to the eastern view here also. So are most of the kivas everywhere except at Hano and Sichomovi, where out of four between them three are embedded in the shaped plazas (fig. VI:43), which again seems to indicate what might be called the courtyard dominance in the conception of those two towns. The only exception, I think a significant one, is the kiva at Hano beside which was its big three-storied building on the north.

Mishongnovi is a balance of solid and void, and its dances are deeply framed. I saw the Hemis Kachina dance there, the Niman home dance, on July 18, 1970, on the day when the kachinas make their last appearance of the ceremonial year before they leave for their home in the San Francisco Peaks.[33] I had seen two Niman dances at Shipaulovi in 1968 and 1969, but neither was the Hemis Kachina, the noblest of them all. He is like an evergreen tree that carries the clouds on its head (figs. VI:59–62). When his file (twenty-six of them on this day) begins to dance, it is as if one had looked down through the

VI:59 Hemis Kachina Dance (Niman Kachina, "Home" Dance), 1919. Not Mishongnovi. They are not wearing evergreen with their kilts for some reason. (*Collections in the Museum of New Mexico*)

ranks of evergreens in the rainy Chuska highlands above Ganado or, probably more to the point, into those of the San Francisco Peaks, and seen the trees all begin to dance together (fig. VI:60). Indeed, the file of kachinas comes into the plaza from its secret waiting place just at the moment when the breeze would be starting to make the trees, if there were any, give off leafy, or rather, pine or spruce needle sounds. That is to say, they do not come really at sunrise, but when the sun wakes the breeze. Just as it stirs on your cheek you begin to hear them coming in the swish, swish of their evergreen boughs.

Rain and water symbolism is very obvious in their costume. Water symbols are sketched in white on their black-painted bodies; there is a full evergreen ruff—the usual Douglas fir, the spruce, deep and furry in the sun, every needle shivering like a conductor of forces—and spruce boughs hanging below the dance kilt: black tree trunk in rain, undying green around it. The moccasins are brown as pine needles, and above the mask the sky altar rides high with eagle feathers standing up and wheat sheaves taut between them. But it is mostly erect phalli stepping up in white and blue, while the soft white breast feathers of eagles are set around the rim so that, as on prayer sticks, they always flutter upward in any breeze, and in the dance the whole crown of the massed dancers lights and shivers together, the clouds and the snow peaks rising above all (figs. I:11; VI:61, 62).

They come on three times in the morning, three in the afternoon, and are complemented by nine kachinas as women. In the usual file arrangements, they dance one dance together and then go into a formation with the women kneeling side by side in a straight line and the men, now also in line side by side, curving in the ends of their rank to face and contain them. The women kneel on mats and begin to scrape notched sticks which are stuck into pumpkin gourds; they scrape them with a shell and produce a most striking noise (I had almost said, incorrectly, ungodly or unearthly). It is a frog noise, pure breck-kek-kek-kek koax koax. Aristophanes again; and it tells us once more that the animal chorus of Dionysos must never be forgotten here.[34] It is a harsh, gurgling voice of earth and water, mindlessly repetitive, deep and wild. Then as it takes hold the kachinas suddenly lift up each his right foot and as it comes down they present their enormous rattles at the women (most of them natural brown gourds, one blue) and raising their own deep hoarse chant, they strike out with the rattles while the frog chorus goes on. The striking motion is aggressive and continuously repeated, while the women are all hunched over below it, grinding down on the gourds. It is an act of copulation, power and release consummate, and a thundershower, too, the same thing: the sky dark as thunderheads, white feathers flying like storm-tossed birds, beating down with all its blackness upon the women, who are colored like the desert in their Hopi blankets of deep red and light tan. The sound is booming and rain-filled, swishing and roaring, and the movement is in and out, up and down, of strike and withdrawal. Then suddenly, after some terrific hesitations, they stop—just like that—and back right up, rattle quickly, with no chanting, and, very straight, dance backward into file before you know it. And you realize now how tremendous it is for Hopi kachinas to dance in line, as they almost never do, because the power we have just seen was awesome: the batteries of the gods unmasked in their broadside.

Then they give out presents and go around and do it all again at two other stations around the plaza. Tall and splendid, they come in and go out from the kivas above the desert like trees walking. (One caught a cramp in the plaza during one of the dances and hung convulsed on the altar: a god in pain and truly terrifying to see.) After the last dance they go to the kiva in the other plaza where they are stripped of their rattles and of some of their evergreen, which is given to Indians from other villages. There were people from the Rio Grande towns who had come all the way for a piece of it this time. The Hopi are strong. Then the kachinas go off against the sky, lightning flashing far off. They pass in silhouette toward the cone of rock to the southeast of the village and are seen no more.

VI:60 Flagstaff, Arizona, with the San Francisco Peaks and evergreen forests. Proto-Strip and proto-Hemis Kachinas. (*Ben Wittick, Collections in the Museum of New Mexico*)

VI:61 Hemis Kachina Dance. Dancing in file. (*Collections in the Museum of New Mexico*)

VI:62 Hemis Kachina Dance. Turning and striking. In 1970 at Mishongnovi the women knelt facing the kachinas. (*Collections in the Museum of New Mexico*)

Against a house near the kivas, in the presence of the lifted wings of the buttes where he may have been caught, one small eagle only was tethered this year. After the dance he was gone: into the kiva to be smothered next morning, one supposes, initiated into the clan, mummified perhaps and so a messenger to the sky. One's thoughts on the matter tend to be complicated. In a sense this Hopi sacrifice is no better, if more reverently handled, than the usual human exploitation of animal life. Mankind fills its emptiness and covers up its fears with every kind of animal hecatomb from covert to slaughter house, altar, and laboratory. The Hopi are no strangers to such thoughts. They know that they exploit other living things but feel that they have to do so not only to live but also to play their part in the scheme of things.[35] They ask the victim's pardon, of course, and hope for its consent always. They are brothers after all. Like all farmers the Hopi kill domestic animals under normal circumstances with dispatch and without compunction.[36] Concerning wild game they are, apparently, ruthless toward rabbits and prairie dogs, respectful to deer. Nor is death that much of an absolute for the Hopi. It is only a change in manner of existence; it is not nonbeing. But the eagle is special; his sacrifice is, in the Hopi view, a tragic and important event. He is the ultimate hero of this mystery play.[37]

The morning after the Niman dance, just after dawn when the sun was beginning to touch the village and the dawn breeze had come cool, four kachinas, three of them Hemis, led by a heavy one in a white head mask, came to the central kiva. They mounted to its roof, circumnavigated it three times, and then, led by the white head, they slowly divested themselves of various objects by handing them down through the ladder hole to some being within: feathers, water gourds, and so on.[38] All of this was done in absolute silence and with the kachinas standing quietly in place as the sun finally flooded them with a still, gentle light that rounded their bodies. Standing thus larger than life and seen from below, immobile in the modeling light against the still delicate soft blue sky, they had all the majesty of Piero della Francesca's blondly lighted figures, motionless and silent. But their eagle down fluttered in the cool morning breeze: hence not wholly closed or still their shapes, but opening to the touch of the morning. It went on a long time. I was bored finally—until the three priests of yesterday, two old and one young, plus another man and a boy, all stripped to the waist in the simple white kilt, climbed up out of the kiva and stood on the roof. They were all brown as the earth. Humanity was being born in the morning, the color of the sand. Then, out of the kiva, wrapped in their bravely colored shawls of normal holiday wear (while the "female" kachinas were in the characteristic and now purely ceremonial mantle), climbed two women, born with the men out of the kiva world. Here as elsewhere it has not seemed worthwhile to contradict the common misconception—so well ridiculed by Hewett anyway[39]—that the kivas are or were exclusively for men. They own and run them, right enough, as the women own the houses, but the latter are by no means categorically excluded, as so many of the dances can show us. Such segregation is the modern clubman's version of the kiva idea; the Indian intention is more complex. Nor do they ever perform a meaningless ceremony. The dullness here as in so many of their rituals is always part of a slow process of growth, in this case of birth. In the end men and women are equally majestic against the sky, framed in the village setting, but more splendid, as they should be, one supposes, than their rather offhand immediate surroundings might suggest.

I saw the snake dance at Mishongnovi in the last year of the life of the renowned snake priest, Joe Sekakuku, though he had by then retired from the dance itself.[40] I remember him sitting with his legs stretched out at the edge of the plaza looking levelly at an approaching rattler, two clan members together, for what turned out to be the last time. The dance was so accurately described long ago, and has been so picked over since, that I have no heart to describe it in detail.[41] (D. H. Lawrence was especially tiresome though mercifully brief on the subject.[42]) It seems enough to say that it is danced early in August after the kachinas have gone away, and it is regarded as a survival of the very earliest Hopi practice, before—whenever that was—the masked dances came (figs. VI:63–74). The song of the snake and antelope priests who perform it does seem to come right out of the earth (fig. VI:67). The only kachina songs which approach it are, it seems to me, those of the Long-Haired Kachinas (fig. V:73), deep prehistoric mutterings as of muffled thunder. But this song is less open than theirs; it is an ominously subterranean sound, as I suppose it is meant to be. The snake dancers are unique among Hopi dancers in that they look utterly savage and unkempt, with faces painted black, chins sometimes weirdly white, hair itself Medusa-like. They come in fast after the Antelope priests have taken station alongside the *kisi*, and they make quick circuits of the plaza and stamp on the *sipapu* (fig. VI:64). Then, no foolishness, they are ready. Their dance is done with precision. They have to be efficient. They move with a fast-stamping, no-nonsense step. They are dedicated to their work, as if they were doing it soberly for mankind as a whole (fig. VI:69). I saw none of the fear among any of them that was mentioned by some early observers. I do not know why they are not bitten. The snakes are

VI:63 Snake Dance. The snakes after being washed in the kiva, 1897. (*D. W. James, Collections in the Museum of New Mexico*)

VI:64 Snake Dance. Walpi, 1899. The Snake priests are circling the plaza and stamping on the *sipapu*. (*H. S. Poley, Collections in the Museum of New Mexico*)

neither defanged nor milked of their venom, nor do the dancers take any antidote. I can understand why they might not be bitten while they are carrying the snake, because their partner distracts its attention with his eagle feathers[43] (figs. VI:68, 69), but I cannot understand why somebody is not bitten when the snakes are finally all thrown together in a pile (figs. VI:71, 72) and smothered with cornmeal by the women (who dump it on them very gingerly and from as far away as possible), and are then grabbed up in blind handfuls by the dancers who rush with them out of the plaza to return them to the four directions in the desert below (figs. VI:73, 74). I cannot understand why nobody seems to be bitten in the kivas, where some of the snakes are kept for as long as nine days, others for only one, and are herded back against the wall, we are told, by laughing kids with bare feet (fig. VI:63). Most of all, there is a ceremony when the snakes are released in the kiva, the men sitting chanting with their eyes closed, while the serpents in their multitude react to the sound like wheat in the wind and climb in the men's laps and look into their faces and—this well attested[44]—coil in the laps of those with open hearts who have grown beyond human hate and fear. And sleep there. It has to be, somehow, after all pseudoscientific, mechanical explanations are shown to be incorrect, that the fact of the matter is precisely that question of fear and its companion hate, and their evil odor. Without it there is nothing to strike at, just plenty of mutual respect among the brothers in the clan. That is a minor point of the dance.

The major point is rain. Here the nature of the sympathetic magic seems obvious. We know from pueblo paintings and petroglyphs of all periods that snakes are associated with lightning and with the descending rain itself. They also penetrate the earth and seek out its springs. But there is a part of the dance which has not been stressed enough in this connection. That is: after the snake carrier has been given his snake out of the leafy *kisi*, and has stamped out his circuit of the plaza with it lifting its (birdlike, catlike) head against his cheek, or whipping around his ears, or just hanging lethargically like a hose, he sets it down, and it is normally allowed to wriggle around in the plaza for quite a while. It is under constant observation from the third member of the team, the gather-upper, but he usually lets it squirm around as it may over as wide an area as possible (fig. VI:70). I saw them let whip snakes get in among the crowd. They are more careful with rattlers, but the principle is the same. And a glance out across the lower slopes of the mesas from the rooftop (a good place to be, in my opinion) can show us what that principle is. The snakes are making the same squirming pattern in the dust that the washes take as they wriggle out and away into the plain. Rain is being brought to the plaza in this way.

Another point that seemed clear to me in this dance is what the feathered serpent, Quetzalcoatl, was: namely wholeness, completeness, a being in touch with each end of reality. Mexicanoid gods with tendril-like snakes in their mouths guard the Reviewing Stand at Classic Mayan Copán, and Quetzalcoatl is a feathered serpent (fig. I:4), and it is the horned and feathered water serpent that the Anasazi so often pecked and painted on the rock (figs. IV:21, 22). It is precisely that being, Avanyu or, in Hopi, Palulukang, that the snake priests, like the buffalo dancers, wear writhing heavily upon their kilts[45] (figs. III:74; VI:66, 68, 69, 73). It is the combination of snake, deep-delving, and bird, high-flying, that counts. So the macaw, sold out of Casas Grandes, is sacred, and of all snakes the diamondback. This rattler has large, feathered, highly articulated scales, and the macaw short, stubby, scaly feathers. The proportions are almost the same, and the scaly, feathery units of both animals mesh and overlap like the same coat of mail. All of that is there in the dance in even grander form. The hero-buffalo had done part of it, standing up to his fate on two legs with the snake on his kilt and the feathers on his horns. Now it is men's turn. Now it is they who must become the conductors of force between earth and heaven. Now they lift the snakes to their mouths; they don't do it to show courage; they do it to raise the snake to where he never

VI:65 Mishongnovi. Snake Dance. The Antelope priests alongside the *kisi* are facing the Snake priests. Altar left. (*Ben Wittick, Collections in the Museum of New Mexico*)

VI:66 Snake Dance. Mishongnovi, 1911. Chanting at the *kisi*. (*H. F. Robinson, Collections in the Museum of New Mexico*)

is, into the air like a bird: ". . . upon thy belly shalt thou go, and dust shalt thou eat all the days of thy life."[46] They lift him intimately out of the dust. And before his face they hold not macaw but eagle feathers, the most high flying there are, showing them to him. And when he is dropped down in the dirt of the plaza and perhaps loses his head and is filled with his own accustomed fear once more and tries to coil, it is with a bird's feathers that the handler strokes him across the back so that he straightens out and can be picked up once again and handled most casually, his head swinging loose sometimes by a handler's thigh. Why not, since he has been touched with wholeness and has forgotten his fear. Not accursed—"And I will put enmity between thee and the woman, and between thy seed and her seed; it shall bruise thy head, and thou shalt bruise his heel"[47]—not cursed, but blessed, and touched with liberty and glory.

Can this be why it rains then—always, they say; it is that time of year. Still the clouds do come up released and churning, with the rain sometimes really blasting and the washes running and all the poor snakes, now back in their holes, getting washed along with it, you think, and then here they come again in their other persona, knifing through the clouds (fig. VI:75), the rainbow.

VI:67 Oraibi. Snake Dance in 1898. Chanting and invoking the forces underground at the *kisi*. (*Ben Wittick, Collections in the Museum of New Mexico*)

VI:68 Snake Dance. Mishongnovi, c. 1910. The carriers have the snakes in their mouths and are making the circuit assisted by their companion with the eagle-feathered wand. Note the horned and feathered water serpent, Avanyu (Palulukang), on their kilts. (*H. F. Robinson, Collections in the Museum of New Mexico*)

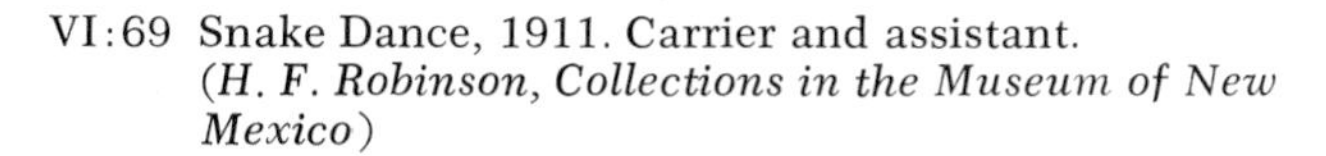

VI:69 Snake Dance, 1911. Carrier and assistant. (*H. F. Robinson, Collections in the Museum of New Mexico*)

VI:70 Walpi. Snake Dance. The snakes are crawling in the plaza under the eye of the gather-upper. Note the washes in the desert. (*Ben Wittick, Collections in the Museum of New Mexico*)

VI:71 Oraibi. Snake Dance, 1896. The Snake and Antelope priests are throwing the snakes by handfuls into the cornmeal circle. (*F. H. Maude, Collections in the Museum of New Mexico*)

VI:72 Oraibi (?). The snakes in the circle about to be grabbed and returned to the desert. (*Collections in the Museum of New Mexico*)

VI:73 Releasing snakes, 1911. (*H. F. Robinson, Collections in the Museum of New Mexico*)

VI:74 The Great Bull Snake, 1911. (*H. F. Robinson, Collections in the Museum of New Mexico*)

VI:75 After the Snake Dance, 1969. The Rainb

VII:1 The Sierra Blanca of the Mescalero Apache. View from the north.

VII

EPILOGUE: THE PUBERTY CEREMONY OF THE MESCALERO

Men are to women as that little star is to that big moon.

—BERNARD SECOND, PRESIDENT OF THE NATIONAL INDIAN YOUTH COUNCIL AND PRIEST OF THE MESCALERO APACHE

We have our sacred mountain too.

—Donni Torres, Mescalero girl

The central ceremony of Mescalero Apache life celebrates the coming of age of their girls. In another ceremony, their Gahan, or Mountain Spirits, Dance, masked beings who live in the caverns of the sacred mountain come forth in power for the healing of the tribe. The two ceremonies have apparently never had any serious or necessary ritual connection with each other.[1] Now, however, they have been woven by the Mescaleros into a single enormous work of art, one that can stand up to (and in fine contrast with) the great achievements of the Pueblos, such as Santo Domingo's animal dance in February and its massed corn dance in August, and Zuni's Shalako in December and the home dance of the Hopi kachinas in late July. It is one of the noble creations of this hemisphere, and an Apache victory over everything: poverty and suicidal drunkenness, military defeat and loss of freedom most of all.

The latter is symbolized by the Fourth of July date (July 2–5 in 1970 and 1971), when the U.S. government allows the ceremonies to take place. Yet that restriction has been turned into an advantage by the Mescaleros, who took it as an opportunity to syncretize the two rituals into one intrinsic form. They also run a rodeo and put on distressing pan-Indian "war dances" in the afternoons to catch every element of the Fourth of July tourist trade. None of this touches the great nighttime ceremonies themselves, which come out pure and strong despite the degrading public-address system, the bleachers, and the white visitors—who are enjoined to leave "quietly" at midnight and are not allowed to take pictures or to record the songs, though the Apaches avidly photograph and record the ceremony themselves.

Credit for this fundamental cultural achievement—this act of growth and liberation, in which ancient ritual becomes consciously expressive modern art without loss of force or sanctity—must go to the rising generation of young Mescaleros and especially to such scholars and teachers as Bernard Second, whose activism is cultural and whose powers as a shaman, if this is indeed what he should be called, are doubly based upon ancient tradition and a new kind of intellectual conviction.

From the Pueblo haven of the upper Rio Grande one approaches the Mescaleros past the old Piro towns and missions—Quaraí, Abó, Gran Quivira and the rest, which were harassed to abandonment by the Comanches and the Apaches themselves (figs. I:1; V:16–19). On this tragic route one's first awareness of the intrusive Athapaskan Mescaleros is of their sacred home mountain, the Sierra Blanca, rising rather ominously southward above the bloody Lincoln County plain (fig. VII:1). It is still a fortress of its once predatory people, and it lifts out of the burning White Sands on the west to a Canadian climate at its summit (fig. VII:2). In winter it is a notched white cone. Its looming presence is well experienced from the prehistoric site of Three Rivers, whose serrated ridge wriggles fatly across the plain like a feathered serpent itself, its projecting stony scales pecked with hundreds of petroglyphs[2] (figs. VII:3, 4). But the

VII:2 The Sierra Blanca. The summit from the southeast.

VII:3 Three Rivers. The rock-spined ridge in the plain before the Sierra Blanca.

major entrance to the Sierra Blanca is from farther south, near Tularosa, through a pass all female in its landscape forms. Here, beside U.S. 70, an almost perfectly conical hill, the famous Round Mountain, marks the entrance (fig. VII:5). Beyond it the road curves on up the mountain until another strikingly conical hill seems to close the way ahead (fig. VII:6). It marks the place where the deep body of the Sierra opens to the upper passes, and it defines the site of the major settlement, the government agency, and the present tribal headquarters of the Mescalero. Directly under the cone, alongside the road, the puberty ceremony was traditionally held—or was at least held there when the ceremony was first permitted again under government auspices. Now it has moved up away from the road to an artificially leveled terrace on the slope. Above and below it, during festival time, spreads a temporary encampment of tepees and

VII:4 Three Rivers. The Sierra Blanca from the ridge. Petroglyphs in foreground.

VII:5 Round Mountain in the pass below and west of Mescalero. (*Photo by Gene Aiken: Courtesy of Schaaf Postcard Co.*)

VII:6 The Conical Hill above Mescalero from the west, seen along the main street.

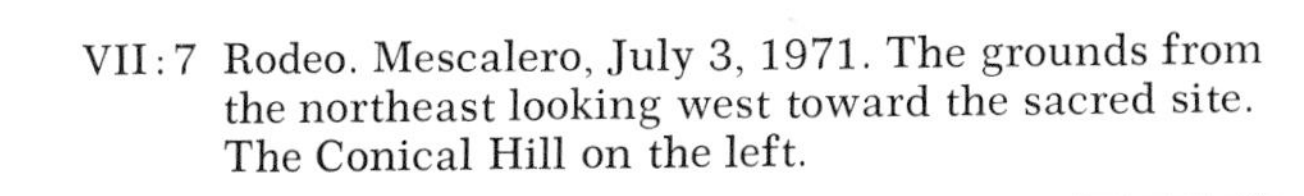

VII:7 Rodeo. Mescalero, July 3, 1971. The grounds from the northeast looking west toward the sacred site. The Conical Hill on the left.

VII:8 The encampment and the Conical Hill from the north. Ceremonial terrace below, with sacred tepee far right. July 1970.

wickiups, with horses, pickups, and sedans parked among them. The rodeo takes place on a higher terrace to the east (fig. VII:7).

Though a Plains Indian specialty—if not in its basic conical form his invention[3]—the tepee is an especially beautiful form in the mountains, and the contemporary Mescalero, with their rather romantic desire to stress the Plains part of their background, much prefer it to the more southwestern wickiup (figs. VII:8, 9). It stands up like a man, and its cone can also be sacred, as the squashed-looking brush wickiup apparently cannot be. So the natural cone in the pass dominates the site, signifies its character, and sets the shape of its major ceremony (fig. VII:10).

The axis of the terrace runs generally east and west and is defined on the south by a long, boughy wickiup with communal cooking fires and with tepees for the participating families behind it (figs. VII:11–13). The big tepee stands at the west end of the terrace, its opening facing east. It is a cone of Douglas fir saplings perhaps thirty feet high with the crowns left on. These lodge poles are thinly thatched with boughs and with a largely symbolic shawl of canvas wrapped around near their tie. The form exactly echoes that of the conical hill across the valley. A fire burns within it, and a funnel of evergreens, stuck in the ground like Christmas trees, opens from it to eastward. The keyhole kivas of Anasazi prehistory are archetypally recalled (fig. I:31). The fire pit occupies the center of the tepee and is flanked by buckskin mats for the maidens to dance on. Four male singers sit on chairs at the east side facing the girls, each of whom is attended by an older woman who sits on the ground. Other members of the family—old men, a child or two—are occasionally present. People are permitted to crowd up behind the singers and watch. The girls dance intermittently through the night. They make a simple herringbone pattern keeping the knees and feet together, moving back and forth laterally on the mat, their clenched hands held up and out at ear level. They are dressed in golden buckskin, their long hair unloosed, a couple of eagle feathers attached at the crown and hanging down

VII:9 Wickiup in the encampment.

VII:10 Ceremonial terrace from the northwest. Sacred tepee center.

VII:11 The Ceremonial Plaza from the west. Sacred tepee center, bleachers left. Large wickiup with communal fires and related tepees right.

VII:12 Tepee in 1939. Note that it was much more regularly constructed in 1970, 1971. (*Bertha Dutton*)

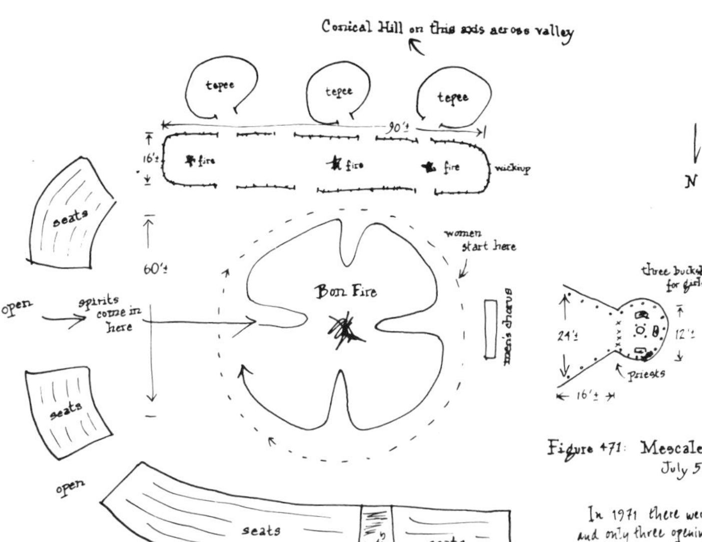

VII:13 Sketch plan of plaza. (*Drawing by Melanie Simo*)

behind. Twelve to fourteen years old, they are just coming into womanhood, and their dance is innocently sexual, a constant, gentle, liquid squirm. The body is the spirit here, as pure as good water (figs. VII:19–21).

Outside, the energy seems at first all male, and it is spiritual as well. The mountain spirits start coming in after sundown. They bless the big bonfire in the middle of the plaza at about eight in the evening, and the main dance begins about an hour later. In the afternoon a party of three dancers, a clown, and two drummers had already blessed the tepee.

Everything really begins just at nightfall, as the moon begins to rise toward Venus in the northwest. The sky is still dark blue and the hills already black. The great tepee sits quietly with its own small fire red within it. As the first spirits come in from the east, emerging, so they say, from their mountain cavern home, they move straight toward the still glowing west and seem to be blessing that direction and the new night. Each group is made up of four spirits, embodiments of the four directions, with a sacred clown (fig. VII:14). One clown is a little eagle, the others rather goatlike eared creatures in coal-scuttle-shaped masks and painted a more or less ashy gray. In this they strongly resemble the ominous Rivermen clowns of Keresan Cochití.[4] But their character here seems much more simpleminded and good-hearted; they frisk and skip about in a playful complement to the spirits' aggressive movements. They appear bemused, fey, perhaps a little mad from their dalliance with the spirit realm. The mountain spirits are painted black, with crosses and other shapes very bold in white on their backs, chests, and arms. They wear black hoods with vast, abstracted tree or antler shapes of slatted Spanish Bayonet (yucca) rising from their heads. Sticks of the same material are held like swords in each hand, and are striped like the arms that wield them with white snake or lightning shapes. Running in, lifting their sticks, dancing with a leaping, rocking, side-to-side step—knees cocked, arms way out, headdresses twirling and clattering—the spirits bless, or greet, the fire (figs. VII:14, 15).

Eventually three such groups are all moving in a quick, shuffling run clockwise around the fire, and about fifteen singers, young and old men alike in their normal work clothes, bunch in two rows in front of the tepee, facing out toward the spirits and toward the blaze of huge cedar trunks now roaring in the middle of the plaza. The chorus begins to sing; at that moment the nearest group of spirits to the south stops. Its leader expresses surprise, consternation, amazement; he postures, sticks out his backside, points to the singers, gestures back to his group as if conferring with them. Then all point with their sticks and their dance begins: a brag, a swaggering march, more or less aimed at the singers. The dancers go fast and wild, bent over, stamping, rearing up, shoulders back, sticks crossed in front, sticks up and out in that wide V toward the fire (figs. VII:15, 16). Splendid swordplay takes place with the two sticks, with more stamping and clacking, while the upper body moves forward and back with an articulated shoulder rhythm which recalls that of West Africa. This counterrhythm between shoulders and rump is unique in America, I think. Indian dancers (not always the buffalo) normally keep the upper body straight and the shoulders still. All the forms of this dance are open, gesticulative, released from constraint. Though wilder and freer than men, the spirits are enormously goodnatured, without aggressive hang-ups. There is challenge but no real threat, only pure energy celebrated in reckless force. Magnificently silhouetted against the fire, and with a fiery energy far from the liquidity of the girls, the spirits leap, squat, and bound, all jagged edges. Finally the song stops and they start running around the fire again in their flatfooted, slightly bent-kneed shuffle. Then it all starts up again.

Soon, groups of women and girls begin a circular dance which moves clockwise too, around the leaping figures between them and the fire. An ancient woman seemed to start it tonight. Another, face alight, danced out with the spirits pretty much in their step. The younger women do not enter the spirits' terrain. They dance a proud sort of show-off step: legs stiff, feet moving forward and back so as to make the whole body strut, heads high, backs very straight, even leaning back a little, wrapped tight in a blanket. They are

VII:14 Part of a team of Mescalero Mountain Spirit, Gahan, Dancers. The clown is concealed and only three dancers are shown, hence not the sacred four directions. (*New Mexico Department of Development*)

VII:15 Gahan Dancer (these accoutrements are of a Western Apache type). (*Bertha Dutton*)

all magnificent, not least the older, fat ones, looking in their nineteenth-century dresses like so many cabbages—but absolutely themselves, fulfilled, belonging, honored and very beautiful. Most have the classic Apache faces, broad and round, with full cheeks and strong chins and noses. Most beautiful of all are some noble young matrons of a Roman splendor: heads high, leaning back, proud. Some of their men are probably dancing as spirits inside their ring—all that open, loose-knit, free and leaping energy inside *their* ring. The dance is, in the end, their triumph, and their circle is lifted in elevation beyond the mountain cone to the circle of their moon with its dependent star (fig. VII:17).

Later a fourth group of spirits runs in almost silently from the east. All the spirits come from the east, while the women all start up just south of the singers. The clown may have a sheep bell. But it is the singers who make the noise, and plenty of it, beating with sticks on a piece of cardboard laid flat on the ground, or the next night on drums and pots with skin covers—and whooping it up as the night goes on, challenging and egging on the spirits with war cries and deep-voiced grunts and roars. One can imagine how they must have loved those raids in the old days and slapped each other on the back and laughed till their bellies shook as the captives danced with them through the night, to be dispatched by widowed

VII:16 Gahan Dancers and Clown. Mescalero, c. 1889. Bows and arrows are not usually carried in this dance. (*Smithsonian Institution*)

women in the morning.[5] And in the intervals when no spirits are present, the song seems redirected to the women, strong, proud too, and full of praise.

It seems to me that the dance as a whole marvelously integrates Plains Indian and Pueblo elements. One would guess at a kachina background learned from the Pueblos but modified to suit Apache ways and Athapaskan shamanistic traditions. The Pueblo dances are normally closed-ranked, in step, disciplined like a phalanx (though the great animal dances are somewhat different, as we have seen, as are the antics of the clowns). But every Pueblo kachina dance—every masked dance, that is—forms a solid line with a coil rippling through it as the dancers turn close back to front, while the Apache dance is all open, wide spaced, emphasizing the posturing of individuals. They come on in file like Hopis, but running, and then they break up into their individually heroic, if richly reciprocative, routines.[6] And the whole is encircled by a Plains round dance, whose social function now takes on a more intensely symbolic focus, as it had done in the ghost dance during those sad years now long ago. It is the ultimate labyrinth, the coil never-ending (fig. VII:17). The costume too is a kachina mask costume, developed from a fundamentally closed to a fundamentally open form. Kachina costumes, even if feathered and wide horned, are all essentially tight packed, plastically

VII:17 "Mountain Spirits Dance," oil on canvas board, 1964, *by Cain Hastings, Western Apache.*

rounded off, close profiled, as is their wearers' bent-and-straight-kneed step. But here everything is out in space and skeletally articulated, recalling Plains Indian costume (so apparent in the Sioux Museum at St. Francis on the Rosebud), where horns spring from the head or hang off the shoulder, feathers stick out, and so on. Here at least two ways of dressing, of dancing, of composing movement, are brought together in an especially striking form.

So the singers shout through the long night, the spirits leap, the fire roars, and clouds sparks sail upward. But the instant of revelation has to be when the file of proudly prancing, backward-leaning women weave their circle between the singers and the spirits, moving between them, tight wrapped and desirable, showing off before the males and enveloping the spirit world with their bodies. Hence the step of the much older women is different, and appropriate to their build: a kind of earthly roll, ponderous, grand and enduring. It is a female version of the spirits' side-to-side prance, through which the old women indeed approach the spirits; old, they have conquered life and move toward the rhythm of the natural world.

All the time, behind the singers, the girls' dance is going on in the tepee, the heart of the rite. Out of them the power comes. Protected but not secret it is open for all who care to take the trouble to come down from the grandstand to see it—looking over the heads of the priests into the body of a sweetness beyond words.

While one is doing so, odds are that an aging man with a broad, seamed, brown face, just down from the high ranges, will come up and gently say, "Hello, gentleman, I was Second Armored," or, "Where you from? Connecticut a long way. Tell them we not bad people here," and another, "We Mescalero no trouble, no Geronimo here." Apologizing to us! Only one man waved to me smiling and said, "Hey, you don't belong here" and then laughed for pure joy. But a note on culture shift: the next year an elderly Apache said, "We Geronimo, you know," to a couple of students, who replied, "Gee, wow."

The second night, after the mountain spirit dance had been going on for perhaps an hour or more, I saw the beginning of the girls' ritual. They do not fast, but they were already very tired. A priest with a rattle (Bernard Second) talked at some length with each girl and her attendant old lady. Then he gave each of them a drink of water and poured a libation from it near the fire. He and the three other priests then began to sing softly. There seemed to be two songs with repetitive phrasing and a gentle tone. Each of the girls danced and rested according to her own pattern of endurance. They varied in grace—one I thought rather awkward, the other two graceful, one of them very beautiful. In the firelight they all look like princesses. They dance within the lightly thatched cone, its poles leaping up to their green crown; overhead the stars wheel and the smoke from the great fire in the plaza blows across them. The high jagged tops of the spirit headdresses can be seen leaping against the blaze behind the singers and the crowd of watchers. Out there the male song, not so different from that of the girls in structure, is roaring and yelling to the fine ki-yis and the drums; but here in the tepee the sense is of something deeper, germinal. Here in this circular, conical place the essential force is being brought forth, growing out of these soft, young, dancing bodies to the sibilance of the rattle and the low-voiced song. It moves out through the funnel of evergreens to envelop the singers and the spirits and the circling women and even the conical hill—moving out to make everything possible through the miracle of life. That is the girls' gift to their tribe.

A year later I was in time to watch the tepee being raised. They began at about seven in the morning and finished in an hour or so.[7] Before that a girl in a yellow shawl (not one of the puberty girls) had been standing facing the old filled-up fire pit for some time while the priest (young, Talmudic, long hair behind, tall hat, the same priest as last year) fussed about among his relaxed companions like the only man in Philadelphia who doesn't read the *Enquirer*. But he is much older, heavier and stronger than last year; that can be seen at once. He has gained power. Finally his crew slowly assembled in the usual, wonderfully casual Indian way. He and they laid out the tepee's twelve slender firs radially from the old fire pit (figs. VII: 11–13). Then a rope compass was made and a circle scratched on the ground. Then the fire pit was deepened a little, and shallow butt holes were opened for the poles. People were slowly gathering. Eventually, the priest faced them and blessed and anointed them with pollen in his right hand. Then three other priests did the same. Next they in turn blessed the poles with pollen—the first, *fifth*, eighth and twelfth poles, and on some of them tied an evergreen bundle near the top. When everything was ready they stood in line facing the fire pit and sang the same gentle song as last year. Then men gathered at the first, *fourth*, eighth and twelfth poles. Then, singing, they raised up number one, with a hanging rope tied in under its topknot of green; then the eighth, then four and twelve: all held up straight like spears in the singing. Next they leaned the first and eighth poles against each other while a man circled with the rope, firmly lashing them together. He skipped around like a goat over obstacles, flicking the rope to clear knots and so on. Then the fourth and twelfth poles were raised and lashed. Finally the others; the lashing went on; now a boy climbed and tied a good knot at the top. It was marvelous to see the man-made shape rising against the hill, the basket cone of the tepee before the solid cone of the mountain. Then the canvas wrap, like a blanket around a maiden, was flung around the shoulders of the tepee under its nodding head of green boughs. A young man climbed up for that too. The agility and utter competence on everyone's part was in striking contrast to the shuffling about, the grinning, and the horseplay that had gone on beforehand—a very Indian contrast, perhaps an especially Apache one. They are so deprecatingly ironic most of the time that one forgets how frighteningly savvy they really are. Next they began to weave leafy boughs horizontally between the poles and to set up the four evergreen trees on a diagonal at each side of the eastern opening. Then they wove vertical cuttings into tepee and funnel-fence of trees alike. At last they piled up vertical boughs, especially thickly around the tepee (more than last year), until the naked poles near the top emerged delicately out of the green cone. Finally they dug out the fire pit and brought up the benches. Now all was complete: a mantled bower, a conical volume opening to the eastern sun, the quickener of the earth's cones, father of all. Indeed, I forgot to say that two of the maidens in their light buckskin, but now with yellow paint like sunlight across nose and cheeks, were present during the raising of the tepee. That, too, was now a sacred form, one with the mountain but a sloping-shouldered maiden too, a bride and an earth shape, blanketed and rich in boughs.

Then the priest spread out four blankets on the ground covering of rushes in the throat of the tepee. Four maidens with their sponsors came out and knelt behind the blankets facing east (figs. VII: 18–21). Then priests knelt in front of them and blessed them with pollen on face and head. The girls reciprocated with their families, most touchingly with tiny children whose hands the mothers reached out to the girls. (Perhaps they were painting each other, as they are reported to do, but I saw no marks.) Then the girls were laid out for a few minutes, full-length and face-down on their blankets. Next a young man placed a basket with evergreen in it perhaps thirty yards to the east—defining the east-west axis firmly. The girls raced one after the other to it, walked around it, and ran back, buckskin fringes flying, little bells jingling on their skirts. The boy then moved it closer three more times, and the girls ran again (first time hardest, rest easier: the stages of life, one supposes).

Then the girls, directed by the old women, were made to shake out their blankets energetically, after which two of them left. Over the other two, with richer families perhaps, or for some other reason I do not know, cartons of small candies in bright wrappers were poured like floods of jewels. Kids raced in to get them. Then, from the shelter, people began throwing candy, oranges, boxes of crackerjacks. And all the

Apaches and a few white kids stampeded to pick them up. Then it began to rain—in general a cold, damp morning. The rising sun did not touch the girls today. But it was out there in everything that was done, its presence invoked always.

The ultimate effect was to define the man-made space and the human presence in relation to the natural world. Such was built into the tepee and acted out in the race—each putting the human stamp on the earth's face, fixing the cardinal points, and charting out the special area which was to be the ceremony's major terrain. So human measure framed human action on the flattened earth surface and in relation to the mountain shapes and the sky. It was the full glory of the act of building, of the process itself and its result: all of it praising in the end life, earth, and sun, merging men and the rest of creation in one calm form.

European architecture has come to explore multiple themes, many of them having to do with the victorious exercise of human energy and wit, dominating the world. A glorious architecture, yes, and counting many victories, but now clearly required by mortal necessity to exhibit a renewed reverence for nature's realities and to explore ways for decent interaction with the earth and its forces in the crowded years to come. Not least with the force in the sun. North American Indian architecture, on the other hand, whether because its builders are less "developed," less powerful, considerably wiser, or merely more practical than their conquerors, has for many centuries been concerned with nothing less than that cosmic theme: celebrating a vast human and natural concordance, oneness, and peace—the same for relentless Apache raiders as for the farmers of the pueblos. Perhaps, especially in the case of the Pueblos, this is so in part because they have seen it all before: the failure of resources, the desolation of the earth, the death of the proud towns—and then their patient, humble, indomitable resurrections. But the tepee is impermanent, the home and symbol of people always on the move. So at sunrise on the last day at Mescalero the process is carried out in reverse. The girls are brides of the morning for the last time; the tepee is dismantled and the whole order disappears.

VII:18 Cibecue, Arizona. Western Apache site of dawn puberty ceremony. This and the following photographs taken at Cibecue of the Western Apache NAI'ES ceremony are included here because of the Mescalero prohibition of photography within the ceremonial grounds.

VII:19 Cibecue. The two girls with singers. The sun has just risen.

VII:20 Cibecue. The girls dance with their presents.
Others begin to join them.

VII:21 Cibecue. The sun touches the girls and the ground before them fills with dancers.

NOTES: SOURCES, CRITICAL BIBLIOGRAPHY, METHODS, COMMENTARY

PREFACE

1. The prehistoric architecture of the Southwest has been more extensively published than historic Pueblo. Its broadest chronological designations in the area under consideration here have generally been: Early Basketmaker (c. A.D. 1–450); Modified Basketmaker (450–750); Developmental Pueblo (750–1100); Great, or Classic, Pueblo (1100–1300); Regressive Pueblo thereafter. Written history began with the coming of the Spaniards in the sixteenth century. Cf. Alfred Vincent Kidder, *An Introduction to the Study of Southwestern Archaeology* (New Haven, 1924; rev. ed., with a summary of southwestern archaeology today by Irving Rouse, 1962); H. M. Wormington, *Prehistoric Indians of the Southwest* (Denver, 1961); Gordon Willey, *An Introduction to American Archaeology*, Vol. 1, *North and Middle America* (Englewood Cliffs, N.J., 1966). For contemporary pueblos (but not primarily concerned with architecture): Edward P. Dozier, *The Pueblo Indians of North America* (New York, 1970). For Pueblo religion in general: Elsie C. Parsons, *Pueblo Indian Religion*, 2 vols. (Chicago, 1939). For the ceremonials and dances in general: John Collier, *Patterns and Ceremonials of the Indians of the Southwest* (New York, 1949); Virginia More Roediger, *Ceremonial Costumes of the Pueblo Indians* (Berkeley, 1961); Erna Fergusson, *Dancing Gods: Indian Ceremonials of New Mexico and Arizona* (Albuquerque, 1931); Frank Waters, *Masked Gods: Navaho and Pueblo Ceremonialism* (Denver, 1950); idem, *Book of the Hopi* (New York, 1963); also B. and M. G. Evans, *American Indian Dance Steps* (New York, 1931). Other studies of Tiwa, Tewa, Keres, Zuni, and Hopi dances, as well as those of the Navaho and the Apache, are referred to later. George Peter Murdoc , *Ethnographic Bibliography of North America*, 3rd ed. (New Haven, 1960), is always of use, as is Edward S. Curtis, *The American Indian*, 20 vols., ed. Frederick Webb Hodge (Cambridge, Mass., 1907–1930). One thinks, in conclusion, of historical essays such as Edgar L. Hewett, *Ancient Life in the*

American Southwest (Indianapolis, 1930), in which, speaking of the dance (p. 135), one of the themes of this book is clearly stated: "The basic art of all groups of the native American race, so far as I know, is the drama. Their finest achievements in architecture . . . are emanations of the drama, and the drama is the expression of their religion."

2. Stanley A. Stubbs, *Bird's-Eye View of the Pueblos* (Norman, Okla., 1950). This contains an aerial photograph and a plan drawn from it of every existing pueblo with the exception of Hopi Hotevilla and Bacavi. The School of American Research is now preparing a new set of photographs and plans to bring this essential work up to date. I will occasionally refer to changes since Stubbs's time, but such are not normally essential to this study.
3. For Hohokam, Mogollon, Patayan, and Sinagua archaeology, which is not treated here: Wormington, pp. 108–69; also John C. McGregor, *Southwestern Archaeology*, 2nd ed. (Urbana, Ill., 1965).
4. Vincent Scully, *The Earth, the Temple, and the Gods: Greek Sacred Architecture* (New Haven, 1962; rev. ed., New York, 1969).
5. Walter W. Taylor, *A Study of Archaeology*, (Carbondale, Ill., 1967).
6. See Dan Budnik, "Black Mesa: Progress Report on an Ecological Rape," *Art in America*, 60 (July–Aug. 1972), pp. 98–105. It now looks as if the entire Southwest, as we know it, may be poisoned and polluted out of existence unless the strip mining and its attendant power plants can be eliminated or controlled. If the present and projected plants—which are, cruelly enough, intended to power the toasters and televisions of the far-off Phoenix, Tucson, Los Angeles, and Las Vegas urban agglomerations—were forced to burn the natural gas which abounds in the region instead of the strip-mined coal, many of the problems would be solved. It would cost them only a little more to do so and would hardly affect their astonishing profits.

I. MEN AND NATURE—PREHISTORY AND THE PRESENT

1. Clark Wissler, *The Relation of Nature to Man in Aboriginal America* (New York, 1926), suggestively titled in this connection, is in fact a study of geographical distribution.
2. Vincent Scully, *The Earth, the Temple, and the Gods*, rev. ed. (New York, 1969), see esp. pp. 41–69, 169–85.
3. These and all ensuing references to Whorf are to his "Linguistic Factors in the Terminology of Hopi Architecture," *International Journal of American Linguistics*, 19 (1953), pp. 141–45; reprinted in *Language, Thought, and Reality: Selected Writings of Benjamin Lee Whorf*, ed. with an intro. by John B. Carroll (Cambridge, Mass., 1956).
4. Victor Mindeleff, "A Study of Pueblo Architecture: Tusayan and Cibola," in the *Eighth Annual Report of the Bureau of American Ethnology, 1886–87* (Washington, 1891), pp. 3–228. Report on Hopi nomenclature by A. M. Stephen, pp. 220–23. There are a few differences between Stephen's and Whorf's transcriptions and interpretations but no critical discrepancies. Nor have subsequent linguistic studies affected this issue. Cf. Clyde Kluckhohn and Kenneth MacLeish, "Moencopi Variations from Whorf's Second Mesa Hopi," *International Journal of American Linguistics*, 21 (1955), pp. 150–56.
5. In the equation of magic with science, one thinks especially of the work of Claude Lévi-Strauss (*La Pensée Sauvage* [Paris, 1962], trans. *The Savage Mind* [Chicago, 1966]), who has also insisted upon the instinct toward complex, "non-natural" formal constructions, as in kinship patterns, body ornament, and mythology. See also his *Structural Anthropology* (New York, 1963) and *The Raw and the Cooked: Introduction to a Science of Mythology* (New York, 1969). The linking of these sometimes contradictory elements of desired function and imagined shape, recognizing as it does the complex relationships

between meaning and form in the making and the experience of human art, can hardly be unfamiliar or unsympathetic to art historians, whether of a morphological (Henri Focillon, *La Vie des Formes* [Paris, 1934; 2nd ed., 1939], trans. *The Life of Forms in Art*, rev. ed. [New York, 1948]) or an iconological (Erwin Panofsky, *Studies in Iconology: Humanistic Themes in the Art of the Renaissance* [New York, 1939] and *Meaning in the Visual Arts* [Garden City, N.Y., 1955]) bent. In point of fact, the physical form eventually becomes the meaning in any work of art, since it must in varying degrees embody and symbolize the meaning, which otherwise is literally not there. (Cf. my "The Nature of the Classical in Art," *Yale French Studies*, 19–20 [1958], pp. 107–24.) A dance, for example, is as it is performed, not as it was intended or projected: hence the insistence in all magical ritual upon perfect performance. The instinctive feeling, very strong among the Pueblos, and realistically so in view of the way art seems to work, is that intentions are important but not enough. They can neither explain the work of art nor substitute for it, since it generates meaning far beyond theirs. Only the formed work possesses the magical power that moves men and the gods. Iconographers, especially, would do well to remember this.

6. For Chaco in general: Edgar L. Hewett, *The Canyon and Its Monuments* (Albuquerque, 1936). There have since been some excellent specialized publications, but Hewett's brilliant study, with many plans and restoration drawings, remains the best general account.
7. Knossos, Phaistos, Mallia, Pylos, Tiryns, etc.: Scully, *The Earth*, figs. 2, 8, 13, 49, 55.
8. Later I note such at Taos, San Juan, Santa Clara, and Zuni.
9. For the Great Kivas and their development, with bibliography: Gordon Vivian and Paul Reiter, *The Great Kivas of Chaco Canyon and Their Relationships*, School of American Research Monograph 22 (Santa Fe, 1960). In the modern pueblos, the Hopis build kivas for clans, the Tewa and Keres for moieties, and the Tanoans when possible, as at Taos, for the six directions, though Taos also has a seventh for reasons peculiar to itself.
10. On these questions see especially R. Gwinn Vivian, "An Inquiry into Prehistoric Social Organization in Chaco Canyon, New Mexico," in William A. Longacre, ed., *Reconstructing Prehistoric Pueblo Societies* (Albuquerque, 1970), pp. 59–83. Some of the channeled tracks identified as canals may in fact have been narrow ceremonial roadways—or footraceways—stretching out across the mesa top.
11. Robert H. Lister, *Site 1086, An Isolated, Above-Ground Kiva in Mesa Verde National Park Colorado*, Contributions to Mesa Verde Archaeology, 4 (Boulder, Colo., 1969).
12. Neil M. Judd, *Pueblo del Arroyo, Chaco Canyon, New Mexico*, Smithsonian Miscellaneous Collections, 138 (Washington, 1959), esp. fig. 49, pl. 51. Again, as in all the Chaco houses, the fundamental geometric order and symmetry are striking. The planning has nothing agglutinative about it; the whole is conceived at once as one shape.
13. R. G. Vivian, *The Hubbard Site and Other Tri-Walled Structures in New Mexico and Colorado* (Washington, 1959); E. H. Morris, *The House of the Great Kiva at the Aztec Ruin* (New York, 1921).
14. J. W. Fewkes brilliantly pursued all these relationships very early, as in his *Excavation and Repair of Sun Temple, Mesa Verde National Park* (Washington, 1916); "The Relation of Sun Temple . . . to Prehistoric Towers," *Journal of the Washington Academy of Science*, 6 (1916), pp. 212–21; *Prehistoric Villages, Castles, and Towers of Southwestern Colorado*, Bureau of American Ethnology Bulletin 70 (Washington, 1919); and "Hovenweep National Monument," *American Anthropologist*, 25, pp. 145–55. Also Paul S. Martin, Lawrence Roys, and Gerhardt von Bonin, *Lowry Ruin in Western Colorado*, Field Museum of Na-

tural History, Anthropological Series, 23 (Chicago, 1936). Ute Mountain is in view of the Great Kiva here as well. The most recent large survey of the Mesa Verde shows many more kiva and tower units along the rims: Alden C. Hayes, *The Archaeological Survey of Wetherill Mesa, Mesa Verde National Park, Colorado*, National Park Service Archeology Series, 7-A (Washington, 1964).

15. Here, with many other titles, the main publications are those of R. J. Fewkes, such as *Antiquities of the Mesa Verde: Spruce Tree House*, Bureau of American Ethnology Bulletin 41 (Washington, 1909) and *Cliff Palace*, Bureau of American Ethnology Bulletin 51 (Washington, 1911). I regret to say that in the first printing of a recent book of photographs of pueblo architecture, for which I wrote an introduction, two of the Mesa Verde ruins were somehow mislabeled: William Current and Vincent Scully, *Pueblo Architecture of the Southwest: A Photographic Essay* (Austin, 1971); fig. 34 should read "New Fire House"; fig. 35, "New Fire House and Fire Temple"; and fig. 37, "Oak Tree House."
16. See Ross Calvin, *Sky Determines: An Interpretation of the Southwest* (Albuquerque, 1965).
17. J. W. Fewkes, *Preliminary Report on a Visit to the Navaho National Monument*, Bureau of American Ethnology Bulletin 50 (Washington, 1911); Ralph L. Beals, G. W. Brainerd, and Watson Smith, *Archaeological Studies in Northeastern Arizona* (Berkeley, 1945). Also: Alfred Vincent Kidder, *An Introduction to the Study of Southwestern Archaeology* (New Haven, 1924; rev. ed., 1962); John C. McGregor, *Southwestern Archaeology*, 2nd ed. (Urbana, Ill., 1965); H. M. Wormington, *Prehistoric Indians of the Southwest* (Denver, 1961).
18. Vivian and Reiter, op. cit., pp. 106–107; for relevant publications by Emil W. Haury: ibid., p. 109. Byron Cummings, *Kinishba: A Prehistoric Pueblo of the Great Pueblo Period* (Tucson, 1940).
19. Alfonso Ortiz, *The Tewa World: Space, Time, Being, and Becoming in a Pueblo Society* (Chicago, 1969), esp. pp. 139–42. Ortiz includes an excellent working bibliography for the study of Pueblo ritual and cosmology.
20. John Peabody Harrington, "The Ethnogeography of the Tewa Indians," in the *Twenty-ninth Annual Report of the Bureau of American Ethnology, 1907–1908* (Washington, 1916), pp. 29–636. A staggering work of scholarship. The reference to the Truchas Peaks: p. 340. Harrington identified Lake Peak above Tesuque as the sacred mountain of the east for all the Tewa (p. 44), but Ortiz, noted above, now identifies the Truchas Peaks as at least San Juan's eastern mountain, to which the actual topographical relationships lend credence. For double-peaked, "horned" mountains in relation to sacred sites in Crete and Greece see Scully, *The Earth*, chaps. 2 and 3, and *passim*; for Mount Kerata above Eleusis (hence the "Gate of Horn"), see chap. 5.
21. Paul Horgan, *Great River: The Rio Grande in American History* (New York, 1954; rev. ed., 1960). Horgan writes sensitively of the Indian relation to nature and notes that the pueblos "looked like mesas" (rev. ed., pp. 29–30). Even without the corroborative linguistic material cited earlier, the intrinsic and essential relationship of modern pueblo and mountain is obvious enough. In the absence of such evidence, therefore, the art historian must have the confidence to explore meaning and intention through his analysis of the physical forms alone. They are, after all, the material in which he is presumed to have special competence and through which he is required to make his own special contribution to human perception.
22. For an aerial view and plan of Taos: Stanley A. Stubbs, *Bird's-Eye View of the Pueblos* (Norman, Okla., 1950), pp. 24–48.
23. J. B. Jackson, "Pueblo Architecture and Our Own," *Landscape*, 3 (Winter 1953–54), p. 11 ff., stresses the room unit and posits a "sacred room"

which the proliferation of other units is symbolically intended to protect. The legend of the deeply buried secret room is persistent; it is heard from Zuni to Taos, though there seems to be no clear physical evidence for it in prehistoric or (more difficult to explore) contemporary pueblos. From an art-historical point of view the development of the form of Pueblo architecture from its so-called Classic to its so-called Regressive period is in fact eerily Wölfflinian: from what he would have called a closed (classic) to an open (baroque) form, from a symmetrical to an asymmetrical, and so on. According to these categories, the north house at Taos, for example, could be contrasted with Pueblo Bonito or Aztec much as Wölfflin contrasts a Rubens with a Raphael (Heinrich Wölfflin, *Kunstgeschichtliche Grundbegriffe* [Munich, 1929], trans. *Principles of Art History: The Problem of the Development of Style in Later Art* [London, 1932]).

24. Kubler, in his standard history of New Mexican churches (George Kubler, *The Religious Architecture of New Mexico in the Colonial Period and Since the American Occupation* [Colorado Springs, 1940]) does not develop this theme. He does note the Indian tendency to "build in horizontal layers . . . following the lines of the landscape" (p. 132), and that façades in European (as distinct from Pueblo) towns "generally [have] well-developed towers of considerable height" (p. 140). He states, without specification, that parapet modulations are Hispanic and Colonial Mexican in derivation and form (p. 54). As they develop, however, they all too closely recall both the Pueblo sky-altar profile and that of the particular mountain to which they are related for those connections to be missed.

25. South of the Anasazi area there may be evidence of other types of connection. The towerlike adobe main building at the Hohokam site of Casa Grande on the Gila River in southern Arizona comes to mind as an example. Harold S. Gladwin, *Excavations at Casa Grande, Arizona*, Southwest Museum Paper no. 2, Los Angeles, California, 1928. Its walls are pierced to provide lines of sight along critical bearings, and it may have served at least in part as an astronomical observatory, ritually serving the cycles of its people's elaborately irrigated agricultural system. In this it recalls the so-called Caracól at Toltec Chichén Itzá in Yucatán—though the actual form of that monument, a tall cylinder rising up through a rectangular block, is more closely approached at Chetro Ketl. A connection has been suggested between rectangular Mexican ball courts and the more or less elliptical, shallowly excavated hollow enclosures with built-up sides and of varying sizes that have been found at Casa Grande and the neighboring Snaketown as well as at Wupatki under the San Francisco Peaks. If these did indeed serve a ceremonial ball game it was one that, so the shape of its "courts" suggests, must have been considerably modified from the Meso-American exemplar—made much gentler, more of a dance—and which that would seem to have escaped, perhaps even reversed the development, which had been from a sloping to a tenser, straight-sided form, of the Mayan-Toltec court itself. Cf. Gladwin, *Excavations at Snaketown: Comparisons and Theories*, Medallion Papers, no. 26, Gila Pueblo, Globe, Arizona, 1942. Also McGregor, op. cit., pp. 201–203, 271–72, 300.

26. Here the main archaeological work has been done by Charles di Peso, Director of the Amerind Foundation, Dragoon, Arizona. See his "Cultural Development in Northern Mexico," in *Aboriginal Cultural Development in Latin America: An Interpretative Review*, ed. B. J. Meggers and C. Evans, Smithsonian Miscellaneous Collections, 146 (Washington, 1963), pp. 1–16. Di Peso's monumental report of the foundation's excavations at Casas Grandes is now close to publication.

27. One cannot help remembering how Morgan focused on this point in the early days of archaeology: Lewis H. Morgan, *Houses and House-Life*

of the American Aborigines (Washington, 1881; republished, with an intro. by Paul Bohannan, Chicago, 1966). Recent related studies of some interest: Amos Rapoport, *House Form and Culture* (Englewood Cliffs, N.J., 1969); Douglas Fraser, *Village Planning in the Primitive World* (New York, 1969); Jorge Hardoy, *Urban Planning in Pre-Columbian America* (New York, 1969). The issues are no less real in terms of mass public housing in the twentieth century. The great Social-Democratic projects of Amsterdam and Vienna in the teens and twenties were ritual monuments no less than shelters. Cf. my *Modern Architecture*, new ed. (New York, 1974), pp. 53–55, figs. 163–65.

II: THE RIO GRANDE—TAOS AND PICURIS

1. John Peabody Harrington, "The Ethnogeography of the Tewa Indians," *Twenty-ninth Annual Report of the Bureau of American Ethnology, 1907–1908* (Washington, 1916), 29:83, pp. 513–14. And in general: E. L. Hewett, J. Henderson, and W. W. Robins, *The Physiography of the Rio Grande Valley, New Mexico, in Relation to Pueblo Culture*, Bureau of American Ethnology Bulletin 54, (Washington, 1913).
2. Harrington, p. 560.
3. Alfonso Ortiz, *The Tewa World: Space, Time, Being, and Becoming in a Pueblo Society* (Chicago, 1969), pp. 19, 140.
4. There is sometimes disagreement on these points; the sacred mountain of the east might now be Tsi'como or Pelado or some other in the Jemez range for example. With Navaho migration moving generally southwestward, the sacred mountains slowly change. Ruth M. Underhill, *The Navajos* (Norman, Okla., 1956), p. 19. James J. Hester, *Early Navaho Migrations and Acculturation in the Southwest*, Museum of New Mexico Papers in Anthropology, 6 (Santa Fe, 1962–1963). Laura Gilpin, *The Enduring Navaho* (Austin, 1968). For the pueblos: Edgar L. Hewett and Bertha P. Dutton, *The Pueblo Indian World* (Albuquerque, 1945).
5. Harrington, map 8, p. 172. In general: M. L. Miller, *Preliminary Study of the Pueblo of Taos* (Chicago, 1898); Elsie C. Parsons, *Taos Pueblo*, General Series in Anthropology, 2 (Menasha, Wis., 1936); idem, *Taos Tales*, Memoirs of the American Folk-Lore Society, 34 (Boston, 1940); Ruth M. Underhill, *First Penthouse Dwellers of America* (New York, 1938), pp. 131–54.
6. San Francisco at Ranchos de Taos: George Kubler, *The Religious Architecture of New Mexico in the Colonial Period and Since the American Occupation* (Colorado Springs, 1940), figs. 13, 83, 123. Frank Waters has characterized the façade of San Francisco as "wholly Spanish . . . open with European extroversion"; he feels the back to be "heavy, down-sinking, impenetrable [with] the secretiveness of the kiva" and senses influence from Taos pueblo in it (*New Mexico Quarterly*, Summer 1951, and in correspondence since). For Taos: Kubler, p. 126. For the old church of San Geronimo at Taos, now a ruin lying on the west edge of the pueblo: Kubler, pp. 113–14. Charles F. Lummis, *The Land of Poco Tiempo* (New York, 1928; facsimile ed., Albuquerque, 1966), has a beautiful photograph showing the gate to the modern church's courtyard echoing the sacred mountain (p. 271).
7. Frank Waters, *Masked Gods: Navaho and Pueblo Ceremonialism* (Denver, 1950), pp. 188–92; Erna Fergusson, *Dancing Gods: Indian Ceremonials of New Mexico and Arizona* (Albuquerque, 1931), pp. 36–40; F. M. Bailey, "Some Plays and Dances of the Taos Indians," *Natural History*, 24 (1924), pp. 85–95.
8. Herodotus, *The Histories*, book 4, chap. 79.
9. For the dog dance as the Pueblos perform it: Gertrude Prokosch Kurath and Antonio Garcia, *Music and Dance in the Tewa Pueblos* (Santa Fe, 1970), p. 237. For the Italic *devotus*: the splendidly blood-curdling article by Louise Adam Holland, "The Purpose of the Warrior Image from

Capistrano," *American Journal of Archaeology*, 60 (1956), pp. 243–47.

10. See Hubert Howe Bancroft, *A History of Arizona and New Mexico, 1530–1888* (Albuquerque, 1962), p. 432.
11. Waters, *Masked Gods*, p. 262. The ceremonies at Blue Lake are absolutely secret and have never been accurately described, though Taos has often been slandered concerning them. Nevertheless, Taos has now succeeded in regaining clear title to Blue Lake and its surroundings. For early stages of the controversy: Waters, pp. 371–76.
12. Though the *Salii* were much more like Comanche dancers. Frank Brown, to whom I am indebted for this analogy, writes that they performed their rite "at the opening and closing of the fighting season, on March 19 and October 19 . . . and wore the antique costume of Bronze or Iron Age warriors—spiked helmets, red tunics, bronze girdles—and carried long lances and the sacred figure-eight shields, *ancilia*. As they danced they sang a hymn, invoking Mars." Livy, *De Urbe Condita*, 1.20.4; Dionysius of Halicarnassus, 2.70–71; Plutarch, *Numa*, 13. The only general study is R. Cirilli, *Les Prêtres danseurs de Rome* (Paris, 1913).
13. See especially: Weston La Barre, *The Ghost Dance: The Origins of Religion* (New York, 1970), chapter 5, "The First Gods," pp. 161–96.
14. In *Phoenix: The Posthumous Papers of D. H. Lawrence*, ed. Edward D. McDonald (New York, 1936; Viking Compass ed., 1972), pp. 141–47. "New Mexico," which is largely about Taos, was originally published in *Survey Graphic*, May 1931. "Indians and an Englishman," about the Jicarilla Apache ceremonies at Stone Lake, was published in *Dial*, Feb. 1923, and is also included in *Phoenix*, pp. 92–99. See also D. Martin, "D. H. Lawrence and Pueblo Religion," *Arizona Quarterly*, 9 (1953), pp. 219–34. Lawrence concludes "New Mexico" by praising the Pueblos' ". . . great religious effort. For the whole life-effort of man was to get his life into direct contact with the elemental life of the cosmos, mountain-life, cloud-life, thunder-life, air-life, earth-life, sun-life" (pp. 146–47).
15. In D. H. Lawrence, *The Complete Short Stories*, 3 vols. (New York, 1955; Viking Compass ed., 1961), vol. 2, pp. 546–81.
16. I am grateful to Frank Waters, who lives on the Arroyo Seco (the water of which flows out of Blue Lake) just below the cavern, and who directed me to it and described the effects of changing light and weather on the waterfall and the peaks.
17. Harry T. Moore, *The Intelligent Heart: The Story of D. H. Lawrence* (New York, 1954; rev. ed., 1962), pp. 533–35, fig. 16b, for Frieda Lawrence, her last husband, Angelo Ravagli, and the shrine.
18. Stubbs, *Bird's-Eye View of the Pueblos*, pp. 27–30; Elsie C. Parsons, "Picuris," *American Anthropologist*, 41 (1939), pp. 206–22. The excavations at Picuris were done by Herbert Dick. A copy of his report to the National Park Service, "Picuris Pueblo Excavations," is available only on microfilm (#PB-177047), Clearinghouse for Scientific and Technical Information, Springfield, Virginia.
19. It has been restored since Kubler's day, when it was in the usual disastrous, gabled, tin-roofed phase. Kubler, *The Religious Architecture of New Mexico*, fig. 87, p. 54.

III. THE RIO GRANDE—THE TEWA TOWNS

1. John Peabody Harrington, "The Ethnogeography of the Tewa Indians," *Twenty-ninth Annual Report of the Bureau of American Ethnology, 1907–1908* (Washington, 1916), maps 1–7, 10–12.
2. William B. Douglass, "Notes on the Shrines of the Tewas and Other Pueblo Indians," *Proceedings of the Nineteenth International Congress of Americanists* (1915), pp. 344–78.
3. Vincent Scully, *The Earth, the Temple, and the Gods*, rev. ed. (New York, 1969), figs. 3, 7, 11, 37, 59, 121, 122.

4. George Kubler, *The Religious Architecture of New Mexico in the Colonial Period and Since the American Occupation* (Colorado Springs, 1940), p. 104, figs. 107, 108, 124.
5. Alfonso Ortiz, *The Tewa World: Space, Time, Being, and Becoming in a Pueblo Society* (Chicago, 1969), figs. 2, 3; pp. 21, 37–38.
6. Stanley A. Stubbs, *Bird's-Eye View of the Pueblos* (Norman, Okla., 1950), pp. 39–42.
7. Ortiz, pp. 142–44, finds four plazas and an "anti-sunwise" pattern. He cites in this connection Gertrude P. Kurath, "Plaza Circuits of Tewa Indian Dances," *El Palacio*, 65, pp. 16–26. For a marvelously detailed and profusely diagramed discussion of what she calls the "Ceremonial Ecology," the "Choreographic and Musical Patterns," and the "Symbolic Pageantry" of every category of dance in all the Tewa pueblos, with an excellent bibliography, see Kurath's *Music and Dance in the Tewa Pueblos* (Santa Fe, 1970). Also, in general: Herbert J. Spinden, *Songs of the Tewa* (New York, 1933).
8. Willa Cather, in *Death Comes for the Archbishop* (New York, 1927), turned this rather stern prelate into one of America's gentlest heroes. The tan stone of his cathedral of Santa Fe, cut, except for its engaged arcades, into hard, linear, flat planes and reflecting the western sun, is probably more appropriate to the contemporary scale of the city than fake adobe would have been, and its spacious vaulted interior offers a welcome expansion of volume and scale after all the flat ceilings and vigas.
9. Harrington, map 22.
10. Stubbs, pp. 43–46.
11. Kurath's diagram of dances at Santa Clara (fig. 9) has them first in the large eastern plaza and then in the small plaza.
12. On the Pajarito Plateau we encounter the lively ghosts of some of the major heroes of Southwestern archaeology—Hewett, in my opinion, occupying a place there along with Lummis and the legendary Bandelier. Lummis and Bandelier mainly roamed south of Frijoles Canyon; Hewett covered a wider area, with many publications, culminating in Edgar L. Hewett, *Pajarito Plateau and Its Ancient People*, rev. Bertha P. Dutton (Albuquerque, 1938). For Puye, which he excavated, see pp. 60–85. Hewett emphasizes the importance of sacred pools of the four directions as well as sacred hills and mountains. He illustrates San Ildefonso's old Sacred Pool of the West under the Jemez (fig. 64).
13. William B. Douglass, "A World Quarter Shrine of the Tewa Indians," *Records of the Past*, 2, (1912), pp. 159–73. Ortiz, p. 141. I visited this shrine with Edward T. Hall in July 1968. I am most grateful to him for dragging me to the summit, which he pretty much had to do.
14. Kurath, figs. 10 ff. A mason of Santa Clara, working on the walls of Puye in the summer of 1966 and for all I know an admirer of Robert Graves, said to me of Tsi′como: "We call her the White Lady." The Sierra Blanca image seems recurrent among sacred mountains.
15. Hewett, pp. 32–35, 101–11; G. L. Beam, "The Prehistoric Ruins of Tsankawi," *National Geographic Magazine*, 20 (1909), pp. 807–22; L. L. Wilson, "Excavations at Otowi," *El Palacio*, 3 (1916), pp. 28–36.
16. Stubbs, pp. 47–50. The central range of houses was still there in 1950; pl. 8, fig. 10. Cf. William Whitman, "The San Ildefonso of New Mexico," in R. Linton, ed., *Acculturation in Seven American Indian Tribes* (New York, 1940), pp. 390–462; idem, *The Pueblo Indians of San Ildefonso: A Changing Culture*, Columbia University Contributions to Anthropology, 34 (New York, 1947).
17. San Ildefonso's record of church building is a tangle of movings, dilapidations, and so on: Kubler, pp. 122–23. He shows an older church now destroyed, with even more dramatic profiles and projecting platforms supported on the choir-loft joists (fig. 122).
18. One thinks of the incomparable Maria and her son Popovi Da. See A. Marriott, *Maria the Potter of San Ildefonso* (Norman, Okla., 1948).
19. Kurath, pp. 233–36.

20. Cf. in general G. B. Grinnell, *The Cheyenne Indians*, 2 vols. (New Haven, 1923); idem, *The Fighting Cheyennes*, 2nd ed. (Norman, Okla., 1970); idem, "Cheyenne Woman Customs," *American Anthropologist*, 4 (1902), pp. 13–16; idem, "Coup and Scalp among the Plains Indians," *American Anthropologist*, 12 (1910), pp. 296–310.
21. Kurath, pp. 198–217. She also discusses animal dances in other pueblos and contrasts the patterns with those of the Keres. See in general: Virginia More Roediger, *Ceremonial Costumes of the Pueblo Indians* (Berkeley, 1961), esp. pp. 184–89.
22. Her fatefulness as Mother of the Animals apparently came to be associated with that of the Mexican Malinche, the guide and mistress of Cortés, whose Spanish and Indian lovers dance with her. See Nancy H. Saldaña, "La Malinche: Her Representation in Dances of Mexico and the United States," *Ethnomusicology*, 10 (1965), pp. 298–309, esp. p. 306. The plumed serpent which the buffalo wear on their kilts also suggests a Mexican connection here, in view of Parsons' insistence on the Mexican provenance of that fundamental symbol (Elsie C. Parsons, *Pueblo Indian Religion*, 2 vols. [Chicago, 1939] pp. 1016–25).
23. Edgar L. Hewett, *Ancient Life in the American Southwest* (Indianapolis, 1930), pp. 132–34, mentions the snowbird dance and quotes Alice Fletcher's translation of an Omaha ritual song to describe its meaning. The last stanza: "Ho! All ye of the heavens, all ye of the air, all ye of the earth, / I bid you to hear me! / Into your midst has come a new life. / Consent ye, consent ye all, I implore! / Make its path smooth—then shall it travel beyond the four hills!"
24. Stubbs, pp. 55–58. The large room south of the plaza (fig. 12), which Stubbs notes as abandoned, is now in good repair as a kiva.
25. Kubler, p. 113, fig. 140.
26. Marsden Hartley, the painter, whose writing about the dances Hewett much admired and quoted at length, was especially taken with the animal dances at Tesuque (Hewett, *Ancient Life in the American Southwest* [Indianapolis, 1930], pp. 135–43; and Marsden Hartley, "Red Man Ceremonials," *Art and Archaeology*, 9, no. 1, pp. 7–14, and 13, no. 3 [1922], pp. 113–19).
27. For the corn-dance patterns and songs: Kurath, pp. 169–85; Charles H. Lange, "Tablita or Corn Dance of the Rio Grande Pueblos," *The Texas Journal of Science*, 9, pp. 39–74.
28. It will be interesting to watch the physical redevelopment of Pojoaque, if any. For Nambé: Stubbs, pp. 51–54. Almost nothing is left now but the kiva and the house rows far south and far north; a north-south row of houses once bisected the plaza. The government houses are mostly spread out north of the road. Also: C. Arnold, "The Dance at Nambe," *El Palacio*, 24 (1928), pp. 26–29.
29. Kubler, fig. 198.
30. Under the direction of Douglas Schwartz, director of the School of American Research, Santa Fe.

IV. THE RIO GRANDE—THE KERES TOWNS

1. John Peabody Harrington, "The Ethnogeography of the Tewa Indians," *Twenty-ninth Annual Report of the Bureau of American Ethnology, 1907–1908* (Washington, 1916), maps 27, 28. Cf. in general: Leslie White, "The World of the Keresan Pueblo Indians," in *Primitive Views of the World*, ed. Stanley Diamond (New York, 1964); and, always a model of completeness, Charles H. Lange, *Cochití: A New Mexico Pueblo, Past and Present* (Austin, 1959).
2. For this whole area the pioneer archaeological and ethnographic exploration was that of Adolph Bandelier, especially as embodied in his *Final Report of Investigations among the Indians of the Southwestern United States*, Papers of the Archaeological Institute of America, American series, 4, 2 parts (Cambridge, Mass., 1890, 1892). Also idem, *Documentary History of the Rio Grande Pueblos of New Mexico* (Santa Fe,

1910); and now: *The Southwestern Journals of Adolph F. Bandelier, 1880–1882*, ed. Charles H. Lange and Carroll L. Riley (Albuquerque and Santa Fe, 1966). Bandelier was often accompanied in his travels by the writer, photographer, and artist—but certainly anthropologist, too—Charles F. Lummis; of Lummis's many titles, the most germane: *The Land of Poco Tiempo* (New York, 1893).

3. Hewett's excavation reports in *American Anthropologist*, 11 (1909), pp. 434–35, 651–73; *Pajarito Plateau*, pp. 41–43, 85–101. Cf. J. W. Hendron, *Prehistory of El Rito de los Frijoles* (Coolidge, Ariz., 1940).
4. Lummis, chap. 6, "The Wanderings of Cochití," p. 143.
5. Written in 1890. A gothic tale of most un-Apollonian romance, intrigue, and warfare between Keres and Tewa. Probably closer to the reality than Benedict's famous, brilliant generalizations about the moderation of Pueblo behavior, with their misleading Nietzschean terminology: Ruth Benedict, *Patterns of Culture* (New York, 1934; Pelican ed., 1946), pp. 52–119. The application of Nietzsche's terms "Apollonian" to the Pueblos and "Dionysian" to the Plains Indians cannot help but confuse our understanding of a culture whose dance-drama is so obviously related to the chorus of Dionysos in its historical actuality. Cf. n. 18, below.
6. Bandelier, *Final Report*, part 2, pp. 152–56, 161–63; Hewett, *Pajarito Plateau*, pp. 44–46; Lummis, pp. 146–47; Lange, *Cochití*, p. 8, pl. 3. Cf. J. B. McHarg, "The Lions of Cochití," *El Palacio*, 20 (1926), pp. 99–104. Also E. L. Watson, "The Cult of the Mountain Lion," *El Palacio*, 34 (1933), pp. 95–109.
7. Vincent Scully, *The Earth, the Temple, and the Gods: Greek Sacred Architecture*, rev. ed. (New York, 1969), figs. 62a, 64, 65, 221.
8. For the lions on los Idolos: Hewett, *Pajarito Plateau*, p. 46; Lummis, pp. 149–51; Lange, *Cochití*, p. 132, pl. 4.
9. Harrington, pl. 18.
10. Stanley A. Stubbs, *Bird's-Eye View of the Pueblos* (Norman, Okla., 1950), pp. 63–66.
11. I think of Estevan, a black man, because he was the first "European" the Pueblos saw; he was killed at Zuni in 1539 and entered into Pueblo mythology. Cf. Adolph F. Bandelier, "Fray Marcos of Nizza," *Hemenway Southwestern Archaeological Expedition*, Papers of the Archaeological Institute of America, American series, 5 (Cambridge, Mass., 1890). The earliest appearance of black men in the chorus long predates the Black Power movement and is therefore no indication in itself of any such connection, although its meaning could change in changing cultural circumstances. Or in the eye of the beholder: in 1939 similar black men at Santo Domingo reminded Goggin of minstrel actors (John M. Goggin, "Notes on Some 1938–39 Pueblo Dances," *New Mexico Anthropologist*, 3 [1938], pp. 31–32).
12. Lange, *Cochití*, includes a long section on ceremonial organization and ceremonies, pp. 227–336, and appends a section by Gertrude Kurath, "Cochití Choreographies and Songs," pp. 534–56, with descriptions of the major types of dances, diagrams, and musical scores.
13. Lummis in the Los Angeles *Globe-Democrat*, July 2 and 9, 1888. We recall his eye for church-gate-mountain relationships at Taos as well. See above, chap. II, n. 6.
14. Lange, *Cochití*, pls. 7, 8; George Kubler, *The Religious Architecture of New Mexico in the Colonial Period and Since the American Occupation* (Colorado Springs, 1940), pp. 112–13, fig. 121. In their day it was in its tin-roofed stage.
15. Stubbs, pp. 67–70. Leslie A. White, *The Pueblo of Santo Domingo, New Mexico*, Memoirs of the American Anthropological Association, 43 (1935). At that time kachina dances were still to be seen here and in the other Keres pueblos, and they are described by White, pp. 88–144.
16. Erna Fergusson, *Dancing Gods: Indian Cere-*

monials of New Mexico and Arizona (Albuquerque, 1931), pp. 56–60; Edgar L. Hewett, "The Corn Ceremony at Santo Domingo," *El Palacio*, 5 (1918), pp. 69–76; G. Huebener, "The Green Corn Dance at Santo Domingo," *El Palacio*, 45 (1938), pp. 1–17; and in general: Frances Densmore, *Music of Santo Domingo Pueblo, New Mexico*, Southwest Museum Papers, 12 (Los Angeles, 1938).

17. Fergusson, pp. 40–44. Charles H. Lange, "An Animal Dance at Santo Domingo Pueblo, January 26, 1940," *El Palacio*, 61 (1954), pp. 151–55. The animals run "to the mountain" and back early on the morning of the dance (Densmore, p. 148).

18. Horned Mycenae: Scully, figs. 59, 61, 62. For the horned son of Zeus, Dionysos, snake-blessed: ". . . and when the weaving Fates fulfilled the time, / the bull-horned god was born of Zeus. In joy / he crowned his son, set serpents on his head . . ." Euripides, *Bacchae*, 100–102 (William Arrowsmith). We are told that when the semi-legendary Thespis introduced a protagonist who stood out from the chorus of Dionysos, classic Greek drama was born (Aristotle, *Poetics*, IV; Diogenes Laertius, III.56; Horace, *Ars Poetica*, 275 ff.). That chorus was sometimes dressed as animals, as later in Aristophanes, *The Frogs*, for example. The protagonist, as above, follows the animal attributes of Dionysus, which are fundamental to his nature. So in its earliest centuries Greece must have known many dances like those of Santo Domingo, where an animal stepped forward as a proto-hero for a while. The word *tragedy*, after all, means "goat song," and in later ages the dramatist's prize in Athens was a bull. Cf. Gertrude Levy, *The Gate of Horn: a Study of the Religious Conceptions of the Stone Age and Their Influence upon European Thought* (London, 1947), esp. pp. 313–15, 322. In general these views are best explored, and Aristotle's position defended, by Gilbert Murray, "Excursus on the Ritual Forms Preserved in Greek Tragedy," in Jane Harrison, *Themis: A Study of the Social Origins of Greek Religion* (Cambridge, 1912; new ed., London, 1963); Gilbert Murray, *Aeschylus: The Creator of Tragedy* (Oxford, 1940), esp. chap. 5; and E. R. Dodds, Euripides, *Bacchae* (Oxford, 1944; 2nd ed., 1960), esp. Dodds's introduction and commentary. These conclusions, convincing to me, have not gone unchallenged, as by Sir A. W. Pickard-Cambridge, *Dithyramb, Tragedy, and Comedy*, 2nd. ed., rev. T. B. L. Webster (Oxford, 1962); and Gerald F. Else, *The Origin and Early Form of Greek Tragedy* (Cambridge, Mass., 1965). I diffidently suggest, to turn the argument around, that the Pueblo analogies tend to support the views of Aristotle, Murray, Dodds, and Levy. One does not, of course, want to pretend that Pueblo dances are the equivalents of fully developed Greek plays; their character is their own, and their relation is to earlier stages of whatever common type of development may be posited here. Cf. V. S. Heath, "Dramatic Elements in American Indian Ceremonials," *Nebraska University Studies*, 14 (1914), pp. 377–415.

19. See, among others, F. G. Roe, *The North American Buffalo* (Toronto, 1951). There are still a few small herds preserved, as in Yellowstone National Park, at Colorado Springs, and in Taos itself. The American bison also stands out impressively in the great zoos of Europe. Though his horns are shorter, he much more closely resembles the prehistoric bison of, say, Altamira than does the smaller-headed, more elongated, rather wry-necked modern European bison, himself almost extinct.

20. Weston La Barre, *The Ghost Dance: The Origins of Religion* (New York, 1970), p. 165. We are again reminded of the Aegean in the Tyrant Mother and Queen, the *potnia* of Linear B script, to whom bulls were sacrificed of whom the horned bull, Poseidon, was the consort, like the king at Knossos. Cf. Scully, pp. 26, 156, 202.

21. Kubler, pp. 107–108, figs. 51, 149, 190.

22. Lange illustrates such a moment at Cochití (pl. 21), and describes rooster pulls on various saints' days, all Spanish-derived (pp. 338, 341, and passim). White describes the event briefly, noting that the sweat of men and horses stands for rain (*The Pueblo of Santo Domingo*, pp. 155–58).
23. Stubbs, pp. 71–74. Leslie A. White, *The Pueblo of San Felipe*, Memoirs of the American Anthropological Association (1932). White observes that the "mother of game" in the Buffalo Dance at San Felipe presses the effigy of a mountain lion to her abdomen during the dance (p. 58), and he notes other variants on the dance (p. 59).
24. Leslie A. White, "Keresan Indian Color Terms," *Papers of the Michigan Academy of Science, Arts and Letters*, 28 (1942), pp. 559–63.
25. Kubler, p. 108, fig. 191.
26. By Frank Waters, *Masked Gods: Navaho and Pueblo Ceremonialism* (Denver, 1950), p. 264, who notes that the crest can be called *huitziton*, with which he would like to connect Huitzilopochtli, the Aztec war god. He also likens the long, pliant staff to a snake.
27. White, *Santo Domingo*, op. cit., pp. 149–55, describes a similar dance at that pueblo. He calls the dancers *sandaros*, a corruption of *soldados*; Santiago-type horsemen are also involved in baiting the bull.
28. John L. Sinclair, *The Story of the Pueblo of Kuaua*, Papers of the School of American Research, 45 (Santa Fe, 1951). Bertha P. Dutton, *Sun Father's Way: The Kiva Murals of Kuaua* (Santa Fe, 1963). These paintings, like those in the kiva at Awatovi, taken in conjunction with prehistoric petroglyphs, show the continuity of pueblo culture from prehistory to the present and the antiquity of its symbolism.
29. Stubbs, pp. 75–78. Leslie A. White, *The Pueblo of Santa Ana, New Mexico*, Memoirs of the American Anthropological Association, 60 (1942), pp. 1–360. One recalls the deathly lancer at Santo Domingo when White, pp. 301–302, mentions a black-painted dancer with a lance in the animal dance at Santa Ana who may represent an "eastern" or "Oklahoma" Indian.
30. Kubler, figs. 78, 82, 148.
31. Lange, pp. 353–62, fig. 24. At Santa Ana one horseman is black, the other usually white, the former receiving gifts out of the earth and appropriate to Indian ways, the other accepting white man's store-bought "doo-dads" (Waters). My notes about them in 1968 have them both black, however, and their whipping around the plaza tense and menacing as I have described it.
32. Stubbs, pp. 79–82; Matilda Coxe Stevenson, "The Sia," in the *Eleventh Annual Report of the Bureau of American Ethnology, 1889–90* (Washington, 1894), pp. 9–157. Also R. B. Regan, "The Story of Jemez and Zia," *El Palacio*, 4 (1916), pp. 24–72; idem, "Additional Notes on the Jemez Zia Region," *El Palacio*, 12 (1922), pp. 120–21. Also R. C. Euler, "Environmental Adaptation at Sia Pueblo," *Human Organization*, 12 (1954), pp. 27–32. Zia has been praised in the past for the vigor of its dances. My impression of weakness, based on the Easter "prayer service" of 1968, may therefore be faulty. The ruined kiva has, after all, been repaired. But repeated visits, though unfortunately without dances, have reinforced my original impression.
33. Very obvious in Kubler's fig. 167.
34. Claude Lévi-Strauss, *La Pensée Sauvage* (Paris, 1962); trans. *The Savage Mind* (Chicago, 1966). Hartley says somewhat the same thing, if I read him aright: ". . . the esthetic of the redman [is] the science of the redman . . ." (Marsden Hartley, "Red Man Ceremonials," *Art and Archaeology*, 13, no. 3 [1922], p. 117).

V. JEMEZ, PECOS, SANDIA, ISLETA, LAGUNA, ACOMA, ZUNI

1. Stanley A. Stubbs, *Bird's-Eye View of the Pueblos* (Norman, Okla., 1950), pp. 59–62. Elsie C. Parsons, *The Pueblo of Jemez* (New Haven, 1925). Also R. B. Regan, "The Story of Jemez and Zia," *El Palacio*, 4 (1916), pp. 24–72; idem,

"Dances of the Jemez Pueblo Indians," *Transactions of the Kansas Academy of Science*, 23 (1906), pp. 241–72; Roy A. Keech, "Pecos Ceremony at Jemez, August 2, 1932," *El Palacio*, 36, pp. 139 ff.; and Bertha P. Dutton, "Hopi Dance of the Jemez Indians," *Research*, 1 (1936), pp. 70–84.

2. George Kubler, *The Religious Architecture of New Mexico Since the Colonial Period and Since the American Occupation* (Colorado Springs, 1940), figs. 172, 173, pp. 126–27.
3. Kubler, pp. 82–84, 118–19; figs. 118, 125, 153.
4. Hubert G. Alexander and Paul Reiter, *Report on the Excavations at Jemez Cave*, Monograph of the University of New Mexico and the School of American Research, University of New Mexico Bulletin 278, series 4 (1935).
5. A. V. Kidder, *The Pueblo of Pecos*, Archaeological Institute of America, Papers of the School of American Archaeology, 33 (Santa Fe, 1916). Also: idem, *An Introduction to the Study of Southwestern Archaeology* (New Haven, 1924; rev. ed., 1962), pp. 61–139; idem, *Pecos, New Mexico, Archaeological Notes*, Papers of the Robert S. Peabody Foundation for Archaeology (Andover, Mass., 1958); Marjorie F. Lambert, "A Rare Stone Humpbacked Figurine from Pecos Pueblo," *El Palacio*, 44 (1937), pp. 93–108.
6. "The shadowy side behind the place of the rock horns" (John Peabody Harrington, "The Ethnogeography of the Tewa Indians," *Twenty-ninth Annual Report of the Bureau of American Ethnology, 1907–1908* [Washington, 1916], 22:14, p. 341).
7. The great early mission church is oriented east-west, and so lies as an intrusive mass directly athwart the major axis of view. Kubler (p. 23) finds this orientation unusual in New Mexico.
8. Kubler, figs. 4, 12, 14, 27, 31, 45, 48, 49, 59, 62, 63, 68, 85, 92, 100, 150, 154, 159–62, 165, 166; Lummis, *The Land of Poco Tiempo* (New York, 1893), chap. 11, "The Cities That Were Forgotten," pp. 285–310.
9. Stubbs, pp. 31–34. Leslie A. White, "Ethnographic Notes on Sandia Pueblo," *Papers of the Michigan Academy of Science, Arts and Letters*, 31 (1945), pp. 215–22.
10. Kubler, pp. 122–23. In 1935 the church had a tin roof and tight gable (fig. 200).
11. Stubbs, pp. 35–38. Cf. Elsie C. Parsons, "Isleta," in the *Forty-seventh Annual Report of the Bureau of American Ethnology, 1925–26* (Washington, 1930), pp. 193–466. Erna Fergusson, *Dancing Gods: Indian Ceremonials of New Mexico and Arizona* (Albuquerque, 1931), pp. 49–63. Lummis was very fond of Isleta: op. cit., pp. 111–30; and idem, *Pueblo Indian Folk Stories* (New York, 1910).
12. Kubler, p. 54, figs. 57, 84, 99.
13. F. Eggan, *Social Organization of the Western Pueblos* (Chicago, 1950), pp. 223–90. H. O. Brayer, "The Land Grants of Laguna," *Research*, 1 (1936), pp. 5–22.
14. Kubler, pp. 54, 63, 65, 66, 110, fig. 114.
15. Stubbs, pp. 83–96, notes that in 1887 there were more three-story houses and the plaza was more completely enclosed.
16. Leslie A. White, "The Acoma Indians," *Forty-seventh Annual Report of the Bureau of American Ethnology, 1925–26* (Washington, 1930), pp. 17–192; idem, "New Material from Acoma," *Bulletins of the Bureau of Indian Ethnology*, 136 (1943), pp. 301–59. Lummis, *Poco Tiempo*, chap. 3, "The City in the Sky," pp. 55–76.
17. Stubbs, pp. 87–90. The house at the northeast corner of the plaza is now two-storied. I have never been able to see a dance at Acoma, and was ejected by the women ("Don't let them see him," they said, Pueblo women being indescribably gentle and kind) one day when I wandered up there by chance while a secret dance was in progress. Cf. Frances Densmore, *Music of Acoma, Isleta, Cochití and Zuni Pueblos*, Bureau of American Ethnology Bulletin 165 (1957).
18. Kubler, pp. 18–19, 92–95, figs. 32, 44, 58, 67, 88. Here, as at Pecos, Kubler emphasizes the place-

ment of the church outside the pueblo and its fortified aspect (p. 18).

19. Cf. Scully, *American Architecture and Urbanism* (New York, 1969), pp. 13, 24–43.
20. Pindar, frag. 64 (Dithyrambi), trans. C. M. Bowra, Oxford Classical Text. "O thou renowned and violet-crowned, sung by poets, shield of Hellas, beloved Athens, god-filled city-state."
21. F. W. Hodge (many excavation reports, culminating in) *History of Hawikuh, New Mexico: One of the So-Called Cities of Cíbola*, Publications of the Frederick Webb Hodge Anniversary Publication Fund, 1 (Los Angeles, 1937).
22. Matilda Coxe Stevenson, "The Zuni Indians: Their Mythology, Esoteric Fraternities, and Ceremonies," in the *Twenty-third Annual Report of the Bureau of American Ethnology, 1901–1902* (Washington, 1904), pp. 5–634. For Corn Mountain, its horns and shrines: plates 11, 12, 50. The bibliography on Zuni is enormous, but Stevenson's and Bunzel's (note 25 below) incomparable works can stand as major references for the ceremonies and dances. One should also refer to the strange genius who knew how implacable the Zuni could be: Frank Hamilton Cushing, "My Adventures in Zuni," *Century Magazine*, 25 (1882), pp. 191–207, 500–511; 26 (1883), pp. 28–47; and idem, *Zuni Folk Tales*, new ed. (New York, 1931), p. 901. The fundamental work: A. L. Kroeber, *Zuni Kin and Clan*, Anthropological Papers of the American Museum of Natural History, 18 (New York, 1971).
23. Kubler, pp. 95–97, fig. 176.
24. Stubbs, pp. 91–94, shows no kivas at all, but there are at least five besides the main one built into the house blocks—at least six when the suburb across the river is considered. See in general: Victor Mindeleff, "A Study of Pueblo Architecture: Tusayan and Cíbola," *Eighth Annual Report of the Bureau of American Ethnology, 1886–87* (Washington, 1891), pp. 80–223.
25. The kachinas are representations of the gods, more or less; they are innumerable. Some are apparently ancestor figures. The mudheads (*koyemshi*) are intended to represent early men who, in some accounts, were the offspring of an incestuous union and thus deformed. Cf. Ruth Bunzel, "Zuni Katcinas," *Forty-seventh Annual Report of the Bureau of American Ethnology, 1925–26* (Washington, 1932), pp. 837–1086; idem, "Zuni Origin Myths," ibid., pp. 545–610.
26. There too the view of the sacred mountain would have been blocked, or partially blocked, by the buildings around the court, but from the flat roofs the effect would have been much the same as at Zuni (Vincent Scully, *The Earth, the Temple, and the Gods: Greek Sacred Architecture*, rev. ed. [New York, 1969], figs. 2, 3, 5, 8, 11). Note also Puye above, where the arrangement is axial down the court, as in most Aegean sites, whereas at Zuni it falls diagonally across the pueblo. There are some stongly diagonal lines of sight at Knossos and Mallia, too, however.
27. Fergusson, pp. 67–91.
28. See Cushing, "My Adventures in Zuni," for a chilling description of the Zuni way with dissidents, deviants, and "witches."
29. Stevenson, pp. 58–60, 354–61, plates, 88, 89. The Texans at Fence Lake are described in E. von Z. Vogt, *Modern Homesteaders: The Life of a Twentieth-Century Frontier Community* (Cambridge, Mass., 1955). A depressing story.
30. Scully, *The Earth*, figs. 3, 4, 50, 51, 53, 60, 63, 67, 76, 94, 95, 115, 121, 122, 143, 160, 166, 167, 263, 272, 346, 373, 377.
31. Stevenson, pp. 227–61, plates 61–64, for Shalako. This dance has been described by many other people, as by Bunzel, above. Also: Fergusson, pp. 91–113; Frank Waters, *Masked Gods: Navaho and Pueblo Ceremonialism* (Denver, 1950), pp. 281–90. For some comments on natural benevolence: Frances Densmore, "Notes on the Indians' Belief in the Friendliness of Nature," *Southwestern Journal of Anthropology*, 4 (1948), pp. 94–97.

32. Stevenson, plates 61, 62. Shulaawi'si reminded Michael Coe of Tezcatlipoca in the dance of 1971.
33. Edmund Wilson, who wrote a rather dry if unsentimental description of the Shalako ceremony in his *Red, Black, Blond, and Olive* (New York, 1956, pp. 23–43), described these bearers (p. 28) as "characters in a production of Romeo and Juliet."
34. Stevenson, plate 60.
35. In 1971 I saw none of the occasional Zuni discourtesy toward white guests that Stevenson and Wilson both describe. The pueblo had, however, threatened to close the ceremony to whites because of disorders the previous year. Hopi now closes up sporadically. Resentment may well be on the increase as a kind of public policy, but I have never experienced it from individuals.
36. Wilson (pp. 41–42) noted the same reaction in himself by late evening. He did not stay for the races the next day, which he describes, inaccurately I should think, as taking place at dawn.
37. Stevenson, pp. 261–73.

VI. THE NAVAHO HOGAN AND THE HOPI TOWNS

1. C. Mindeleff, "Cliff Ruins of the Canyon de Chelly, Arizona," *American Anthropologist*, 8 (1895), pp. 153–74; idem, "The Cliff Ruins of the Cañon de Chelly, Arizona," *Bulletin of the American Geographical Society*, 30 (1897), pp. 111–23.
2. Ruth M. Underhill, *The Navajos* (Norman, Okla., 1956), p. 19; and Clyde Kluckhohn and D. C. Leighton, *The Navaho* (Cambridge, Mass., 1946). Also: G. A. Reichardt, *Navaho Religion*, 2 vols. (New York, 1950); Edward T. Hall, "Recent Clues to Athapaskan Prehistory in the Southwest," *American Anthropologist*, n.s. 46 (1944), pp. 98–105; A. O'Bryan, *The Diné: Origin Myths of the Navaho Indians*, Bureau of American Ethnology Bulletin 163 (New York, 1950); and James J. Hester, *Early Navaho Migrations and Acculturation in the Southwest*, Museum of New Mexico Papers in Anthropology, 6 (Santa Fe, 1962–63).
3. As in the painting *The Earth Mother*, by Fred Stevens (Gray Squirrel), which is produced here with Mr. Stevens' description. I am grateful to Mr. Stevens and to my son, John Scully, who commissioned the painting and made me a present of it.
4. Clyde Kluckhohn, "Navaho Witchcraft," Peabody Museum Papers, 22 (Cambridge, Mass., 1944); W. Morgan, *Human-Wolves among the Navaho*, Yale University Publications in Anthropology, 11 (1936). A. H. and D. C. Leighton, "Some Types of Uneasiness and Fear in a Navaho Indian Community," *American Anthropologist*, 44 (1942), pp. 194–209.
5. Washington Matthews, *The Night Chant: A Navajo Ceremony*, Memoirs of the American Museum of Natural History, 6 (New York, 1902). Erna Fergusson, *Dancing Gods: Indian Ceremonials of New Mexico and Arizona* (Albuquerque, 1931), pp. 203–47. Frank Waters, *Masked Gods: Navaho and Pueblo Ceremonialism* (Denver, 1950), pp. 238–58.
6. C. Mindeleff, "Navaho Houses," *Seventeenth Annual Report of the Bureau of American Ethnology, 1895–96* (Washington, 1898), pp. 475–517. W. R. Hurt, "Eighteenth-Century Navaho Hogans from Canyon de Chelly National Monument," *American Antiquity*, 8 (1942), pp. 89–104. B. Haile, "Why the Navaho Hogan?" *Primitive Man*, 15 (1942), pp. 39–56. M. A. Tremblay, "Navaho Housing in Transition," *American Indigena*, 14 (1954), pp. 182–219.
7. Vincent Scully, *The Earth, the Temple, and the Gods: Greek Sacred Architecture*, rev. ed. (New York, 1969), esp. figs. 51, 52, 60.
8. Fergusson, 206–208. Kluckhohn and Leighton, pp. 222–23.

9. Clyde Kluckhohn, "Hopi and Navajo," *New Mexico Quarterly*, 3 (1933), pp. 56–64.
10. In general: Frederick R. Eggan, *Social Organization of the Western Pueblos* (Chicago, 1950), pp. 17–138; H. R. Voth, *The Traditions of the Hopi*, Field Museum of Natural History Anthropological Series, 8 (Chicago, 1905); W. Hough, *The Hopi Indians* (Cedar Rapids, 1915); A. M. Stephen, *Hopi Journal*, ed. Elsie C. Parsons, Columbia University Contributions to Anthropology, 23, 2 vols. (New York, 1936).
11. Paul Coze's relief map seems the clearest that shows all the villages (Paul Coze, "Living Spirits of the Kachinas," *Arizona Highways*, 47 [1971], pp. 4–5). The Navaho Tribal Council's tourist relief map referred to above is a graphic if quaint presentation of the whole area.
12. The use of mesa features to mark critical sunrises is described in Leo W. Simmons, ed., *Sun Chief: The Autobiography of a Hopi Indian*, (New Haven, 1942; 11th printing, 1972), pp. 58–59. This autobiography of Don C. Talayesva, an Indian of Oraibi, is an invaluably candid first-hand account of Hopi life, belief, and customs during the first half of the twentieth century.
13. H. R. Voth, "Notes on the Eagle Cult among the Hopi Indians," in *Brief Miscellaneous Hopi Papers*, Field Museum of Natural History Anthropological Series, 11, no. 2 (Chicago, 1912), pp. 105–109.
14. Frank Waters, *Book of the Hopi* (New York, 1963), pp. 137–53. See photo facing p. 190, and fig. 51, p. 108, for representations of the Two and One Horns. For Masau'u: Hamilton A. Tyler, *Pueblo Gods and Myths* (Norman, Okla., 1964), pp. 3–48; and Simmons, *Sun Chief*, p. 179, where Masau'u "guards our village." (The gulf between the Hopi and the Greek view of the relationship of human society to nature and fate is expressed in the character of the major male divinity. For the Hopi it is Masau'u, a death, fire, and earth god, who is most evoked as the protector of towns. For the Greeks it was Zeus, a sky god of war and, later, of legal justice.) Also: H. R. Voth, "Oraibi New Year Ceremony," *Brief Miscellaneous Hopi Papers*, pp. 111–19. Elsie C. Parsons, "The Hopi Wöwöchim Ceremony in 1920," *American Anthropologist*, n.s. 25 (1923), pp. 156–87. In Don Talayesva's dream vision of climbing up "Mt. Beautiful," which, according to him, lies west of Oraibi and in the dream is staired like a Mexican temple base, it is a horned man, a Kwanitaka, who receives him at the top (Simmons, *Sun Chief*, pp. 95, 123, 423, 436).
15. That is certainly what emerges from Waters' recent account after allowance is made for a certain amount of Hopi hoodwinkery (Waters, pp. 3–108). Talayesva has the clans gathering from the four quarters of the compass (Simmons, *Sun Chief*, pp. 420–22), but the drift is the same. Coze, p. 4, Waters, pp. 109 ff.
16. The sequence of colonization is summarized by Coze, p. 4, Waters, pp. 109 ff.
17. R. G. Montgomery, W. Smith, and J. O. Brew, *Franciscan Awatovi*, Peabody Museum Papers, 36 (Cambridge, Mass., 1949).
18. Christy G. Turner, II, and Nancy T. Morris, "A Massacre at Hopi," *American Antiquity*, 35, no. 3 (1970). Waters, pp. 258–66, states that the Hopi have suffered feelings of guilt ever since.
19. Edward P. Dozier, *Hano: A Tewa Indian Community in Arizona* (New York, 1966).
20. Stubbs, pp. 117–20. Sadly, Oraibi is even more ruinous now than in Stubbs's time (1950).
21. Victor Mindeleff, "A Study of Pueblo Architecture: Tusayan and Cíbola," *Eighth Annual Report of the Bureau of American Ethnology, 1886–87* (Washington, 1891), pp. 13–79, 100–223; for Oraibi, pp. 76–77 and passim.
22. Stubbs, pp. 113–16. Victor Mindeleff (who calls it Shumopavi), pp. 73–76, and passim.
23. Camillo Sitte, *Der Städtebau nach seinen künstlerischen grundsätzen* (Vienna, 1889); *City Planning According to Artistic Principles*, trans. George R. and Cristiane Crasemann Collins (New York, 1965).

24. Stubbs, pp. 95–98; Victor Mindeleff, pp. 63–66 and passim.
25. Stubbs, pp. 99–104; Victor Mindeleff, pp. 61–63 and passim; and Dozier.
26. D. H. Lawrence, "Just Back from the Snake Dance—Tired Out," *The Laughing Horse*, Sept. 1924, and in *Selected Essays* (Harmondsworth, 1950), pp. 199–202. Lawrence, who loved spectacular Taos, hated the Hopi country: ". . . hideous . . . with death-grey mesas—like broken edges of bread crust . . ." (p. 199).
27. Stubbs, pp. 109–12. Not much changed. Victor Mindeleff, pp. 71–73 and passim.
28. J. W. Fewkes, "Hopi Kachinas," in the *Twenty-first Annual Report of the Bureau of American Ethnology, 1899–1900* (Washington, 1900), pp. 3–126; Fergusson, pp. 177–78.
29. Cf. Elsie C. Parsons and R. L. Beals, "The Sacred Clowns of the Pueblo and Mayo-Yaqui Indians," *American Anthropologist*, n.s. 36 (1934), pp. 491–514. There is much less written about the clowns than one might expect.
30. *The Southwestern Journals of Adolph F. Bandelier, 1880–1882*, ed. Charles H. Lange and Carroll L. Riley (Albuquerque and Santa Fe, 1966), pp. 341, 367, 374. "The whole is a filthy, obscene affair" (p. 367). ". . . Protestantism has no effect upon the Indians" (quoting George Pradt, p. 374). And, "The morality of the Pueblos is very evidently fearfully low" (p. 374).
31. Stubbs, pp. 105–108. Victor Mindeleff, pp. 66–71 and passim.
32. Cf. J. W. Fewkes, "The Sun's Influence on the Form of Hopi Pueblos," *American Anthropologist*, 8 (1906), pp. 88–100.
33. Idem, "A Few Summer Ceremonials at the Tusayan Pueblos," *Journal of American Ethnology and Archaeology*, 2 (1892), pp. 1–160. H. Jones, "Niman Katcina Dance at Walpi," *El Palacio*, 33 (1932), pp. 68–71. There is a lively account of the Hemis dance, with splendid photographs of July 30, 1927, in Elizabeth Compton Hegemann, *Navaho Trading Days* (Albuquerque, 1936), figs. 153–73. She notes that brides are blessed in the downward-striking sequence, two in that year, fig. 170. This book contains many delightful photographs and anecdotes of Hopi and Navaho life—including a Navaho chicken (burlap bag) pull, figs. 307–309.
34. Aristophanes, *The Frogs*, the opening song of the frog chorus. See note 18, chap. IV.
35. J. W. Fewkes, "The Sacrificial Element in Hopi Worship," *Journal of American Folk-Lore*, 10 (1897), pp. 187–201.
36. For domestic animals, some of which Don Talayesva also buggered, at least in his youth: *Sun Chief*, pp. 55, 65, 78–79. For wild game: pp. 54, 92, 103. Don, possibly as a courteous cross-cultural gesture to his Yale collaborators, expresses compassion for the rooster in the chicken pull (p. 106).
37. J. W. Fewkes, "Property-Right in Eagles among the Hopi," *American Anthropologist*, 2 (1900), pp. 690–707; and Voth, "Notes on the Eagle Cult," op. cit., note 13, above.
38. To the Powamu chief (Waters, pp. 207–209).
39. Edgar L. Hewett, *The Chaco Canyon and Its Monuments* (Albuquerque, 1936), p. 68. This is one of the humane inspirations that Hewett seems to have had so often, as when in the same discussion he ridicules our use of "deflector" for what in the kivas the Indians call an "altar," and of "ventilator" for what they call a "spirit tunnel" (p. 70). It is his usage that I try to employ in my description of kivas in chapter I.
40. Joe Sekakuku as a young man figures largely in Hegemann's *Navaho Trading Days*.
41. The bibliography is staggering. Among the most interesting accounts are: J. G. Bourke, *The Snake-Dance of the Moquis of Arizona* (London, 1884); J. W. Fewkes, A. M. Stephen, and J. G. Owens, "The Snake Ceremonials at Walpi," *Journal of American Ethnology and Archaeology*, 4 (1894), pp. 1–126; H. R. Voth, *The Oraibi Summer Snake Ceremony*, Field Museum of Natural History Anthropological Series, 3, no. 4 (Chi-

cago, 1903), pp. 267–358; M. L. Oliver, "The Snake Dance," *National Geographic Magazine*, 22 (1911), pp. 107–37; as well as in Elsie C. Parsons, *Pueblo Indian Religion*, 2 vols. (Chicago, 1939); and idem, *Hopi and Zuni Ceremonialism*, Memoirs of the American Anthropological Association, 39 (1933). In 1969 at Mishongnovi I noted only one major difference from the earlier descriptions but perhaps a major and disquieting one: the snakes were not produced from the *kisi* as they happened to be grabbed out of the bag, as earlier accounts all seem to indicate, so that one large man might get a whip snake, a small boy a diamondback, and so on. That way seems in accord with the meaning of the dance, with all snakes, poisonous or not, treated the same, since it is not intended as a theatrical horror show. In 1969, however, and, I am told, again in 1970 (in 1971 the dance was closed to whites), they produced first all bull snakes, then all whip snakes, and last all rattlers—and only small ones. This development, while it might have some special ritual significance I am not aware of, and while it is not up to me to complain, does seem a rather sinister theatricalism, an editing of the dance for spectator effect, perhaps a major step toward its corruption and disappearance.

42. "Just Back from the Snake Dance." Lawrence hated the snake dance too. Curious, considering his respect for the depths of experience at Taos that he should have called it a "circus," and "the hopping Indian . . . cute" (p. 301). He seems to have been reacting to the white crowd more than to the dance and writes as if he were trying to shock his readers. It is a pettish little article; perhaps Lawrence was in fact just "tired out" when he wrote it. One tends to suspect, though, that Lawrence loved the primitive when it came to him in a form around which he could himself construct an emotional edifice but hated it when, like the snake dance, it both cut too close to his bone and was too hopelessly matter of fact. Some of his comments in *The Plumed Serpent* and elsewhere also indicate that, like many of us, he was in reality deeply sickened by snakes.

43. Waters was told that the "snake-whips" of the gather-uppers were, like those used by the snake hunters and in the kiva, made of buzzard feathers; the gray spots on their undersides are thought to mesmerize and soothe the snake (*Book of the Hopi*, pp. 220, 229). The feathers used by the snake bearer's partner in the dance, however, look to me like eagle, as they have to other observers. I have raised this point with Waters, and he has been good enough to say that they look like eagle to him, too, and that the Hopi say of them only that they can be of any kind, since the snake has already been tamed, "befriended," in the kiva and does not need to be charmed while being carried. The eagle, Waters further points out, is, like the antelope whose priests assist in the dance, "a representative of the higher power." There are those, including Waters, who have reported seeing rattlers strike their carriers on the jowls, but to no effect (*Masked Gods*, p. 313). Perhaps they are not striking but caressing, as when: "The Bacchae then returned where they had started, / by the springs the god had made, and washed their hands / while the snakes licked away the drops of blood / that dabbled their cheeks . . ." (Euripides, *Bacchae*, 765–68, William Arrowsmith).

Closer to home, Don Talayesva describes a snake "licking" his "face and nose" and coiling around his neck and doing him no harm, which would not have been the case "if my heart had been evil" (*Sun Chief* pp. 206–207). Characteristically, the snake is not identified as to type. Earlier he had described how as a boy he had refrained from killing a bull snake which had coiled around his neck and frightened him as he was practicing the snake dance with it (pp. 72–73). The Hopi are wary of bull snakes anyway; they are big and can be very aggressive and (p. 426) they may contain the souls of sorcerers.

For snake handling in another context, where

the devotees are sometimes struck and die: Weston La Barre, *They Shall Take Up Serpents: Psychology of the Southern Snake-Handling Cult*, Minneapolis, 1962.

44. Fewkes; Parsons; Waters; et al.
45. Again, for the Mexican derivation of the plumed serpent: Parsons, *Pueblo Indian Religion*, pp. 1016–25.
46. Genesis 3:14 (King James Version).
47. Genesis 3:15.

VII. EPILOGUE: THE PUBERTY CEREMONY OF THE MESCALERO

1. These ceremonies, annotated by Hulda Hobbs as in 1939, and with a couple of photographs by Bertha Dutton, are briefly described in Dan Nicholas, "Mescalero Apache Girls' Puberty Ceremony," *El Palacio*, 46 (1939), pp. 193–204. Opler, the major interpreter of Mescalero culture, regarded the Gahan dance as largely curative and stressed the importance of the clown in it: Morris E. Opler, "The Sacred Clowns of the Chiricahua and Mescalero Indians," *El Palacio*, 44 (1938), pp. 75–79. He regarded the Gahan participation in the girls' festival as "not of a serious nature," and "really displays of virtuosity" (p. 78). The curative function of the Gahan is stated by Henry Kane, "The Apache Secret Devil Dance," *El Palacio*, 42 (1937), pp. 93–94. For something on the songs: J. F. Bartoli, "The Apache 'Devil Dance,'" *Musical Courier*, 152 (1955), pp. 8–10. Erna Fergusson, *Dancing Gods: Indian Ceremonials of New Mexico and Arizona* (Albuquerque, 1931), pp. 257–69, wrote up the ceremonies in a most disheartened and depressing way in 1931. The existing standard history of the Mescaleros, C. L. Sonnichsen, *The Mescalero Apaches* (Norman, Okla., 1958), also describes the ceremonies as in decay (pp. 25–27, 30). It is fair to state that by 1970 at least that process had been reversed.
2. Cf. Eugene B. McCluney, "The Hatchet Site: A Preliminary Report," *Southwestern Lore*, 26, no. 4 (1961).
3. Weston La Barre, *The Ghost Dance: The Origins of Religion* (New York, 1970), pp. 125, 151–52. But also: Reginald and Gladys Laubin, *The Indian Tipi: Its History, Construction and Use* (Norman, Okla., 1957). This stresses the originality of the Plains Indian development of wind flaps, the asymmetrical cone, and so on.
4. Charles H. Lange, *Cochití: A New Mexican Pueblo, Past and Present* (Austin, 1959), p. 338.
5. That was apparently Western Apache practice at any rate, including that of the Chiricahua, with whom the Mescalero had close affinities. Cf. Grenville Goodwin and Keith H. Basso, eds., *Western Apache Raiding and Warfare* (Tucson, 1971), pp. 284–86.
6. The Apache adaptation of Pueblo influence could hardly contrast more with that of their Athapaskan cousins, the Navaho, whose *yeibichai* is a night-haunted affair, spoon-packed in grouping, of strangled coyote yips and eerie mewings. But the tepee and fire cones, with the moon and star above them, were much the same at Mescalero and in the squaw dance I described seeing south of Gallup. A general structure of ritual among Pueblos, Navahos, Apaches, and others is traced in Ruth M. Underhill, *Ceremonial Patterns in the Greater Southwest*, Monographs of the American Ethnological Society, 13 (Locust Valley, N.Y., 1948).
7. I illustrate the dawn ceremonies with photographs from the Western Apache site of Cibecue, in Arizona, where photography is allowed. Cf. Keith H. Basso, *The Cibecue Apache* (New York, 1970), pp. 53–72. By present Mescalero standards, the ceremony at Cibecue is a touchingly threadbare one. Basso mentions no Gahan connections and seems to specify that the rite has no nighttime sequences (p. 64). Still, mountain spirits are often shown with the girls in popular publications, and are described as dancing on the four nights among the Western Apache as well, as by Tom Bahti, *Southwestern Indian Ceremonials* (Flagstaff, 1970), p. 48.

PHOTO SOURCES

All photographs in this book are by the author unless otherwise credited. The following books were sources for several of the photographs, as noted, which are reproduced with permission:

Harrington, John Peabody. "The Ethnogeography of the Tewa Indians," *Twenty-ninth Annual Report of the Bureau of American Ethnology*. Washington, 1916. Figs. III:9, IV:3, 21.

Hewett, Edgar L. *Pajarito Plateau and Its Ancient People*, rev. ed. School of American Research, Museum of New Mexico, Albuquerque, 1953. Figs. III:33, IV:22.

Hoegler, R. G. *Kreta*. Lucerne, 1966. Fig. III:47.

Kidder, Alfred V. *An Introduction to the Study of Southwestern Archaeology*, rev. ed. Yale University Press, New Haven, 1962. Figs. I:17, 18, 31; V:11.

Kubler, George. *Religious Architecture of New Mexico*. Taylor Museum, Colorado Springs Fine Arts Center, Colorado Springs, 1940. Figs. III:89; V:2.

Stevenson, Matilda Coxe. "The Zuni Indians," *Twenty-third Annual Report of the Bureau of American Ethnology*. Washington, 1904. Figs. V:75, 76, 77, 82, 84.

Stubbs, Stanley A. *Bird's-Eye View of the Pueblos*. University of Oklahoma Press, Norman, 1950. Figs. II:7, 45; III:14, 23, 58, 79, 84; IV:24, 35, 52, 62, 66; V:3, 22, 25, 34, 38, 62; VI:27, 32, 37, 43a, 52, 57.

Torrijos, Enrique Franco. *Prehispanic Mexican Art*. Putnam, New York, 1972. Fig. I:7.

Willcox, A. R. *Rock Paintings of the Drakensberg*. Max Parrish, London, 1956. Fig. II:38b.

INDEX

Page numbers in italics indicate illustrations.